Daughter of the Game

Daughter

of the Game

TRACY GRANT

WM

WILLIAM MORROW
An Imprint of HarperCollins*Publishers*

HarperCollins books may be purchased for educational, business, or sales promotional use. For information please write: Special Markets Department, HarperCollins Publishers Inc., 10 East 53rd Street, New York, NY 10022.

FIRST EDITION

Designed by Renato Stanisic

Printed on acid-free paper

Library of Congress Cataloging-in-Publication Data

Grant, Tracy.
  Daughter of the game / by Tracy Grant.—1st ed.
    p. cm.
  ISBN 0-06-621133-6
    1. Berkeley Square (London, England)—Fiction.   2. Missing children—Fiction.
  3. Married people—Fiction.   4. Kidnapping—Fiction.   I. Title.
  PS3607 R423 D38   2002
  813'.54—dc21   2001044506

02   03   04   05   06   RRD   10 9 8 7 6 5 4 3 2 1

For Penny
with thanks for believing in the book and in
me, and not letting me give up on either one

Daughters of the game.
—SHAKESPEARE, *Troilus and Cressida,*
ACT IV, SCENE V

. . . Truth is truth
To the end of reckoning.
—SHAKESPEARE, *Measure for Measure,*
ACT V, SCENE I

Acknowledgments

A profound and heartfelt thank-you to my agent, Nancy Yost; to my editor, Lucia Macro; to Carrie Feron; and to Marion Donaldson, for believing in this book, understanding what I was trying to do, and helping me do it better.

Thank you to Monica Sevy, John Lampe, and Carol Benz for telling me the story was worth telling, when it existed largely in my head and publication seemed a distant dream.

Thank you to Ross Sevy for helping me understand early-nineteenth-century weapons. If I've made any mistakes, the fault is mine entirely.

Thank you to Jim Saliba for brainstorming character motivations, helping me dream up the history of the Carevalo Ring, searching out Shakespeare quotes, and making me laugh when I needed to.

Thank you to Penny Williamson for endless plot discussions over lattes and glasses of red wine; and for helping me trace Charles and Mélanie's steps across London (even if we did get thoroughly lost round Covent Garden). Thank you to Paul Seaver for inspiring me to study history and teaching me to love primary-source documents.

I would not have been able to take the time to write this book without the generosity of my parents, grandparents, great-aunts, and great-uncles. Most writers do not have that luxury, and I am very grateful.

Finally, thank you to my mother, Joan Grant, for introducing me to Jane Austen, Shakespeare, and the magic of creating worlds and characters. And to my father, Doug Grant, who taught me about ambiguity tolerance and truth by approximation.

Prologue

London
November 1819

*I*t was the sort of night that cloaks a multitude of sins. Clouds drifted across the three-quarter moon. Mist hovered over the cobblestones, like cannon smoke after a battle. Yellow pools of lamplight glowed with murky radiance. Even in the classical expanse of Berkeley Square, with its pedimented houses and stately trees and decorous gravel walks, damp and soot choked the air.

Two passersby in sturdy wool cloaks stuck close to the shade of the plane trees by the square railing. They could have passed for a pair of manservants returning home from their evening off, the better for a pint or two in a Covent Garden tavern or even a few glasses of blue ruin in a St. Giles gin mill. Which was exactly the impression they intended to give.

The slighter of the two paused to tug her felt cap more firmly over her hair. A long apricot-colored strand slipped loose and swung over her shoulder. The woman, whose name was Meg, muttered a dockside curse and pushed the telltale hair back into its pins. She knew she should have cropped the whole mass short. Vanity had no place in games where one played for life-and-death stakes.

Her companion cast a sidelong glance at her. She could feel the impatience rising off of him, like the stench of damp in the lodging house where she'd been born. That was the problem with Jack. His quick temper had been the ruin of more than one promising job. A knife blade could be right handy, but at the wrong time it was as likely to land you in hot water as to get you out of it.

Music sounded from one of the larger houses across the square. Not the sort of music she and Jack danced to in the taverns of Seven Dials, their blood hot from the exhilaration of a job well done. No, this was the genteel tones of a waltz. A party was in progress. A decorous party. An expensive party.

The jangle of bridles and the clop of hooves echoed through the damp, sticky air. A whiff of pine and pitch came from the torches carried by the linkboys who ran alongside to light the way for the carriages. Perfectly matched horses tossed their glossy heads. Crested door panels glittered in the mist.

Jack turned his head. Curse the man. A glimpse of riches could distract him as easily as a woman's smile could most men.

The door of the house swung open, and candlelight spilled onto the portico, bright as the glint of gold coins. Two footmen hurried down the steps. Christ, *they* were perfectly matched, too, from their silver-buckled shoes to their powdered wigs. Neither could be more than an inch under six feet. Perhaps their employers bred them, like the horses.

Dark-coated gentlemen and pastel-gowned ladies stepped down from the carriages. A month's pickings in gold and gems sparkled on Grecian knots of hair, round white-gloved wrists, in the snowy folds of a cravat, on the ebony head of a walking stick.

Jack's eyes gleamed with a lust hotter than he'd ever shown for her. Meg gave a quick shake of her head. There'd be riches enough for them tonight, but their work wasn't here.

A gust of wind came up, sharp with the bite of November. The sweet, flowery smell of expensive scent and fancy soap drifted from the partygoers. Meg clapped a hand on Jack's shoulder and urged him forward. He jerked away. When he looked at her like that she knew she was playing dice with her life.

Jack turned his gaze from the party and strode forward. A knot of tension Meg had barely acknowledged eased in her throat.

They walked on, the branches black overhead, fallen November leaves crunching underfoot. They knew the house they wanted. Four stories of smooth gray stone, a chimney-studded slate roof, and sixteen tall, ivory-framed windows across the front alone. A house whose owners had no need to worry about the window tax, nor the candle tax either, judging by the glow that came from the front hall even at this hour.

Meg and Jack had made a fair study of the building in recent days. Now they moved past the columned portico, with its shiny mahogany door and gilt-tipped fanlight and lacy wrought-iron lampposts, as if it was no different from any other house that lined the square.

They rounded the corner and turned into the mews. The air smelled of dung and saddle soap. A horse whinnied in its stall as they passed. Another stamped its feet. They paused to make sure there was no human disturbance, then moved on.

Jack had promised that the gate to the back garden was well oiled. For once, he was true to his word. It swung open without a sound. The garden was a mass of shadows. Meg paused and let her eyes adjust until she could make out the trees and shrubs, the metal furniture and stone statues.

She started forward. Her soft-soled shoes skidded on the mist-dampened flagstones, and she nearly went crashing into a bench. Jack caught her arm in a rough grip. His fingers had a bite like iron. She was glad, not for the first time, that she'd never been on the receiving end of one of his blows.

The window they wanted was on the second floor, at the right-hand corner. A faint glow shone behind the curtains. They paused for a moment, staring up at the house. A staff of twelve lived behind those stone walls, not counting the coachman and grooms who had quarters in the stable. But the servants would all be snug abed now, save for one footman on duty in the hall, who had a tendency to doze at his post. The master of the house, Charles Fraser, and his lady were out for the evening. It would be near dawn before they returned home.

Charles Fraser was a grand nob indeed. A Member of Parliament. The grandson of a duke. This house, so quiet and still tonight, was the scene of some of Mayfair's most glittering parties. Fraser's wife was said to be one of the most beautiful women in London. They'd glimpsed her on the previous day, stepping out of her lacquered sapphire phaeton. A flash mort indeed. Even Jack's eyes had sparked with an interest that could not be put down wholly to Mrs. Fraser's pearl earrings and diamond brooch.

Jack unfastened his cloak and swung it off his shoulders. A shaft of moonlight caught the steel handle of the knife in his belt. Meg took off her own cloak and began to unwind the long rope that was wrapped round her waist. Her senses quickened with anticipation. If they played their cards right tonight, they'd end up with enough money to let them live like kings for months.

Provided, of course, that she could keep Jack's temper in check. Their employer had made it clear that violence might become unavoidable. Meg was prepared for it. But dead bodies could be a damned nuisance.

Colin Fraser peered down at his sister in the tin-shaded blur of her night-light. A red mark spread across her forehead, like a big, ugly inkblot on smooth white paper. Colin's neck prickled with shame. He wanted to run to the long-case clock in the hall and turn back the hands so that the last eight hours had never happened. But a traitorous part of him also wanted to shake his sister. It had been her idea to play with the new wooden weapons Uncle Edgar had given him. Jessica had grabbed the battle-ax and refused to put it down. To be honest, Colin hadn't minded. Jessica was the only opponent at hand, even if she was not quite three.

The sword and ax hadn't made a true clanging, like proper weapons, but the sound had been very satisfactory. Jessica had screamed with delight while their bare feet slithered over the nursery floorboards and the weapons met again and again.

Colin wasn't sure what had happened next, except that instead of striking the battle-ax, his wooden sword had crashed against Jessica's head. She'd fallen to the floor, screaming in earnest. Laura, their governess, had thrown open the door and gathered Jessica up. Mummy had come running, in her dressing gown, with her hair in curl papers, and Daddy, without any shirt at all and with shaving lather on his face.

They'd all fussed about Jessica, of course. None of them had seen the truth of what had happened. Finally Jessica had buried her head in Mummy's sleeve, and Daddy had turned to him, his eyes as hard as the gray marble of the drawing room mantel. "Do you know what you've done, lad?" His voice had gone rough, the way it did when he was angry or upset, so that he sounded like the people who lived near their house in Scotland.

The memory gave Colin a sick feeling, like the time the milk in his chocolate had gone sour. It scared him to think that he had hurt Jessica without meaning to at all. He didn't understand how he could be so sorry she was hurt and at the same time want to scream and jump up and down because everyone saw her side of the story rather than his.

Berowne, the family cat, stirred in his nest of quilt at the foot of the bed and opened one yellow eye. "I'm sorry," Colin mouthed.

Berowne closed his eye and put a gray paw over his face. Jessica's head sank deeper into the pillow. Her arm tightened round her stuffed rabbit. Colin bent down, careful not to touch the red mark, and brushed his lips against her forehead. "I'm sorry, Jessy."

Jessica didn't open her eyes. Colin watched her a moment longer. Then he scratched Berowne behind the ears, picked up his candle, and slipped out of the room.

The footmen had long since snuffed the candles in the wall sconces, except those in the downstairs hall, which was left lit for Mummy and Daddy. Colin hesitated in the corridor. He'd scarcely touched his supper, because his throat had been tight and his insides had been all twisted up, but now he was suddenly starving.

Michael would be on duty in the hall. Even though he often nodded off, Colin didn't want to take any risks. Michael was a capital fellow, but he might think it was his duty to send Colin back to bed and Colin didn't want to get him in trouble. So instead of walking to the big central staircase with the curving rail he liked to slide down, he went to the green baize door that led to the servants' stairs.

His candle flickered when he opened the door. He shielded the flame with one hand and gripped the pewter candlestick tighter with the other. He made his way down three flights of stairs and pushed open the door to see the comforting glow of the coals in the kitchen range.

But for some reason he paused on the threshold. In the small circle of light from his candle, the room looked just the same as it always did. The big mass of the range against the wall and the smaller stewing stove beneath the window; the long outline of the deal table where he sometimes sat and licked the cake bowl; the blurs on the wall that were copper pans and enamel tins; the bell board with its row of bells for every room in the house.

Maybe it was something about the smell that didn't feel right. Something he couldn't put a name to, except that it was different from the scent of yeast and charcoal and the salt and lemon skins the maids used to clean the copper pans. For a moment, his throat went tight and he had the funniest impulse to run back up the stairs.

But that was silly. He was six years old and he wasn't afraid of shadows or ghosts or ogres under the bed. He stepped into the room and pushed the door shut behind him.

The stone floor felt cold and slithery. He took a step forward. And then he paused, because his eyes had made out something else in the shadows by the doorway to the scullery. It looked like a person.

"Michael?" he said. Michael was the only person up at this hour.

He felt a stir of movement beside him. Something hard shot out and covered his mouth, driving the breath from his lungs. Something else gripped his arms behind his back. His candle fell from his fingers, fizzled, and went out. A scream rose up in his throat, but he couldn't give voice to it. He kicked out with his feet.

Whoever was holding him gave a strangled yelp of pain. "Christ, you little bastard." It sounded like a woman. "What the hell were you standing there for, Jack?"

"Didn't have much choice, did I?" The second voice came from near the range. It was definitely a man's. "Here's where I was when I heard the door open. Talk about rotten timing."

"No time for talk at all. Bloody hell, Jack, shut him up, so we can finish the job."

The man crossed the room, a swift, shadowy blur. Colin screamed into the hand that was muffling his mouth. The grip on his arms tightened until it felt as though they were being pulled from their sockets.

The man hovered over him for a moment. Colin couldn't make out his face, but he saw him draw back his arm.

A fist slammed into his jaw. He saw a blaze of light, brighter than all the candles in the drawing room chandelier. Then everything went black.

Chapter 1

"All the world may be a stage, but sometimes the dia-logue's too bloody ridiculous for any self-respecting playwright." Charles Fraser set down his candle and shrugged out of his evening coat, sparing a silent curse for the close-fitting fashions of the day. "What is it about diplomatic receptions that always brings on the most god-awful lapses in tact?"

"Don't tell me you expect diplomats to be diplomatic, dar-ling." Mélanie unwound the voluminous cashmere folds of her shawl from her shoulders and began to peel off her gloves. "That would be much too logical."

Charles tossed his coat over a tapestry chair back, turned up the crystal Agrand lamp that had been left lit in readiness for them, and moved to the fireplace. They never had his valet and Mélanie's maid wait up, but a fire was laid in the grate. He picked up the poker and stirred the coals.

"What particularly appalling dialogue caught your attention tonight?" Mélanie asked.

Charles turned from the fire to look at his wife. She was sitting at her dressing table, her feet drawn up onto the striped damask chair so she could remove her evening slippers. Her glossy dark ringlets fell about her face, exposing the curve of her neck. The pearl-embroidered skirt of her gown was tucked up as she unwound the ivory satin ribbons that crisscrossed her silk-stockinged ankles. Strange, when he knew every inch of her, that his breath still caught at the sight. "Lady Bury told Ned Ellison that his wife looked charming dancing with Peter Grantham and hadn't they been dancing to the same waltz at the Cowpers' only two nights ago?"

Mélanie looked up, one slipper dangling by the ribbons from her fingers. "Oh, dear. That would seem glaringly obvious on any stage. Though if Ellison doesn't know his wife's sleeping with Peter Grantham, he's the last person in London not to be in on the secret."

Charles moved to the satinwood table that held his great-grandmother's Irish crystal decanter and glasses. "Poor bastard. One of those mad fools besotted with his own wife." He shot her a glance. "Not that I'd know anything about that."

She returned the glance, a glint in her eyes. "Of course not."

He took the stopper from the decanter. Ellison's gaze, as he watched his wife circle the floor with her lover, had stirred images of a past Charles would just as soon forget. He paused, the heavy cut-glass stopper in his hand, an uncomfortable weight in his memory.

Mélanie flexed her foot. "I rather think his adoration may be the problem. Too much can be smothering. Literally. Think of Othello."

Charles jerked himself out of the past. "Ellison doesn't strike me as the violent sort." He poured an inch of whisky into two glasses.

"He's a quiet brooder." She dropped her slippers to the floor and got to her feet. "They're the ones who snap."

Seven years of marriage and her perceptiveness about people could still surprise him. He set down the decanter and replaced the stopper. "Am I the sort who'd snap?"

She turned from lighting the tapers on her dressing table, laughter in her eyes. "Controlled, dispassionate Charles Fraser? Oh, no, darling. Anyone who's been to bed with you knows you aren't nearly as cold as you let on."

He walked over to her, carrying the glasses of whisky. "So I'm the perfect sort of husband to betray?"

"Not quite." Her gaze was appraising, but her lips trembled with humor. "You're much too intelligent, dearest. You'd be damnably difficult to deceive."

He put one of the glasses into her hand. "Sounds as though you've considered it."

She leaned against the dressing table and took a meditative sip of whisky. "Well, I might." Her eyes, a color between blue agate and the green of Iona marble, gleamed in her pale face. "Except that it would be quite impossible to find anyone who's your equal, my love."

He regarded her, aware of a smile playing about his mouth. "Good answer."

"Yes, I rather thought it was."

He lifted one hand and ran his fingers down the familiar line of her throat. The puffed gossamer that was an excuse for a sleeve slipped from her shoulder. His fingers molded to her skin. The scent of her perfume filled his senses, roses and vanilla and some other fragrance that still remained elusive after all these years.

A lump of coal fell from the grate and hissed against the fender. He swore, shrugged his shoulders, and went to pick up the poker.

"You warned me about it," Mélanie said from the dressing table. "The night you proposed."

He pushed the coal into the grate. "Warned you about what?"

"That—in your words—you weren't a demonstrative man.

That you'd thought you'd never marry, your parents had set a miserable example, and you weren't sure how good you'd be at it."

He looked at her over his shoulder. "I didn't really say that."

"You did." She curled up, catlike, on her dressing table chair. "You pointed out all the potential pitfalls with scrupulous care. It might have been a white paper you'd drawn up for the ambassador on the advantages and disadvantages of a treaty. You didn't even try to kiss me."

"I should think not. That might have risked biasing your judgment. One way or the other." He returned the poker to its stand. "Of course, if I had, perhaps you'd have given me an answer straightaway, instead of going off to think about it for the most uncomfortable three days I have ever spent."

"Charles, given what you've been through in your life, that has to be hyperbole."

He kept his gaze on her face. "Not necessarily."

She unfastened her pearl earrings without breaking eye contact. "Terrified I'd accept?"

"Mel, the most terrifying thing I can imagine is life without you."

Mélanie looked at him a moment longer, her eyes dark. Then she gave one of her wonderful smiles. The smile she'd given him after their first, awkward kiss in a drafty embassy corridor, with a military band blaring in the street outside. The smile he'd opened his eyes upon when he'd recovered consciousness after a gunshot wound to find her sitting beside his camp bed, three months into their strangely begun marriage.

Charles returned the smile, then looked away, because sometimes, even now, what they had together was so miraculous it scared him. He stared into the leaping flames in the grate. Thinking about their betrothal made him think about their son and the scene that had been enacted earlier tonight. "Were we too hard on Colin, do you think? I hate to ring a peal over him to no purpose."

"Is that what your father would have done?" Mélanie said.

His fingers curled round the glass. The Fraser crest, etched into the crystal, bit into his skin. "Hardly. Father wouldn't have come to the nursery at all, unless Edgar or I were spilling our lifeblood onto the carpet. And even then he'd have taken care the blood didn't seep onto his boots. More likely he'd have summoned me to his study when the dust had settled and told me if I must murder my brother could I have the decency to do it outside on the lawn."

"And you'd have much preferred it if he'd beaten you?"

He swirled the whisky in his glass. "At least that would have implied he had a passing interest in whether we lived or died."

An emotion he couldn't have defined flickered like a shadow across Mélanie's face. She unclasped the pendant he'd commissioned from a Lisbon jeweler for their first anniversary. The candlelight gleamed against the rose gold of the Celtic knotwork and the green gold of the Spanish poppy at the center. "It's never easy to be betrayed, least of all by those one should be able to trust the most."

"Even at my most maudlin, I can hardly claim either of my parents betrayed me. Unless you consider lack of affection a betrayal."

"The worst betrayal of all. Your father was certainly guilty of it."

Charles took a sip of whisky, savoring the smoky bite of the liquor. He was seized by a sudden longing for their estate in Scotland—clean air and open space and cool, peaty streams. The house he loved, though he could hardly claim to love the man from whom he had inherited it.

"Always assuming that he was my father," Charles said. It was something he had questioned more and more in the two and a half years since the death of Kenneth Fraser, the man he had grown up calling Father.

"He claimed you as his son," Mélanie said. "He owed you his love. Just as you love Colin."

Charles looked into her eyes. She returned his gaze steadily. After a long moment, he said, "I'm not sure Kenneth Fraser was capable of loving anyone."

"That's no excuse. Damn the man, if he hadn't got himself killed I could cheerfully strangle him."

Charles smiled in spite of himself. "Bloodthirsty tonight, aren't you?" He hadn't meant to mention his mother, but he found himself saying, "As for Mother, whatever her faults I wouldn't claim she didn't love her children."

"No. But one could say suicide is the worst betrayal of all."

Charles's fingers tightened on the whisky glass. For a moment, he thought it would shatter in his hand. The image of his parents' faces pierced years of denial: the cool, ironic arch of his father's brows, the cutting line of his mouth; the hectic flush of his mother's cheeks, the brilliant, quixotic torment of her eyes. It almost seemed that he could reach out and demand the answers they had never given him. Answers that shouldn't matter, but that did, far more than he would admit, even to Mélanie.

The images of his parents gave way to the careless, handsome features of his brother, from whom he was estranged for reasons he himself did not fully understand. And then he thought fleetingly of a honey-haired woman, whom he had failed and who had left him, as surely as his mother had.

He looked at his wife. A crooked smile came to his lips, because that seemed the only possible response to what could not be changed. "Put that way, you could say you're practically the only person I've trusted who hasn't betrayed me, one way or another."

Mélanie's eyes turned unexpectedly luminous. "Darling—" She put out a hand, then let it fall to her side. "Thank you. That's one of the nicest things you've ever said to me. Though it's rather a large burden to place on any one person."

"Never mind, I'm sure you're equal to the task." He held her gaze for a moment, then shook his head and raked a hand through his hair. "Sorry. I must have had more to drink than I realized. Usually I have to be three sheets to the wind before I give way to self-pity."

"Dearest, if you can't indulge in self-pity in front of your wife, when can you?"

"Even the most patient of wives must have her limits." Charles flung himself into his favorite wing chair, the moss-green velvet he steadily resisted reupholstering. Even now, even with Mélanie, talking about his parents cut through too many defenses, until it nicked at feelings he preferred to keep buried.

Mélanie turned back to her dressing table, as though she were quite unaware of the undercurrents in the room. He rested his head against the worn velvet of the chair and watched as she went through the familiar ritual of taking down her hair. Amazing how many pins it took to create that elaborate arrangement of curls and loops. The walnut-brown strands fell one by one about her shoulders. The metal pins clattered as she returned them to their porcelain box. Her face was reflected three ways in the trio of looking-glass panels. The fine bones and ivory skin of her French father, the vivid hair and eyes and brows of her Spanish mother. Mélanie's parents hadn't been beastly and she had loved them and they'd both been killed before her eyes. What she had gone through then had been worse than anything he or his brother and sister had endured.

He saw her for a moment as he had first seen her in Spain, in the Cantabrian Mountains, her face smeared with dirt and blood, her eyes bright with a reckless will to live. In a dank, moldering alley, aiming a pistol at a fleeing man with one arm and cradling their one-year-old son with the other. In a makeshift hospital, face blue-shadowed with exhaustion, hands steady as she stitched up a wound. He wondered, not for the first time, where he'd be if they hadn't met. Dead, more than likely, one way or another. Certainly alone.

The brush swept rhythmically through her hair. The firelight flickered over the gray and cream wall hangings, the French blue upholstery, the theatrical prints on the walls. Airy, soothing, yet whimsical. Mélanie's touch was everywhere in the room. He felt it lap away the painful memories, as surely as a soothing caress.

He loved the Perthshire house, but he had never thought he would live here, in the house that had been the center of his parents' lives, the house he had only visited rarely, the house in which he had never felt at home. After his father's death, his first impulse had been to get rid of it as quickly as possible. Mélanie, he knew, had fully expected him to do so. But he'd caught the wistful look in her eye at the beautifully proportioned rooms, the Robert Adam ceilings, the graceful plasterwork and moldings. He'd realized how wonderful it would be for the children to have to walk only a few paces from the house to the square garden. He'd thought of the rare luxury of a house that looked out on the leafy expanse of a square rather than the narrow width of a street. There were few spots in London as lovely as Berkeley Square.

And so they'd moved into his parents' house, and Mélanie had engaged painters and plasterers and knocked out walls and hung wallpaper and laid tile until it was no longer his parents' house but their own.

"Speaking of being undiplomatic," Mélanie said, "don't you think your talents might have been better employed than spending the entire evening hiding out in the library with Henry Brougham and David Mallinson?"

"On the contrary." He tugged his cravat loose and unwound the confining folds of muslin, unstarched in defiance of fashion, from about his throat. "We rehashed the slavery issue and the abolition of rotten boroughs. By the time we broached the second bottle of port we were quite impressed with our own eloquence."

"You see them practically every day."

"They were two of the only people at the reception who had anything remotely interesting to say. Present company excluded, of course, but I see you even more frequently."

She made a face at him in the mirror. "Charles Fraser, for a politician, your social skills are positively atrocious."

"Why do you think I need a wife?"

She pretended to throw her rouge pot at him. He ducked. "Speaking of infidelity," he said, "what was Antonio de Carevalo whispering in your ear after supper?"

"Darling." She set the rouge pot back on the dressing table. "I didn't think you were paying attention."

He stretched his legs out in front of him. "My dear wife. I would hardly have been any use in military intelligence if I wasn't able to observe without being seen to do so."

She cast a glance at him over her shoulder. "Carevalo whispered a variety of suggestions, most of which seemed to have been cribbed from bawdier bits of Lope de Vega. I'll say this for him, his flirtation is as good-natured as it is crude."

"Did he say anything about his reasons for coming to England?"

"He said a great deal about the Elgin Marbles and the female form, quite as if he'd come to England expressly to view them." She propped her arm on the back of the chair and rested her chin in her hand. "Do you suppose he really thinks anyone doesn't know he's here to muster support for an uprising in Spain?"

"I shouldn't think so. Carevalo's a shrewd politician." Charles looked into his glass, watching the crystal and the pale gold liquid catch the light of the fire. "I must have been asked a dozen times tonight if I thought Spain was going to erupt into revolution."

Mélanie pushed her hair back from her face. "What did you answer?"

"That I couldn't say, but that if I were Spanish I wouldn't be overjoyed to have spent six years fighting the French only to be stuck with the same corrupt monarchy I'd had before Napoleon invaded."

She got to her feet. "Talk about being undiplomatic, darling."

He let his shoulders sink deeper into the chair. "I'm not a diplomat anymore, I'm a politician. An opposition politician. I'm supposed to raise people's hackles."

"And you do it superbly, love." She crossed the room and dropped into his lap with a swish of her skirt. "Strings. They're beginning to pinch. I must have had too many lobster patties. Thérese's chef has a heavy hand with the cream."

The light fabric of her gown was gathered into dozens of pleats at the back, where the bodice was closed by impossibly tiny silk strings. He pressed a kiss to the nape of her neck and went to work on the strings. She gave a contented sigh. "Mmm . . . You have witchcraft in your fingers, Charles."

He loosened the last string. The bodice slithered down over her shoulders. He brushed aside the champagne-colored silk, turned her in his arms, smiled into her eyes, and put his mouth to hers.

Her arms came round him at once. Her body curved into his own. The passion was familiar. The urgency took him by surprise. He lifted his head and looked at her with the faintest of questions.

Her eyes were like rain-streaked glass. "Charles." There was a slight catch in her voice.

He took her face between his hands. "Soul's idol?"

She regarded him for a moment, her brows drawn together. Then she smiled in an awkward sort of apology. "Nothing." She touched her fingers to his lips. "Just—I love you."

He stroked her cheek. "That's hardly nothing, at least not to me. Will it sound hopelessly redundant if I say I love you, too?"

She leaned her cheek against his hand. "Amazing how easily those words come to your lips, considering how much trouble you once had saying them."

"You've changed me in a number of ways, *mo chridh*." He caught her hand and lifted it to his lips. "I'm sorry. I should say it more often."

"Save your impassioned speeches for Parliament, dearest." She smiled again, but there were still demons lurking in her eyes. The same demons that made her wake trembling, her nightdress plastered to her skin, from nightmares she never fully described.

He didn't question the nightmares and he didn't question what had brought on her change of mood now. They had an unspoken rule not to press each other for confidences. They both had too many ghosts in their pasts. Instead he brushed his lips against her temple, the tip of her nose, the corner of her mouth. Gentle, feather-light kisses such as he'd given her on their wedding night, when for all her vitality he'd felt as though he held something made of spun glass in his arms, something that had been shattered once and was barely mended.

She twisted her head so his kisses fell on her lips. He stood, cradling her in his arms. She curled against him and wrapped her arm round his neck. Her laughter vibrated through the silk of his waistcoat and the linen of his shirt. "Don't drop me."

"Don't insult my abilities, *mo chridh*. When have I ever dropped you?"

"The inn in Pamplona."

"I tripped on the carpet. I hung on to you."

"The Granvilles' house party."

"We collapsed on the sofa together."

"Scotland last Christmas Eve."

"Ah, there you have me." He set her down on the embroidered coverlet they'd brought back from Lisbon. "As I recall, we never made it to the bed that time."

"That's what I mean. I don't like the floor." She caught hold of the loose ends of his cravat and pulled him down for a kiss. "That's better." Her vulnerable moment was gone. She went to work on the buttons on his waistcoat. She was still half-wearing her gown. He decided it was in the way. He helped her wriggle out of it, carefully, because he knew it was one of her favorites. His sleeve-link caught on one of the gauzy sleeves. She made him hold still while she disentangled it.

He lost his balance and half fell on top of her. Her chemise had slipped down over her shoulders. He pushed up the hem and reached for the string on her drawers. Even now his fingers shook when he touched her.

He was kissing the underside of her arm and she was trying to pull his shirt over his head when the knock sounded on the door. The blood was pounding so loudly in his head that it was a moment before he heard it.

"Mr. Fraser? Mrs. Fraser?"

It was Laura Dudley, the children's governess. Mélanie was on her feet in an instant. She ran across the room clad only in her chemise and pulled the door open. "What is it?" Charles, two steps behind her, heard the sharpness in her voice. "Is Jessica worse?"

Laura shook her head. "No. She's asleep. I'm sorry to disturb you, but I thought—" She swallowed. Her blue eyes were dark with worry. The light from the candle she held flickered and jumped, as though her hands were shaking. Laura Dudley could cope with scraped knees and bumped heads and pencils up children's noses without batting an eyelash.

"We always wish to be informed when there's anything amiss with the children," Charles said. "What is it?"

"It's Colin." Candle wax dribbled onto Laura's fingers, but she didn't seem to notice. "He's missing."

Chapter 2

A spasm of fear gripped Charles's heart, a fear he hadn't known existed until he had children. He dropped an arm round Mélanie's shoulders. "Right." He took the candle from Laura before her long titian plait could catch on fire. "He probably couldn't sleep—qualms of conscience—so he went down to the kitchen to scrounge up something to eat. Guilt has a way of bringing on hunger pangs, at least in the Fraser family."

"I thought of that." Laura gripped her hands together. "I checked. He's not in the kitchen."

Bloody hell. Of course she would have looked everywhere she could think of before knocking on the door of their bedchamber at this hour. He squeezed Mélanie's shoulders. "Where haven't you looked?"

"The servants' rooms. The other bedchambers." Laura pushed her plait back over her shoulder. "I heard Jessica cry out but she must have been talking in her sleep, because she was fast asleep when I went in. I looked in on Colin before I went back to bed. He wasn't in his room. I checked the schoolroom and the kitchen and the reception rooms downstairs. I didn't look in all the cupboards and under the furniture, though."

"It's all right, Laura." Mélanie put a hand on Laura's arm. "Colin's probably hiding somewhere to give us a good fright. We'll have to wake the servants and organize a search."

Charles had already crossed the room and was tugging the bell pull. Mélanie pulled on her dressing gown, and brought Charles his own. They were both decently covered by the time his valet, Addison, and her maid, Blanca, hurried into the room. Addison and Blanca had been with them since their days in the Peninsula and were well used to times of crisis. Neither fussed nor asked unnecessary questions.

The rest of the staff were soon assembled in the ground-floor hall. Higgins, the butler, and Mrs. Erskine, the cook; Morag and Lucy, the housemaids; William and Michael, the footmen; Polly, the laundry maid; Jeanie, the kitchen maid; and Kip, the boot boy. Charles apologized for waking them, explained the problem, and divided them into teams assigned to various parts of the house.

"Don't worry, Master Charles." Higgins, who had been a footman in the Fraser household in Charles's youth, patted his arm with the familiarity of an old friend. "We'll find the little devil. I hope you won't be too hard on him. You and Master Edgar got up to a lot worse in your day, as I recall."

It was perfectly true. It did nothing to quench the queasy feeling in Charles's stomach.

He and Mélanie searched the second floor. Mélanie went through the guest suite while Charles examined the nursery and schoolroom more thoroughly than Laura had done. He looked under desks and tables, inside cupboards, and behind chests of drawers, moving cautiously because despite the lamps, he still needed his candle to see into the dark corners. His throat grew hoarse from calling his son's name. He would never feel the same about the smell of chalk and beeswax again.

He found a sapphire earring Mélanie had been missing for weeks, a crumpled Latin exercise in Colin's round, careful hand, a yellow silk tassel that looked as if it had come from a Hessian boot, and something that seemed to be an ear torn from a stuffed toy. There was no sign of his son. The embers of alarm smoldered and sparked and finally, as the minutes ticked by with no shout of discovery from the rest of the house, flared into a raging blaze that tightened his chest and drove the breath from his lungs. He emerged from the schoolroom to find Mélanie closing the door to the dressing room of the guest suite.

"Nothing." She came down the corridor toward him with a shake of her head. "Charles, do you think he could have run away?"

He set his candle, now sputtering, on a demi-lune side table and gripped her hands. "It's beginning to look that way. Christ, I'll wring the little blighter's neck." *Except that I'll be too busy hugging him to do so.* "Damn it, he should have known we weren't that angry."

Mélanie squeezed his fingers. "You can kick yourself later, Charles. The question is, where would he have gone?"

"To the stables to visit the horses. Or out into the square. Possibly to Edgar's or the Lydgates'—he's walked there often enough in daylight. But let's not jump to conclusions. We don't know he *has* run off." He took her hand and drew her down the corridor. Someone had lit the candles in the gilt sconces on the landing and the curving stair wall. He leaned over the mahogany rail to call down two flights to Michael, the second footman, in the hall below. "Anything?"

Michael shook his head. He was a carefree young man, recently come from Charles's grandfather's property in Ireland and a great favorite with the children. Like Charles, he was wrapped in a dressing gown, his dark hair standing on end.

There was a concern in his eyes that Charles had never seen before. "No sign of him on the ground floor or the first. We're still having a go at the third floor and the attics. Addison's gone out back to the stables." He flashed a smile at Mélanie. "We'll find him, Mrs. Fraser, don't worry."

"Mummy!" Jessica's voice carried across the landing. Laura came down the corridor, Jessica in her arms. Jessica's hair was tousled and her face sleep-flushed, but she stared about her with eyes that were all too alert.

Laura gave a smile that did not quite reach her eyes. "I'm afraid all the excitement woke someone up."

"It's all right, *querida*." Mélanie took her daughter from Laura and stroked Jessica's golden brown hair. "Colin's just being silly."

Jessica twisted her fingers in the blue satin ribbon at the neck of Mélanie's dressing gown. "I didn't want him to go 'way. He didn't hit me that hard."

"No, of course you didn't." Mélanie's voice was bright. Charles suspected only he could see the effort it cost her. "And Colin hasn't gone away. He's just . . . hiding."

Charles cupped his hand round his daughter's head. "I'll have a look at Colin's room, Mel. See if we missed anything."

The night-light was still burning in Colin's bedchamber. Charles lit the lamp on the chest of drawers as well. The light spilled over the green-sprigged curtains, the wallpaper border painted with scenes from Robin Hood, the green and blue quilt. Charles looked under the pillows, smoothed out the covers, picked up the quilt and shook it, so hard the fabric snapped like a banner in the wind.

"What are you looking for?" Mélanie appeared in the door-way behind him.

"A note. If he did run away, I thought he might have left one. Is Jessica all right?"

"Laura's telling her a story in our room." Mélanie crossed to the bed and picked up Colin's stuffed bear. "I can't believe he'd run away without taking Figaro." She hugged the bear to her chest, smoothing its fur. "Charles—"

He looked into her eyes. "No." The word came out more harshly than he intended. "There's a simple explanation, Mel. There has to be."

Mélanie moved to the writing desk they had given Colin just last year, picked up his Latin primer, glanced in the drawers, riffled through the sheets of drawing paper.

Charles was looking through the wardrobe. "None of his clothes seem to be missing."

"That's not surprising. Colin's far less interested in his clothes than he is in his bear."

The door creaked softly. Berowne, the cat, pushed his way into the room and wound against Mélanie's legs. Mélanie scooped him into her arms. "Did you see anything, Berowne?" She pressed her face against the cat's fur and moved to the window. "It's started to rain."

Charles closed the wardrobe. He realized he had been aware of the patter on the roof and the creak of branches for some time, without registering what they meant.

Mélanie pushed up the sash with her left hand, while she held Berowne against her shoulder with her right. A blast of wind blew the hair back from her face and ruffled the papers on the desk. Berowne yowled. Mélanie started to close the window, then went still. "Charles."

He was at her side in an instant. "What?"

She plucked something from the ivory-painted sash and held it out to him. It was a scrap of linen, almost indistinguishable against the paint. "It looks like a bit of Colin's nightshirt," she said.

Charles let out a low whistle. "Christ, I *am* going to wring his neck. He must have climbed down the side of the house." Yet he was relieved to have found tangible proof of Colin's flight. Surely Colin himself could not be far behind.

Mélanie stared at him. "Why, for heaven's sake? He can

unbolt the doors. If he wanted to slip out, he had his choice of the hall or the garden or the kitchen— Oh, of course, I'm being silly. Going out tamely through the door wouldn't be nearly as much of an adventure."

"Precisely. This explains why he didn't take Figaro. Edgar and I climbed out the nursery window more than once. Only our nursery was in the attic, so it was a longer way down." He didn't add that he'd turned his ankle more than once and Edgar had broken his arm. He'd be more alarmed about Colin, save that they'd know by now if he'd fallen and hurt himself. He picked up the lamp from the chest of drawers, pushed the sash higher, and leaned out the window. The wind drove the rain against his face and whipped the branches of the apple tree by the garden wall. A light flickered across the mews in the stable, where Addison was searching. Charles studied the wall below, seeking signs of Colin's descent. The stone was smooth, but there were possible footholds and handholds in the grouting.

Mélanie leaned out the window beside him, holding the cat against her shoulder with one hand and pushing her wind-spattered hair back from her face with the other. "He probably doubled a rope up over something at the window level." She gestured to a corner of the window ledge, which protruded from the wall. "Then he could climb down maneuvering with both ends and pull the whole thing down after him when he reached the ground."

"Quite," Charles said. They had done the same themselves in Spain on more than one occasion. "I was telling Colin about the time we got out of Salamanca only a few days ago. It never occurred to me he'd actually try it himself."

"Charles." Mélanie shifted the compliant cat against her shoulder. "Our son climbed down two stories using a rope that was only draped over a bit of wood and is now hiding outside somewhere in the midst of a rainstorm. And we're talking as if we're *proud* of him."

"Well, I am. Concerned but proud. Aren't you?"

"That's not the point. As I remember, by the time we got out of Salamanca you had a cracked rib and my hands were torn to ribbons."

"That was a medieval fortress and we had French snipers to worry about. A London town house is a lot tamer." Charles tilted the lamp so the light fell flush against the wall. No telltale strands of rope were caught against the stone in the part he could see. But something caught his eye just above the peaked pediment of the first-floor window, something showing dark against the pale gray stone. He tilted the lamp further, anchoring the glass chimney with his hand. A chill that had nothing to do with the night air ran along his nerves.

"What is it?" Mélanie said.

"Dirt. On the wall." He kept his voice conversational.

There was a brief pause. When Mélanie spoke, her voice was equally conversational. "You mean Colin didn't climb down. Somebody else climbed up."

"Possibly." He saw torchlight crossing the mews and heard the creak of the garden gate. "Addison," he called.

"Sir?" His valet disengaged himself from the shadows of the garden wall, one hand raised to shield his face from the rain. "He's not in the stable, I'm afraid."

"Come over here," Charles said. "Take care to stay on the flag-stones. Tell me if there are any footprints beneath the window."

The moonlight picked out Addison's pale hair as he crossed the garden. Charles took Mélanie's hand and gripped it. Her fingers closed hard round his own. Otherwise she was absolutely still. The cat gave a distressed mew that echoed out into the night.

"Blimey." Addison looked up at them, his face a white blur. "Sorry, sir. But it looks as if someone's been tramping about in the primrose beds."

A lead weight settled in Charles's chest, equal parts inevitability and disbelief. Mélanie clenched his hand, so tight he could feel the scrape of bone against bone. "Look at the wall," Charles said. "Do you see any dirt? As though someone's been climbing it?"

"Yes." The word was clipped, but the edge of fear in Addison's voice said that he too realized the significance. "Especially near the bottom. Looks as though it scraped off someone's shoe."

Charles drew a long, uneven breath. Mélanie's hand was ice cold in his own. "All right, we'd better call off the search. Thank everyone for their hard work and send one of the footmen round to Bow Street. It looks as though someone's taken Colin."

Colin's head felt as though someone had been jumping on it. He opened his eyes, but all he could see was blackness, which was funny, because Laura always made sure the night-light was lit.

He turned his head. Something wet and scratchy rubbed against his face. It seemed to be draped over him or wrapped round him. It didn't feel like a bedsheet or even a blanket. The floor beneath him seemed to keep shifting and jolting, only it was hard to tell because his head was spinning so badly.

Memory jabbed at him, sharp as the pain in his head. Rough hands, harsh voices, a fist smashing into his face. He tried to sit up and found he couldn't. His feet and hands were tied. He let out a scream into the rough stuff that covered his face.

"Oh, Christ." A voice cut through the blackness. "He's awake. Pull over, Jack."

Colin heard a muffled curse, felt a quick, sideways jerk, and then all of a sudden the floor beneath him stopped moving. He heard a horse whicker. He wasn't in a room, he must be in a carriage or cart or something.

He drew a deep breath. Daddy always told him to breathe when he was frightened.

The boards creaked as though someone had climbed into the back of the cart. "Don't scream, lad, or we'll have to clout you again." It was a woman's voice. There'd been a woman before, in the kitchen. He remembered now.

The scratchy stuff was jerked off his head. He didn't scream, not because of the warning so much as because his throat had gone tight and all his fear seemed to be bottled up inside him.

Raindrops spattered against his face. He found himself staring at a triangular face set beneath a dark felt cap. It was a man's cap, but it was a woman's face. Long strands of hair hung from beneath the cap, glinting red in the faint glow of the moon. Her eyes were dark and set wide apart. Her mouth was full and looked as if it could smile. It wasn't the sort of face that went with hitting.

"That's more like it." The woman pulled a flask from her pocket and unscrewed the top. "Drink this down, there's a good boy."

The flask had a funny, sickly smell. Colin stared at it. He wasn't sure he could have managed to drink it if he wanted to, and he knew he didn't want to.

"Don't be balky, boy. There's no time for it." She grabbed him by the shoulders and tilted his head back. Pain lanced through his temples. He gave a cry that got clogged in his throat.

"Drink it," the woman said again. She put the flask to his lips. "It won't hurt, it'll just make you fall asleep. Better than Jack hitting you again."

The memory of Jack hitting him was enough. She tipped the flask, and Colin tried to swallow. The stuff tasted even more sickly than it smelled. He gagged, but he managed to choke some of it down.

"All right, that should do it." The lady took the flask away. She laid him back down in the cart and pushed something under his head that felt like straw.

"Not a peep out of you, mind." She laid the rough stuff—a burlap bag—on top of him but didn't pull it over his face. "You'll soon be asleep."

He looked up at her. "Couldn't I go home, please? I won't tell anyone I saw you."

The woman got to her feet and shook her head. "Sorry, lad. That would make a right mess of everything."

The boards creaked. The lady must have climbed back onto the box.

"All right?" A man's voice, low and rough, rose above the stillness. It had a funny lilt to it, sort of like Daddy's but not quite.

"He's had enough laudanum to put him out till we're safe settled. I couldn't risk you hitting him again or our job'd have been over before it was begun."

"You told me to keep him quiet. What the hell'd you expect?" The cart lurched forward. "Anyway, what's it matter if we get our money? You really think his high and mightiness means to hand the whelp back alive?"

"That's his business." The woman's voice got louder, as though she'd turned her head. "But I'm not throwing away our prize chip just as the cards are dealt."

"We've made our bargain. Five hundred pounds."

"Why settle for five hundred when we could have two or three times that?"

The man gave a low chuckle. "Christ, Meg. You can still surprise me."

"Why not? We've got the boy. We keep him till we get what we want. Then his lordship can do what he wants with the brat."

Colin's head was beginning to feel as though it were filled with cotton wool, but he tried to think past the fuzziness. They had *meant* to take him. It hadn't been an accident. Someone called his lordship had paid them to take him. Mummy and Daddy knew lots of lordships. Some of them let him ride their horses and even snuck him ices when he peered over the stair rail during parties. Some frowned when he made too much noise in the drawing room. Some ignored him. But he couldn't think of a reason why any of them would want to steal him away from home. There was Great-Grandpapa, of course. But he would never do something so mean and anyway people called him "Your Grace" or sometimes "Duke."

"You always know just how to handle a man, Meggie," the man said after a moment. "One way or another."

"Handle him?" The woman's laugh was like the scrape of

nails on a writing slate. "I'd sooner handle a snake. He's the most dangerous man we've ever had dealings with, and don't you forget it."

"Don't exaggerate, girl."

"I'm not."

"What makes him so dangerous, then?"

The lady was silent for so long that Colin didn't think he'd be able to keep from falling asleep. When she finally spoke, it sounded as though the words were drifting down a tunnel. "Because he has nothing left to lose."

Mélanie murmured the words of a Spanish lullaby. Jessica snuggled against her, as though she could burrow into safety. Her hand was fisted round the falling collar of Mélanie's gown, but she was losing the fight against sleep. Berowne sat washing himself on the bed beside them. *The harmless, necessary cat.* Perhaps he knew that the sight of him smoothing his soft gray fur and rubbing his ears was the best comfort he could offer.

Mélanie's gaze drifted over the room. Her lip-rouge-stained glass of whisky stood abandoned on the dressing table beside the rouge pots and perfume flasks and jewel boxes. Her throat closed at the sight. Little more than an hour ago, she and Charles had been laughing in this room in blithe unconcern. Little more than an hour before that she had been fending off the Marqués de Carevalo's attentions and eating overrich lobster patties, as though this night were no different from any other.

Colin, her son, was missing, taken from his bedchamber and spirited into the dark London night. The knowledge reverberated through her with a force that bone and muscle could scarcely contain.

Logic said that whoever had taken Colin was long gone and the best way to help him was to wait for the Bow Street officers, but her body screamed with the impulse to run from the house and scour the streets of Mayfair shouting her son's name.

Yet beneath the fear and disbelief, guilt twisted her guts. She had thought she was safe in this beautiful house, with her beautiful children and her brilliant if self-contained husband. She had thought she had put the past behind her. There were moments when she had feared otherwise, when she had known that one couldn't separate what one had been from what one was now and what one would become. But never, *sacrebleu!* never, had she thought her children would pay for her crimes.

Jessica made a protesting sound. Mélanie willed the tension from her arms. *Was* that why Colin had been taken? Because of who his mother was? She could not make sense of it, yet the fear that it was true gnawed at her insides.

The knife's edge on which she had balanced for so many years turned inward, slashing through elaborate layers of defense and pretense, laying bare the cold, hard fear that had always lurked at the heart of her marriage. Should she tell Charles the whole? Would the truth serve any purpose? Or would it merely smash their marriage to bits without doing Colin any good?

"Mel." Her husband's voice came from the doorway.

She jerked her head up. She looked into the deep-set gray eyes that could see so much and yet from which she had kept her deepest secrets hidden for seven years. For a moment, she doubted her own ability to dissemble.

"The Bow Street officers are here," Charles said. "They've gone outside to look at the garden. They made it clear I wasn't to get in the way. Since I'd already drawn my own conclusions, I left them to see if they come up with anything different." His mouth hardened, and she could feel the need for action rippling through him. He walked toward the bed. "Jessica asleep?"

She was, Mélanie realized. Her head had flopped against Mélanie's arm, and her breathing was deep and even. "At last. I think she should stay in here. The Bow Street men will want to go through the nursery rooms."

Charles turned back the covers. Mélanie uncurled Jessica's

fingers from the collar of her gown and laid her on the Irish linen sheet. Jessica stirred but didn't open her eyes.

Mélanie straightened up to find Charles looking down at their daughter, his face knit in a fierce combination of love and fear and rage. She touched his arm. "She was asking for Colin. She knows something's wrong. We'll have to find a way to explain."

He nodded, the muscles in his arm bunched tight beneath her fingers. She studied his face. His hair was damp and he had got a smudge of soot on his cheek, marks of the investigating he had done himself while they waited for Bow Street. "What conclusions did you draw?" she said.

He lifted his gaze to her. "I couldn't find anything outside, except the footprints in the primrose bed. There were two of them. One man's feet are longer by a good two inches. Inside—they definitely climbed in through the window, but it looks as though they left by way of the kitchen."

Mélanie started. "But the scrap of fabric on the windowsill—"

"Doesn't match Colin's nightshirts. I compared it to one in his wardrobe. The scrap must have come from one of the thieves' shirts. I found a faint scrape of dirt on the carpet in the corridor and more on the back stairs."

"You mean they climbed in through Colin's window and then carried him down to the kitchen?"

"I think it's more likely Colin went downstairs on his own."

"Of course," she said. "Midnight hunger pangs."

"Quite. When the thieves didn't find him in his room, they guessed the kitchen was the likeliest place to look. They found him there and went out through the kitchen door into the garden."

The image flickered before Mélanie's eyes with the blinding pain of sunlight striking snow-covered ground.

Berowne stirred on the coverlet, stretching a paw toward them. Charles reached down to give the cat an absent pet. "I told the Bow Street Runner—Roth is his name—that we'd be in the small salon."

"Then we should go down." Mélanie rubbed at the smudge on his face. "I'll ask Laura to sit with Jessica."

He caught her hand and pressed it to his lips. Mélanie took a deep breath, gathering her forces for the interview with the Bow Street Runner. Questions had to be asked. God knew questions needed to be asked.

How they were to be answered was another matter entirely.

Chapter 3

Jeremy Roth, runner in the employ of the Bow Street Public Office, stepped through a swan-pedimented doorway into an airy room with sea-green walls and pristine ivory moldings. The small salon, the footman had called it. You could fit two of his own parlor quite neatly beneath the coffered ceiling and not even scrape the paint.

The Frasers were standing in front of the veined cream marble fireplace, flanked by matched silver candlesticks, the porcelain mantel clock between them. Mélanie Fraser had her back to the door, her dark head held at a proud angle, the pin-tucked skirt of her pale blue gown falling in perfect folds round her. Charles Fraser had one hand on his wife's shoulder, the other on the mantel, his claret-colored coat an unexpected jolt of color among the cool tones of the room.

They could have been posing for a portrait of a typical Mayfair couple, at home in their perfect jewel box of a world. Save that this was an hour when no fashionable couple would be awake. Unless, of course, they had failed to go to bed, in which case they would probably not be in each other's company.

Charles Fraser lifted his gaze to the doorway. "Oh, Roth, good. Come in." The rough Scottish lilt in his voice was more pronounced than it had been when Roth arrived. Otherwise he sounded perfectly in command of himself. Roth marveled, as he had on his arrival, at Fraser's composure. The result of training from the cradle, no doubt. In his place, Roth would have been tearing his hair out and smashing things.

"You haven't met my wife," Fraser said, as Roth advanced into the room.

"Mrs. Fraser." Roth inclined his head, then felt the breath catch unexpectedly in his throat. He had heard Mélanie Fraser described as beautiful. He had seen an engraving of her once, in a print shop window. Neither the description nor the picture had done her justice. He had seen women with more perfect features, more flawless complexions, more voluptuous bodies, but there was a radiance about Mélanie Fraser that made it impossible to look away. His inner defenses slammed into place. His own wife had taught him not to trust beauty.

"Please sit down, Mr. Roth." Her voice was as well-modulated as her husband's, but she had a slight accent that, while not obviously French or Spanish, betrayed that English was not her native tongue. She moved toward a green satin sofa, her gown rustling softly. The only sign that she had dressed hastily was the few strands of dark hair that had escaped about her face—that, and the absence of any jewelry. She looked like a woman who always wore earrings. "I've had coffee sent in," she said. "I imagine you could use it as much as we can."

Roth glanced at the sofa table, where a silver coffee service and an array of porcelain cups were set out on an intricately patterned blue-and-white tray that was probably Wedgwood. He wasn't sure what startled him more, the fact that Mélanie Fraser was composed enough to make such an offer or that she had been thoughtful enough to do so. In truth, the coffee would be welcome. He'd been questioning a trio of robbery suspects in the Brown Bear Tavern until past three in the morning. He had just returned to the Public Office to write up his notes when Charles Fraser's message arrived.

He crossed to a chair opposite the sofa, a spindly thing upholstered in a shiny cream-colored fabric. He found himself wondering how they managed to keep the upholstery clean. Perhaps they simply had it recovered every year.

Charles Fraser dropped down on the sofa beside his wife. He moved with the loose-limbed elegance of one bred to command. "You saw the garden and Colin's room?"

Roth nodded. "I was hoping there'd turn out to be some mistake. But I'm afraid there's no doubt your son was taken."

Mélanie Fraser set down the coffeepot with a thud that echoed through the room. Coffee spattered onto the glossy surface of the table and the delicate folds of her gown. "We know that." Her voice shook, cutting through the cinnamon and cloves of the potpourri-scented air. "We wouldn't have sent for you otherwise."

Charles Fraser put a hand on his wife's arm. She drew a harsh breath, stirring the pleated muslin at the neck of her gown. "I'm sorry." She jabbed the loose strands of hair behind her ear. "It's just so bloody awful."

The light from the branch of candles on the sofa table fell full on her face, revealing what Roth hadn't been able to see from the doorway. Her posture might be perfect, her voice controlled, her manners impeccable—but her eyes held a raw anguish that Roth had seen in the eyes of Billingsgate fishwives and Oxford Street milliners and Covent Garden harlots. The sick terror of a mother who fears for her child was a universal language, whatever the woman's accent. He felt a rush of cold shame. Mélanie Fraser might not deserve more consideration than a woman of lower station, but neither did she deserve less.

"There's no need to apologize, Mrs. Fraser. Bloody awful sums it up very well." He leaned forward, hands clasped between his knees. "You have a good eye, Mr. Fraser. It looks as if it happened just as you guessed. They came through the garden gate and probably tossed a rope up over the ledge of the window to your son's room. I found a few strands of rope stuck to the wall."

Mélanie Fraser tugged a handkerchief from her sleeve and pressed it over the spilled coffee. "You're sure they *meant* to take Colin? They couldn't have been after the silver and simply stumbled across him?"

"I'm not sure of anything, Mrs. Fraser. But they entered the house through your son's bedchamber window, a silly thing to do if they were bent on robbery. And as far as we can tell, nothing else is missing from the house. So yes, I'd say it's likely your son was their target."

She twisted the coffee-soaked handkerchief in her hands, as though she could knead answers out of the damp linen.

Fraser was looking at his wife. Lines were etched deep into the sharp Celtic planes of his face, but otherwise his control hadn't faltered. "They didn't go to all this trouble to take Colin in order to do him a mischief, Mel."

It was not the sort of comfort most husbands would offer their wives, but Mélanie Fraser nodded. "No. There is that." She picked up the coffeepot again and poured out three cups with painstaking care. "Cream, Mr. Roth?"

"Black." He leaned forward to accept the silver-rimmed cup she was holding out, close enough to catch the spicy floral scent of her skin and to see the smeared traces of blacking round her eyes.

Charles Fraser stared into his own cup. "London is full of boys it would be all too easy to snatch off the street. So whoever took Colin must want him to extract money from us or to use as leverage against one or both of us."

Roth took a welcome sip of the strong, hot coffee. "That seems the likeliest explanation." He balanced the fragile cup in his hand. "To own the truth, I've never come across a case like this nor heard tell of one. Young heiresses are sometimes abducted in the hope of forcing a marriage, but this is obviously something very different. As I said, the men were professionals, probably hired for the job. I don't believe in false reassurance.

But if they've taken your son for ransom or to use as a bargaining chip, they'll keep him safe and healthy."

Fraser gave a quick, contained nod. Mélanie Fraser's fingers whitened round the ecru porcelain of her cup.

Roth set down his coffee cup, reached into the frayed pocket of his brown wool coat, and drew out a notebook and a pencil. "I know it's difficult to think clearly at a time like this—"

Fraser set his own cup down with a clatter. "My wife isn't given to hysterics, Roth. I'll do my best not to succumb to them myself. For God's sake, don't waste time sparing our sensibilities."

Roth met the other man's gaze. Fraser's gray eyes had the hard glint of tempered steel. Roth recalled that before he had been a politician, Charles Fraser had been posted at the British embassy in Lisbon, where he had earned fame for exploits beyond the usual diplomatic line. A man of action with a cold intellect. A volatile combination.

"It was carefully planned," Fraser continued, in a tone that made Roth wonder just who was conducting the interview. "They'd have learned the routine of the house, the arrangement of the rooms." He looked at his wife. "My wife and I were discussing who we've seen about in the last few days. Tradesmen making deliveries. Hackney drivers. Coachmen and grooms. It would be easy enough for a stranger to blend in."

Roth nodded. "Judging by the break-in, they're too accomplished to have drawn attention to themselves, but the patrol I brought with me is having a word with the servants in case anyone noticed anything. Which brings us back to the question of the motive."

Fraser picked up his coffee cup, then set it down again without touching it. "Money would seem likeliest. Isn't it at the root of most crime?"

"It is indeed, Mr. Fraser. And it's surprising how often the culprit proves to be a family member." Roth looked from husband to wife. "Any relatives who've applied to you for a loan or whom you know to be in debt?"

Roth expected shocked denial at this accusation against one of their own. In his experience, the higher one moved up the social ladder, the more people wanted to believe that crime was something that only existed in the dark reaches of the underworld.

But Fraser merely said, "My brother's a captain in the Horse Guards. Fraternal feelings aside, he married an heiress. Their income is probably larger than ours. My sister and her husband live in Scotland and they're too proud to ask for money, let alone extort it. I have an aunt and uncle who are in Paris at the moment and a widowed aunt in Brighton. She has a taste for amorous intrigue, but she's far too well off to indulge in anything this sordid. None of my cousins is in straitened circumstances. Oh, and there's my grandfather. But he hasn't left Scotland in years and he's quite comfortably situated."

This last was a wild understatement. Charles Fraser's maternal grandfather was the Duke of Rannoch. Roth inclined his head. "I appreciate your frankness." He made some notes. "Mrs. Fraser?"

Mélanie Fraser plucked at the skirt of her gown, her nails scraping against the sheer fabric. "I'm an only child. Both my parents were killed during the war in Spain. Between the war and the revolution, I don't have any family left that I know of."

Roth, ardent supporter of the French Revolution, more than passingly sympathetic to Napoleon, looked into the eyes of this blue-blooded woman and found himself smiling in an awkward attempt to ease her fears. "Friends, then." He jotted down a note. "Hangers-on. Former servants, though it would have to be someone with the resources to carry out such a plot."

The Frasers exchanged glances again. "No one I can think of," Mrs. Fraser said. "The only servant who's left recently is our little girl's nurse who got married last summer. My husband and I were at the wedding."

"My friends aren't all saints," Fraser said. "But if they wanted money they'd simply ask for it."

"Of course it's possible he was taken for ransom by someone unknown to you," Roth said. "But while money's the likeliest motive, it's not the only one. You're a prominent politician, Mr.

Fraser. Perhaps the culprit wishes to force your hand in the House of Commons."

"You can't have followed my career too closely. It's highly improbable that any of my proposals will be enacted in the immediate future. It's more likely *I'd* take someone hostage as leverage."

"You ruffled a lot of feathers with your speeches against suspension of habeas corpus. Suppose someone took the boy to force you to be silent. Or to get you to change your vote."

"Unfortunately, they're hardly in need of my vote to suspend habeas corpus."

"No, but it would make a powerful statement to silence critics if you changed your position."

Fraser leaned back on the sofa, his eyes narrowing.

"I do read the papers," Roth said. His voice was mild, but there was an edge to it.

"I don't doubt it." Fraser watched him a moment longer. "You're an unusual man, Mr. Roth. You work for the chief magistrate of Bow Street, who works for the Home Secretary. The Home Secretary is a government minister. Yet you've just suggested that someone allied with the government's interests may have been behind the disappearance of our son."

"It's my job to explore all possibilities, Mr. Fraser." Roth shifted his gaze to Mélanie Fraser. "Mrs. Fraser? Is there any reason you can think of why your son might have been taken to target you?"

She shook her head, strands of hair stirring about her face. "No. I'm sometimes accused of being too outspoken, but I can't see anyone going to this much trouble to quieten me."

Her fingers clenched tight in her lap. Her gaze shifted toward the painting on the overmantel. Roth followed the direction of her gaze. The painting had only registered before as a blur of colors. Now the candlelight seemed to cluster about the luminous whites and pastels the painter had used. It was a portrait of Mélanie Fraser and the children. They were sitting on a wrought-iron bench in the same garden where Roth had looked for clues to Colin Fraser's disappearance. In the painting it was not a November night but a spring afternoon. The linden trees in the background were thick with leaves, not stark and barren. Mélanie Fraser's face was bright with laughter, not shadowed with fear. A little girl of perhaps eighteen months sat in her lap, reaching for the rose-colored ribbons on her dress. A small boy stood beside her, leaning against her arm.

Colin Fraser must have been about five when the portrait was painted, Roth guessed, judging by his own sons. The boy wore a shirt and breeches, not ruffles and velvet. His hair was dark, almost as dark as his mother's. His face was fine-boned and serious, but curiosity sparkled in his eyes and a hint of mischief danced in the slant of his brows.

Roth's throat closed unexpectedly. "He looks like a bright lad."

"He is." Mélanie Fraser's voice broke, like crystal hurled against a rock. She drew a sharp breath. "He'll keep his head. I keep telling myself that."

Charles Fraser took her hand and gripped it between his own. "He has his mother's nerves of steel as well as her looks."

In truth, the boy did look very like his mother. Roth studied the picture a moment longer, searching for some echo of Charles Fraser in his son. You could see it in the little girl—the strong, determined bones of the face were visible even beneath the baby fat. But the boy was pure French-Spanish, with no hint of the Celt. Not that it was surprising for a child to take strongly after one parent. And yet—

Roth turned a page in his notebook and jotted down a random note, to give himself a moment to think. The Frasers seemed a happy enough couple, but Charles Fraser was a damned cold bastard and fidelity was rare in their set. Some women of fashion made it a matter of pride to have each of their children by a different father. It was rare for an eldest son and heir to be illegitimate, but accidents could happen to even the cleverest woman. If another man had fathered Colin Fraser, if that man knew or guessed and wanted to lay claim to his child . . . Roth scribbled over the page. It would explain Mélanie Fraser's startling combination of self-possession and fear if she suspected who had taken her child and why.

It was nothing he could pursue with the Frasers, but he could make discreet inquiries later. No doubt it would be damnably difficult. What the polite world did and what they were willing to talk about were two very different things. "Anything else either of you can think of?" he said. "Anything anyone might pressure you to do, not to do, anything anyone might want from you—"

"We've had our share of adventures in the past," Charles Fraser said, "but nothing— Oh, Christ." Fraser stared across the room, as though he had been slapped hard across the face.

"Darling?" Mélanie Fraser squeezed her husband's hand.

Charles Fraser pushed his fingers into his brown hair. "It's absurd. But—"

"What?" His wife's voice was tense with strain.

Fraser looked at her. "The Carevalo Ring."

Mélanie Fraser's eyes widened. "Why—"

"What ring?" Roth asked.

Fraser drew a breath. "You've heard of the Marqués de Carevalo?"

"Spanish nobleman. War hero."

"Yes. He was one of the *guerrillero* leaders whose forces were allied—somewhat uneasily at times—with Wellington's troops in driving the French from Spain. Carevalo was reckless to the point of insanity, but he was a brilliant enough commander that his crazy risks paid off more often than not. The Carevalos are an old Spanish family. Carevalo saw his service to Spain as part of his family's tradition. He was inclined to view the royal family as incompetent upstarts, with little understanding of what was due to the Spain he believed in. Like many Spaniards who opposed the French, Carevalo isn't best pleased with the course his country has taken under the restored monarchy. He's now working with the Spanish liberals, who are in increasingly vehement opposition to the king."

Roth nodded. In his view, the British government had woefully betrayed their Spanish allies. Many of the Spaniards had seen the struggle against Napoleon's occupation as a time to enact long-needed reforms in their own country. At the end of the war, the Spanish king had been restored under an extremely progressive constitution. But the restored King Ferdinand had promptly repealed the reforms made in his absence, restored the Inquisition, stifled all freedom of speech and discussion, and refused to honor the constitution. All the while, the British government continued unwavering in their support of him.

"Carevalo's in England now, isn't he?" Roth said. "Trying to turn British opinion against the Spanish monarchy."

"Yes, he— No, I'll have to start at the beginning. It's a hell of a long story." Fraser looked as though the last thing he felt like doing was telling it while more time ticked by with his son missing.

"If there's any chance it has a bearing on your son's disappearance—"

"Quite." Fraser pushed himself to his feet and took a turn about the room. "To understand what the ring means today, you have to understand its history. What came to be known as the Carevalo Ring is a gold signet ring, a lion with rubies for eyes. It was forged in Andalusia in the eleventh century, when Spain was divided between Moorish and Christian princes who fought each other and often fought on the same side, in a complex web of shifting alliances. Ramón de Carevalo was a friend and comrade in arms of El Cid. Like El Cid, he fought in the service of both Christians and Moors."

Fraser continued to pace, speaking with the crisp precision Roth imagined he would use to outline a strategy for steering a bill through the House of Commons. "There are different stories about how Ramón de Carevalo came to possess the ring. The ring was commissioned by Princess Aysha, wife of Tariq ibn Tashfin. She and her husband presided over a court that was known for its tolerance and artistic achievements. The ring represented what was best in the court. A Jewish sculptor designed it, a Christian gem-cutter cut the rubies, a Moorish goldsmith forged it. According to some versions of the story, Aysha commissioned the ring as a gift for her husband. After Prince Tariq was killed in battle, Carevalo stole the ring and abducted Aysha. According to other versions, Aysha commissioned the ring not for her husband but for Carevalo, who was secretly her lover. After her husband's death the two of them ran off together."

Fraser's mouth tightened for a moment, perhaps with impatience. "Whether it was an abduction or an elopement, they were pursued by Aysha's brother. Carevalo and the brother fought. Supposedly the magical power of the ring protected Carevalo. Less fanciful versions of the story say that Carevalo put up his hand to ward off a death blow and the sword point glanced off the ring. Or perhaps Carevalo was simply a better swordsman. What does seem certain is that Carevalo survived and he and Aysha escaped to an estate he had been given in Léon.

"Whatever the reasons for the marriage, apparently it was a success. Carevalo more or less retired from fighting. Aysha brought a small but talented group of artists to their estate from various cultures and religions. The castle they built is still standing today. It has some of the most beautiful frescoes and metalwork in Spain. They—"

The crisp voice broke off. Fraser stopped pacing and drew a sharp breath. He stood stock-still, his back to Roth and his wife, his fingers pressed over his eyes, as though he could not remember what he had been saying or the point of the conversation.

Mélanie Fraser watched her husband for a moment, then turned her gaze to Roth. "Aysha and Ramón's great-great-grandson wore the ring on the Third Crusade," she said, her own voice taut with self-control, "which is decidedly ironic, considering the spirit of tolerance in which the ring was forged. He was the only one of his party to return alive. He came home to find that his younger brother had usurped the title and estate in his absence. An armed guard awaited him, but when he rode up to the castle, the peasants rose up on his side."

"Because he showed them the ring?" Roth said.

"According to the legend," said Mélanie Fraser. "Whether the ring had come to the Carevalos through conquest or as a gift to a beloved, it had come to symbolize power. People often find it easier to follow a symbol than a person."

"That certainly seems to have been the feeling in the Carevalo family." Charles Fraser strode back into the center of the room. "In the time of Ferdinand and Isabella, a Carevalo cousin stole the ring and then apparently had the current Carevalo heir murdered and usurped the title. He went on to become the first Marqués de Carevalo. His grandson, the third marqués, failed to wear the ring when he went off to fight in the Spanish Armada. Not only did he perish at sea, so did all the other men from the Carevalo region who went with him. So, of course, did a number of other Spaniards who were part of the Armada, but that minor historical detail hasn't dimmed the legend of the ring's power. During the War of the Spanish Succession, the eighth marqués and his son supported rival claimants to the throne. They stole the ring back and forth from each other several times in the course of the conflict. The loyalty of the people in the Carevalo region seems to have gone to whoever possessed the ring."

Roth leaned forward. "You know a great deal about the history of the Carevalo family."

Fraser grimaced. "I've had reason to learn. Sometime in the middle of the last century, the ring disappeared. No one is sure exactly when—it was a while before the Carevalos admitted it was no longer in their possession, and no one wanted to take credit for being the one to have lost the ring. One story is that it was taken by bandits but the Carevalos were too proud to admit it. Another is that one of the Carevalo sons lost it in a card game and then was afraid to tell his father. Or that a Carevalo secretly presented it to his mistress as proof of the extent of his devotion. But the ring's loss only seemed to make the legend stronger. The story grew up that whoever recovered it would be invincible in battle. Which brings us to November of 1812."

Fraser paced the carpet, as though mapping out the terrain of a battlefield in its scrolls and medallions. "Wellington's troops were wintering in cantonments near Ciudad Rodrigo, just beyond the Portuguese border. The French were spread about Spain. It was clear that the real push of the war would come with the spring thaw. I was on the staff at the British embassy in Lisbon. We got word that a group of bandits in the Cantabrian Mountains had stumbled across something that looked like the Carevalo Ring in the course of plundering a village."

Fraser stopped pacing and met Roth's gaze across the room. "You can understand the significance. The current Marqués de Carevalo was a noted *guerrillero* leader, but the people of his own region were slow to rally to the Spanish cause. Or perhaps I should say the British cause. We'd rather taken over their war."

"And it seemed the recovery of the ring would rouse the populace to battle?"

"That was our hope. The Carevalo lands were strategically situated for the spring campaign." Fraser strode to the fireplace. "The bandits were willing to turn the ring over to us, but only for a substantial payment in gold. Carevalo was away fighting in the south. The ambassador wanted to act quickly before the French got wind of the ring. There were a fair number of French sympathizers in the Carevalo region. If the French had recovered the ring it might have turned the tide in their favor. The ambassador thought the fewer people who heard the story, the better. So he sent me to retrieve the ring."

"You'd undertaken such missions before." It wasn't a question.

"From time to time. When they found it convenient to use someone without direct links to the military." Fraser leaned his arm on the marble mantel as though to anchor himself. "I went off to the Cantabrian Mountains. I had a detachment of soldiers with me, but none of them knew the point of our mission. I was half-convinced I was on a wild-goose chase."

"We still don't know for a certainty that you weren't," Mélanie Fraser said.

Roth swung his head round to look at her. "You and Mr. Fraser were already married at the time?"

"No." She was worrying the narrow ruffle on her sleeve with her left hand. The lace had frayed between her fingers. "We met on his journey into the mountains. I'd been stranded. I couldn't believe my good fortune when a gallant British gentleman came to my rescue."

She looked at her husband. His eyes went dark with an emotion Roth couldn't put a name to, save that for a moment there was nothing cold or self-contained in his gaze.

Fraser turned back to Roth. "We continued on to the rendezvous point. The morning we were to meet with the bandits we were ambushed by a French patrol." He picked up the poker and jabbed it into the fireplace, though the fire was burning briskly. A puff of smoke gusted through the room. "When the bullets stopped flying, our whole party was dead, save Mélanie and me, a sergeant, and our servants. The two bandits who had come to make the exchange must have been caught up in the crossfire. We found their bodies. The ring was gone. We thought one of the escaping Frenchmen must have made off with it."

The firelight caught the stark weight of failure in his eyes. He returned the poker to its stand. "We made our way back to Lisbon," he said after a moment. "Wellington's forces were victorious in the spring campaign. The French were driven out of Spain altogether. Napoleon was crushed in Russia and forced to abdicate. The ring seemed irrelevant."

"Until?" Roth said.

Fraser turned to look him full in the face. "Until three weeks ago. Antonio de Carevalo came to see me and demanded I hand it over to him. He said the ring was his family's birthright."

Roth frowned. "But—"

"But I don't have the ring. I tried to tell Carevalo that. He refused to believe me. He said now the war was over he'd managed to track down one of the French soldiers who attacked us.

The Frenchman claimed the ring never found its way into French hands."

"The French never used it to rally support on the Carevalo lands?"

"No." Fraser glanced down at the fire, his thick, dark brows drawing together. "We kept expecting them to. I rather suspect one of the French patrol appropriated the ring for himself."

"Why wouldn't Carevalo believe you?"

"I'm not sure, save that the war left him with little trust in anyone British. He was adamant that I must have kept the ring for myself. He refused even to consider other possibilities. You can see why he wants to get his hands on it. If Carevalo and the Spanish liberals rise up against the king, the ring could be just as valuable a symbol now as in 1812."

"What did he say when you insisted you didn't have the ring?"

"That I'd be sorry." A muscle tightened along Fraser's jaw. "I took it for bluster. He was half-drunk at the time, which isn't unusual for Carevalo. When I saw him a few days later, he acted as though nothing had happened."

Roth tapped his pencil against his notebook. "Has Carevalo ever seen your son?"

"Oh yes. Carevalo dined with us occasionally when we lived in Lisbon."

"Alliances shift. Friends turn into enemies."

Fraser was looking into the coals again. "Yes, but—"

"Honor among gentlemen?" Roth tried to keep the irony from his voice.

Fraser lifted his head. "The war taught me that men of all ranks can find honor elastic, Mr. Roth. I was going to say I knew Carevalo. I thought I knew him."

Mélanie Fraser stared at the unraveled mess she had made of the once pristine lace on her sleeve. "We saw Carevalo at the reception this evening."

"Did he say anything that could relate to your son's disappearance?" Roth asked.

"Not in the least. He flirted with me." She shivered, as though the memory made her feel unclean. "Why didn't you tell me he'd asked you for the ring, Charles?"

"I didn't see any point in dredging up the past."

Their gazes met. Roth couldn't begin to guess at the memories that echoed between them, but the intimacy of that look went far beyond what he expected from husbands and wives or even lovers.

A rap at the door broke the stillness. Fraser turned from his wife. "Come in."

"Sorry to interrupt, sir." A slender man with straight fair hair and pale blue eyes stepped into the room. It was Addison, Fraser's valet, who had shown Roth the footprints in the primrose bed. "Polly has something you and Mrs. Fraser and Mr. Roth had best hear." He looked at Roth. "I told Officer Dawkins I'd bring her in. She's a bit upset."

It was a classic bit of British understatement. The girl who followed Addison into the room was pale with fright and red-eyed with weeping. Roth would swear her legs were shaking beneath the printed cotton skirt of her gown. Her arms were folded across her stomach as though she was going to be sick.

Her gaze went from Charles Fraser to his wife. "Oh, sir. Ma'am. I'll never forgive myself. It was all my fault."

Chapter 4

*M*élanie Fraser pushed herself to her feet and crossed to the girl's side. "It's all right, Polly, we're all overset. Sit down and tell us what happened." She put her arm round Polly and steered her to the sofa.

Polly sank down on the sofa and drew a shuddering breath. She was scarcely more than a child herself, perhaps fifteen or sixteen. She looked at Mrs. Fraser out of wide, troubled hazel eyes. "I didn't think anything of it at the time. Well, I was flattered, truth be told. And he was so . . . so . . . ."

"He?" Charles Fraser's voice was surprisingly gentle, though Roth could feel the force of his impatience.

Polly raised her anguished gaze to him. "I didn't know him for a criminal, sir, truly. Well, I still don't rightly know it. Only Officer Dawkins, he was asking us questions and I had this dreadful thought of a sudden—"

"And very clever of you to make the connection." Mélanie

Fraser pressed a cup of coffee, liberally laced with milk and sugar, into the girl's trembling hand. "And brave of you to tell us." She paused for a moment. Roth applauded her technique. You never got far flustering a witness. "Who was he, Polly?" Mrs. Fraser asked.

"A deliveryman from Hatchards. I saw him in the mews when I was hanging out the laundry. He tipped his hat—ever so much the gentleman—and then he said wasn't it a fine day and it would have been proper rude not to answer—"

"Just so." Mélanie Fraser's hands were white-knuckled, but her voice was coaxing. Roth stayed silent. She was handling this interrogation much better than he could have done. "What then?" she said.

Polly took a gulp of coffee, sloshing it into the saucer. "He asked me was this a pleasant house to work in and how long had I been here and was the family large. Then he said he'd best be off, but—" She drew a breath and spoke in a rush. "He said did all the houses hereabouts have gardens because he was afeared the gate might be locked. I said—I said I couldn't answer for the other houses, but our garden gate was always unlocked."

"It's all right, Polly." Mrs. Fraser put her hand over Polly's own. "All you did was tell him the truth. Did you see him again?"

"A week later. Just two days since. He said he was going a bit out of his way, but"—she colored—"he couldn't help stopping in the hopes I'd be out with the laundry again. He said he'd had a hard morning, he'd had to take a load of books up to a schoolroom clear in the attics and why was it children were always packed away out of sight. And I said— Oh, ma'am, I'm sorry."

Mélanie Fraser swallowed, but her voice and gaze remained soothing. "You said it wasn't that way in our house?"

"I said you and Mr. Fraser liked to have the children nearby. I—God forgive me, I pointed out Master Colin's and Miss Jessica's windows."

Roth saw the full realization register in both Frasers' eyes— one of the men who had taken their son had been so close they could have stepped into the garden and looked him in the face. Instead, he'd had all the information he needed handed to him on a silver salver.

Charles Fraser looked at Polly and smiled, the first genuine smile Roth had seen from him. It lit his cool eyes with unexpected warmth. "They'd have learned what they wanted one way or another, Polly. At least this way we know how they came by the information."

"Can you tell me what he looked like, Polly?" Roth asked.

Polly raised her head and fixed her gaze on him. The Frasers' tacit forgiveness had wiped some of the strain from her face. She was a pretty girl and her eyes, cleared of weeping, were bright with intelligence. "He was tall. Not so tall as you or Mr. Fraser, but taller than Mr. Addison." She nodded toward Fraser's valet, who was sitting quietly on the sidelines.

"Hair?" Roth asked. "Eyes?"

Polly's level brows drew together in an effort of memory. "His hair was brown—darker than yours, Mr. Roth, but a bit lighter than Mr. Fraser's. I suppose his eyes must've been brown, too— No, they were blue." She colored again. "I remember thinking they looked just like a bed of larkspur in the spring."

"Right." Roth jotted down the description and gave her an encouraging smile. "Anything else? How old would you guess he was?"

She frowned again. "Older than William and Michael, but younger than Mr. Addison."

"William and Michael are one-and-twenty or thereabouts," Charles Fraser said. "Addison's thirty-two, like me."

Polly stared down at her hands, still frowning. "He had a dimple in his right cheek when he smiled. And his voice—I don't think he was London-born. He had a bit of the sound of a Welshman."

"Does it sound like anyone you know of?" Fraser asked Roth.

"No, but even I can only boast acquaintance with a fraction of London's criminal class. We'll circulate a description and offer a reward for information. I'll make inquiries at Hatchards, though I'd lay you money he's no deliveryman." Roth nodded at Polly. "This is a good start. You've done well." He returned his notebook and pencil to his pocket, then added, "Mr. Fraser is right, Polly. They'd have got the information they wanted, one way or another. There's no way you could have known what they were planning. No one could."

Polly gave him a tremulous smile, got to her feet, and dropped a quick curtsy before Addison escorted her back to the kitchen.

"I'd best be off," Roth told the Frasers. "I want to get this description circulated as soon as possible." He took a last swallow of coffee and stood up. "You'll tell me what you learn from Carevalo?"

Both the Frasers were silent for a moment. "I didn't say I was going to see Carevalo," Fraser said.

"But you are, aren't you? It's what I'd do in your place."

Mélanie Fraser rose from the sofa and went to stand beside her husband. "We're both going to see him."

Roth looked into her eyes and caught a glimpse of iron beneath the porcelain surface. He nodded. "You know Carevalo, you'll know to handle him. Did you think I'd try to stop you? I don't see how I could. Besides, if Carevalo is behind the boy's disappearance, he'll scarcely admit it to a Bow Street Runner. But presumably he'll admit it to you. I only ask that you keep me informed. No rash heroics, Mr. Fraser."

For an instant the coolness in Fraser's eyes cracked like a sheet of ice. Beneath lay a white-hot rage that was one step short of violence and a self-recrimination that went bone-deep. "I'm not a fool, Roth."

"I didn't say you were."

Mélanie Fraser reached for her husband's hand. "Charles wouldn't do anything that might jeopardize Colin's safety. Neither of us would."

Which, Roth thought as he left the house, answered his question without promising anything at all. Charles Fraser might be a master at control, but sooner or later the fury roiling beneath the cool surface was bound to break free. Roth wondered if the Marqués de Carevalo had the least idea what he'd unleashed.

"Ah, Mr. Fraser." The desk clerk at Mivart's Hotel turned his head between his well-starched shirt points. "We've been expecting you."

Oh, Christ. It was true. "Expecting us?" Charles said.

"The Marqués de Carevalo thought you might call." If the clerk thought it odd that they had done so at half-past six in the morning, he gave no sign of it.

Charles barely refrained from reaching across the polished counter and grasping the clerk by the well-tailored lapels of his coat. "Where is he?"

"I'm afraid I can't say, sir. The marqués left this morning."

"Left?" Mélanie's voice shook, frayed to the breaking point. "But he was at the Princess Esterhazy's only a few hours ago."

"The marqués returned to the hotel at about four this morning, madam. A short time later he settled his account and departed." The clerk's face was carefully wooden. "He said if you or Mr. Fraser asked for him I was to direct you to Mr. O'Roarke in room 212."

"O'Roarke?" For a moment Charles wasn't sure he had heard correctly. "Raoul O'Roarke?"

"I believe that is the gentleman's name. He arrived at the hotel yesterday evening."

Charles didn't even stop to look at Mélanie. There was no point. They crossed the lobby and made for the stairs without speaking.

Raoul O'Roarke. A name from the past, a force to be reckoned with, a piece that shook the emerging pattern of the puzzle. O'Roarke and Carevalo had both been leaders in the Spanish resistance to French occupation, but O'Roarke's hardheaded pragmatism was the antithesis of Carevalo's extravagant intensity.

Charles had known Raoul O'Roarke since boyhood. O'Roarke's five-times-great-grandfather had fled to Spain from Ireland after ending up on the losing side in a struggle with the English in the time of Elizabeth. Successive generations of O'Roarkes had intermarried with Spanish noblewomen, but Raoul O'Roarke's mother was an Irish Catholic aristocrat. O'Roarke had grown up in both countries and had been educated in Dublin. Charles had childhood memories of O'Roarke as one of the throng of guests always overflowing his grandfather's Irish estates. O'Roarke had been friendlier than most, with a kind word to spare for the curious Fraser children and a genuine interest in their activities. Charles still had a copy of *The Rights of Man* that O'Roarke had given him for his tenth birthday, and he could still remember the thrill not only of the present but of the fact that O'Roarke had made time to discuss it with him.

In those days, O'Roarke had been one of the young Irish radicals who spoke and wrote against British rule. Just how much O'Roarke had had to do with the United Irish uprising of 1798 was still open to debate. No formal charges had been laid against him, but O'Roarke had slipped out of the country in the aftermath of the uprising and returned to Spain.

O'Roarke's letter of condolence, after Charles's mother's death, had been one of the least sentimental and most comforting Charles had received. When Charles joined the British embassy staff in Lisbon, he met O'Roarke again, a clever man, committed to his cause, willing to be ruthless when necessary. O'Roarke had made it clear that he remembered Charles as a boy, but at the same time had been quick to treat Charles as an adult and an equal. Yet though O'Roarke had fought alongside the British as part of the Spanish resistance to Napoleon, he had no liking for the English and never pretended otherwise.

"I didn't know Raoul O'Roarke was in England." Mélanie spoke when they were halfway up the first flight of stairs.

"Nor did I. He must have just arrived."

"He and Carevalo were never particular friends."

"No. I've heard O'Roarke call Carevalo a romantic fool on more than one occasion. But they were allies against the French and they'd be allied now in their hatred of the Spanish monarchy. It's not surprising to find they're working together. Perhaps O'Roarke thinks he'll have more luck than Carevalo's had mustering support in London for Spanish liberalism. Or perhaps he was forced to leave Spain. Last I heard he was setting Madrid on its ear with his antimonarchist pamphlets."

Mélanie paused on the first-floor landing. Beneath the blue velvet brim of her bonnet, her eyes looked enormous. "Charles, you don't think O'Roarke—"

"I don't know what I think. Except that I'm going to kill Carevalo when I get my hands on him. Let's see this message he left for us."

He started for the next flight of stairs. She caught at his hand. "Charles."

He scanned her face. "What?"

She drew a breath, then gave a slight shake of her head. "It doesn't matter. Nothing else matters if they have Colin. Let's go."

They half ran up the stairs and down the second-floor corridor to room 212. Charles turned the handle without bothering to knock. The door was unlatched. "O'Roarke?" he called, pushing the door open.

"Fraser?" A familiar voice, light with mockery, carried into the narrow entryway from the sitting room beyond. "Come in and tell me what the devil's going on."

The air in the sitting room smelled of toast and marmalade and coffee. O'Roarke was seated at a linen-covered table, his long fingers curled round a cup, a newspaper spread before him. He wore an immaculate white shirt and a rich paisley silk dressing gown. He had always been elegant, even in the blood and grime of the field.

"Look here, Fraser—" O'Roarke broke off as his gaze fell on Mélanie. "Mrs. Fraser." He pushed himself to his feet. "I didn't realize."

"Where's Carevalo?" Charles said.

"I was hoping you could tell me." O'Roarke tightened the belt on his dressing gown. "He hammered on my door at an ungodly hour this morning to say he was leaving and I was to deliver a letter to you if you called. Very cloak-and-dagger. Typical Carevalo."

Charles's gaze had already fallen on the letter, leaning against a black basalt candlestick on the mantel. He crossed to the fireplace, snatched up the letter, and broke the seal. Mélanie was beside him.

It was a single page, written in English in a flowing black hand.

> *My dear Fraser,*
>
> *Congratulations. How long did it take you to work it out, I wonder? But that's neither here nor there, as you British say. You know now of course. I have the boy. I want the ring. You have until this Saturday evening. When you are ready to hand over the ring, place an advertisement in the* Morning Chronicle. *I will respond with instructions. If you value your son's life half as much as I think you do, you won't fail me.*
>
> *Carevalo*
>
> *P.S.*
>
> *Don't make the mistake of thinking I don't mean what I say. I'm not the man you knew in Lisbon. I can play the cheerful boon companion when it serves my purpose. But believe me, antagonist is a role to which I am much better suited.*

Charles opened his fist, dropped the letter, crossed to the table, and grabbed O'Roarke by the shoulders. "Where is he?"

O'Roarke stared at him. "Don't be an idiot, Fraser. I told you—"

"Goddamnit, O'Roarke." Charles pushed him up against the

wall. The plate-glass windows rattled in their frames. "Where's Carevalo?"

The early-morning light flickered over the finely molded bones of O'Roarke's face. "What's Carevalo done?" he said.

"He's taken Colin." Mélanie spoke from across the room. "He wants us to give him the Carevalo Ring."

"Oh, Christ." O'Roarke closed his eyes for a moment. "Oh, sweet Jesus. The damned fool."

Charles tightened his grip. "I need answers. I'll beat them out of you if I have to."

"That would be a lamentable waste of time for us both, Fraser. I don't have answers to give you, however many of my bones you manage to break." O'Roarke drew a breath. "For God's sake, Charles. You've known me all your life. Do you really think I'd be party to abducting a child?"

"If you thought it was the only way to further your cause." Charles stared hard into O'Roarke's eyes. The man was more than capable of lying. Charles had seen him do so with great agility. But he realized, too, that Carevalo would know the lengths to which he would go to get information. So unless Carevalo was more fool than Charles thought, he'd make sure O'Roarke didn't have any information to give. O'Roarke was most likely telling the truth.

Charles released O'Roarke and took a step back. "Tell us what you know."

"I arrived in London last night and came straight to the hotel." O'Roarke's voice had the rifle-shot crispness Charles remembered from moments of crisis in the Peninsula. "I expected to meet with Carevalo this morning. Instead he woke me sometime after four and said he'd been called away on private business. He wouldn't say what business or where he was going."

"Did you ask?"

"Of course." O'Roarke took a quick turn round the room. "I had no particular desire to twiddle my thumbs waiting for him. He refused to tell me anything else. Had I been a little more awake I might have pressed him further, but I doubt I'd have been successful. He gave me the letter and said you'd probably call for it sometime today." O'Roarke whirled round and faced Charles across the breakfast table. "I had no idea how important the letter was. I'm sorry."

"*Sorry*—" Mélanie said.

"Where would he go?" Charles asked.

"Somewhere none of us will be able to trace him."

"And he probably doesn't have Colin with him in any event. He'll have left the messy bits up to his hirelings." Charles pressed his hands over his eyes. "Whom does Carevalo know in England?"

"Lord and Lady Holland. Lord John Russell. The Lydgates. You and Mrs. Fraser. A score of others, I imagine."

Charles moved to the table, keeping O'Roarke within striking distance. "Does he have a mistress?"

"I expect he has more than one. But he's of far too jealous a disposition to share their names with anyone, let alone me."

"Damn it, O'Roarke." Charles slammed his hand down on the table. "He's your friend. He must have written to you."

"Don't break the china, Fraser, it won't get us anywhere. He's not my friend, he's my ally. There's a world of difference."

"Allies write to allies," Mélanie said.

"Oh, Carevalo wrote to me." O'Roarke rested one hand on a chair back with the deceptive nonchalance of a panther. "He wrote to me about the stubborn loyalty of the British government to the monarchy in Spain. About the arrogant contempt British soldiers have for their former Spanish comrades. About the way the liberals at Holland House lectured him on the virtues of British constitutionalism. He didn't include personal details." O'Roarke looked at Charles, his expression not unkind. "You don't have the ring?"

"*Of course* I don't have the ring."

"There's no *of course* about it, Fraser. The ring disappeared in the ambush. The men who had it were killed. The French soldier claims the French never got their hands on it."

"They must be lying."

"Or you are. Carevalo has evidently decided you are."

Something snapped inside Charles. He reached out to grab O'Roarke. O'Roarke caught his arm. "Steady, Fraser. For what it's worth, I'm inclined to believe you. Though I can't for the life of me say why. There was little to choose between your side and the French. In the end you both used us. You used Spain as a private battleground to fight your war. You used our people as cannon fodder, you used our women as whores, you used our land for pillage. And when it was over, you threw your support behind our incompetent tyrant of a king."

Charles wrenched his arm away. "I'm no supporter of King Ferdinand. I never have been."

"Your country is. The government you served are doing their damnedest to keep Ferdinand in power while he rips to shreds any of the reforms that came out of the war. That's what Carevalo would say."

Mélanie, who had been watching in silence, moved to the table. "You seem to be forgetting that I'm half-Spanish," she said. Her hands closed hard on a chair back. "Just as you are, Mr. O'Roarke."

O'Roarke turned his gaze to her. His eyes were hard and unyielding. "But you've clearly decided your loyalties lie with your husband's country, madam."

Mélanie looked back at him, as though she could cut through to his soul. "He's six years old. He still worries about ogres under the bed, though he won't admit it. He can't go to sleep without his stuffed bear. He woke screaming from a nightmare only last week and I had to go sit with him. He—"

"Mrs. Fraser—" O'Roarke stretched out his hand to her, then let it fall to his side. "If I hear anything from Carevalo, I'll let you know."

"You expect us to believe that?" Charles said.

O'Roarke's mouth lifted in a faint smile. "About as much as you can expect me to believe you know nothing about the ring."

Charles looked at him a moment longer, then gave a brief nod. "Quite. Mel? There's no sense in wasting any more time."

"Charles," O'Roarke said as they turned to the door.

They both turned round. O'Roarke was still leaning against the chair, but despite the languid drape of the silk dressing gown, he had the unmistakable air of a commander. "Don't underestimate Carevalo. He doesn't make idle threats. You've heard how he lost his own son?"

Charles took a step closer to Mélanie. "I thought his family were killed by the French."

"His wife and the younger children, yes. The eldest son fought with Carevalo's *guerrillero* band. I met him once or twice. A boy of fourteen, who worshipped his father. Before the British were in the war—early '08, it must have been—the French besieged Carevalo's forces, who were hiding in a ruined castle near Burgos. Young Carevalo was carrying messages. He fell into French hands. The French commander told Carevalo to surrender if he wanted his son back alive."

"And?" Mélanie's voice was bone dry.

O'Roarke looked straight into her eyes. He had the look of a man with an intimate acquaintance with hell. "Carevalo sent back a message telling his son he loved him and he knew he'd die like a man. They shot the boy within view of the castle walls."

Mélanie made a small, strangled sound. Charles reached out and gripped her hand.

"Carevalo's not a monster," O'Roarke said. "But he's a man who'll give up anything for his cause. He loved his children. He'll never forgive himself for sacrificing his son, yet if he had to do it again, he'd make the same decision. And if he could sacrifice his own son, he won't hesitate to sacrifice yours."

The rain had stopped and a gray light was fighting its way through the morning mist when Charles and Mélanie emerged from Mivart's. Charles paused on the pavement before the hotel, his senses assaulted by light and sound, his brain battered by his own anger.

A post chaise had drawn up in front of the hotel and two porters were unloading bandboxes and portmanteaux onto the pavement. A third porter was struggling to lift a hamper from the boot while a gentleman in a many-caped greatcoat abjured him to be careful not to bruise the port. The rattle of wheels and the snap of reins filled the air. More carriages were abroad than when they had arrived at the hotel. It must be getting on toward seven. More than three hours since they'd discovered Colin's disappearance.

Rational thought came flooding back and with it a sense of purpose. Charles took Mélanie's arm and drew her toward their waiting carriage. "Hell," he said when they were inside the carriage and the coachman had given the horses their office. "Bloody, bloody hell. How could I have been such a fool?"

"You couldn't have foreseen this." Mélanie folded her arms over her stomach, as though she could physically force down a wave of fear and nausea. "Neither of us could."

He wrapped his arm round her and pulled her against him. "Colin's a survivor. He's our son." He pushed back her bonnet and put his lips to her hair. "We're going to have to find the damned ring."

"Yes." He felt her tremble, felt her control the tremors. "The question is where to begin."

He took her hand and held it between his own. "Where it was lost. In the past."

Chapter 5

The Cantabrian Mountains, Spain
November 1812

Even in winter, their rocky slopes dusted with snow, the mountains looked parched. The sight reminded Charles that he could do with a drink. Perhaps it was in keeping with the barren waste he had made of his life that he was riding along a barren waste of a mountain track, in the midst of what increasingly seemed to be a barren waste of a war.

The track was so narrow that they had to go single file. Lieutenant Jennings led the way, his shoulders set with weary nonchalance. Charles's valet, Addison, Sergeant Baxter, and five soldiers of the 43rd Foot tramped behind Charles, their booted feet thudding rhythmically against the frozen, rocky ground.

The track widened a bit. Jennings fell back beside Charles. "We should look for a place to make camp. There's little more than another hour of daylight." He squinted at the slate-gray sky. "And it looks like we may have snow."

Charles nodded. "There are wine caves a mile or so on."

Jennings lifted his brows. "You know these mountains well."

"I've been here once or twice."

Jennings regarded him for a moment. His blue eyes held a glint of mockery. "I suppose you still wouldn't care to tell me why the devil we're traipsing across the mountains in the middle of winter?"

Charles smiled and shook his head. "You wouldn't believe me if I told you, Jennings."

Jennings gave a laugh that was sharp with the cynicism of the hardened soldier. "Very likely not. As I suspect the last thing you'd tell me would be the truth. You're a damned cold bastard, Fraser."

"I don't know about the bastard part," Charles said without inflection, "but I'd have to be inhuman not to be cold in this weather."

In truth, the cold was so intense you could taste it on your tongue. It sliced like a knife blade through the wool of his greatcoat and the Cordoba leather of his top boots. Patches of snow littered the ground, though none was falling at the moment, thank God for small mercies. He wondered what Jennings would have said if he'd told him they'd come all this way, in the chill of oncoming winter, in search of a piece of jewelry.

Charles turned up the collar of his greatcoat. If he were warm and dry before a fire in Lisbon, the search for the Carevalo Ring would be an excuse for a good laugh. Even now, cold and tired and saddle-sore, he suspected he ought to see the humorous side of the situation.

He flicked a sidelong glance at Jennings. Tempers were frayed to the breaking point. None of the soldiers were happy at having been sent on this mission when they had expected to be snugly bivouacked for the winter. It was understandable that they were curious about what Charles expected to receive in exchange for the gold they were escorting north.

Charles tightened his grip on the reins. The leather of his riding gloves crackled in the chill air. As missions went, this was not a particularly complicated one. Perhaps if it presented more of an intellectual challenge, he would care more.

But even as the thought crossed his mind, he knew it was untrue. Long before he reached adulthood he had developed a personal code of sorts, based on the idea that one's actions mattered, that though the world might be a bleak and unfair place, with perseverance one could make a difference. The events of the last few months had shattered that code. Guilt gnawed away at him until nothing was left but numbness.

The track curved sharply, snaking round a lichen-crusted wall of rock. Charles pulled up to let Jennings go first. Spiny bunches of rosemary and thyme and gorse clung to the ground above. Pine trees towered over them, misshapen by the wind, an endless mass of gray and green. And suddenly, in the midst of it, an unexpected flash of white.

Something crackled in the bushes. A musket rattled behind Charles. He flung out an arm to stop the soldier from shooting. "No."

A cry came from the hill above. The white flashed again.

Jennings had wheeled his horse round. "Don't shoot," Charles said, both to Jennings and to the men behind. "They've got a white flag."

"We're unarmed." A voice, speaking in accented English, came from the mountainside. A woman's voice, sharp with desperation. More crackling in the bushes, tearing cloth, slithering feet.

Charles swung down from his horse. Two figures burst through the pine trees, half running, half tumbling down a break in the rock in a swirl of dark hair and wool cloaks. Charles caught the first woman as she slid to the track. She fell hard against him in a shower of loose pebbles. Sergeant Baxter steadied the second woman.

Charles started to release the woman he held, but she swayed on her feet. He put a steadying hand on her shoulder.

Her breath shuddered through her in quick, painful gasps. He could feel the chill in her body through the folds of her cloak. "Breathe," he said. "Deeply. It's all right, whatever else we are, we're safe."

The woman drew a harsh breath. She held a bandbox in one hand and a stick in the other, with a bit of torn petticoat knotted to it to make a white flag. She dropped both to the ground and pushed her tangle of dark hair back from her face. Clear eyes the color of the Hebridean sea stared at him from beneath dark, winged brows. Her pale skin was smeared with dirt, but it would take more than dirt to dim a face such as hers. For a moment, he forgot to breathe.

"Thank you." The woman's voice had a raw, cracked sound, as though her throat was parched from fear or cold or thirst. Or all three.

He reached into the pocket of his greatcoat for a flask of whisky, unstopped it, and put it into her chilled fingers.

She took a quick swallow, then turned and gave the flask to her companion, who now stood within the protective circle of Sergeant Baxter's red-coated arm.

The other girl dropped the bandbox that she, too, carried, gripped the flask in both hands, and took a grateful swallow. Her eyes looked enormous in her thin, heart-shaped face. She was a slip of a thing, even younger than the other woman. Her hair was darker than her companion's, inky black against skin tanned by the Spanish sun.

The aquamarine-eyed vision turned back to Charles. "I'm afraid we're in rather desperate straits." She gave a wobbly attempt at a smile. Her lips were full, and they curved sweetly. He wouldn't be human if he didn't feel the force of that smile. Without looking round, he knew that every other man present, from the phlegmatic Addison to the world-weary Jennings, had felt it as well.

Charles returned the smile. Then he realized that some of the dirt on her face wasn't dirt at all. It was dried blood.

"You'll have to tell us about it," he said. "When we've

found shelter and built a fire." He shrugged out of his great-coat and wrapped it round her shoulders. Addison took off his own greatcoat—he was the only other man wearing one—and handed it to Baxter to put round the younger woman.

Charles exchanged a quick glance with Jennings, then looked back at the woman before him. "Can you sit a horse?"

She nodded. Charles boosted her into the saddle and swung up behind her. Baxter handed the younger woman up to Jennings, who for once didn't ask any questions. Addison picked up the bandboxes.

Charles set his horse into motion, riding in the lead this time. "There are wine caves not far off," he told the woman. "Don't try to talk if it's too much of an effort."

She twisted her head round to look at him. "My name's Saint-Vallier." Her voice was a little less raw. "Mélanie de Saint-Vallier."

His eyes must have widened at the French name, for she added, "All Frenchmen—or women—aren't supporters of Bonaparte."

"I'm well aware of it. But you're a long way from home, Miss Saint-Vallier."

She shivered beneath the greatcoat. "Not so very far. My home is near Acquera. We moved there during the Terror, when I was a baby. My mother was Spanish, my father French."

Her voice was curiously flat as she said this last. He noted the past tense, but this was not the time to ask what had happened to her parents or what had left her stranded on the road with only another young girl for a companion. "My name's Fraser," he said, in the tone he'd use in a London drawing room. "Charles Fraser. I'm an attaché at the British embassy in Lisbon."

"You're a long way from Lisbon."

"Don't I know it."

"Whatever you're doing, it must be important."

"That depends on the definition of importance. At the moment, my sole objective is to find shelter and build a fire. We should reach the caves in half an hour. Can you make it that far?"

"Yes," she said, though her shivering was more pronounced and he didn't think it was entirely owed to the cold. She was a tall woman, but she felt fragile within the circle of his arms. Her unpinned hair, a rich walnut-brown, fell forward, exposing the curve of her neck. He turned the collar of the greatcoat up round her throat.

"Thank you." Beneath the hoarse voice was an echo of governess-trained manners. But he hadn't missed her instinctive moment of recoil when his fingers brushed her throat. It stirred uncomfortable images of the events that might have left two women alone and bloodstained on a mountain pass.

Despite her assurances, he nearly called a halt before they reached the caves. He could feel the strength ebbing from her with each passing minute. The younger girl was drooping against Jennings. But the wind had picked up, whistling through the mountains with a bite that cut like glass, and there was an ominous promise of snow in the air. The shelter of the caves would mean a lot.

His memory, at least, had not played him false. The two wine caves were where he remembered, up an even narrower track that cut away from the path they'd been following. The wooden doors were overgrown with gorse and securely locked. Jennings glanced at him with raised brows.

"Not a problem," Charles said. "Excuse me," he added to Miss Saint-Vallier, reaching into the pocket of his greatcoat. He drew out his picklocks and swung off his horse. Within a matter of minutes, he had unlocked both caves. The pungent, sour smell of wine spilled out into the mountain air.

"Your talents continue to amaze me, Fraser." Jennings had dismounted and helped the two women from the horses. "I begin to think a stray diplomat or two would be handy to have on a long campaign." He jerked his head at his men. "Firewood."

Whether it was the promise of the wine or the presence of the women, the soldiers worked with a crisp efficiency they had not shown heretofore on the journey. Charles helped the women into one of the caves. The stench was overwhelming as they bent under the low wooden frame of the door, but neither woman hesitated. They sank down on the hard ground and slumped against one of the barrels, as though it had just occurred to them that they were no longer required to move.

Charles gave them blankets he'd taken from the saddlebags. "Give us another quarter-hour and we'll manage a fire and something to eat."

Within short order, they had fires going in the mouths of both caves. Jennings sent Baxter and the other five soldiers into one cave, with strict instructions that no man was to drink so much he wouldn't be fit to march in the morning. He gave Baxter a purse to pay for what they drank. Then he, Charles, and Addison joined the women.

Miss Saint-Vallier and the younger girl were huddled close together, hands held out to the fire. They both started as the men ducked through the doorway. Charles glimpsed a rush of terror in Miss Saint-Vallier's eyes, swiftly suppressed.

He dropped down on the far side of the fire. "Right. Time we all knew each other's names. Lieutenant Jennings of the 43rd. Miles Addison, my valet. Miss Saint-Vallier and—?" He looked in inquiry from Miss Saint-Vallier to the younger girl.

"Blanca Mendoza, my maid." Even in the warmth of the firelight, Miss Saint-Vallier's face was a ghostly white, but her voice had lost the harsh sound. It had the clear, musical ring of sterling silver clinking against crystal.

Jennings swept his shako from his head and managed to give the semblance of a bow beneath the low ceiling of the cave. "Enchanted."

While Addison set up a tripod over the fire and filled a cooking pot from the contents of their saddlebags, Charles broached one of the wine barrels and filled five tin cups. Jennings handed them round.

Miss Saint-Vallier smiled her thanks and took a swallow of wine. Her throat worked, her fingers clenched the cup, her shoulders hunched inward. She drew a deep breath and looked from Jennings to Charles. Her eyes were wide and dark and what Charles saw in their depths made him go cold in a way that had nothing to do with the night air. "I suppose," she said, "that you're wondering why we were mad enough to be traveling through the mountains in the middle of November without an escort."

Charles leaned against a barrel across the fire from her. "I imagine you had an escort when you started."

"Yes." She looked down into her cup. The firelight flickered over her face, sharpening her delicate bones, exaggerating the shadows round her eyes. "My father opposed Bonaparte. Perhaps too vehemently. A French patrol attacked our house a month ago." Her voice had gone flat again, as it had when she spoke of her parents earlier. "My mother and father were killed. I was persuaded I'd be safer in Galicia."

Jennings frowned. "But surely—"

"Our house was burned, Lieutenant." She tugged at the neck of her gown. The fabric had been rent in two, Charles realized, then tacked together with a hairpin. "The livestock were taken. Half the household were killed, and I had no way to support those who were left. I paid them what I could and bought horses from a neighboring farm. Blanca and I set off for Galicia with one of the grooms."

Silence hung uneasily in the wine-scented air. The fire gusted smoke out the open door of the cave.

Miss Saint-Vallier twisted her cup in her hands. She seemed to be unaware of the shudders that wracked her body. "We were attacked in the mountains, near where we found you. *Afrancesados*, I think, though I didn't stop to ask their political affiliations. They killed my groom and took our horses. They debated what to do with us, but they didn't have the stomach to kill us and it was too complicated to take us with them. So in the end they simply left us."

"*Bastardos*," the girl Blanca muttered, her voice sharp with venom. She was huddled against the cave wall, legs drawn up to her chin, arms wrapped round her knees. "I bit one of them. I hope his arm turns poisoned."

Jennings's eyes widened. Addison was startled into looking up from the cooking pot.

"I hope he suffers a good deal worse," Charles said. "When was this?"

Miss Saint-Vallier tried to lift her wine cup to her lips, but her fingers were shaking too badly. "Early yesterday."

More than twenty-four hours with no food and no protection from the elements save their cloaks. "We found a rock to shelter under," Blanca said. "We drank melted snow."

Miss Saint-Vallier steadied her fingers, as if from sheer effort of will, and took a sip of wine. "We knew there weren't any towns within walking distance. Our only hope was that someone would pass by on the road. We couldn't believe our luck when we saw the British uniforms."

Jennings lifted his cup in a toast. "It appears you are as courageous and resourceful as you are beautiful, Miss Saint-Vallier. I'm afraid we can't take you to Galicia, but I hope you will accept our escort to Lisbon."

Charles didn't care for the glint in Jennings's eyes. He told himself it was because Miss Saint-Vallier was in no state for flirtation, but he knew that was only part of the reason. "You may have friends or relatives in Lisbon," Charles said. "If not, I'm sure the ambassador will offer you assistance." In fact, the ambassador was all too ready to offer more than that to pretty women, though he wouldn't go beyond the line with an unmarried girl of good family.

Blanca rubbed her hand over her face. "She doesn't have anyone. She's the last of her family, thanks to those foul toads of French soldiers."

"Blanca." Miss Saint-Vallier gave a slight shake of her head. Then she smiled at Charles and Jennings with the formality of a lady accepting a gentleman's escort on a morning ride. "We'd be very glad of your escort, Lieutenant Jennings. Mr. Fraser."

There was little more that could be said. There was a great deal that remained unspoken. Such as what exactly had happened to Miss Saint-Vallier and Blanca when the French soldiers attacked their house and what the *afrancesados* had done to them before they left. Those incidents had almost certainly left scars, both physical and mental, which should be attended to. But three men they had never met before were scarcely the appropriate choice to minister to either.

Addison had returned his attention to the cooking pot with his usual tact. "Supper," he said, as he ladled out the stew. "We've no meat left, I'm afraid, but I can promise you it's the best corn and chickpeas you've tasted."

The women ate as though they had thought they would never do so again. Jennings launched into a series of amusing, well-edited battlefield anecdotes. Charles sipped his wine in silence. The wine was sweet, but the bite of irony was bitter on his tongue. He was the last possible person who should be playing the role of protector to vulnerable young women. He had an abysmal past record. But for the moment, at least, it seemed there was no one else.

Miss Saint-Vallier set down her bowl and leaned back against the wine barrel. The skirt of her gown was tangled about her legs, and she twitched the dark blue fabric free. Her hand lingered for a moment, curled over her abdomen.

Charles's wine cup tilted in his fingers. Damn and double damn. He righted the cup, his fingers clenched hard on the tin. Damn the French soldiers and damn the *afrancesados* and damn this damnable war. Miss Saint-Vallier's situation was even worse than he'd feared. He'd seen women from harlot to duchess make that fleeting but unmistakable gesture. They'd all had one thing in common.

They'd been carrying a child.

Chapter 6

The sound of retching told Charles where to look. He'd
heard it every one of the three mornings since they'd
found Mélanie de Saint-Vallier and Blanca Mendoza. The first
time he hadn't been sure. The second he'd lain awake, debating
what to do, until she slipped back into the camp. This morning
he'd been ready. He moved quietly over the rocky ground, past
Jennings and the other soldiers, past Blanca and Addison, all still
wrapped in their sleeping blankets. The fire he'd kindled flickered red amid the rocks. Fog hung thick in the air, clinging to
tree trunks, shrouding the predawn glow in the sky. The brush
of damp air on his skin brought a memory of home.

He'd slept little the night before. The meeting with the bandits who claimed to have the Carevalo Ring was to take place
later this morning, at a rendezvous point just beyond the clearing where they'd camped for the night. He was ready for any-

thing, including an attempt to take the gold at gunpoint without producing anything that remotely resembled the ring.

But at the moment, the ring seemed of far less consequence than Mélanie de Saint-Vallier. Patches of dirty snow crunched beneath his feet as he picked his way out of the clearing. One of the horses whickered, and he stopped to stroke its muzzle.

She was kneeling by a line of pine trees that bordered a streambed. The fog blurred his view, but he could see that she had one hand wrapped round a moss-covered tree trunk. Her head was bent, her dark hair spilling loose over the green wool of her cloak.

"Miss Saint-Vallier." He pitched his voice to be heard over the rushing of the stream, but he kept his tone gentle. He knew what cause she had to start when approached unawares.

She went still for a moment, then pulled herself to her feet and turned, gripping the tree trunk. "Mr. Fraser." Through the curtain of fog, it sounded as though she was farther away than she was. "I didn't realize anyone else was awake."

"I thought perhaps you could do with some tea." He held out the tin cup he carried.

She wiped her hand across her mouth. "Thank you." She walked forward, her steps firm and deliberate. "The stew last night must not have agreed with me."

He put the cup into her hand. "Very likely not."

Her hands curved round the warmth of the cup. A gust of wind riffled through the pine trees, tugging at her cloak. "For once I think Shakespeare got it wrong," she said, her voice bright with determination. "I don't think man's ingratitude could possibly be more unkind than this wind."

"Shakespeare was a genius, but I doubt he had experience of the Spanish mountains." He looked into her eyes, seeking a bridge to the painfully personal topic that needed discussing. "Not many Franco-Spaniards quote *As You Like It* in adversity."

"My father got me to learn English by promising I couldn't really appreciate Shakespeare in translation." She took a swallow of tea, gripping the cup in both hands. "You're fond of him yourself? Shakespeare, I mean."

"Next to my brother, he was the closest companion of my youth. My brother would tell you I have an unfortunate tendency to prefer the company of books to people."

She regarded him through the steam that rose from the cup. "You find you're less likely to be bored or disappointed that way?"

"And then there's the fact that I don't have to worry that *I'll* disappoint the books."

"I find it hard to imagine you disappointing anyone, Mr. Fraser. I've met few people so adept at coping in a crisis."

The smile that tugged at his mouth was more bitter than he intended. "That depends on the crisis. Some are more easily resolved than others." He paused. "The first step is always to face the problem. Talking to a friend can help."

She drew in her breath. For a moment, they looked at each other without speaking. He wasn't going to force a confession, but he was very much hoping for one. It would make things a great deal easier.

The wind cut the fog so that it swirled and re-formed round them. She released her breath, a sound as harsh as the crack of dry needles. "You're an observant man, Mr. Fraser. Or is it obvious to everyone?"

"I shouldn't think so. To own the truth, I was concerned from the moment I heard your story."

She let out a mirthless laugh. He cupped his hand round her own so she wouldn't spill the precious tea. "My old nurse said a cup of tea soothed any trouble." He smiled into her bleak eyes. "I'm not sure she was right, but it can't make it worse."

Miss Saint-Vallier gave a weak attempt at a smile. Even that brightened her face. He steadied her hand as she lifted the cup to her lips and took a careful sip. Warm metal, cold fingers, soft skin.

"How sure are you?" he asked.

She looked straight into his eyes. "I'm never ill like this, Mr.

Fraser. I'm sure." Her mouth went taut. " 'She is a woman, therefore may be woo'd; She is a woman, therefore may be won.' But there was precious little wooing about it, and I refuse to say that I was won."

He kept his hand cupped round her own. "It's too soon for it to have been the *afrancesados*. The French patrol who attacked your parents' house—"

"Yes. I'm carrying a French soldier's bastard. I couldn't tell you his rank. I doubt I'd recognize him if he passed me on the street. There was more than one, and I didn't get a very good look at their faces."

Oh, Christ. For a moment he thought he was going to be sick himself. He murmured the first words that came into his head. " 'Cry "Havoc!" and let slip the dogs of war.' I've always fancied myself a humanist, but I sometimes think this war will strain my faith in humanity to the breaking point." He tightened his fingers over her own. "What about Blanca?"

"She's all right. Oh, God, that sounds ridiculous. I mean, the French soldiers didn't plant a babe in her belly. I don't know about the *afrancesados*. They . . . used us, too."

"I'd like to kill them for you." The words came out with a violence he hadn't intended. "Though I'd be a poor match for a pack of bandits, not to mention soldiers. And it would do nothing to solve your predicament."

She gave a desperate sound that might have been a laugh or a sob. "I'm afraid solutions to this predicament don't exist."

"On the contrary. It's not unheard of, even in the best families in London." He hesitated. She was sharp-witted and well-educated, but it was difficult to judge how much an unmarried girl of little more than twenty would have been told. "There are ways—" He sought for the right words, for once quite out of his depth.

"Of getting rid of it?" Her gaze was clear and candid.

"It can be dangerous." He looked straight into her eyes. They couldn't afford to waste time on embarrassment. "But there are doctors who know the business and can be counted on to be discreet. I could make inquiries when we reach Lisbon. Or you could retire somewhere secluded to have the child. Then a home could be found for it."

Her lips twisted. "And everyone could pretend it didn't exist, including me?"

He studied the fragile bones of her face, the delicate point of her chin, the pure line of her throat. The fog misted her skin and made damp tendrils of hair cling to her forehead. "No one could blame you if you couldn't bear to look at this child after it's born. Or if you couldn't bear to carry it at all."

Her fingers stilled beneath his own. She glanced down into the steaming liquid in the cup they held between them. She looked as though she was seeing places he could only begin to imagine. "Perhaps not." She drew a breath that shuddered through her, stirring the folds of her cloak. "I've wondered, sometimes, if I'll be able to forget how the child was made. The problem is, I'm quite sure I won't be able to forget that the child is mine. The only relative I have left in the world."

"You have time. It's not a decision to make lightly."

She put her free hand over her abdomen, the way she had three nights ago in the wine cave. "After the *afrancesados* left, I was terrified that what they'd done would make me lose the baby. I knew then." She looked up at him, her eyes as bright and clear as a Highland loch on a summer day. "I'm not going to get rid of the child, Mr. Fraser. And I'm not going to give it away."

He nodded and said the only thing left that he could say. "Then I'll do whatever I can to help you."

Her mouth curved in a genuine smile. "You're a kind man, Mr. Fraser."

That smile cut through to a place somewhere inside him that he had thought no longer existed. His breathing turned uneven. At the same moment his ears caught something he'd been a damned fool not to hear earlier. Not a specific sound so much as a shift in the creaks and rustlings of the forest. Noises that weren't caused by birds or rodents or the wind.

He caught Miss Saint-Vallier's arm in a hard grip and gave a warning shake of his head. She nodded. He slid his hand into the pocket of his greatcoat, feeling for his pistol. His gaze swept the area round them. Nothing save fog, trees, and the damnably tell-tale glow of the fire.

A crack sounded from beyond their camp some fifty feet away. A booted foot, landing on a dry branch. A stir of movement followed, then a startled curse and a sharp report. One of their own men had wakened, reached for his musket, and fired off a shot.

A hail of answering bullets ripped through the fog. Someone cried out. A flock of birds rose from the trees, squawking in fear. The horses whinnied. A woman screamed.

Blanca. Miss Saint-Vallier started forward, but Charles pulled her back. "No," he mouthed against her hair. "Not that way. It won't do any good."

Jennings was shouting orders to his men. They fired off a volley of musket shots. Bullets ricocheted off the rocks. The smell of gunpowder choked the air.

Charles had his pistol out, and the leather bag that contained dry powder. He loaded the powder and rammed the ball into place, but he couldn't see enough to make out how many stood or had fallen. He reached out to grip Miss Saint-Vallier's hand again.

"Drop the gun." A voice, disembodied in the fog, spoke in French-accented English. "Or I shoot the lady."

Charles mentally called himself six kinds of fool and dropped the pistol. Miss Saint-Vallier was standing very still not two feet away. He twisted his head to the side. A man in the brass helmet and scarlet-faced green coat of a French dragoon had his own pistol pressed against her back.

"Kick the pistol over here," the dragoon said, his voice raised above the blare of musket fire.

Heroics were an impossibility. Charles nudged the pistol with the toe of his boot. It scuttered through the pine needles. The dragoon bent and scooped it up, keeping his own pistol trained on Miss Saint-Vallier.

In the clearing beyond, shots still rang out. A voice called out. A Spanish voice. Oh, Christ. The bandits had arrived to collect their gold and hand over the ring.

"Right." The dragoon tucked Charles's pistol into his belt. "Now—"

Miss Saint-Vallier let out a soft moan and crumpled to the ground. She crashed into the dragoon as she fell. The cup she still carried spattered hot tea onto her captor. He stumbled, and the pistol that had been pressed against her back tilted toward the ground.

Charles lunged forward and delivered a swift blow to the dragoon's chin. The dragoon staggered. His pistol slipped from his fingers. Charles hit him again. The dragoon blocked the blow with his arm, and his fist came up and caught Charles full in the face. Charles fell against the hard, rough bark of a tree. Pain sliced through his temples. He heard the click of a hammer and found himself staring down the muzzle of his own pistol.

He had a moment to think, with faint surprise, that he didn't want to die. Then the dragoon gave a strangled cry and collapsed face-first on the ground, the pistol clutched in his hand, a knife hilt protruding from his back.

Mélanie de Saint-Vallier stood over him. "He was going to shoot you." Her voice was flat. "Is he dead?"

Charles bent over and felt for the pulse in the dragoon's neck. "Very." He looked up at her. Her face was a still, pale blur in the fog. "My compliments, Mélanie." It was the first time he'd called her by her name.

"I've kept a knife in my bodice ever since—since the other time. I didn't have a chance to use it on the bandits. But my father taught me how to stab a man."

Charles snatched up the pistol the dragoon had dropped earlier. "Did your father also teach you how to shoot?"

"Yes."

"Good." He put the pistol into her hand and took his own pistol from the dragoon's still-warm fingers. The Frenchman also carried a musket. Charles slung it over his shoulder.

Musket balls whistled through the air fifty feet away. A man screamed. Jennings shouted an order. His voice broke off in midsentence. Charles grabbed Mélanie's hand and pulled her down the bank of the gully.

The bank was steep. He couldn't see the stream, but he could judge the distance to its edge by the sound of the water rushing over the rocks. Mélanie's cloak caught on a thornbush. She tugged it free. Then they both went still. The ever-present gunfire had stopped.

Someone moaned. A horse whinnied. Boots crunched over twigs and earth, careless now of the noise. A voice barked out a command. Charles couldn't make out the words, but the accent was French.

He looked at Mélanie, weighing her safety against that of those in the camp. He knew enough of her now to know that she wasn't one to run, any more than he was. He jerked his head down the bank. She nodded, her hand going to the pistol in the pocket of her cloak. They crept forward, over snow and rocks and brittle pine needles.

A French voice carried through the fog. "One move and we shoot." The speaker was not addressing them but whoever remained in the camp. "Where are the others?"

"There aren't any. Just us and the dead."

That last was Addison, in impeccable French. At least his valet had survived the attack. A breath of relief whistled through Charles's lungs.

"You're lying." This was another French speaker. "There's bedding for at least two more. Where are they?"

Silence followed, and then the smack of a hand connecting with a cheek.

"I don't know," Addison said, his voice as cool and controlled as ever. "Away from here, if they have any sense."

"Impudent bastard." The words were accompanied by the sound of another slap.

"The lieutenant needs tending to," Addison said. "He's badly wounded."

"No one gets cosseted until we find the others. Georges! Michel! Search the woods. We don't want them sneaking up on us unawares."

In the cold frozen earth of the gully, Charles's hand had closed round a large rock. He hurled it as far as he could in the opposite direction, away from him and Mélanie, away from the dead dragoon.

An old trick, perfected in his boyhood to throw his tutor off the scent, but as the rock crashed through the underbrush, the French leader gave an excited cry. "That way! They may be armed."

Boots tramped across the ground in the opposite direction. Two of the French soldiers were out of the clearing for the moment. Charles couldn't tell how many were left. He motioned for Mélanie to stay where she was and crawled on his stomach to the edge of the gully.

The smell of blood washed over him, sweet and choking. He gagged, swallowed, then squinted through the tangle of thorn-bushes.

The rising sun pierced the fog. The light glared against the snow, but he could see enough to make out the two French dragoons left in the clearing. Both were armed with muskets. The stocks glinted in the light.

Addison was leaning against a large boulder, his arm round Blanca. Blanca appeared to be unhurt, but Addison's right leg was stretched out at an awkward angle. Sergeant Baxter and fresh-faced Private Smithford sat across the clearing from them. Blood showed on the white facings of their coats, but it might not be their own. The other red-coated figures were sprawled over the ground. One of them, probably Jennings, gave another low moan. Charles couldn't tell whether any of the others lived. The horses, miraculously, appeared to be unharmed.

One of the dragoons walked up to Blanca. "She's a pretty thing, Corporal. She'll liven up the journey back to camp." He bent and stuck his hand down her bodice. Blanca spat full in his face. The soldier lifted his musket and swung it against the side of her head.

The blow fell half on Blanca, half on Addison, who had flung up his arm to protect her. Charles reached for his pistol, then stilled his hand. That wouldn't solve anything, not with the French soldiers positioned as they now were, both armed.

Smithford jumped to his feet with a roar of outrage. He couldn't be much more than eighteen and he'd been making eyes at Blanca ever since they'd found her.

The second dragoon, who had the insignia of a corporal, whirled round and fired a musket ball straight into Smithford's chest. Smithford's eyes opened in astonishment. He made a gurgling sound low in his throat. Then he collapsed face-first in the dirt.

"*Asesino,*" Blanca cried.

"I said I'd shoot anyone who moved." The corporal was ramming a fresh ball into his musket. "You, the pasty one who speaks French. You tell them."

Addison murmured to Blanca and Baxter in English. The underbrush stirred beside Charles. Mélanie crawled up next to him. Charles turned to her. Even before she began to whisper in his ear, he knew what she was going to suggest. It was madness. And it was their only hope.

Charles held himself motionless behind the thornbushes and watched as Mélanie stumbled into the clearing, gasping, her cloak billowing round her, her hair whipping about her face.

"Blanca! *Dios gracias!*" Mélanie flung herself down beside the younger girl, seemingly heedless of the dragoons.

Blanca turned her head, the red mark clearly visible on her face. "Oh, Mélanie, *porque—*"

"So. Another *señorita.*" The dragoon who had hit Blanca stared down at Mélanie. Charles couldn't read his expression, but he could hear the combination of anger and lust in the Frenchman's voice.

"Sir?" One of the soldiers who had gone to search called out through the trees. "Have you found them?"

"Only one. Do you see anything?"

"There are a couple of dead Spaniards, but no sign of an Englishman."

"Keep searching." The corporal looked at Mélanie. "The other man," he said in halting Spanish. "Where is he?"

"Who?" Mélanie shrank back against the boulder. Her hands were tucked into the folds of her cloak, as though for protection. Behind the thornbushes, Charles eased the musket onto his shoulder and sighted down the barrel.

"The man with you." The corporal gestured toward the empty sleeping blankets.

"At least now we know why they slipped away from camp," the other dragoon murmured in his own tongue. "Too fastidious to do it in front of his men. I expect he's left her nice and warm and wet."

Blanca looked up at him. She had understood the implication if not the words. "*Bastardo.*"

The dragoon raised the butt of his musket again. Mélanie coughed once, loudly. Then all at once her left hand wasn't tucked into her cloak but was pointing at the dragoon. She shot him before he had a chance to see the pistol she held. At the same moment, Charles fired off a musket shot that caught the corporal full in the chest.

Both Frenchmen fell. Mélanie sprang to her feet. Charles ran into the clearing.

Footsteps crashed through the underbrush. Charles pulled his unfired pistol from his belt. Baxter snatched a musket from one of the dead dragoons.

The footsteps raced past. "Running away," Baxter said. "They've got horses in the trees yonder. I don't think they'll stop to bury their own dead. They must know they're outnumbered now."

Mélanie dropped down beside Jennings, who was making incoherent noises. His chest was soaked bright red, and blood dribbled out the corner of his mouth. She took off her cloak and spread it over him. "Lie still, Lieutenant. It's all right now.

Blanca, we need fresh water from the stream. Are both the dragoons dead, Mr. Fraser?"

"Without question." Charles straightened up from checking the pulse of the second dragoon. The other four British soldiers were flung about the rocks, their bodies twisted and bloodied and shattered by bullets.

"Smithford's gone, too, poor devil," Baxter said.

"Are you hurt, Baxter?"

"Me? Nay, untouched, sir." Baxter brushed his hand over the blood on his coat as though surprised it was there.

Charles dropped down opposite Mélanie. She sat back on her heels and looked up at him. Her face was smeared with blood that must have sprayed from the dragoon she'd shot. Her eyes held a look that was part shock, part horror, part sheer guts.

Charles brushed his fingers against her cheek. He stripped off his greatcoat and laid it over Jennings, then turned to his valet, who was still slumped against the rock. "How bad's your leg, Addison?"

"Broken, I think. I'm afraid you may have to give me the use of your horse, sir."

"Gladly. But you had only to ask, you know. You needn't have gone to the trouble of getting your leg broken." Charles got to his feet and jerked his head in the direction the French had run. "I'll reconnoiter. Make sure they're gone."

They *were* gone, as best he could tell. They'd left three of their own dead sprawled among the trees. Not twenty paces off, he found the bodies of the two Spanish bandits. Poor bastards. They'd come to the rendezvous early. It was their bad luck to have arrived in the middle of the fight.

Charles returned to the clearing to find that Baxter had kindled a fresh fire beside Jennings, and the women had contrived a splint for Addison's leg.

Jennings died just after eleven, with barely a sound. It took them nearly the whole of the morning to tend to the dead—English, French, and Spanish.

They found nothing resembling the Carevalo Ring, but one of the Spanish bandits had a leather pouch on a cord round his neck. Someone had ripped his shirt open and loosened the draw-string on the pouch. It seemed the Carevalo Ring had existed after all. And it was now in the hands of the French.

Chapter 7

London
November 1819

"Suppose Carevalo's right, damn his eyes," Charles said. "Suppose the French soldiers didn't make off with the ring."

Melanie turned her head to look at her husband. His voice was level, almost conversational, but the light slanting through the carriage window glanced off his clenched hands. His knuckles were white. She could see him sifting through the pieces of the past, rearranging them in his head, searching for a break in the pattern. She had been doing the same herself since they left Raoul O'Roarke at Mivart's Hotel scarcely ten minutes ago. Save that for her, the picture was different.

She put her hand over her abdomen, flat again—how proud

she had been of it, how inconsequential it now seemed—nearly three years after Jessica's birth. For all the danger seven years ago, at least Colin had been with them, tucked safely inside her.

She reached for Charles's hand. "Perhaps you were right that it was a wild-goose chase and that the bandits never had the ring. It was all a trick to lure you into the mountains so they could steal the gold."

"Perhaps. But one of them did have something hidden in that pouch round his neck. Which brings us back to the French dragoons. Unless one of our own party somehow managed to steal it after the fight. Baxter, Blanca, you, or me. Addison couldn't have moved with his leg." Charles laced his fingers through her own. She could feel the warmth of his hand through the ecru kid of her glove. "Well, *mo chridh*?" he said. "Are you hiding it in your jewel box?"

She managed a smile, but it turned wobbly. "I wish to God I were."

He stared down at their clasped hands. "Suppose Blanca stumbled across the dead bandits when you sent her to the stream for water after the French soldiers ran off."

"Blanca might rip the shirts off a pair of live men, but she'd scream bloody murder at the sight of dead ones. And she wouldn't steal."

"You can't know that, Mel." His fingers tightened round her own. "You can never really know what another person might be capable of."

Beneath the velvet of her pelisse and the sarcenet of her gown and the linen of her chemise, her insides twisted, as if someone had turned a knife in her gut. "No," she said. "I suppose not. What about Baxter?"

"I don't see how he'd have had time. Unless the ring wasn't in the pouch after all, and Baxter found it later, when we were burying the bodies. I still think the likeliest explanation is that the French soldiers made off with the ring and disposed of it for their own purposes."

She drew in her breath. The air in the carriage was close and choking, thick with the smell of Charles's shaving soap and her perfume and the smoke from the charcoal brazier at their feet.

"Stiffen up your sinews, my sweet," Charles said. "I'll talk to d'Arnot at the French embassy. He has contacts among the former Bonapartist officers. If Carevalo traced the dragoons, we can, too."

"I should think so. In half the time." She made her voice light, but panic closed tight round her heart. Her free hand curled into a fist, so hard she heard a stitch give way in her glove. She had an impulse to smash her hand through the watered-silk upholstery, the polished mahogany fittings, the plate-glass window. "Oh, God, darling, I want him back. I'd give anything—"

"So would I," Charles said. Blue shadows of fatigue drew at his face. He had looked like that on the night of the battle of Waterloo, when their house in Brussels shook from cannon fire and the hall was filled with wounded soldiers. And on the nights Colin and Jessica had been born, when he'd sat beside her, in defiance of custom. He'd held her hand then, too.

She had a sudden memory of how Colin had felt when the doctor first placed him in her arms, so small and insubstantial, with a wobbly head and squirmy limbs. Charles had reached out and cupped his hand round the baby's head. The warmth and wonder on his face had brought tears to her eyes.

"We'll talk to Blanca and Addison," Charles said, in the voice of an outnumbered commander recounting a desperate battle plan with calm certainty. "We'll call on Baxter. We'll go to the French embassy and talk to d'Arnot."

She nodded, only half hearing, because she had come to her own decision. She was going to have to tell Charles the truth, all of it. She had known that from the moment they read Carevalo's letter, though she hadn't fully admitted it until now.

She was not as sick or terrified at the prospect as she ought to be. Perhaps her fear for Colin left little room for other emotions. If they could get him back, nothing else mattered. And they were not going to get him back unless Charles learned the truth.

She looked up at her husband. The familiar, ironic eyes, the full, generous mouth, the thick hair that would never quite lie smooth. She remembered the moment he had proposed to her, on a chill December night on a balcony overlooking the Tagus River. She had thought then that he was mad. She had wondered if he would ever be able to think of himself as Colin's father. She had been a fool. Charles was the sanest man she knew, and once he gave his loyalty, he was unswerving. His capacity for love was a well she had not plumbed the depths of.

Yet.

Blanca sprang to her feet, poplin skirts snapping. "How can you accuse me of such a thing? You think I am a thief? You think I have no honor?"

Mélanie crossed the small salon and took the younger woman by the hands. "We're not accusing you, *querida*. We're asking a question. We have to be sure, for Colin's sake."

Outrage, fear, and compassion flickered across Blanca's face. She let out a sigh that ruffled the muslin collar of her gown and made her hands tremble. "I'm sorry, Mélanie." She rarely called Mélanie by her given name when Charles was present. It was a sign of how greatly her composure had been shaken. She looked straight into Mélanie's eyes. "I didn't take the ring. I wouldn't have even if I'd seen the dead bandits. And I never saw them."

Mélanie squeezed Blanca's hands. Her gaze went to the Meissen clock on the mantel. The filigree hands inexorably marked the time she had already allowed to slip by since her son's disappearance. It was twenty-five minutes past seven. Four hours since they had learned Colin was missing. Longer since he had been taken. Less than five days until Carevalo's Saturday-night deadline.

Blanca was looking past Mélanie at Charles. "I may only have been fifteen. But I gave you my word. I do not go back on my word."

"I know, Blanca." Charles gave her one of his smiles that were as warm as a cashmere shawl and as fortifying as a glass of whisky. "But we've had to question all our assumptions about the people we know. I thought I knew Carevalo. I couldn't have been more disastrously mistaken."

Melanie returned to the settee, and Blanca moved back to the sofa.

"Sir?" Addison was standing beside the sofa. He had been sitting next to Blanca but had punctiliously risen to his feet when she did. "Don't you want to ask if I took it?"

"You're a remarkable man, Addison, but slipping out of the clearing and dodging through the trees with a broken leg seems beyond even your capabilities."

"I could have been pretending about the broken leg."

"So you could. Were you?"

"No," said Addison, in precisely the same tone. "And I didn't take the ring. Though I was probably the only one of the party who knew we were in the mountains to fetch it."

"There was speculation among the soldiers?" Charles asked.

"Constantly. The odds-on favorite theory was that you were delivering the gold to support a surprise attack on the French garrison at Palencia. But there was also some talk about funneling the gold to British agents, and a rather ingenious theory that the bandits were blackmailing either Wellington or the ambassador over an amorous intrigue. I don't think the lieutenant believed any of the stories."

"Jennings?" Charles perched on the arm of the settee and rested his hand on Mélanie's shoulder. His fingers were as cold and tense as she felt inside. "Why not?"

Addison seated himself on the sofa again, carefully smoothing the creases from his trousers. Unlike Blanca, whose hair was only half pinned up and whose gown wasn't buttoned properly, he looked as immaculate as ever, his linen spotless, his pale hair combed smooth, his pearl-gray coat without a wrinkle. "Jennings kept himself aloof from the men," he said at last. "Well, he would, he was an officer. But I'd catch him watching you some-times, sir, with an odd look in his eyes. If I had to put a name to it, I'd call it calculating."

"Jennings asked me outright about the reasons for the mis-sion," Charles said, "though I don't think he really expected an answer. He didn't care much for having to play nursemaid to a civilian."

"Jennings was a clumsy oaf." Blanca leaned forward, elbows on her knees, and scowled at the shiny black toes of her shoes. "Oh, his face was nice enough and the rest of him wasn't bad, either, but he was too quick and he didn't have the least idea what to do with his hands."

Addison swung his head round to stare at Blanca. "Good God," he said after a moment. "Do you mean you let Jennings—"

Blanca straightened up and shrugged, though she avoided meeting Addison's gaze. "I told you he had a nice face. And you were refusing to so much as touch my hand."

"But you'd just been—" Addison swallowed. His face was even more bloodless than usual.

Blanca flushed. "That was war." She lifted her chin and looked him straight in the eye. "I wanted pleasure to erase it."

Their gazes locked. It was Addison who looked away, his own cheeks stained with color. Under normal circumstances, he and Blanca kept up a scrupulous pretense of being no more than friends when Charles and Mélanie were present.

Charles was silent for a tactful moment. "Did Jennings say anything to you about the ring, Blanca?"

She shook her head. "He didn't talk much at all. He had other things on his mind."

Charles looked from her to Addison. "What about Sergeant Baxter? Do you remember how long he was out of the clearing when we were putting things to rights after the attack?"

Addison shook his head. "Everyone was milling about. I don't think any of you were gone for long."

Blanca folded her arms over her chest. "Baxter is a nice man. He wouldn't steal."

Addison stared at a bit of lint on his coat, as though somehow it held an answer. "Baxter has a tavern now. In Covent Garden. Called the Thistle. I visit it occasionally."

"Yes, I know," Charles said. "I stopped by once myself just after he opened it. He must have had some capital to start a tavern."

"A legacy from an uncle of Mrs. Baxter's, I understand." Addison flicked the lint from his coat. "For what it's worth, Baxter mentioned the legacy to me on the journey into the mountains, before he could have known of the ring, let alone planned to steal it. I assume you'll want to visit the tavern, sir. You know the direction?"

"In Henrietta Street. Near the Piazza." Charles squeezed Mélanie's shoulder. "We can call at the French embassy and see d'Arnot on the way."

Mélanie nodded. She remained where she was while Charles walked to the door with Blanca and Addison. The smell of cinnamon and cloves washed over her, a potpourri she'd arranged for autumn. Her own face and the faces of her children looked down at her from the painting over the mantel. She stared at the sunny, luminous image. Why was it that the most perfect pictures always shattered the most easily? Once she spoke the words, there would be no going back, for either of them. Like the loss of virginity, which could take one from maiden to harlot in one clean stroke.

She recalled a moment from a visit to their Scottish estate last spring. She had stood on the gravel walk, watching Colin and Jessica race across the lawn in the fading light of early evening. The sky was a heavy gray smudged with charcoal. A curl of mist hovered between the mountains, and snowcapped peaks shimmered in the distance. The crisp wind tugged at her skirt and pushed her hair back from her face, the clean air filled her lungs, the prospect of a quiet candlelit dinner lay before her. She had thought that in that moment she was perfectly happy.

Charles closed the door, and they were alone in the room. The time had come. She swallowed, drew a breath, and twisted her wedding ring once round her finger. "Before we go, darling, there's something I have to tell you."

Charles was halfway to the bellpull. "We can talk in the carriage."

"No." She was on her feet. "This needs to be said here."

Many men would have objected. Being Charles, he didn't. Instead, he crossed back to her side, close enough that she could see the circles beneath his eyes, the stubble on his chin, the laugh lines that bracketed his mouth.

"What is it, *mo chridh*?" He reached out as though to take her hands.

She pulled away. He stood watching her, his face dark with concern.

A film of perspiration dampened her palms. Absurd on a November morning. She had a mad impulse to go up and see Jessica, to hold their little girl in her arms, before she told him. She was being a fool. In the end, the only way to do it was as simply as possible. "The French soldiers didn't make off with the ring, Charles." The words seemed to scrape against her throat as she spoke them. "It never found its way into French hands."

Surprise filled his face, followed by confusion, and then a search for answers. "How do you know?"

She forced herself to look straight into his eyes. "I had it on the best authority. French Intelligence."

"I see." He studied her for a moment. "And how did you happen to be in the confidence of Bonaparte's agents?"

It was the tone of a man who loved his wife and didn't doubt her. Had never doubted her. Never could. Or so he thought.

She drew a breath. Her chest hurt. Her throat felt raw. "Because they confide in their own. Because I was one of them. Because, my darling, you married a French spy."

Chapter 8

A shutter slammed shut in Charles's brain, leaving him in a sick, black void. *You married a French spy*. The words echoed in his head, but his bruised, battered mind refused to comprehend them. Then his vision cleared and he was looking at his wife's familiar face. Because her words made no sense at face value, he sought for the logical explanation that must exist. At any other time, he would have thought she was joking, but not now. Not with their son in jeopardy. "Then you'd better tell me about it," he said.

The light pouring through the windows fell across Mélanie's face with crystalline, autumnal purity. "We'd heard the ring had been found and that an English diplomat was being sent to fetch it. We knew how valuable it could be. Blanca and I hid in that mountain pass for three days waiting to intercept you."

Charles scoured her face with his gaze. The features he

could mold with his fingers from memory. The eyes he had let see into his soul. The mouth whose taste was as familiar as air. "How did they make you do it?" he said. "Did your family not die after all? Were the French holding one of them hostage? Or was it something else?"

She shook her head. Sweat beaded her forehead and plastered strands of dark hair to her skin. "Oh, Charles. Oh, my sweet. Sometimes I forget how quick you are. But you're reasoning under a false assumption. You think there must be an explanation that exonerates me. And there isn't."

"Or you think there isn't." He took her chin in his hand. "Tell me the rest, Mel."

The pulse in her throat hammered against his fingers. "I wasn't blackmailed, Charles. I wasn't coerced. Make your mind up to that now. We don't have time for self-deception."

Her eyes were dark and opaque, as though she was afraid to let him inside. He sought for a way to breach the wall she had erected between them. That it could be breached he had no doubt. "Who sent you to fetch the ring?" he asked.

She hesitated the barest fraction of a second. "Raoul O'Roarke."

He dropped his hand from her face. "You're telling me O'Roarke was a French agent?"

"He wasn't just an agent. He ran a network that covered half of Spain. A lot of his people were infiltrated into the resistance. As he was himself."

"So instead of fighting for Spanish freedom he betrayed his comrades to the French?"

A hint of challenge flashed in her gaze. "Raoul wouldn't put it that way. He wanted a new Spain. He thought the best hope for it lay with Bonaparte."

The puzzle pieces shifted and fell into place in his head. Loyalties and alliances in the Peninsula had been as complex as a multifaceted gem. A lot of Spanish intellectuals had supported the French occupation as the quickest route to progressive reform. O'Roarke, with his liberal principles and his Irish heritage, would have had reason enough to side with the French against Britain. It fit. It fit all too damnably well. But how the man had managed to acquire a hold on Mélanie—

"Charles." Mélanie seized his face between her hands. Her fingers trembled, but her gaze pinned him like a lance. "Raoul was a French agent. I was a French agent. I committed a great crime against you when I married you. I don't expect you ever to forgive me. But right now it doesn't matter. All that matters is what this means for Colin."

Her eyes bored into his own. They stared at each other for a moment that seemed at once as slow as torture and as brief as a musket shot.

Realization slammed into him like a punch to the gut. He pulled away from her, crossed the room, and smashed his fist into the wall.

The sea-green plaster gave way beneath the force of his blow. His knuckles struck a beam. He pulled his hand free of the ruined plaster and walked to the door. "Let's go."

"Where?" Mélanie came after him.

He didn't look at her. He might never be able to look at her again. He turned the door handle. "To see Raoul O'Roarke again and find out just how much he really knows about Carevalo and the ring he tried to have you steal seven years ago."

"Charles." Mélanie caught his hand as he strode through the door.

He jerked away. His hand clenched. He came closer to striking her than he would have imagined possible. "What?"

"Your hand's bleeding." She held out her handkerchief.

He glanced down at his ragged knuckles. The gash was dripping blood onto the rose and cream of the carpet. He tugged his own handkerchief from his sleeve and wound it round his hand.

"Charles, listen, there's more, that's why I had to—"

He strode to the stairs without listening. Mélanie ran after him. Michael's voice echoed up from the entrance hall. "If you'll wait a moment, sir, I'll inquire if Mr. and Mrs. Fraser are at home."

"Thank you."

Two words, but the voice was unmistakable. Charles had heard it in Mivart's Hotel scarcely an hour before, denying any knowledge of Colin's disappearance. He'd actually taken O'Roarke at his word. Then.

He rounded the first-floor landing and took the rest of the stairs in a half-dozen strides.

O'Roarke, now formally attired in a dark gray coat and flawless cravat, was standing beside the console table where callers left cards. He lifted his head and met Charles's gaze. His face was still and intent, as though he was searching for something. Understanding flashed in his eyes. For a raw, angry moment, anything might have happened. If the air between them had been made of a solid substance, it would have been smashed to bits by the crossfire.

Charles couldn't have said what checked his impulse to violence. The training of a lifetime. The memory that his daughter was upstairs. The need to maintain some sort of control. He jerked his head toward a pair of double doors across the hall. "Come into the library."

He crossed the hall without waiting for an answer and flung open the doors. O'Roarke followed. So did Mélanie. Charles stood to the side until they were both in the room. Somehow, beneath the black knot of rage that filled his brain, he knew that he couldn't speak until the doors to the hall were closed.

He pulled the doors to behind Mélanie, then turned to face her and the man she now claimed to have been working for. The light from the tall windows slanted across their faces. Mélanie's face stood out parchment-white amid the golden oak and brown velvet of the room. O'Roarke's gaze was veiled and friendly once again, as though he were no more than a concerned bystander.

"I know what a great shock your son's disappearance has been, Fraser," O'Roarke said.

"You can spare the playacting." Charles pressed his shoulders against the solid oak of the doors in an effort to stop himself from crossing the room and throttling them both. "She's told me the whole."

"I see." O'Roarke nodded, a man accepting the inevitable and making the necessary transition. "I feared as much. That's why I came."

Mélanie crossed to O'Roarke's side in two strides, the pale blue folds of her gown whipping round her legs. "Did you know about what happened to Colin, Raoul?" She dragged him round to face her. "Did you?" She gripped his face between her hands, as she had gripped Charles just a short time ago. "Because if you did, so help me God I'll cut off your balls and stuff them down your throat."

"Why would I be fool enough to abet Carevalo, *querida*? I know better than anyone that you never had the ring."

Mélanie's fingers pressed into his skin. "That isn't a straight answer."

"Would you believe me if I gave you a straight answer?"

"No. But I want one anyway, damn you."

He lifted a gloved hand and brushed his fingers against her cheek. "I wouldn't hurt your son, Mélanie. I wouldn't be party to any plot that did. I think you know that."

Mélanie's gaze raked his face. "You bloody bastard." She released him and took a step back. "I can almost always tell when you're lying. Almost. But not without fail."

O'Roarke looked straight into her eyes. "No one can tell that without fail, *querida*."

Charles pushed himself away from the doors, knocking against a table that held a chess game he and Mélanie had been playing. "Was Carevalo one of your creatures, too?"

"Carevalo a French agent?" O'Roarke gave a shout of laughter that echoed off the coffered ceiling. "Christ, no." He put up a hand to straighten his cravat. Mélanie's fingers had left red marks on his skin. "How much has she told you?"

Charles strode to a walnut armchair that had once belonged to his grandfather and gripped its high back. "You were a French agent. So was she."

"That's it in a nutshell." O'Roarke's gaze flickered to Charles's bandaged hand, then back to his face. "You were an agent of the British yourself."

"I did the occasional fetching and carrying. I fear I was a rank amateur compared to you and my wife."

"You underrate yourself, Fraser."

Charles's grip on the chair tightened. The carved tracery pressed into his hands. "You sent Mélanie to intercept me and steal the Carevalo Ring."

"There's more, Charles," Mélanie said. "That's what I was trying to tell you on the stairs. According to our informant, one of the British soldiers in your party had the ring all along. He set up the exchange with the bandits as a cover to extort money for the ring."

Charles stared at her. "Who the hell was your informant?"

"The mistress of one of the bandits." Mélanie glanced at O'Roarke. "You were the one she talked to. What did she say?"

"That a British soldier had somehow got possession of the ring. He knew the British would never pay him for it. So he hired the bandits to pretend they had it."

Mélanie turned back to Charles. "That must be why the bandits were hiding in the trees the morning of the attack. They arrived early to collect the ring from the British soldier so they could sell it to you at the rendezvous a few hours later."

Charles closed his eyes for a moment. "Who was the British soldier?"

"I don't know," O'Roarke said. "The bandit's mistress didn't know his name."

"Was he an officer or an enlisted man?"

"She didn't know anything about him, save that he was British and a soldier."

"You expect me to believe that?"

"Why would I lie about it at this point?"

"Probably just for the hell of it," Charles said. He remembered, with sickening clarity, that he used to like this man. "Who the devil are you working for now?"

"For Spain. For a government with some belief in the rights of man. Not to mention women," he added with a glance at Mélanie. "During the war the best hope for that lay with Bonaparte. Now it lies with supporting Carevalo and his friends against the monarchy."

"I take it Carevalo doesn't know you worked for the Bonapartists?"

"Carevalo the French-hater? No, and God help me if he ever learns the truth." O'Roarke stripped off his gloves and tossed them onto the marble library table. "Mélanie has given you the power to ruin me in Spain. I'm sure you realize that. There's little point in discussing it. You'll come to your own decision one way or another."

"At the moment I don't give a damn about your future, O'Roarke. All that concerns me is my son." Charles strode toward the other man. "You say you'd have no reason to take Colin because you know we don't have the ring. But you could scarcely tell Carevalo that. So if Carevalo confided his plan to you, you'd have little choice but to go along with it."

"Well reasoned, Fraser. But as it happens, he didn't confide in me. I think he knows I find his obsession with the ring rather juvenile."

"And yet you went to great lengths to recover it seven years ago."

"Oh, I can't deny its power as a symbol. I won't say it would have turned the war in our favor if we'd got our hands on it seven years ago, but it certainly wouldn't have hurt."

"We're not talking about seven years ago."

"No." The light from the windows emphasized the circles beneath O'Roarke's eyes, the hollows of his cheeks, the long, sharp line of his nose. He looked older than he had a few moments before. "I'm not without sympathy for your fears, Fraser. If I'd had any inkling that Carevalo meant mischief for the boy, I'd have warned Mélanie. You'll have to take my word for that."

"Why the hell would I take your word for anything?"

O'Roarke turned to look at Mélanie, and she returned his gaze in a kind of silent duel. The fire crackled in the grate. The long-case clock ticked with precision.

"We can't take Raoul's word for anything," Mélanie said at last, her gaze still fixed on O'Roarke. "You can never be sure of what another person might be capable of doing. Raoul told me that, and you said it yourself only today. But I don't think Raoul would hurt Colin."

Charles looked from O'Roarke to his wife. The sunlight fell between them in a glittering arc. Their profiles, set with twin determination, were reflected in the glass-fronted bookcase on the wall behind. "Why?" he said.

Mélanie drew in her breath, then released it. O'Roarke watched her, as though waiting for a cue.

"Because he's Colin's father," Mélanie said.

Chapter 9

Of course. Of course. Of course. The obviousness of it pummeled him, a series of blows he should have seen coming. But he was so used to thinking of Colin as his son that he rarely considered who had performed the biological act.

The library was suspended in stillness. The sunlight burnished the oak and velvet and struck sparks off the gilded book spines. The smell of ink and leather hung in the air with pungent familiarity. Books had been his retreat since boyhood. Now even this haven proved to be one more chamber in the house of cards that was his home.

He looked at Colin's mother. "I must be very slow. You were in the mountains to intercept me. The rest was a cover story. So of course you weren't raped and that isn't how you became pregnant."

"No." Mélanie's gaze was steady, though her pulse was beating very fast just above the muslin at the neck of her gown.

Charles turned to O'Roarke. Colin could have inherited his dark hair and fine bones from Mélanie as easily as from this man. But the slanting, quizzical brows and the long, mobile mouth were unmistakable, now that one knew where to look. "Did you know Mélanie was pregnant?" Charles asked. His voice was a hoarse rasp, alien to his own ears. "Was marrying her to me part of the plan?"

The quizzical brows lifted. "I'm a good strategist, Fraser, but not that far-seeing. I didn't know Mélanie was pregnant when I sent her after the ring. She didn't know it herself. Nor did we bargain on the extent of your gallantry. We improvised from there."

Gray predawn light, clinging mist. An unlooked-for shock of kinship. An unexpected whiff of a happiness he had never thought to find. "So you lost the ring but gained a French agent as a British diplomat's wife. You can't have considered the mission a complete failure."

"On the contrary." O'Roarke smiled briefly. "Mélanie was my greatest success as a spymaster."

Charles pressed his hand to his temple. His image of the life he and Mélanie had built together—against all odds, with painstaking care—had been blasted to bits. There was no coherent picture to take its place, merely fragments which swirled painfully in his head, like bits of shrapnel in a wound. "How long?" he asked, without thinking, without planning.

"Since the start of the war, or very nearly," Mélanie said. "It was 1809 when I met Raoul."

Charles forced his gaze to focus. He stared into the blue-green depths of her eyes. "And you worked for him all through the war?"

"Yes." She answered without hesitation.

"And afterwards? When we were in Vienna at the Congress? When we were in Brussels before Waterloo? *During* Waterloo?"

"Yes."

He drew a breath that seemed to grate through him. "And now?"

She looked at him in that way that only she could, as though she was seeing straight into his soul. "It's over, Charles. It ended after Waterloo. We lost."

"You expect me to believe that?"

She swallowed. Lines he had never before noticed stood out against her finely textured skin. "I told you," she said, with a control so tight it seemed to crackle through the air, "I no longer expect you to believe anything I say to you."

"But it happens to be the truth," O'Roarke said. "She told me after Waterloo that in the future she'd no longer act as my agent."

Charles looked at his wife's lover. He would have hit him, but that seemed a woefully inadequate response in the face of what had been revealed. "Shut up, O'Roarke. If I don't believe Mélanie, I certainly won't believe you." He looked back at his wife. "Is Jessica mine?"

Mélanie sucked in her breath as though he'd slapped her. "Don't be ridiculous, Charles. You can see it in her face."

"Convenient."

Her hands clenched at her sides. "I didn't need to see her face to know that no one else could be her father." She hesitated a moment. "There hasn't been anyone else for a long time."

"You'll have to tell me more someday. I'm afraid there isn't time now." Charles wrenched his gaze away from her and spread his hands palms-down on the cold, uncompromising marble of the table. He couldn't seem to stop them from shaking. "O'Roarke, I'm going to give you the benefit of the doubt and assume you want to get my—your—our son back. What else do you know about Carevalo?"

"No more than I told you at Mivart's. Do you know whom he employed to actually take the boy?"

"Not by name. We have a Bow Street Runner looking for them."

O'Roarke's eyes narrowed. "The Bow Street Runners are in charge of ferreting out foreign spies."

"Among other things. That should make Roth right at home

in this mess. Tell me again that the ring never found its way into French hands."

"If it had found its way into French hands, we'd have used it."

Charles looked at O'Roarke a moment longer, then nodded. "If one of the British soldiers really had the ring, then it must have been on his person when he died. Unless Baxter had it. Baxter's the next person to talk to." He glanced at Mélanie. "Are you coming with me?"

"Of course."

O'Roarke's gaze flickered between them. "I don't know where Carevalo is, but there are one or two places I can make inquiries. Mélanie can tell you I used to be rather good at tracking people. I'll see what I can learn."

"Tomás might learn more asking questions among the servants," Mélanie said.

"I'm afraid my loyal valet left me last spring. My new man is decent at starching the linen but no earthly good as an agent. I'll do my best on my own." O'Roarke picked up his gloves. "I have no doubt Carevalo will be getting reports on events in London. I need hardly say that the less he knows about any connection between us, the better. For all our sakes—and the boy's."

Charles bit back the impulse to fling O'Roarke's tacit offer of help in his face. He needed the man, damn his soul to hell. "You know where to find us. I presume you and my wife are experts at sending messages without detection."

"We've done it once or twice." O'Roarke tugged on his gloves. "How the two of you settle matters between yourselves is your own affair. But take care you don't let Carevalo guess even a hint of the truth about Mélanie's past. He's been longing to wreak vengeance on the French ever since his own family were killed. The last thing you want is for him to realize he has the child of a French agent in his power."

Mélanie tucked her disordered hair into the knot at the nape of her neck. "I'm not a fool, Raoul. By now you should know Charles isn't, either."

The three of them left the room in a sort of strange solidarity, like rival MPs forced into an uneasy alliance by parliamentary expediency. Charles retained no coherent memory of the next ten minutes. Somehow he must have said and done what was necessary. O'Roarke was shown from the house. The carriage was brought round. He and Mélanie settled themselves inside, wrapped in the appropriate outer garments. He directed the coachman to Covent Garden, then turned to Mélanie and spoke the words that most needed to be said. "*Do* you believe O'Rourke"

"As much as I believe anything. Raoul can be ruthless, but he has his own loyalties."

He leaned back into his corner of the carriage. They were at opposite ends of the seat. "Was he loyal to you?"

She turned her head and met the full force of his gaze. "After a fashion. He never forced me to take a risk I didn't understand."

"Including marrying me?"

The pleated silk that lined her bonnet cast cool, blue-tinged shadows over her face. Her eyes were very dark, almost black. "He wanted me to accept your offer. But he left the decision up to me."

"Kind of him."

"Charles—" She reached out to him, then let her hand fall in her lap. "You'd better ask me whatever you need to ask now, or we'll never get through this."

They rounded a corner. He gripped the strap harder than was necessary. "No, I think I'd better not. Or we'll never get through this."

She watched him with that damned look that could always slash through his defenses. "I think Raoul cares about Colin more than he'd admit even to himself. But Colin's your son in every way that matters."

"Of course he's my son." His hand tightened round the strap. The leather cut into his bandaged palm. "I can understand that you used me. I was fair game. But you used Colin. Before he was even born."

"Darling—"

His hand jerked, wrenching the strap from the carriage wall. "You bloody bitch, don't you dare try to make excuses for yourself."

She sucked in her breath. "What could I possibly say that would excuse what I did?"

"Nothing." And yet even as he spoke, he knew that a part of him would clutch at any excuse she offered, as a drowning man clutches the flimsiest shard of timber. Christ, he was a fool.

He fixed his gaze across the carriage. The patterns on the watered silk squabs wavered and shimmered before his eyes. Questions he hadn't meant to ask came unbidden to his lips. "Surely O'Roarke could have used your help even after Waterloo. Why the hell did you stop working for him?"

"Because I'm your wife."

The carriage lurched over a loose cobblestone. He gave a laugh that was as rough as the scrape of the iron-bound wheels. "You've been my wife for seven years." He swung his head round and met her gaze. "Or had you forgotten?"

"That's something I've never forgotten, darling." She drew a breath, as though she meant to say more. Then she checked herself, hands folded tight in her lap.

He looked from her still hands to her pale, shadowed face. "Where did you meet O'Roarke?" he asked.

She jerked her chin up a fraction. The ribbons on her bonnet rustled. "In a brothel."

"You continue to surprise me. What was the Comte de Saint-Vallier's daughter doing in a brothel?"

"I'm not the Comte de Saint-Vallier's daughter, Charles. My parents were traveling actors." She paused a moment but kept her gaze on his face. "I was in the brothel because I worked there. Before Raoul introduced me to a new game, I was a daughter of one of the oldest games of all. I was a whore."

He was silent for the length of a heartbeat. "Of course. And O'Roarke suggested you sell your body for military secrets instead of a few paltry coins?"

"Why not?" Her voice went sharp. "If one's been forced into the gutter, why not make the most of it?"

"Why not indeed. Though surely when it came to selling yourself in marriage, you could have done better than a mere attaché."

"I told you, I never meant—" She slammed her fist against her mouth. "When Raoul sent me after the ring, seduction wasn't any part of the mission."

"No, apparently that was an added benefit." He pressed his hands over his eyes, but a thousand memories deluged his senses. The whiff of roses and vanilla. The slither of a silk stocking. The taste of champagne in her mouth. The feel of her body clenched round his own and her lips against the hollow of his throat. "Tell me one thing," he said. "On our wedding night I told you I wouldn't rush you into intimacy. I said we could wait until after the baby was born. Why the hell didn't you take me up on it? Who knew what the future held. You might never have had to sleep with me at all."

She was silent. He dragged his hands from his face and stared at her. "Damn it, madam, you owe me an answer."

"I knew I'd done an unspeakable thing to you, Charles. I thought—" She looked at him the way she looked at the children when she had to put a particularly harsh truth to them. "A real wedding night was the least I owed you."

He had thought nothing she could say could sicken him further. He had been wrong. "I see," he said, over the bitter bile of memories turned to ash. "So it was payment."

"I prefer to call it reparations."

"Dear Christ." Moonlight shimmering through the linen of her nightdress. A hand trembling in his own. Eyes that shone with fear and trust. A communion that seemed absolute. A lie that cut deeper than any words. The fragile woman he'd held in his arms that night had staged the whole scene. It was a fitting start to their marriage.

"Charles—"

"Don't. Whatever it is, don't say it. We're going to get Colin back. And then so help me God I never want to see you again."

Her eyes turned as impenetrable as a fathoms-deep sea. "I didn't expect that you would, darling," she said.

He wrenched his gaze away. He didn't let himself look at her again until they reached Covent Garden. He was shaking as though with a fever. Rage choked his throat, flayed his skin, clawed at his vital organs. He had a sudden image of his mother hurling a crystal scent bottle against a silk-hung wall. The memory of her scream echoed in his head.

No. Damn it, no. He wasn't his mother. He could control this. He could control anything if he put his mind to it. His marriage might be over, but his son still needed him.

The coachman pulled up as close to the Thistle as he could. Charles jumped down and nearly skidded on a rotted cabbage leaf. The smell of overripe oranges and a babble of hawkers' cries filled the air. Two women with liberal amounts of rouge on their cheeks and scant covering on their bosoms were leaning against the wall of the tavern. They moved toward him, then subsided against the wall as he handed Mélanie from the carriage. He kept hold of Mélanie's arm and steered her past a trio of young men in grubby corduroy jackets who were warming their hands at a fire laid in the street. One man's gaze slid sideways toward Mélanie's shot-silk reticule.

The Thistle was a narrow brick building, with a wood-faced lower story and brightly polished brass lamps flanking the door. The air in the common room smelled of sour ale and freshly brewed coffee. Charles scanned the dozen or so customers who lounged about the tables. Two gray-haired men were bent over a backgammon board. A man in a greengrocer's apron was gulping down a mug of coffee and eating a paper-wrapped sausage, one eye on the mantel clock. A woman in a low-cut gown and a tattered lace shawl was slumped at one of the tables, listening to the attentions of a stringy young man in a flashy coat as though she was too tired to shoo him away. A potboy threaded his way between the tables with a pot of foaming ale.

Charles signaled to the potboy, but as he did so, Baxter himself came through the doorway from the room beyond and let out an exclamation of pleased surprise. "Good God, it's Mr. Fraser. And Mrs. Fraser. An honor, ma'am."

Charles subdued his impatience and shook the tavernkeeper's hand, pleased to find his own hand relatively steady. "Could we have a word in private, Baxter?"

"Of course, of course." Baxter led them up a narrow staircase to the family quarters and opened a door onto a cheerful, floral-papered room with dried flowers on the mantel and a child's building blocks strewn over the hearth rug. "Tea? Or a spot of ale? No? I suppose it is a bit early. Just let me light the fire."

Mélanie sank down on a black horsecloth settee. Charles moved to a straight-backed chair several feet away from her. Baxter's gaze flickered at the seating choice. He busied himself adjusting the cabbage rose fire screen. He had grown a bit thicker about the waistline, but otherwise he was unchanged since their days in Spain. "Well, now. Very kind of you to call, but it can't be just to chat about the past." He turned to face them. "What's amiss?"

Charles told him, as succinctly as possible, omitting only Mélanie's revelations. Baxter's eyes went wide with surprise, then dark with anger. "By God, sir. Begging your pardon, ma'am, but Mrs. Baxter and I have three little ones of our own. What kind of fiend would do that to a child?"

"Someone willing to go to any lengths to achieve his objective." Charles was relieved to find that his voice still sounded rational. He was putting to use every lesson he'd ever learned about self-control in a crisis, every trick mastered in boyhood to hold feelings at bay.

Baxter unclenched his hands. "Carevalo wants the ring that much?"

"Apparently. My mistake was not to realize it sooner." "Mistake" was a woefully inadequate way to describe such a sin of omission. But there would be time, later, to curse himself for the fool he'd been. Time to remember that whatever sins Mélanie had committed, he was the one who had failed their son.

Baxter stared at Charles, a dawning realization on his face. "You think I'm the British soldier who had the ring all along?"

Charles watched him with an unwavering gaze. "We don't know what to think. We're investigating every possibility."

"No, you're right to wonder." Baxter slicked his sparse dark hair back from his forehead. "It would have to be me, wouldn't it. That would explain why the ring didn't turn up on any of the dead men. But as God is my witness, Mr. Fraser—"

" 'Saint-seducing gold,' " Mélanie murmured. "It would have been a great temptation. After all, the British would still get the ring. Why shouldn't you gain by the transaction?" She was tugging off her gloves, as though she couldn't bear to be still. A pearl button snapped off and rolled to the floorboards.

Baxter bent down and retrieved the button. "I'm not a liar, ma'am. I don't know how to prove it to you, save to say it plain out." He held out his hand to her.

Mélanie leaned forward and took the button from him. "Truthfully, I never thought you were, Mr. Baxter."

Baxter's shoulders relaxed. He stared at his broad hands, smeared with soot from lighting the coals. "It's odd, I don't talk about the war much as a rule—don't like to upset Mrs. Baxter. Don't think about it much neither, truth be told. It was an ugly time. Hard sometimes to believe it really happened." He looked at the children's blocks on the hearth rug for a moment, then turned his gaze to Charles. "So that ring was the reason we were in the mountains. I wasn't sure whether or not to believe the gentleman who was here last week."

Charles gave a jerk of surprise. "What gentleman?"

Baxter looked up at him. "A gentleman by the name of Lorano came to see me last week. He told me this same story about the ring. I assumed he'd have been to see you, too."

Charles glanced instinctively at Mélanie. "What did the man look like?"

"Nothing very much to speak of, sir. About your years. Tallish. Dark hair. Not too heavy. Seemed to be a Spaniard. Least-ways he had the coloring and a bit of an accent and the name sounds Spanish. I had no reason to think he wasn't who he said he was."

"No, of course not." Mélanie scrunched her gloves in her lap. Her nails pressed into her palms. "What did this Mr. Lorano say to you?"

"That he was trying to trace the ring. I insisted the French must have got it, but he said he had doubts. Asked if there was a chance we buried it with any of the dead. I assumed he was a friend of this Marqués de Carevalo, though come to think of it he didn't come right out and say so." Baxter rubbed at the soot on his hands. "Do you think it was my answers made Carevalo decide you must have the ring yourself?"

"I doubt it," Charles said. "Carevalo's been convinced I have the ring ever since he talked to the French soldier. If he was going to make inquiries, he'd have come himself. I doubt this Lorano is his friend, or even working with him."

"Who the devil is he, then?"

"I'm not sure. But we may have competition in finding the ring." Charles leaned forward, hands clasped between his knees. "*Is* there any chance we buried it with the dead after the attack?"

"I don't see how, sir. I went through their pockets careful as can be, in case there was anything to send on to their families."

"What did you take out?"

Baxter frowned. "The Spaniard asked me the same thing. One fellow had a watch. Another had a lock of his sweetheart's hair. I think that was all, except that Lieutenant Jennings had a letter on him."

Charles straightened up. "What sort of a letter? How many pages?"

"I couldn't rightly say, sir. But it must have been longish. It was a fair fat packet."

"Fat enough for the ring to be tucked inside?"

Baxter's eyes went wide. He nodded slowly. "Aye. More than fat enough."

Charles regarded him for a moment. "You didn't say any-thing about it at the time."

Baxter glanced down at the scuffed toes of his boots. "Well, no, sir, I didn't quite like to. It—ah—the letter wasn't addressed to Mrs. Jennings at their house in Surrey. Seemed more discreet just to send it on to the lady quiet-like. If I'd known—"

"But you couldn't have, of course. Did you tell Lorano about the letter?"

"I mentioned it, sir. Didn't see any reason not to. I'm not sure he put it together that the ring might have been inside. I didn't myself properly until just now."

Charles sat forward in his chair. "Do you remember the lady's name?"

Baxter's face screwed up with concentration. Out of the cor-ner of his eye, Charles saw Mélanie twisting her gloves round her fingers.

"Ellen something," Baxter said at last. "No, Helen, that was it." His face cleared. "Helen Trevennen. Like Helen of Troy, I thought. I suppose that's why it stuck in my head."

Charles released his breath and gave thanks to a God he had long since ceased to believe in. "Did you mention her name to Lorano?"

"No. I said I couldn't remember—which was true until just now. Seemed best to leave well enough alone."

"I don't suppose there's any chance you remember her direc-tion as well?"

"Oh, I remember that right enough. She must have been an actress or a dancer or something of the sort. The letter wasn't directed to her lodgings. It was sent to the Drury Lane Theatre." He shook his head. "Fancy my remembering after all these years."

Chapter 10

Mélanie gripped the edges of the carriage seat to steady her hands. It was not far to the Drury Lane Theatre, but the narrow streets were thronged with carts and drays going to and from the market. They were crawling along at a maddening pace. "Seven years is a long time," she said. "I don't recall seeing a Helen Trevennen on the program at the Drury Lane since we've been back in Britain."

"No." Charles turned his gaze to her. He'd been staring out the window with a fixed expression. "The odds are she's not at the theater anymore."

Don't let your hopes carry you away, his voice said. It was difficult when hope and fear churned within her, clogging her throat, tearing at her chest. "What about this man Lorano who asked Baxter about the ring?" she said. "Who do you think he's working for?"

"The royalists most likely, perhaps even the Spanish

embassy. If there's a rebellion in Spain, the royalists could make as much use of the ring as Carevalo and the liberals."

"Wouldn't they have to return it to the Carevalo family?"

"Why?" He scanned her face with a cold gaze. "Your people weren't planning to turn the ring over to Carevalo seven years ago. All the royalists need to do is dig up a Carevalo relative who supports the monarchy and parade him about with the ring. They could repeat the legends about the ring with a strategic emphasis on the links between the ring's power and the Spanish throne. Like most legends, the story of the Carevalo Ring can be bent to serve a multitude of purposes."

She couldn't argue with that. It was much the same thing Raoul had said to her seven years ago. "And if the people on Carevalo's lands saw a pro-royalist Carevalo cousin with the ring, they might side with him rather than Carevalo and the liberals."

"Precisely. If the royalists get their hands on the ring, there's not a chance in hell they'll surrender it to Carevalo, even if we could explain what that means for Colin."

"We'll just have to hope Mr. Lorano hasn't traced Helen Trevennen to the Drury Lane."

"Yes." Charles pushed his hair back from his forehead. She caught a telltale tremor in his hand. For a moment his controlled expression wavered. It was like looking into a glass at the reflection of her own terror.

"So Lieutenant Jennings found the Carevalo Ring," she said, recapitulating what they had learned thus far in the hope it would still the panic welling up in her chest. "It must have been hidden in some village or town the British occupied. Jennings heard the legends about the ring and realized how valuable it could be to the British. But he knew his superiors in the army wouldn't pay him for it. In fact, given Wellington's strictures against pillaging, he might get asked some uncomfortable questions about how he'd acquired the ring. So he hired the bandits to sell the ring to the British for him. Somehow he arranged to lead the detachment of soldiers who traveled with you when you went to buy the ring from the bandits. He wouldn't trust the bandits with the ring until the last minute, so he carried it with him and hid it in a letter he'd written to his mistress, Helen Trevennen."

"It's largely conjecture," Charles said, "but it's the only explanation that fits the facts as we know them."

"What do we tell them at the Drury Lane?" Mélanie said. "The truth?"

"The truth?" Charles's voice cut like ice. "Surely not. Do you even know how to tell it? Besides, it might frighten Helen Trevennen or her friends into silence. I think Lieutenant Jennings had better have been a good friend of mine. I was going through a trunk of his belongings recently and I found a letter from him leaving a bequest to Miss Trevennen. I didn't want to tell his wife, so I'm seeking out Miss Trevennen myself."

"That's simple and fairly plausible." She adjusted the brim of her bonnet, as though she could anchor herself. "What time is it?"

He pulled his watch from his pocket and opened it. "Just past ten."

"There's sure to be a rehearsal starting by now. The stage manager's a better bet for information than the manager. Stage managers know everything."

He nodded, returned his watch to his pocket, then swung his head round to look at her. "How long were you an actress?"

Even now, even with his mind on Colin, he missed nothing. She tightened the ribbons on her bonnet, tugging harder than was necessary. The ribbon cut into her skin. "My father had a traveling theater company. I was performing before I was Jessica's age. I went on doing so until I was fifteen."

"And then?"

He deserved an answer. She gave him the bare minimum. "He died."

Charles's eyes asked a great deal more and, she feared, saw more than a glimmering of the answers, but he merely said, "Evidently he taught you well."

A rich voice, smiling eyes. A hand ruffling her hair, a challenging question, a love she had never doubted. "My father was a man of integrity," she said. "I think he'd have liked you. I expect he wouldn't be very happy with what I've become."

"If he was a man of integrity," Charles said, "I can't imagine he would be."

His cool words cut her to the quick, because she knew he was right. Her father, like Charles, could never have made sense of letting the ends justify the means.

The porter at the stage door of the Drury Lane greeted their entrance with a frown, which changed to a look of surprise when Charles produced his card. It was not politic for a theater to offend influential politicians. He waved them in.

The smell was instantly recognizable. Not the scented candles, French perfume, and ripe oranges one smelled in the audience, but a sharper scent composed of cheap gilt paint, musty costumes, thick greasy cosmetics, and rehearsal tea brewed over a spirit lamp. Her father's company had never played in a theater half so grand, but some things were universal, whatever the size of the house.

The slither of booted feet on floorboards and the clang of foils came from the stage.

" 'Good king of cats, nothing but one of your nine lives,' " a voice muttered in desultory tones.

"No, no." Another voice interrupted from beyond the stage. "You're supposed to be the best swordsman in Verona, Tony. Try to look confident. Crispin, Mercutio should swagger. You look as though you're a stripling trying to remember the steps of the waltz."

Mélanie hesitated for the barest fraction of a second, teetering on the edge of a forgotten world. She'd long since severed this play from the demons of her past, but being behind the scenes was different from watching it comfortably seated in a box or even saying the lines herself in amateur theatricals.

No one noticed their entrance at first. Murky, strong-smelling rehearsal lamps cast giant shadows over the wings, the slotted scene panels, the stage itself. Two men in their shirt-sleeves were dueling across the stage. Two women—Juliet and the nurse, from the sound of it—were running lines in the upper stage left corner. A girl in an apron hurried by, holding a brocade robe that rattled as if it were full of pins. Two stagehands staggered out of the wings, carrying an enormous canvas flat that smelled of fresh paint. Mélanie stopped them with a smile and a question. Five minutes later, a tall, thin man in a paint-smeared smock appeared beside them.

"I'm Ned Thurgood, the stage manager." He wiped his hands on his smock. "Mr. Fraser? Mrs. Fraser? What brings you to the Drury Lane?" His manner was polite, even deferential, but though he looked them in the eye, his attention seemed to dart about the theater, taking in the movements of the duelists, the young man bent over a prop table, the voices running lines, the pounding of nails echoing through an open door at the back of the stage.

Charles shook Thurgood's hand. "It's a delicate matter, I'm afraid, Thurgood. We're looking for a woman named Helen Trevennen who was employed at this theater seven years ago."

Mélanie was torn between the hope that Thurgood would say Miss Trevennen was even now in the theater and the fear that he would claim never to have heard of her. Instead, his bushy brows shot up. "Helen. Good lord. Yes, she was one of our actresses, though she left the company some time ago. Was she— No, we'd best speak in private. Tim," he shouted to the young man at the prop table. "Make sure the paint's dry on the fountain. We need it this afternoon. Balcony scene," he explained to Charles and Mélanie as he ushered them round coils of rope, a rack of costumes, a thronelike chair with the upholstery stripped off, and a stack of papier-mâché rocks. "Supposed to give the effect of spring and young love. Weighs a ton. We have enough pulleys on this production to rig a ship. Artistic vision's all very well, but sometimes ideas that sound perfectly good on paper prove dam—devilish hard to execute."

" 'O! for a Muse of fire,' " Charles murmured. Somehow he made the words friendly and conversational, though Mélanie knew he must be as desperate for information as she was herself.

Thurgood turned his head, as though he was really looking at Charles for the first time. "Quite. Unfortunately, I have to make do with a crew of all-too-human stagehands." He opened a door onto a small office that seemed to contain a desk and two rickety chairs, though it was difficult to tell, as every surface was stacked with scripts, musical scores, playbills, and odd scraps of paper. Thurgood shifted some papers to the floor, waved them to the two chairs, and perched on the edge of the desk. "Sorry for the chaos. We open in less than a week and it's a new production. I'll do what I can to help you, Mr. Fraser, but I haven't seen Helen Trevennen since she left the company."

In as few words as possible, Charles outlined the story of his friend Jennings's death, the trunk of his belongings, and the paper leaving a bequest to Helen Trevennen.

Thurgood scratched his hair, which was of the curly variety that never quite lies straight. "Helen wasn't a woman one forgets easily." A reminiscent smile crossed his face, then was quickly erased. "Begging your pardon, Mrs. Fraser. This is an unpleasant business for a lady."

"Please don't hesitate out of concern for my sensibilities, Mr. Thurgood." Mélanie calculated her tone and expression to strike a balance between refined wife and woman of the world. "I wouldn't have accompanied my husband if I wasn't prepared for the realities of the situation."

"Ah—quite." Thurgood coughed.

"Where did Miss Trevennen go when she left the theater?" Charles asked, impatience breaking through in his voice.

"I'm afraid I don't know, Mr. Fraser." Thurgood fidgeted with the papers on the desk beside him. "It's odd. I haven't thought of Helen—Miss Trevennen—in years. But another gentleman was asking about her only a few days ago."

Mélanie could almost hear Charles's silent curse. "Oh?" he said. "Another acquaintance from the past?"

"So he claimed. Foreign gentleman. Spanish. Said he met Helen on a visit here during the war."

"Do you remember his name? It might help us in tracing Miss Trevennen."

Thurgood smiled. "Iago. Can't expect anyone who works in a theater to forget that. Iago—was it Morano? No, Lorano, that was it. Iago Lorano."

"Midthirties?" Charles asked. "Black hair? Tallish?"

"Yes, that sounds right. More a Cassio than an Iago. A bit too stiff for Romeo. Might have made a good Harry Five, he had the right military bearing. Do you know him, Mr. Fraser?"

"I think I may have met him once in Spain." Charles leaned back against the sagging slats of the chair, as though willing the tension from his body. "What were you able to tell him about Miss Trevennen?"

"Not a great deal. I—"

The door was jerked open. "Mr. Thurgood—" A young man with carrot-red hair poked his head through the doorway. "Sorry to interrupt, sir, but we can't find either of the poison flasks."

"I think Rosemary took them to make sure they fit in the costume pockets."

"I'll ask her. Oh, and Dobson wants to know if the musicians are stage left or right at the ball?"

"Left, last I heard."

"Thanks." The carrot-haired man ducked out.

"Sorry," Thurgood said. "You'd think they could keep track of things themselves. Oh, thunder." He jumped to his feet and pulled open the door. "Tim! Make sure Friar Laurence's prayer book is on the prop table." He closed the door. "Damn fool can't ever remember to put it back himself. We spent an hour hunting for it yesterday. Sorry, Mr. Fraser, where were we?"

"You were telling us about Iago Lorano."

"Oh, yes." Thurgood returned to the desk. "I wasn't able to tell him much, but I introduced him to Violet Goddard, our current Juliet, who was friendly with Helen—Miss Trevennen." He pulled a pencil from behind his ear and jotted a note on a nearby script. "Must remember to make sure the tombs are anchored properly. Yesterday they went slithering and nearly toppled Romeo and Juliet into the pit." He looked up at them. "I can ask Miss Goddard to have a word with you."

"Yes," Charles said, "in a moment. I'd like to ask you one or two questions first."

Thurgood, who had started to get up, leaned back against the desk.

"When did Miss Trevennen leave the Drury Lane?" Charles asked.

Thurgood folded the paper he'd written on and tucked it in his sleeve. "Must be five or six years ago. No, more than that. We were doing the new *As You Like It*, with the Forest of Arden after the style of Turner. So that would make it . . . early 1813. Nearly seven years."

Just about the time she would have received Jennings's letter. Charles shot Mélanie a glance. "Why did she leave?" he asked Thurgood.

"I wish I knew. She simply didn't show up one night. Very unprofessional. Phebe had to play Celia, and Audrey had to play Phebe, and one of the seamstresses actually went on as Audrey." He shuddered at the memory. "Miss Trevennen was no saint, but she'd always been punctual before."

"What about her friend Miss Goddard or others in the company?" Charles asked. "Did she contact them?"

Thurgood thumbed his finger through a loose sheaf of music on the desk beside him. "I never heard that anyone had had news of her. I didn't ask questions, if that's what you mean. We engaged another actress and that was the end of it."

Mélanie disentangled her skirt from a bit of rough wood on the chair. "Did she have other particular friends in the company? Besides Miss Goddard?"

Thurgood scratched the side of his face. "Helen Trevennen was the sort of woman more likely to be in the company of men than women. And no," he added, in response to the unspoken question in Mélanie's eyes, "she wasn't—ah—entangled with any of the men in the company. She set her sights higher than actors and stagehands." He got to his feet. "Miss Goddard may be able to tell you more. If you wait a moment or two, I'll bring her in."

"Hell and damnation," Mélanie said, when the door had closed behind Thurgood. "How the devil did Iago Lorano or whatever his name is find his way here? Baxter didn't even tell him Helen Trevennen's name."

Charles stood and took a turn about the small room. "If Baxter hadn't been able to remember her name, what would you have suggested we do next?"

Mélanie forced her mind to focus on the question. "Probably that we travel to Surrey and visit Mrs. Jennings. Wives often know more than their husbands realize." It occurred to her that this last phrase had unfortunate reverberations, but she plunged on without waiting for Charles's reaction. "Mrs. Jennings may have known her husband had a mistress and she may even have known the woman had been an actress at the Drury Lane. Do you think that's how Lorano tracked Helen Trevennen here?"

"It seems the likeliest explanation." Charles realigned the edges of a stack of scripts on the desk. "His questioning technique doesn't sound particularly subtle. It's a good bet we can learn something he overlooked."

"Violet Goddard is a very good actress," Mélanie said, thinking back to various performances they had seen Miss Goddard give at the Drury Lane.

"Yes." Charles prowled the narrow length of the room again, a tall, lean, impatient figure, like Raoul a few hours ago at Mivart's. "It won't be easy to get her to say anything she doesn't want to say."

Thurgood returned a few moments later accompanied by a slender young woman with pale gold hair that flowed loose about her shoulders and gave her something of the look of a Renaissance Madonna. She wore a gold silk shawl and a heavy wool rehearsal skirt over a stylish gown of chestnut lustring. Violet Goddard was slighter in person than she appeared onstage, but she carried herself with the same graceful bearing. She paused just beyond the doorway and gave a full, deliberate smile, brighter than a dozen wax tapers. Her fine-boned face went from passably pretty to incandescent.

"Violet Goddard." Thurgood pulled the door closed behind them. "Mr. and Mrs. Fraser, Violet. We'd like to help them in any way we can."

Charles held out his chair to Miss Goddard. The gesture earned him a faint look of surprise. She sank into the chair in one elegant, economical movement, so that the bulky overskirt fell about her in graceful folds. Thurgood excused himself to return to the stage.

"Thank you for seeing us, Miss Goddard," Charles said, as though she might have had a choice about it. "We know you are in the last days of rehearsal."

Miss Goddard smiled, this time with an ironic tilt to her mouth, as though to say the interview had been a command and she knew it. "It's of no moment, Mr. Fraser. They'll be rehearsing the fight for at least another hour. For some reason, duels are much more difficult to choreograph than love scenes."

Sensations teased at the edges of Mélanie's memory. Clashing swords. The swish of a velvet cape. The rustle of a brocade gown. The feel of standing in the wings, waiting to step onstage, more heady than champagne, more nerve-racking than her first presentation at court. "I've always thought it unfair that Juliet is excluded from such an exciting part of the play," she said. "It gives the actress entirely too much time to think."

"Yes." Miss Goddard's eyes brightened with fellow feeling. Then she caught herself up short. How much fellow feeling could there be between an actress and a political hostess? Little did she know.

Charles gave an easy smile that was a tribute to his own acting ability. "We saw you as Lady Teazle last year. The scene with the screen was the funniest I've ever seen it."

"Thank you, Mr. Fraser. It's one of my favorite roles." Miss Goddard folded her hands in her lap with the delicacy of a woman who has learned to infuse her every gesture with grace.

The dazzling charm, her professional armor, was in place once again. Her eyes sparkled, part Juliet, part Cleopatra. "What was it you wanted to talk to me about?"

Charles repeated his story about Jennings and the bequest to Helen Trevennen.

Miss Goddard listened in silence. She had shrewd eyes, set in an elegant, well-groomed face. The face could have belonged to any lady in Mayfair, but the eyes had seen things no gently bred girl was meant to witness. Mélanie wondered if her own gaze could betray her past as easily. Perhaps it took one who shared the experience to recognize the signs.

"I wish I could be of more help," Miss Goddard said when Charles finished. The words sounded just the slightest bit too rehearsed. Her voice was cultured, with an underlay of Spitalfields. "But I fear I can tell you no more than I told the Spanish gentleman who was here last week. I haven't seen Helen in nearly seven years."

Charles was leaning against the desk, arms folded across his chest. "But you weren't as surprised as everyone else by her disappearance?"

Her eyes widened. "How did you know?" she said, and then bit her lip at the easy trap she had fallen into.

Charles hitched himself up on the edge of the desk. "She talked to you before she left?"

Miss Goddard stared down at her well-tended nails.

"I assure you we mean Miss Trevennen no harm," Charles said. "Surely she would appreciate my friend's bequest and the sentiment behind it."

Miss Goddard gave a faint, unstudied smile that made her appear more girlish. She was probably not yet five-and-twenty, Mélanie realized, younger than she was herself. "Helen had little use for sentiment, but she would undoubtedly appreciate the bequest. However, as I said, I haven't heard from her in seven years."

Charles wandered about the room and stopped to study a framed notice advertising Mrs. Siddons in *Fatal Marriage*. "I've always been very fond of the theater. Simon Tanner, the play-wright, is one of my wife's and my closest friends. You perhaps know that I am a Member of Parliament, Miss Goddard, and my grandfather is the Duke of Rannoch. It is unfortunately all too easy for persons of influence to create difficulties for a theater—the government censor is entirely too efficient, and a disparag-ing comment dropped at one's club can have a tiresome effect on the success of a production. It would desolate me to be the cause of any difficulties for the Drury Lane." Charles, ardent advocate of free speech, turned and fixed Miss Goddard with a cold stare. "But believe me, I am quite capable of doing so."

Miss Goddard drew in her breath. "Mr. Fraser, I meant what I said."

"Miss Goddard, so did I."

Her gaze flickered over his face. "Your determination to carry out your friend's wishes is extreme, Mr. Fraser."

"Trust that I have my reasons, madam."

She regarded him a moment longer. Mélanie could see her weighing the consequences in the blue depths of her eyes. Then Miss Goddard gave a slight shrug, fluttering the gold silk of her Norwich shawl. "I don't know why I'm so determined to protect her. It's more, I'm sure, than Helen would do for me."

"She was your friend." Now that he had achieved his objec-tive, Charles's voice turned gentle.

"I suppose you could say that." Miss Goddard ran her fin-gers over the shawl. "Helen made a friend of me because she found me useful. I can't tell you how many pairs of my silk stock-ings she ruined, how many scarves and earrings she borrowed and never returned." She wrinkled her nose in distaste. "I was only sixteen when I met her. Helen wasn't that much older, but she was a font of useful advice about how to get on in the world. Besides"—Miss Goddard hesitated a moment, then continued, her head held high—"Helen knew how to speak and how to carry herself and which fork to use with the fish. I'll always be grateful she taught me that. And she could be tremendous fun, even if she had a tendency to leave others to pay the reckoning and cope with the consequences."

Charles returned to the desk. "You shared confidences?"

"Helen wasn't the sort to confide much in anyone. But—" Miss Goddard was silent for a moment, then spoke in a rush. "The night before she disappeared she asked me to go to a tavern with her after the performance. There was nothing unusual in that. But she insisted we choose a tavern where we wouldn't encounter anyone else from the theater. And when we got there, she told me she was going away."

"Where?" Charles's face was unreadable, but he held her with his gaze.

"She didn't say. She wouldn't say." Miss Goddard's artfully plucked brows drew together. "It sounds completely mad now. It sounded mad then, and Helen was one of the least fanciful women I've ever known. She said I shouldn't expect to hear from her and she wouldn't be coming back. She said it wouldn't be—safe."

There was a brief silence in the cramped, dusty room. "Not safe how?" Charles said, in the same patient voice.

"She didn't explain."

"Was that why she was leaving? Because she was afraid of something? Or someone?"

"Yes. No." Miss Goddard disentangled a strand of hair from one of her antique gold earrings. "She didn't seem to be running blindly. Truth to tell, she looked disgustingly pleased with herself."

Charles leaned back and rested his long-fingered hands on the desk behind him. "Why do you think she told you she was leaving and no one else?"

"Oh, she explained that straight out. She asked me to visit her uncle and tell him she'd left London. She said she wouldn't be able to say goodbye to him herself."

"Her uncle lives in London?"

"He's imprisoned for debt in the Marshalsea. He used to be

an actor. Hugo Trevennen. Some of the company still remember him. He was quite talented apparently, but he had extravagant tastes and a weakness for the horses. I went to see him as Helen asked. A thoroughly charming man."

"Did you ask him where he thought his niece might have gone?"

"Naturally, I was curious. He said he never had the least idea what Helen might do from one minute to the next."

Charles swung his booted foot against the side of the desk. "Did she have any other relatives?"

"Not that I know of." Miss Goddard pulled the folds of her shawl about her throat. "Until then she'd never spoken about her family."

"Were there other men?" Mélanie said, hoping to catch her off her guard with the bluntness of the question. "Besides Lieutenant Jennings?"

Miss Goddard's eyes widened. She looked at Mélanie as though reassessing her opinion of the decorous Mrs. Fraser. "Helen flirted with men by the stage door. We all did. I expect she did more than flirt, though I couldn't swear to it. But the only man I ever met in her presence was someone she called 'Will.' He may have been your friend Lieutenant Jennings. He had the bearing of an army officer."

"Dark hair?" Charles asked. "Blue eyes? Tall, midtwenties?"

She nodded. "He called to take her out after the performance every so often, though his visits stopped some time before Helen disappeared. She said he'd been posted abroad with his regiment."

"Did you know he'd died?"

"Yes, I heard about it just before Helen disappeared." Miss Goddard twisted the end of her shawl round her shapely fingers. Some further words hung unspoken in the air.

"But?" Charles said in a gentle voice.

Miss Goddard looked up at him. "That's all, Mr. Fraser."

"Oh, come, Miss Goddard, surely an actress knows how much can be read into a pause." Charles hesitated a moment. "I know it sits oddly with my threats and I'd no doubt say it anyway. But I told the truth when I said I mean Miss Trevennen no harm."

No one could look more compellingly honest than Charles when he put his mind to it. Perhaps because the honesty was genuine. Miss Goddard studied him for a long moment, an actress judging the authenticity of a performance. "That last night, Helen said she'd meet me at the tavern. But I forgot my gloves, so I ran back into the theater after most of the company had gone home. I heard Helen crying in her dressing room. Or laughing, I couldn't be sure which—it sounded a bit hysterical. The door was ajar, so I peeked inside. A packet of papers was spread on the dressing table in front of her. When I asked her what was wrong, all she'd say is that she'd lost the person in the world who meant most to her and her life had just changed completely."

"And you think she was crying with grief?" Charles said.

"At the time I did, though she didn't act at all brokenhearted later in the tavern. But perhaps she cared for Lieutenant Jennings as much as she was capable of caring for anyone. She certainly must have meant something to him or he never would have sent her such a precious keepsake."

Mélanie's pulse quickened, as though she had been running. "What sort of keepsake?"

Violet Goddard raised her brows at the urgency in Mélanie's voice. "He sent her a piece of jewelry with the letter. I couldn't see it properly, but it was gold and there was some sort of red stone."

Chapter 11

For a moment, Charles forgot to breathe. "Did Miss Trevennen say anything about the keepsake?"

Miss Goddard shook her head. "She pulled the pages of the letter over it. I don't think she realized I'd seen. I don't think she wanted me to see. Helen was free enough with other people's property, but she was jealous of her own."

"Did she say anything else?" Charles kept his voice even, stripped of all but essentials.

"No, just that she'd be ready in a minute. I fetched my gloves and she met me in the corridor. When I tried to offer my condolences on her loss, she laughed it off and said no man was worth crying over. We went to the tavern and had the conversation I told you about. It was the last time I saw her."

"Did you mention any of this to Iago Lorano?" Charles said. "Did you tell him about her uncle in the Marshalsea?"

"No." Miss Goddard smoothed the fabric of her shawl, a gesture that seemed uncharacteristically nervous. "I didn't particularly trust his story—if he was someone who'd known Helen in the past, he might have had something to do with why she ran away." The ironic look crossed her face again. "Besides, he didn't threaten to use his influence against the theater."

Charles got to his feet. "Believe me, Miss Goddard, I wouldn't have resorted to such despicable tactics had I seen an alternative."

Miss Goddard gave him one of her incandescent smiles. "Do you know, I have the oddest inclination to believe you, Mr. Fraser. You're either a very honest man or an exceedingly good actor."

When they returned to the stage, the foils were still clanging. " 'Tybalt, you rat-catcher, will you walk?' " said one of the actors, sounding more natural now.

"Thank God," Miss Goddard murmured. "Perhaps we'll actually get to one of my scenes before the midday break."

Ned Thurgood emerged from the wings, a jeweled flask in one hand, a feathered mask in the other.

"Miss Goddard was a great help," Charles said. "We appreciate her cooperation. And yours."

Thurgood nodded, one eye on the duelists. "I'm glad to hear it. I wish you well in your search."

Miss Goddard stared at the mask. "Please tell me that isn't for me."

"For the ball scene."

"Neddie. Dearest. Chicken feathers make me sneeze."

"Well, at least—"

Charles and Mélanie left them to argue it out and made their way out of the theater in silence. Charles turned toward the corner where Randall was waiting with the carriage. The full reality of what they had learned washed over him. He stopped and gripped a lamppost with one hand. "God," he said, his forehead against the iron of the lamppost, his voice so wracked with relief it trembled. "Sweet Jesus."

Mélanie laid a hand on his arm. Her fingers were shaking. "I know. I didn't really believe Helen Trevennen had the ring until now."

Charles released the lamppost. "She may have sold it. Do you have any paper?"

She dropped her hand and took a notebook and pencil from her reticule.

Charles propped the notebook against the iron lamppost and scribbled a brief note as he spoke. "I'll have Addison start making inquiries among London jewelers while we visit Helen Trevennen's uncle at the Marshalsea."

"Mr. Trevennen told Miss Goddard he didn't have any idea where Helen had gone."

"But he must know something about her friends or at the very least her family. At present he's our only lead."

They returned to the carriage, and Charles gave Randall the note. "This is for Addison. Stop back at the Thistle and ask Baxter to have someone he trusts deliver it to Berkeley Square. Then take us to the Marshalsea."

"Right you are." Randall pocketed the note and accepted the direction to the debtors' prison as matter-of-factly as if Charles had asked to be driven to Parliament or his club in St. James's.

When they were settled in the carriage, Mélanie looked at Charles as though about to ask something, then clamped her lips shut.

Charles pulled his watch from his pocket and snapped it open. The fitful sunlight fell on the inscription inside the cover.

My bounty is as boundless as the sea,
My love as deep; the more I give to thee,
The more I have, for both are infinite. M.

The familiar engraved words slashed like a sword cut. "It's twenty-five minutes past eleven," he said. "Colin's been missing for at least eight hours."

She nodded without looking at him. "Thank you." Her voice was parched.

He returned the watch to his pocket. "Blanca can help Addison with the jewelers. Between the two of them they can cover a lot of territory." At the mention of his wife's maid, a hitherto unconsidered thought occurred to him. "Oh, Christ. I suppose Blanca was a French agent, too?"

"No, Blanca was my maid. I was a French agent."

"And Blanca knew it."

"Charles, you know as well as anyone it's impossible to keep secrets from one's maid or valet."

"But disgustingly easy, apparently, to keep them from one's husband. I think Addison may be in love with Blanca."

"Of course he is. He's been in love with her since they met, though they only actually became lovers in the last couple of years—Addison kept worrying she was too young or he was compromising her virtue. I have no doubt Blanca loves him just as much. And, believe me, I didn't put her up to it."

Her words grated on his nerves like nails on a schoolroom slate. "Believing you does not come easily at present, madam."

She turned her head to look him full in the face. "Blanca was a fourteen-year-old orphan when I met her, Charles. Raoul and I rescued her from her uncle's filthy tavern where she had to fight off her uncle's blows and the wandering hands of the customers. She would have done anything for me after we took her away from there. Lay the blame for the deception where it belongs. At my door."

"Damn you, there's blame enough to go round." Nausea gripped him for a moment, like a vise. He looked at his wife. She was as familiar to him as the salt breeze off the Perthshire coast or the smell of snuff and the crack of walnuts from the back benches in the House of Commons. And at the same time, she was as much a stranger as Helen Trevennen. "How old were you?"

"How old was I when?"

"When you went to work for O'Roarke." He ran his fingers through his hair. He had laid himself open to her in an intimate detail it seared him to remember, yet he did not know even the simplest facts of her life. "Christ, how old are you now?"

"Six-and-twenty. My birthday is the sixth of October. Raoul taught me it's best to stick to the truth when you can."

O'Roarke's name was like salt poured on a raw wound. He wanted to hurt her with a savageness he could scarcely recognize in himself. "I'm surprised you can even remember the truth. Am I supposed to feel less a fool because I've been presenting you with jewel boxes on the correct date every year? How old were you when O'Roarke found you?"

"Sixteen."

"A year after your father died."

"Yes."

Charles looked at her for a moment. He'd been constructing defenses for too long not to recognize them in others. Mélanie would answer questions about working in a brothel, about being a spy and betraying her marriage vows, but she shied away from any mention of her father's death.

He wanted to batter her defenses and force her to confront whatever she was hiding from, because that might inflict on her some fraction of the pain she'd inflicted on him. He wanted to ask more about her father, because with the part of his brain that could still think at all, he wanted to understand her.

But he said nothing. Perhaps he did not press her out of his old habit of not pushing past the boundaries she set. Or perhaps his childhood hurts were still too raw for him to force her to speak of her own, whatever else she had done.

They pulled up in front of the Thistle, and Randall ran into the tavern to deliver Charles's message. Mélanie turned her face to the window. "Charles, what do you think was in the letter from Lieutenant Jennings? Jennings wouldn't have known he was going to die when he wrote it. He wasn't planning to send the ring with it. He was probably just using the letter as a temporary hiding place until he gave the ring to the bandits to sell to you."

Charles stared at the bland emptiness of the carriage seat

opposite. "Romantic drivel. Erotic imaginings. He could even have written to her about his swindle with the ring, though I doubt he'd have been stupid enough to put it down in writing. And if Miss Trevennen knew what the ring was, she'd have been a fool not to try to sell it to the British government."

"So what was she afraid of? Was Jennings protecting her from something, so that once he was gone she had to run?"

"Jennings didn't strike me as much of a protector." Charles folded his arms across his chest. "She could have been lying about being afraid. I get the feeling Miss Trevennen lied with great agility."

"Yes." Mélanie put the grimy fingertips of her gloves up to her temples. "Considering how like me she seems to have been, one would think I'd understand her better."

Charles shot a quick look at her. She sounded serious, not self-mocking, and her dark brows were drawn in concentration. "Perhaps she was running off with a wealthy lover," he said. "That would explain why she told Violet Goddard she'd made her fortune and her life had changed."

"Jennings's death freed her to go off with this other man? That assumes she took her loyalty to Jennings seriously."

"Some women do," Charles said.

Mélanie jerked as though he'd struck her. "Very true," she said. "But that doesn't explain the secrecy surrounding her disappearance."

Charles scanned her face, looking for something he couldn't have defined and wouldn't have believed if he'd found it. "No," he said, "it doesn't."

Randall swung back onto the box and gave the horses their office. Mélanie fell silent as they wended their way through the London streets. They often sat thus, on their way to a rout or a reception or an evening at the theater or on an expedition to buy books for the children or attend a public meeting or see the latest Royal Academy Exhibition at Somerset House. Her profile looked as it always did, outlined against the green silk that covered the carriage walls. He would have recognized the angle of her head in the shadows of twilight. He would have known the elusive scent of her skin in cloaking darkness. How could her outward person be the same, when everything about her was false? How, through seven years of marriage, could he have been such an utter fool as never to have guessed the truth of what she was?

He had an unexpected memory of one of the rare, perfect days he had spent with his mother. He must have been about ten, because it was before his sister was born. His mother had taken him and his brother riding along the Perthshire coast, and they'd picnicked on the beach. While his brother built a sand castle, his mother had pulled out a notebook and taught Charles the key to an ingenious cipher. That night she'd eaten supper with them in the nursery and tucked them into bed. He could still remember her promising them another such day tomorrow as he drifted off to sleep. But when they woke in the morning, she'd already packed her bags and left for London. They hadn't seen her again for three months.

He'd long since accepted that he hadn't known his mother. He would never know what had finally driven her to take her life, if she had thought of her children in those last moments or if he and his brother and sister had been as tangential to her then as they had the rest of the time.

He certainly hadn't known his father. He would never know if Kenneth Fraser had accepted him as his heir out of duty or uncertainty. He would never know who actually had fathered him, in the crudest sense of the word.

He thought, with the stab of guilt her memory always brought, of his first love, Kitty. God knows he hadn't understood her or he wouldn't have failed her so badly. It was too late now to understand his parents or Kitty. In recent years, he had begun to realize that he might never know what had gone wrong between him and his brother, either.

But he would have sworn he knew Mélanie to the core.

The sharp smell of the river seeped into the carriage. Mélanie broke the silence as they rattled across the dilapidated stones of

London Bridge toward Southwark. Her voice was unusually husky. "Will we have trouble getting into the Marshalsea?"

Charles tore his gaze from the broad, greasy expanse of the Thames, thick with barges and lighters and skiffs. "They lock the gates at night, but there's no trouble getting in during the day. My classics tutor at Oxford spent a year there. He was a brilliant man with a weakness for cards and not a lot of skill to go with it. I visited him in prison several times."

"I remember. You told me about him when you proposed the bill to change the debt laws."

Another image flickered across his memory. Sitting at his desk in the early hours of the morning with a dull pain in his head and a scribbled-over paper before him. Mélanie bringing him coffee, perching on the edge of his desk, reading the speech, suggesting changes . . .

He stared at her. Betrayal wasn't a single blow, but a series of sword cuts, each one uniquely painful. "You helped me with that speech. Not to mention God knows how many others. I let a foreign agent pen the words I spoke in the House of Commons. I suppose that ought to be funny. I suppose you thought it *was* funny."

She turned to him with a sharp twist of her head. "Charles, whatever else you think of me, you must realize I believe in the same things you do. The freedom to speak and write what one believes. A legal system that doesn't throw people in prison without charge. A life in which children don't starve on the streets or die in workhouses or lose their limbs in factories. A say in one's own government."

"Liberty, equality, and fraternity?"

"In a nutshell."

"Your Napoleon Bonaparte changed the French republic into an empire long before he lost at Waterloo."

"I'd be the last to call Napoleon a saint or even a hero," Mélanie said. "Perhaps he betrayed the revolution and trampled on its ideals. Perhaps we all did. But I'd take what Napoleon did for France and Spain over what's come after any day."

"And that justifies everything you did?"

"What do you want me to say? That my belief in a tarnished ideal gave me the right to lie to you and betray you at every turn? That I see now that I was wrong, that I should have fought fairly when we both know war isn't fair? That I turned my back on everything I believed in the moment I realized I loved you? None of those answers would be true."

"Least of all that you love me." Anger welled up on his tongue like fresh blood. "There've been enough lies between us already, Mel."

" 'Doubt truth to be a liar; But—' " She shook her head. "I don't expect you to believe me. I wouldn't believe it, were our situations reversed. But I do love you, Charles. I always will."

He returned her gaze, barricading himself against the plea in her eyes. "God," he said, sick with her, sick with himself for wanting to believe her, "you just don't quit, do you?"

Chapter 12

Charles sprang down from the carriage in front of the Marshalsea prison and offered his hand to Mélanie. Chivalry or force of habit, he supposed. He released her as soon as she'd descended the carriage steps.

They were a world away from the decorous precincts of Mayfair or even the familiar chaos of Covent Garden. The air smelled of sour rot and the stench of refuse from the laystalls that overflowed the street. Windows were cracked or boarded over or missing entirely. Coal porters and dustmen, barefoot children, and men and women in shapeless, water-stained garments, who looked as though they scavenged on the river, pushed their way along the crowded street. Carriages clattered by, windows and doors securely locked.

The gray brick walls of the prison reared up before them, stolid, uncompromising, unrelenting. Charles surveyed the prison gates, shutting his mind to the fact that if Helen Trevennen's uncle could give them no clue to her whereabouts, they might have reached a dead end.

As he and Mélanie crossed the pavement to the prison, a boy of no more than seven caught at the skirt of his greatcoat. Charles stared into the boy's saucerlike eyes, thought of his son, and pressed some coins into the lad's hand.

The sky had clouded over again, adding to the gloom of the place, but the porter who admitted them at the main gate was cheerful enough. He nodded at the mention of Mr. Trevennen, gave them a set of directions that sounded like the key to a maze, and said he was sure the old gentleman would be glad of company.

The Marshalsea was like a small, walled city. They made their way along grimy cobblestoned alleys, between high, smoke-stained brick buildings that might have passed for lodging houses if one forgot about the locked gates. A group of children were playing blindman's buff in the wider space where two alleys intersected. A woman was taking her laundry down, one eye on the darkening sky. A terrier nosed round the garbage by the steps of one of the buildings. The sound of an ill-tuned spinet came through an open casement window, the hiss of a fire through another, voices raised in argument through a third.

Many people spent the better part of their lives here. You couldn't get out of debtors' prison until you paid off your debts and you couldn't earn any money to pay off your debts while you were locked up. Yet another example of the profound wisdom of the British system of justice. The same system under which, until a mere five years ago, a parent could legally sell a child to be a climbing boy or a pickpocket or a prostitute. The only crime had been the sale not of the child but of the child's clothes.

Trevennen's rooms were on the first floor, through a decaying wooden archway, up a sagging staircase, down a long gallery that was open on one side. Charles knocked on the splintery door. Heavy, ponderous footsteps sounded within, and the door opened.

Pale blue eyes surveyed them out of a broad, strong-boned

face. "Yes? How may I help you? I don't believe I've—" The blue gaze slid past Charles and fastened on Mélanie. "Good Lord." The eyes widened. The shoulders straightened. The voice deepened with the resonance of a cello. " 'Tis beauty truly blent, whose red and white/Nature's own sweet and cunning hand laid on.' "

Mélanie had been looking ill a moment before, but she gave a laugh that had the sparkle of fine champagne. "How very flattering. I can't answer for the Countess Olivia, but I fear in my case nature gets assistance from a shocking amount of paint and lotions."

A look of pure delight crossed Hugo Trevennen's face. "A beauty *and* versed in Shakespeare." He peered at Mélanie down the bridge of his aquiline nose. "Do I know you, my dear? Appalling that I could have forgotten such a face, but living in this place does strange things to the memory."

Mélanie gave him a smile that was a perfect combination of the daughterly and the flirtatious. Charles watched Trevennen melt like candle wax beneath its warmth. "No, we haven't met. I'm Mélanie Fraser and this is my husband, Charles. We'd be very much obliged if we could have a word with you. It's about your niece, Helen."

Trevennen's brows shot up. "My word. Nelly. Yes, of course. Delighted to be of help—if I can." He smoothed his coat. The coat was threadbare and cut in a frocked style that was thirty years out of date, but the fabric was expensive and the frayed shirt beneath was spotless and carefully starched. "Do come in."

He ushered them into a small, low-ceilinged room. Theatrical prints hung on the peeling wallpaper, and racing forms were stacked on the tabletop. The carpet looked like a Turkey rug but on closer inspection was painted canvas. Two high-backed chairs of a cheap pine painted to resemble walnut might have once graced the set of a Shakespearean drama. Charles suspected the painted screen in one corner had come from a production of *The School for Scandal*.

Trevennen waved them to the chairs. "Would you care for

refreshment?" He swept his arm toward the tarnished brass kettle that hung from a hook over the fireplace, as though he were Prospero and could conjure crystal decanters and plates of cold salmon.

Mélanie sank onto one of the Shakespearean chairs. "Please don't trouble yourself."

"I'm afraid I don't entertain much these days." Trevennen scooped some coal from the coal scuttle and threw it on the fire. "When I think of the supper parties we used to have after a performance . . . But I fear my large style agreed not with the leanness of my purse."

Charles sat in the other high-backed chair. "We understand Miss Trevennen inherited her acting talent from you."

"You could say that." Trevennen sank into an armchair, flicking back the skirts of his coat as if it was a sweeping cloak. "My Hamlet was considered quite good. In the provinces, you know. Of course, by the time I came to London, I played supporting roles. Quite a collection of Shakespearean dukes, and Hazlitt was pleased to comment on my Jaques. 'And so, from hour to hour we ripe and ripe,/And then from hour to hour we rot and rot,/And thereby hangs a tale.' " He frowned, as though this cut a bit too close to the bone. "Oh, you wanted to talk about Helen, didn't you? What's she been up to, then?"

Charles recited the story about Jennings and the legacy left to Helen Trevennen.

Trevennen listened with the detached interest of an actor hearing the plot of an amusing new play. Perhaps after so many years in the Marshalsea, everything in the outside world seemed like theatrical illusion. "Nelly. Such a pretty little girl. A wheedler from the first, mind, but even then 'custom could not stale her infinite variety.' "

"When did you see her last?" Charles asked.

Trevennen stared out the window. The iron spikes on the outer wall of the prison were visible through the mildew-filmed glass. "Must be seven or eight years ago. She was never one for regular visits, but she used to appear every so often, usually when she wanted some sort of advice about the theater or racing. She was almost as fond of the horses as I am, though a bit less prodigal. I helped her get her position at the Drury Lane. She made a charmingly innocent Hero and I heard she did a very fetching Constance Neville in her last season. I wasn't able to attend the performances by that time, of course. Still, I quite looked forward to her carrying on the family name. Then one day this friend of hers—charming young lady—called to say Helen had been obliged to leave London. Do you know where she took herself off to, then?"

"No," Charles said. "We were hoping you would know, or at least have some idea."

Trevennen blinked. "Sorry, dear boy. Always fancied myself a fair judge of women, but never could predict what Nelly would do from one moment to the next. She drove my poor brother to distraction."

"Is your brother still living, Mr. Trevennen?" Mélanie asked.

"No, Theodore went to his maker some ten years since. He was a parson with a living in Cornwall, near Truro. Lost his wife early and hadn't the least idea how to bring up the girls, poor fellow. He was a dreadful puritan, which only served to make them more wild, if you ask me, but of course he never did."

Charles seized hold of the new information in this speech. "Girls?" he said.

"Nelly and Susy. You haven't met Susan? No, no reason you should, I suppose." Trevennen smoothed his gray-brown hair back from his high forehead, less Prospero now than Falstaff, looking back with rueful regret. "She's two years younger than Helen. Looks quite like her, though Nelly's a blonde and Susy got her mother's red hair. Nelly ran off to London when she was seventeen. Susy followed a year later. My brother washed his hands of the pair of them. Never saw them again as far as I know. But he'd stopped speaking to me to all intents and purposes when I took to the stage. It was quite a surprise when Helen appeared on my doorstep and said she wanted to tread the boards herself. Tried to do what was best for her."

"I don't doubt it, Mr. Trevennen." Mélanie smiled at him. "Were the girls close?"

Trevennen snorted. "Close as Hermia and Helena."

"I see. Sewing on the same sampler one minute, ready to tear each other's eyes out the next?"

"Exactly. Do you have sisters, Mrs. Fraser?"

"One younger sister. It can be a complicated relationship." One would swear Mélanie was telling the truth. Perhaps, Charles realized, she actually *was* telling the truth. He knew nothing about her real family, save that her father had been an actor and had died when she was fifteen. "Susan hasn't heard from Helen in the last seven years either?" Mélanie asked.

"Susy hasn't mentioned Nelly at all for longer than that. They had some sort of falling-out, though neither of them saw fit to explain it to me, and I thought it best to keep well clear. They shared rooms when Susy first came to London. Nelly was at the Drury Lane and Susy was an opera dancer at the Covent Garden. Then they must have quarreled about something or other. Nelly moved to finer rooms and Susy moved to Clerkenwell and neither of them mentioned the other when they came to visit me."

"Is Miss Susan Trevennen still in Clerkenwell?" Charles asked.

"No." Trevennen shifted his position in the chair as though he was trying to inch away from something. Falstaff gave way to Desdemona's deceived father. "I know nothing of Nelly's life in recent years. What I know of Susan's I fear has been . . . unfortunate. A true daughter of the game."

Charles felt Mélanie go still at this echo of the words she had quoted about herself, but her face betrayed nothing.

Trevennen's shoulders sank deeper into the chair. "Susan is now employed at the Gilded Lily. In Villiers Street, off the Strand."

He seemed to think the name would not mean anything to Mélanie. Charles was fairly certain that it did, but he didn't disabuse Trevennen.

Mélanie got to her feet with a gentle swish of her skirts. Before the men could rise, she dropped down beside Trevennen's chair and pressed his hand. "Mr. Trevennen. Do you have any idea where Helen went?"

Trevennen looked at her with the air of a man longing to transform himself back into Hotspur or Prince Hal. His pale blue eyes filled with regret at having to disappoint her. For an instant, Charles had a sheer craftsman's admiration for his wife's technique. "I'm afraid not," Trevennen said. "Knowing Nelly, she hasn't immured herself in some backwater."

"Did she ever mention any friends, in London or outside of it?"

"Nelly was never one to volunteer information, unless she thought it could get her something, and then the odds were it wouldn't be truthful."

Mélanie sat back on her heels. "Did she ever seem afraid of anything? Or anyone?"

"Nelly?" Trevennen threw back his head and gave a rich laugh that echoed off the low ceiling as though it were the rafters of the Drury Lane. " 'Of all base passions, fear is most accurs'd.' Or so Nelly would have claimed. We Trevennens may be a foolish lot, Mrs. Fraser, but we don't frighten easily, and Nelly had more courage than my brother and I put together."

Charles got to his feet. "One last question, Trevennen. Has anyone else asked you about your niece recently?"

"About Nelly?" Trevennen shook his head. "Good God, no. I don't get many visitors and I doubt most of the people here even remember I have two nieces."

Charles nodded. "A dark-haired man with a Spanish accent was asking questions about her at the theater. I'd advise you not to talk to him. We have reason to think he doesn't wish Miss Trevennen well."

Trevennen squared his shoulders with the dignity of King Lear. "Don't worry, Fraser. I don't volunteer information to anyone I don't care for."

A light rain was falling when Charles and Mélanie stepped

back out onto the gallery. The wind slapped against the stone, bringing a sour smell from the ground below and warning of a more violent storm to come. The gallery was crowded with visitors hurrying home and Marshalsea residents hurrying back to their rooms before the storm hit.

"I take it the Gilded Lily is a brothel," Mélanie said. The press of the crowd forced her to walk close to Charles, but she hadn't taken his arm.

"It is."

"I won't ask how you know," she said, as they reached the head of the stairs. "Shall we try it first or—"

She got no farther. Charles, his gaze focused inward, didn't see what actually happened. One moment Mélanie was speaking. The next, she gave an abrupt cry and fell headlong down the steps to the hard stone below.

Chapter 13

Mélanie came to to the feel of rain falling and the brush of fingers against her face.

"Mel." Her husband's voice, low and urgent. She opened her eyes and looked into his own. His brows were drawn, his mouth set. He released his breath in a harsh sigh. "Can you sit up?"

"I think so." She reached back against the rain-slick stone, then winced as a burning pain tore through her side. Charles's arm came round her or she would have fallen backwards. She felt him stiffen, heard his quick intake of breath. "What is it?" she asked.

"You're bleeding." He looked up and spoke more loudly. "My wife has injured herself. I need a quiet room, warm water, bandages."

A murmur of conversation followed. Mélanie realized a small crowd had gathered at the base of the steps where she was lying. Solicitous hands helped her to her feet. The voices kept fading in and out round her. Her vision blurred, clouded, faded to black, then returned in a burst of color that sent a stab of pain through her head.

Charles's voice sounded in her ear. "Can you walk?"

"Yes," she said, because it seemed ridiculous that she could not, but she swayed when she tried to take a step. In the end he half carried her across an alley, through a low doorway, and then through another into a small sitting room. She sank into a worn blue velvet wing chair before the welcome warmth of a fire. She heard Charles say he could tend to his wife himself and then deliver some instructions she couldn't follow. Her head was spinning and her side burned and she couldn't seem to stop shivering.

A few moments later, Charles returned carrying a tray with a steaming bowl of water, a stack of cloths, a bottle, and a glass. He dropped down beside her, splashed something into the glass, and put it in her hand. "Drink. It'll help."

"What is it?"

"Brandy, supposedly. I wouldn't swear to the quality." He cupped his hand round hers and guided the glass to her lips. It tasted as harsh as sandpaper, but its warmth spread through her, and she stopped shaking. She had a memory of him giving her whisky to drink in the Cantabrian Mountains. With that memory came another. She jerked, spilling the brandy. "Charles, we don't have time for this."

He put the glass on the floor. "Hold still, Mel. You can't afford to get killed just now." He undid the ribbons on her damp, crushed bonnet and set it on the hearth rug to dry. "Can you move your arm? I need to look at the wound."

She lifted her right arm and gasped at the jolt of pain that ran down her side. "I can't think what I cut myself on. Was there broken glass?"

"Someone stabbed you. We need to get your pelisse off. Lean forward and I'll manage the fastenings."

He unclasped her pelisse and slipped it off her shoulders, unhooked her gown and did the same. Instead of trying to pull her chemise over her head, he ripped the linen in two from shoulder to waist, which was a good thing because it hurt quite damnably to move her arm.

He wrapped a blanket round her shoulders as best he could without covering the wound, then dipped a cloth in the water and pressed it against her side. "How much do you remember?"

Her head had stopped spinning and her senses were flooding back. She could see the black smoke stains on the fireplace tiles, smell the damp and the coal smoke, hear the drip of rain on the roof. The pain was sharper, in her side and her back and her head, but her memory had sharpened as well. "I was pushed."

"So I thought." He took the cloth away, splashed some brandy on a fresh cloth, and dabbed at the wound. "Did you see who pushed you?"

She winced. The brandy burned as much against her side as it had down her throat. "No. All I remember is a hand on my back and then pain and falling. I didn't realize I'd been knifed. But it couldn't have been an accident or a robbery attempt. Whoever it was didn't grab for my reticule and in any case it would be silly to—"

She sucked in her breath. White-hot pain closed her throat.

"Sorry," Charles said. "Almost done." He put the brandy glass into her free hand.

She took another long sip. "In any case, it would be silly to stab someone when all you wanted to do was steal her purse."

"Very silly." He pressed a clean pad of linen against her side. "Hold that, will you? No, there's no doubt the attack was deliberate. Someone doesn't want us to find the ring."

She set the brandy glass on the arm of the chair and held the makeshift bandage in place with her left hand. "Iago Lorano hasn't been to see Mr. Trevennen. You'd think he would have if he knew Helen Trevennen had an uncle in the Marshalsea."

Charles unwound a long strip of linen and wrapped it round her chest to hold the bandage in place. "Suppose Lorano paid someone at the Drury Lane to send word to him if anyone appeared inquiring about Miss Trevennen."

Mélanie forced her mind to focus. Her head had a tiresome tendency to throb. "And this same person overheard you direct Randall to the Marshalsea? He sent word to Lorano, Lorano rushed to the Marshalsea, lingered outside Trevennen's rooms, and then knifed me. Or else hired someone else to do it while we were with Trevennen." She calculated the time. "It's possible. Just."

Charles tied the linen into a smooth knot. "He might see it as a way to delay us while he picks up the trail of the ring himself."

"In which case he'll be talking to Trevennen right now." She gripped the threadbare arms of the chair. "Charles!"

"Sit down, Mel." He drew the ruined remnants of the chemise about her with gentle fingers. "I have a lad keeping watch on Trevennen's rooms. He'll let us know if Lorano appears. Though if Lorano's got a grain of sense—which is debatable—he'll wait until we're out of the prison. Let's get your dress back on before you catch a chill."

She struggled back into the dress, or rather he pulled it back over her shoulders. "How hard is it to breathe?" he asked as he did up the hooks.

She started to draw a deep breath to prove she could do so, then thought better of it. "Not very."

"Surely you can lie more adroitly than that. You may have cracked a rib, I couldn't tell for sure. The wound's long, but not too deep, and it didn't hit anything vital."

A knock sounded at the door. Charles went to open it. A woman's voice, cheerful and with a faint Yorkshire accent, said, "I made you some tea and sandwiches, Mr. Fraser. Is your poor lady recovered? Are you sure we shouldn't send for a doctor?"

"I don't think that will be necessary, thank you. But the refreshment is much appreciated."

"Never you mind that, Mr. Fraser. We don't get much company, not since my poor husband lost everything on the Exchange after Waterloo. Even the children don't come above once a quarter. It's a treat to have someone to fuss over."

Charles came back into the room, carrying a second tray,

this one bearing a chipped cream lustre tea service and a plate of sandwiches. Mélanie started to protest, but the part of her mind that had learned to survive at all costs reasserted itself. Neither of them had had anything to eat since the lobster patties at the Esterhazys' sometime before three in the morning. It was now the middle of the afternoon and God knew when they would have a chance to eat again. They needed sustenance if they were to keep going, and for Colin's sake they had to keep going. She pulled off her gloves, accepted the cup of tea Charles held out to her, and bit into a salty fish paste sandwich.

Charles walked to the fireplace, teacup in one hand, sandwich in the other. "There's another possibility," he said, as though there'd been no pause in the conversation. He set his teacup on the mantel and looked at her. "Your friend O'Roarke may have decided it's safer to eliminate us than to risk the chance that we'll tell Carevalo he was once a French agent."

She straightened up, so suddenly that the tea spattered into the saucer and pain slashed through her side. "No."

"Damn it, Mel." Charles slammed his hand down on the mantel, sending a bit of cracked plaster into the grate. "Just because you made the beast with two backs with the man doesn't mean you know him, any more than I know you."

She forced a mouthful of the strong, bitter tea down her throat. "Sleeping with him is the least of it, Charles. And don't assume you don't know me just because you weren't aware of all my activities."

He picked up his cup with whitened fingers, but didn't drink. "I'm not assuming. I'm stating a fact. The woman I thought I knew, the woman I married, the woman I—loved—wouldn't have done the things you've told me you've done. O'Roarke may not be the person you think he is, either."

She cupped her hands round the warmth of the teacup. "Raoul's capable of a lot. I expect he'd be capable of killing me, if the stakes were high enough. He might even be capable of sacrificing Colin. But not simply to protect himself from Carevalo."

"No?" Charles's eyes were chips of gray ice. "If Carevalo

learned the truth about O'Roarke, he'd probably kill him. He could certainly ruin him in Spain, with the royalists and the liberals alike."

"But Raoul would never act out of fear of a man like Carevalo. He's much too proud. He'd be sure he could outwit him. Besides, I told you he has his own code. If he did sacrifice me or Colin—or anyone else—it wouldn't be simply to save his own skin. He'd never—"

"For God's sake, Mélanie. Have you forgotten how to think?"

Given the value Charles placed on intellect, it was just about the most scathing thing he might have said to her. "It's not a question of thinking, darling, it's—"

"Stop it, Mel. Stop sounding so damned all-knowing." He stalked across the room, then whirled to face her. She could see the urge to destroy something in his eyes. "You may have run rings round me for seven years, but you don't understand what the hell's happening now any more than I do. It's criminal folly to pretend otherwise. If you'd been thinking about Colin from the first—"

"I wouldn't have married you. I'd have turned my back on anything that smacked of espionage and devoted myself to my child." She flung the words at him. "I'm no bloody Madonna, Charles."

"No, by God you aren't." He stared down at her, his face white with anger. "You lied to me from the moment we met, you used your son to get me to marry you, you betrayed our friends. You played me like a damned pianoforte—with, I'll grant you, every bit as much skill as you show at the keys. If you owe me nothing else now, you owe me honesty. If you'd been honest with me sooner—"

"Then Colin might not have been taken?" She gave herself the sharpest cut before he could do so.

"If I'd known the French—if I'd known your people never got the ring, I'd have taken Carevalo's threats more seriously."

"If you'd told me Carevalo was demanding the ring—"

"Yes? What then?" His voice battered the stone walls. "You'd have told me the truth about your past?"

"How can I know—" Shame washed over her in a cold deluge. "No, probably not. I was too afraid of losing you."

"I hadn't realized you valued me so highly. How can you lose what you only had under false pretenses?"

She set her cup down with a clatter. "This isn't about what's between you and me, Charles. I know you must be fearfully jealous of Raoul—"

"*Jealous?* You give yourself too much credit, madam. I can't feel anything for you anymore. Why should I care what you feel for another man?"

"Whatever I felt for Raoul—"

"Don't." The word was like a hand slammed across her mouth. "I don't want to know. When this is over the two of you can run off to Spain or Ireland or South America and plot revolutions to your hearts' content. But meanwhile, don't think I'm going to stand by if he's trying to kill us."

"Charles, if Raoul was behind the attack—"

"You'd deny it even as he stuck the knife in your ribs. The man's obviously bewitched you."

"Damn you, Charles, don't you dare shrug off what I did as romantic infatuation." She gripped the arms of her chair, heedless of the pain in her side. "Call me whatever names you like, but at least credit me with the wit to make decisions for myself. Do you think I'd have run the risks I've run and blackened my soul simply for the love of a man?"

"Hardly. I'd be shocked you know the meaning of the word."

"Five minutes ago you said you didn't know me at all."

"I know love doesn't act the way you've acted."

"Charles, you can't—"

"Can't *what*? You're not in any position to dictate to me, madam."

"If you can't be rational—"

"Who the hell are you to talk? If you'd thought anything through, if you'd had a scrap of sheer common sense, decency and honor aside—"

"Yes?" she stared at him, willing him to give her the coup de grâce.

"Damn it, Mélanie—" He caught himself up short, breathing hard, like a winded boxer. "Christ, listen to us. I thought I'd had my fill of parents who put their own problems before their children."

The anger drained from her body, leaving her sick with guilt and disgust. "You're right. If you'd known the truth about the ring, you'd have taken Carevalo's threats seriously and Colin wouldn't have been taken."

He fixed his gaze on a faded print of a waterfall on the wall opposite. "I should have taken Carevalo more seriously, regardless. That's my sin."

That last word hit her like a blow. "If it wasn't for me—"

"No sense repining on the past. Not now." He strode across the room again, stirring a cloud of dust from the threadbare red carpet. "In a sense it doesn't matter who was behind the attack. It doesn't change our objective. We have to find the ring, only now we have the added complication that we have to manage not to get killed while doing so."

She picked up her sandwich and stared at the thin, crustless triangle. What were they feeding Colin? Were they feeding him at all? She forced down a wave of nausea. "At least we should be able to find Helen's sister at the Gilded Lily."

"And we can only hope she's not as estranged from Helen as their uncle thinks." Charles prowled about the room, picked up another sandwich, set it down untasted. "Before we go to the Gilded Lily, we should stop by Bow Street and see Roth."

"And tell him about the attack?"

"It's possible he can learn something about Iago Lorano. And it won't hurt to have more people hunting for Helen Trevennen. He can have someone help Addison and Blanca with the inquiries among the jewelers." He picked up a spool of thread from the tray with the bandages. "Give me your pelisse. I'll mend the rent. If you keep it fastened, your gown will be all right." He held the needle up to the meager light from the window and threaded it.

She moved, with care, to the edge of the chair and eased the pelisse out from under her. "Charles. You realize the fact that no one's heard from Helen Trevennen in seven years could mean she's dead?"

"It could." He took the pelisse from her, dropped down in a ladderback chair beside the window, and began to stitch up the rent made by the knife. "But she had the ring, and the quickest way to find it is to find out what happened to her." He held out the pelisse. "There. It might not pass muster with Blanca, but it'll do from a distance. Can you walk?"

"It's my side that's hurt, Charles. My legs are fine." She stood up quickly to convince him and regretted the motion at once. But as long as she didn't move her right arm too much, the pain was tolerable.

Charles slipped the pelisse over her arms and did up the frogged clasps that ran down the front. "Do you want more brandy?" he asked. "Or some laudanum?"

"Stop fussing, darling. Just put my bonnet back on."

He looked at her for a moment, then set the bonnet on her head and tied the ribbons. "Under the circumstances," he said, "don't you think it's a bit ridiculous to go on calling me darling?"

"I can't help it," she said, an unexpected lump in her throat. "It's the way I think of you."

Charles went to open the door without making any reply.

Chapter 14

The lad Charles had employed to watch Trevennen's rooms reported that no one had approached Trevennen since Mélanie was attacked. Charles pressed some coins into the boy's hand and asked him to take a message to their coachman. Randall was to remain by the Marshalsea for another quarter-hour and then return to Berkeley Square.

Mélanie could feel Charles's appraising gaze on her as they made their way along the rain-splashed maze of cobblestone alleys. Finally, as they neared the prison gates, she answered his unvoiced concerns. "Darling, don't even think about not taking steps to throw off pursuit. I won't collapse on you, I promise. Thank goodness you had the sense to beg an umbrella along with the brandy and bandages."

Charles cast a brief glance at the sky, which if anything had grown even darker. Then he nodded and tilted the umbrella farther over her head.

They encountered a large family party by the gates. A stoop-shouldered man who kept checking his watch as though he was late for an appointment; a lady in a well-worn pelisse with the cuffs turned; a teenage girl whose legs were several inches too long for her bombazine skirt; and two boys who kept asking their parents why Grandpapa couldn't come home with them.

She and Charles slipped out of the prison in the family's wake. Outside they rounded two street corners, flagged down a hackney, then at the last minute waved it on, rounded another corner and did the same, then finally hailed a third hackney (no easy task in the rain), climbed in, and directed the driver to Bow Street.

Mélanie fell back against the squabs. The umbrella had not kept out all the rain and she was more chilled than she cared to admit to her husband.

Charles looked at her for a moment, but he merely said, "There's no reason to hold anything back from Roth. Except the fact that you and O'Roarke were French agents. Not to mention lovers."

"Good God, no. Being arrested would be nearly as debilitating as being killed." For a moment, the future crowded in on her, a myriad of unpleasant possibilities that drove the air from her lungs. Charles could turn her in to Bow Street as a French spy. One part of her mind said that he never would, but another shouted back, *How can you be sure?* How could she really know how far hurt and anger and an outraged sense of honor might drive him? He might not know himself.

Even if he didn't expose her as a spy, he had every right to want his freedom. She owed him that at the very least.

Her breath stuck in her throat, as she forced herself to confront what lay before her. Separation. Annulment. Divorce. A friend of theirs who had been sued for criminal conversation by her husband had lost all access to her children. The woman's drawn face flickered before Mélanie's gaze, a ghost of what was to come.

She should be prepared for this. The threat of exposure had

always been there, a constant tension beneath the polished surface of her life. Sometimes she had been able to bury the fear so deeply she was scarcely aware of it herself. But a trick of memory, a turn of phrase, a look into Charles's trusting eyes would bring it welling to the surface. Shame and guilt and sheer, bloody terror would wash over her in a cold sweat. And then she would force them all back to a place deep inside, because that was the only way she could continue with her life.

Now there could be no hiding from Charles or from herself. She had lived on borrowed time for seven years, and she would have to take the consequences.

They had crossed back over the bridge, but traffic had slowed to a maddening crawl. She rubbed at the condensation on the glass and peered out the window. A curricle had locked wheels with a brewer's dray on the rain-soaked cobblestones. The patter of rain and the curses of other drivers echoed through the windows.

"Do you have a sister?" Charles said.

The question was as unexpected as a knife cut. She turned her head to look at him. "I had a sister. A younger sister."

"She died." It wasn't a question.

"Yes." It would have been better if she could have kept looking at him as she spoke, but instead she stared down at her hands. The remembered stench of blood invaded the moldering air of the hackney. "Eleven years ago."

"When your father died." The angry edge that had been in his voice when he asked his first questions about her life was gone. Something in his quiet tone was close to Charles her husband and she shied away from it. There were some things she hadn't spoken about to anyone, not even Raoul.

"Yes," she said again. Her hands curled into knots.

Their hackney lurched forward, veering round the accident. Charles looked at her for a moment across the width of the carriage. "It can't be easy to lose a sibling," he said. "I find it painful enough that Edgar and I aren't the friends we once were. Gisèle's so much younger that we were never companions in the

same way, but I always felt it was my job to protect her. If anything had happened to her, I think I'd have felt responsible, no
matter where the blame lay."

How, when every feeling he had ever had for her must have
turned to hate, could he still read her with such devastating
accuracy? Her own sister's face swam before Mélanie's eyes.
Promises made, promises broken. Surely that had not been her
first betrayal, but it was the first she remembered. "One can't
dwell on one's failures," she said. "Or we'd all go mad."

"Did O'Roarke tell you that?" His voice turned harsh.

"No, you did. After those documents got lost that you were
supposed to collect from Count Messelrode."

She watched understanding dawn in his eyes. She wasn't
sure why she had said it, save that his anger was easier to bear
than the excruciating hint of softness that had crept into his
expression.

"Of course," he said. "There seems to be no end to my
idiocy. To think it never occurred to me that those papers disappeared because my wife had taken them."

"It was damnably difficult." She made her voice brittle,
slashing at him, slashing at herself, reminding them both of
everything that had been destroyed between them. It was a form
of self-mutilation. Better to sink into the gutter of hatred than to
delude herself into thinking anything was left of what he'd once
felt for her. "You never were an easy man to deceive, Charles.
Raoul warned me you were dangerous when he sent me after the
ring. He said you notice details most people would ignore."

"Probably because I overlooked the most important detail of
all where you were concerned. Oh, Christ." His hands clenched.
He stared at her with eyes that were dark and hate-filled. "Do
you have any idea how many people went to their deaths because
of your duplicity and my criminal stupidity?"

"It was war, Charles." She kept her gaze steady, because this
was a demon she was used to battling. "People die. Good people,
innocent people. Different people may have died because of
things you told me, but people would have died anyway."

He was silent for a moment. When he spoke his voice was low and raw. "But they wouldn't have been on my conscience."

She shook her head. "I know you think the world is your responsibility, Charles. But you of all people should know that if they're on anyone's conscience, they're on mine."

"But you could have done nothing without my complicity. It seems we continue to be partners. You betrayed me, but in trusting you I betrayed my friends, my country, and any shred of honor I possessed."

"Oh, Charles." Tenderness for him welled up in her chest. "Underneath the radical reformer, you're still a British gentleman to the core."

"It isn't only gentlemen who take their word of honor seriously."

"No, but you've been bred from the cradle to place it above all else."

He turned his gaze to the hackney window. "Perhaps I'm being a bloody, idealistic fool. But in this shifting sands of a world we live in, I'd like to believe my word at least counts for something. Otherwise I don't see that I have much integrity left."

She studied the bleak outline of his profile. "Yes, but your word to whom, darling? The line between honor and dishonor is often a matter of definition. After all—" She bit back the words.

He swung his gaze toward her. "What?"

She hesitated a moment. "*You* were a spy, Charles."

He gave a rough, incredulous laugh. "Oh, for God's sake, Mel. Don't compare us. I'm far out of your league."

"I know you don't like to use the word. Partly out of modesty; partly, I think, because you don't like the associations of what it means to be spy. But you can't deny that your errands for the ambassador were a lot more than fetching and carrying."

"Fetching and carrying can be damnably difficult. But all I did was—"

"Steal documents. Slip behind enemy lines. Pose as a French soldier or a Portuguese *conde* or a Spanish priest or anything else that would help in gaining information. What the devil do you think a spy does?"

"You know the answer to that better than I do."

"Call it what you will, Charles, you couldn't do the things you did in the war without being an expert at—"

"Lying?"

"I was going to say deception. But what is deception but a form of lying?"

"You give me too much credit, madam." Charles's voice cut so sharply she could feel it scrape against her skin. "Whatever my minor accomplishments, I can't even begin to understand the lies you've told."

She looked into his eyes, as cold now as January ice. With the sharp finality of a tolling bell, she realized how truly wide the chasm was between them. She would have said she'd known there was no hope for them from the moment she told him the truth. Yet in some small, unacknowledged corner of her mind, she had thought that if Charles could see past his anger, maybe, just maybe they somehow could find a way to go on together.

She had reckoned without the inbred training of a lifetime. However much Charles might reject the values of his world, his gentleman's code of honor would make it impossible for him ever to forgive her for forcing him to break his word and betray his comrades. He was a remarkable man in many ways, but she doubted he'd ever be able to see beyond the limits of the code he'd been raised on.

She said nothing for the rest of the drive to Bow Street and neither did Charles. "Stay in the carriage," he told her in an impersonal voice when the hackney pulled up in front of the Public Office. "I'll see if Roth's here."

A few moments later he returned to report that Roth was next door in the Brown Bear Tavern. He took her left arm in a grip that was a little firmer than necessary and guided her into the narrow brick building. Despite the rainy gloom outside, the smoky light in the low-ceilinged room took a moment to get used to. The smell of gin and tobacco made her head spin.

The low murmur of conversation stopped at their entrance. Ladies in fashionable bonnets and pelisses—even if those garments were decidedly the worse for wear—would be a rare sight at the Brown Bear.

The sound of a chair being scraped back came from the far corner of the room. Roth had been sitting at a table with a young man in the red and blue of the Bow Street Patrol and an older man with a raffish spotted handkerchief round his throat and a nose that looked as if it had been broken more than once. Roth got to his feet, said something to his companions, and came toward Charles and Mélanie. "I'm glad you're here," he said. "I was beginning to wonder."

Without further speech, he led them upstairs to a small room furnished with a round table, two chairs with peeling varnish, and a thin cot covered with a blue blanket. "Not very commodious, but at least it's private. The Brown Bear's popular with thieves, but it's also very friendly to thief-takers. We use this room to interview suspects and occasionally to keep them overnight. Can I get you anything? Tea? Something stronger?"

They shook their heads. Roth waved them to the chairs and perched on the edge of the cot. "You learned something from Carevalo? I thought— Are you all right, Mrs. Fraser?"

"Yes." Mélanie folded her hands in her lap, careful not to jar her side. "Or rather, no, but that's part of the story."

"We were right about Carevalo," Charles said. He recounted the day's events thus far, neatly excising all mention of her revelations and their second encounter with Raoul.

Roth's eyes widened slightly, but he refrained from questions or even exclamations of surprise. He scribbled in his notebook as Charles talked, chewed on his pencil, scowled. When it came to the attack at the Marshalsea, his head jerked up and he stared at Mélanie. "Good God."

"It's not as bad as my husband makes it sound, Mr. Roth," Mélanie said, though in truth Charles had taken care not to sensationalize the incident. "But it does indicate someone is trying to stop us from finding the ring or Helen Trevennen."

Roth leaned forward and tapped his pencil against his notebook. "This Iago Lorano—you have no idea who he is?"

"I'm quite sure Lorano isn't his real name," Charles said. "It seems likeliest he works for a royalist faction who also want the ring. He could even be in the employ of the Spanish embassy."

"You've thought about talking to the embassy? You must have friends there."

"Acquaintances. I've made too many speeches in support of the liberals in Spain to make me popular with the royalists. Talking to the embassy would be a waste of time we don't have. Assuming I could make them believe the story, I'm not sure they'd think my son's safety was worth the sacrifice of giving the ring to Carevalo. And if they aren't already on the trail of the ring, I don't want to rouse their interest in it."

"Fair enough." Roth flipped to another page of his notebook. "We've circulated a description of the man Polly saw. We have four leads that sound likely. Harry Rogers, a cutpurse who works round the docks; Jack Evans, a former prizefighter turned thief; Bill Trelawny, a highwayman last heard of working with a gang on Hounslow Heath; and Stephen Watkins, a cardsharp who claims he'll take on any job if the money is right. I have patrols questioning their associates."

Mélanie's fingers clenched. "Carevalo may have ordered them to kill Colin if they think they'll be taken."

"We won't stage a foolhardy rescue attempt. Though if they're half as good as they seem to be they'll have gone to earth where not even their friends can find them. Men can disappear for years in the rookeries of Seven Dials and St. Giles." He leaned back, resting his hands on the cot. "Can you find the ring?"

"We don't have any choice," Charles said.

Roth nodded. "I'll make inquiries about Iago Lorano, see if we can at least find out who he is. I'll have a man circulate questions among fences we know to see if we can find news of the ring. You might have Mr. Addison and Miss Mendoza report to me when they finish their inquiries among the jewelers."

"I've already instructed them to do so," Charles said. "Between them, Addison and Blanca can cover a lot of territory in short order."

"What about Carevalo? Any idea where he might be hiding?"

"None, but O'Roarke is making inquiries. He's the likeliest to know Carevalo's associates."

"I'll have one of the patrols make inquiries among the Spanish expatriates as well." Roth scribbled on a page from his notebook and tore it out. "My direction. Don't hesitate to send word to me, at any time of the day or night. If not here, at my house, number Forty-two, Wardour Street. My sister lives with me. She'll know where to find me if the people here don't."

Charles tucked the paper inside his coat. "Thank you."

Roth chewed on the tip of his pencil. "Thus far the chief magistrate knows only the sketchiest details of this case. Should you wish it, of course, you could have the Home Secretary himself take an interest in the matter. I take it you don't wish it?"

"No. We want our son back. The last thing we want is people questioning the political and diplomatic implications of putting the ring in Carevalo's hands."

"So I thought. The chief magistrate is a busy man. There's no need for me to burden him with the details of Carevalo's involvement."

Mélanie forced her fingers to unclench. "Thank you."

"It's the least I can do, Mrs. Fraser. I wish there was more." He started to get up from the cot, then sat back down. "One more thing." He flipped through his notebook again and studied what he'd written. It seemed to Mélanie that he was making rather too much of a show of it. "This morning you were convinced the French had ended up with the ring seven years ago, despite Carevalo's accusations. What changed your mind?"

Charles leaned back in his chair, his pose deliberately casual. "With Carevalo insisting, we had to consider other possibilities. We didn't know for a certainty until Violet Goddard told us she'd seen the ring."

Roth leaned forward, elbows on his knees, notebook dangling from his fingers. "So when you first read Carevalo's demand, you still thought there was a good chance the French had the ring. But instead of pursuing that scenario, you went to see Sergeant Baxter and then to the Drury Lane. You made a lucky choice. In your place, I'd probably have wasted hours at the French embassy, trying to get word of the soldiers who escaped the ambush seven years ago."

"We knew it would take time to get any information at the embassy," Charles said. "We hoped we could get answers from Baxter and the Drury Lane company more quickly."

"Yes. Of course, if the French had been involved, it would have been important to start the inquiries at the embassy as soon as possible. But fortunately that wasn't the case."

"No," Charles said.

Roth closed his notebook. Mélanie could see him toting up the incongruous details—the inconsistencies in their actions, the time gaps in Charles's story, the changes in their body language since he'd seen them this morning. His mind was working very much as her own would in a similar situation. Jeremy Roth could prove to be a more powerful ally than she had realized.

And a very dangerous opponent.

Charles glanced up and down Bow Street as they emerged from the Brown Bear. It was not yet three o'clock, but with the soot-stained buildings leaning over the street, the rain clouds massed overhead, and the steady downpour obscuring vision, it felt like twilight. A crossing sweeper was clearing away the mud and horse manure at the intersection with Russell Street, shoulders hunched against the rain. Greatcoated men with umbrellas hurried toward the shelter of taverns or coffeehouses. Charles hadn't asked the hackney to wait for them, on the chance that they were being followed. No new hackney was immediately within view. He looked at Mélanie. "We'd better walk toward Covent Garden. How's the wound?"

"I'm fine."

He studied her face beneath the brim of her bonnet as they walked along the muddy pavement. She was paler than usual and the tension in the set of her mouth betrayed just how hard she was working to control the pain of the wound. But that she could control it, he had no doubt. He shook his head at his own certainty. The very fabric of her life was alien to him, yet he could still read the clues in her face as though it were his own.

In the space of a few hours, he had learned that everything about their marriage was a lie. And then an unknown assailant had stuck a knife in her ribs. If the blade had struck a few inches higher, he might well be a widower.

The possibility, not quite articulated before, slammed home in his mind. To all intents and purposes he had lost her when she told him the truth of what she had been and done and why she had married him. Yet the prospect of losing her to death brought a prickle of sweat to his skin and stripped his throat raw. He recalled the words a friend of his, a French journalist, had used in describing the Reign of Terror. *We'd nourished ourselves on the dream for so long, you see, that we couldn't let go of it. Even when it had turned into a nightmare.*

The rain had whipped up, a deluge that fell in sheets off the umbrella and blew icy drafts in their faces. Charles caught sight of a hackney up ahead and waved, but the driver took off without seeing him.

"Charles." Mélanie's fingers tightened on his arm. "We're being followed. No, don't look round. It's better he doesn't know we've spotted him."

"Are you sure?"

"I caught his reflection in the window glass a moment ago. A man in a dark greatcoat with a hat pulled low over his face."

He took a few steps in silence, weighing possibilities. "Are you up to a diversion?"

"Dearest, I'm up to whatever needs doing."

"Stay in this shop"—he steered her into the nearest doorway, a tobacconist's—"as though you're waiting while I find a hackney. If he takes the bait and walks past, you can follow him.

I'll round the corner and see if I can lead him into a court or alley."

"Don't take unnecessary chances. We don't know if he can tell us anything."

He turned up the collar of his greatcoat. "I'm not a complete fool."

"You keep the umbrella."

"Mel—"

"Don't be pigheaded, Charles. It will look odd otherwise. You'd keep the umbrella if I was waiting inside."

He nodded, then hesitated a moment. "If it turns nasty, stay out of the fray. We can't afford to have you bleeding all over the street."

She put the umbrella into his hand. "I'm the last person in the world you ought to be worrying about just now, darling."

He stepped out of the doorway, stopped as though scanning the street for a hackney, and walked on. The only other pedestrians visible were a cherry-seller pushing his barrow toward the shelter of an overhang and a rain-soaked errand boy laden down with parcels. Charles kept one eye on the window glass. He caught a flash of movement, but he could not make out anything more clearly.

He rounded the corner into Russell Street. Rainwater sluiced off the umbrella. Shop signs flapped overhead—the golden balls of a pawnshop, the striped pole of a barber, the gilded key of a locksmith. He quickened his pace and ducked beneath a low stone archway into a narrow court. Once there, he snapped the umbrella shut and flattened himself against the rotting wood of the nearest doorway.

Thirty seconds later a man in a dark greatcoat and a low-crowned hat appeared in the mouth of the court. The faint light from the street behind him outlined his form but left his face in shadow. He paused and scanned the court. *Come on, you bastard,* Charles thought.

Seconds ticked by. The man walked forward.

Charles lunged out of his hiding place and hurled himself on the shadowy figure. The force of the assault knocked them both to the slimy cobblestones. They landed in a tangle of damp wool and flailing boots. Charles sat up, gripping the man's throat with both hands, and found himself staring into the blue eyes of his brother.

Chapter 15

Charles slackened his hold and sat back on his heels amid the litter of rotting apple cores, moldy orange peels, and discarded sausage wrappers. He stared through the curtain of rain at the familiar face. The blue eyes, the guinea-bright hair, the features that were so like his own, save that Edgar was a handsome devil, with the gift of careless, unthinking laughter.

"What the hell are you up to?" Charles said.

"I might ask you the same." Edgar pushed himself to a sitting position, then let out a yelp of pain. "Christ, Charles, I think you've broken my arm."

"You're lucky I didn't kill you, you damn fool."

Footsteps pattered against the sodden cobblestones. "Charles— Edgar!" Mélanie hesitated a moment, then ran forward and bent over them. "Are you all right?" she said, addressing both brothers impartially.

Edgar brushed the decaying debris off his greatcoat. "No

thanks to my brother. What's he got you in the middle of, Mélanie?"

"We can't talk in the rain." Charles pushed himself to his feet and held out his hand to pull his brother up. "I saw a coffee-house in Russell Street."

Edgar stared at his brother as though he'd taken leave of his senses. "We can't take Mélanie to a coffeehouse."

Mélanie unfurled the umbrella, which she'd retrieved from the doorway. "It's all right, Edgar, I've seen a lot worse today."

Charles picked up his beaver hat and Edgar's own, both of which had fallen to the ground in the struggle, shook the rain off them, and returned Edgar's to him. Edgar frowned as he settled the curly-brimmed hat on his head, but in seven years he had learned better than to argue with Mélanie. They walked back to Russell Street, a motley trio, soaking wet and far from clean.

Steam and tobacco smoke clouded the air in the coffeehouse. The smell of coffee mingled with the stench of damp wool from the garments drying on a bench by the fire. The patrons were a diverse lot, as they would be anywhere near Covent Garden. Actors studying scripts; journalists scribbling in notebooks; merchants and lawyers, with charts and ledgers spread on the tables before them; a couple of young sprigs who looked as if they'd been sent down to rusticate from Oxford or Cambridge; and mixed in among the crowd, no doubt, a handful of men who might find themselves facing the magistrates in the Bow Street Public Office, should ever they have the bad luck to get caught.

There were no other women present. Heads turned in Mélanie's direction. One of the young sprigs started to say something, but his companion grabbed his arm. The proprietor of the coffeehouse blinked once in surprise, then took Charles's and Edgar's greatcoats and Mélanie's pelisse and showed the three of them to a table with high-backed benches, which afforded a small measure of privacy. At least they hadn't been followed into the coffeehouse, Charles was sure of that much. He glanced briefly at the torn side of Mélanie's gown. No sign the bandage had bled through.

Charles surveyed his brother across the table. He saw Edgar nearly every week, at their club, at balls and receptions, at dinners carefully orchestrated by Mélanie and by Edgar's wife, Lydia. But it was a long time since Charles had talked to his brother about anything this serious. It was a long time since they had talked at all, in any but the most superficial sense. "You first." Charles fixed his younger brother with a firm stare. "Why, Edgar?"

"Orders." Edgar leaned against the high back of the bench. "You got some people in the government very nervous, brother. Sneaking off to meet with Spanish rebels in the early hours of the morning is hardly conventional behavior, even for you."

Damnation. It was one possibility Charles hadn't considered. "You were sent to trail us?"

Edgar nodded. "Lord Castlereagh summoned me to the Foreign Office this morning. He gave me one of those damned cold looks of his—no offense, Charles, but at times he reminds me of you—and asked me if I knew what the devil my brother and his wife were doing conferring with Raoul O'Roarke before dawn."

"How did he know—" Charles scraped his hand through his damp hair. "The Foreign Office have spies watching Carevalo and O'Roarke?"

"Not spies exactly. But I think they engaged one of the clerks at Mivart's to send them word of any suspicious behavior by Carevalo. Surely that doesn't surprise you. It's common knowledge that Carevalo's trying to muster support for a rebellion against a government that our government consider an ally."

"That our government are going to great lengths to prop up." Charles dropped his hands to the rough wood of the table. "I don't suppose anyone thought to follow Carevalo when he left Mivart's?"

"No. The clerk who'd been hired to keep an eye on him couldn't leave his post. No one expected Carevalo to leave the hotel. Isn't he coming back?"

"I seriously doubt it. Go on. What exactly had the Foreign

Secretary heard about Carevalo and O'Roarke and Mélanie and me?"

"That O'Roarke arrived at Mivart's late last night, and Carevalo left unexpectedly in the early hours of the morning. That you and Mélanie then arrived at an hour when no self-respecting members of the polite world would be out of bed and spent some time closeted with O'Roarke. I said it was news to me, I didn't even know O'Roarke was in England and I thought you'd spent last night at the Esterhazys'. Castlereagh replied that you had, that he'd been at the Esterhazys' himself, as had Carevalo, who spent a lot of time talking to Mélanie."

Mélanie opened her mouth as though to interject something, then appeared to think better of it.

"Why—" Charles broke off as a waiter approached their table bearing three mugs of steaming coffee liberally laced with brandy. He curled his fingers round the warmth of the mug. He hadn't realized how numb they were. "Why was Castlereagh so interested in what Mélanie and I might have been discussing with Carevalo and O'Roarke?"

"Oh, admit it, Charles." Edgar took a long swallow from his mug and clanked it down on the table. "Your friends at Holland House have been doing their damnedest to put the Spanish liberals in power for years. When a prominent Opposition politician pays a clandestine visit to a Spanish rebel, it's bound to raise interest. You may disagree with Castlereagh, but it's understandable that he'd be miffed at the Opposition carrying on a separate foreign policy behind his back."

"So Castlereagh set you to spy on us?"

Edgar flushed in the murky light of the oil lamps that hung from the coffeehouse ceiling. "He didn't put it quite so baldly. He said I should find out what the hell—devil you were up to. He was said I was to consider myself on leave and he'd make it right with my superiors. I knew damn well that if there was any truth in Castlereagh's suspicions and I asked you straight out, you'd refuse to tell me or fob me off with some story—"

"Thank you."

"It's true. If you thought you were doing something good for Spain, you'd hardly spill it all to Castlereagh just because I asked you." Edgar took another deep swallow from his mug. "Castlereagh'd had a report that you were seen going into the Drury Lane. I must have got to the theater just after you left. I went in and made inquiries." He shook his head. "Who the devil is Helen Trevennen and what does she have to do with O'Roarke and Carevalo?"

"Later." Charles pushed his mug aside. "If you were making inquiries in the theater, you couldn't have followed us when we left the Drury Lane."

"No, but the porter had heard you direct Randall to the Marshalsea. Why—no, I'll finish my story first. When I got to the Marshalsea, I saw your carriage waiting in front, so I waited, too. It was raining by then—of all the foul-smelling places to have to stand about. The things we do for our country."

The coffeehouse door banged open and shut to admit two young men with books over their heads in place of umbrellas. A blast of chill wind tore through the heavy air. "Finally you came out of the prison and got into a hackney," Edgar continued, "though I must say it was dashed hard to keep up with you. Did you know you were being followed?"

"We thought we might be." Charles glanced at Mélanie. "So much for our subterfuge."

Edgar wiped a trickle of liquid from the black enamel of his mug. "Your subterfuge very nearly worked. I almost went off after the first hackney, and if it hadn't taken you so long to get the third one, I would have lost you for sure. I say, Mélanie, are you all right? You were walking rather oddly."

"I daresay you would be too if you'd been wearing my half-boots." Mélanie had been sitting very still beside Charles, her untouched mug clutched between both hands. "You followed the hackney to Bow Street?"

"Yes. I seem to have spent most of the day waiting on rainy

street corners." Edgar sat back, arms folded across his chest. "So much for my story. Any chance you'll tell me the truth, brother mine?"

"As a matter of fact there is," Charles said.

At the table behind them, a lawyer and his clerk were droning on about a contract. Charles took a sip of the coffee and brandy, mostly to give himself a moment to collect his thoughts, although the fiery jolt did not come amiss. Only the truth would ensure that Edgar stopped prying into their visit to O'Roarke. Though they were not as close as they had been as boys, he knew he could trust his brother. With all but the truth about Mélanie. It wouldn't be fair to ask Edgar to keep that secret.

He set down the mug and recounted the story of Colin's disappearance in brief, factual terms. He omitted only Mélanie's revelations about her past as a spy and her links to Raoul O'Roarke.

Edgar's expressive face went pale with shock, then dark with rage. "By God. Christ, Charles, I'm sorry." He looked into his mug for a moment. Then he pushed his bench back, scraping it against the broken floorboards. "What are we doing sitting here? There's no time to be lost."

"Sit down, Edgar." Charles gripped his brother's wrist and forced him back into his seat before they had half the coffee-house staring at them. "Of course there's no time to be lost. Which is why we can't afford to go blundering about without knowing what we're doing."

"I'm sorry." Edgar raked his fingers through his hair. "I'd give my right arm— You know that, don't you? Why didn't you send word to me when it first happened?"

"We haven't stopped to breathe, let alone tell anyone. Besides, your links to the government would have put you in an awkward position. I don't think Castlereagh and others would be too sanguine at the prospect of putting the ring into Carevalo's hands."

Edgar's eyes widened. "Charles, do you seriously think anyone in the government would put political considerations before a child's safety?"

Charles returned his brother's gaze. "Without a doubt."

Edgar stared at him for a moment. "Do you think *I* would?"

Charles studied his brother. However strained their own relationship had become in the years since their mother's death, there was no doubting Edgar's love for his nephew and niece. "No. Of course not. But there was no need to put you in the middle of the dilemma."

"No *need*." Edgar dragged his gaze away from Charles and took a long swallow from his mug. "Oh, all right, I won't argue with you. But I'm in the middle of it now. I'll do whatever I can, that goes without saying. Tell me how I can help."

"Thank you," Charles said. "But I think it would be best if you—"

"For God's sake, Charles, I know you pride yourself on never needing anyone's assistance, but you can't afford a misstep here. I love Colin like he's my own. Unless Lydia's and my marriage changes in more ways than one, Colin's the closest to a son I'm ever likely to have." Edgar slammed both his hands down on the table. *"Let me help."*

The last three words were a plea. For a moment, Mélanie was gone and the Fraser brothers were locked in a silent confrontation across the scarred table. It was an odd sort of intimacy, an intimacy that they had not shared in years. In their childhood, each had been the central person in the other's world, allies against their father's coldness, their mother's bouts of giddiness and depression, their tutor's strictures. Their sister hadn't been born until Charles was almost eleven and Edgar nine. In the wilds of Perthshire, the Fraser brothers had had few companions but each other.

That had changed when they went to Harrow. Charles had still preferred the company of his books, but Edgar had quickly become the center of a circle of friends. Yet though their interests diverged, they had remained close. Until the December when Charles was nineteen and staying late at Oxford to finish an essay on David Hume, while Edgar went back to Perthshire by himself. The December Edgar saw their mother put a bullet through her brain a week before Christmas.

It was Edgar who had drawn away then, but now his eyes were pleading for the opposite. And he was right. They needed every scrap of help they could get. "Mélanie and I would be grateful for any assistance you can give us," Charles said.

Edgar's shoulders relaxed beneath the smooth blue fabric of his coat. "Thank you." He turned to Mélanie. "Shouldn't you see a doctor?"

"No."

"She wouldn't go, and there isn't time anyway." Charles took Mélanie's wrist between his fingers for a moment. "Still no fever, despite the drenching. You aren't chilled?"

She removed her wrist from his grasp. "Charles, you seem to be forgetting I've given birth to two children. This is a minor nuisance in comparison."

Her dry voice didn't convince Charles, but it seemed to reassure Edgar, which perhaps was what she'd intended. "What's the next step?" Edgar asked.

"A visit to Susan Trevennen," Charles said.

"I thought you said the sisters were estranged."

"But they were close once. If I disappeared from London, wouldn't you have a fair idea of where to look for me?"

Edgar's eyes narrowed. "Yes, I expect I would," he said, making no comment on the reference to estrangement. "And if she hasn't heard from Helen, either?" he asked after a moment.

Charles fished some coins from his pocket to pay their reckoning. "There's always Mrs. Jennings. But I don't want to waste time traveling to Surrey while we have possible leads in London." He tossed the coins onto the table. "You could be of help there, Edgar."

"You want me to go to Surrey to see her while you look for the sister? It's a bit late to leave tonight, but I'd be happy to do so if you think it would help."

Charles glanced at Mélanie. She shook her head. "Better to set off in the morning if you need to go at all," she said. "But you could go back to Berkeley Square and see if Addison and Blanca have discovered anything."

"Of course." Edgar rubbed his hand across his eyes. "God. It's like looking for a needle in a haystack. You realize that, don't you? What if it can't—"

He trailed off under the combined pressure of Charles's and Mélanie's gazes. "It can be done," Mélanie said, "because there's no alternative. One step at a time, Edgar. That's the only way we'll manage."

Edgar swallowed. "Yes. Yes, of course."

Charles got to his feet and held out his hand to Mélanie. "Wait for us in Berkeley Square, Edgar."

"Yes, all right." Edgar stared at him as though the full implications of his words had just sunk in. "Charles, you can't take Mélanie to the Gilded Lily."

"Dear Edgar," Mélanie said. "He's not taking me. I'm going with him."

Edgar tugged at his cravat. "Mélanie, I don't think you understand—"

"It's a brothel, Edgar. I understand very well. They'll just think Charles and I are there for an assignation. It's amazing the places women of fashion go."

Edgar stared at her as though he would be more shocked if he could take in the full import of what she was saying. "Suppose"—he coughed—"suppose you meet someone you know?"

Mélanie picked her gloves up from the bench and tugged them on. "Then I suspect they'll be more surprised than we are."

They threaded their way through the tables and the rain-spattered customers, collected their outer garments, and walked to the door. "Go to the right," Charles told his brother. "Take the second hackney that stops. Yes, I know it didn't manage to shake you off, but it may work with Iago Lorano or his hirelings."

Edgar shot Charles a look of concern as they parted. Charles ignored it. Edgar was extremely fond of Mélanie, but like most people, he was deceived by the polished, decorous veneer. Charles had thought he himself was one of the few people who understood her. While her vulnerability had roused his protective instincts, it was her sheer guts he'd fallen in love with. The irony, of course, was that he'd been more deceived by her than anyone.

He and Mélanie turned left outside the coffeehouse, rounded the corner back into Bow Street, and followed the same process of taking the second hackney.

"I'm glad you didn't refuse Edgar's help," Mélanie said when they were settled inside the hackney. "We can use it."

"Yes, Edgar can be quite handy at fighting dragons. As long as we make sure he attacks the right ones."

She shot him a glance. "He's more straightforward than you, but he's not a fool."

"I never said he was."

"And he loves Colin." She rested her head against the worn squabs. "I remember when I first met him. It was just after I came to Lisbon, before we were betrothed. Some sort of embassy party—he looked very dashing in his dress uniform. You'd retreated to the library in one of your black moods. I told Edgar I was worried about you. He said it was only to be expected, considering all the men you'd lost on the trip into the mountains. I said I didn't see why, you couldn't have known about the ambush, and it was a miracle you'd got the survivors home in one piece. Edgar told me that just because you preferred to have your nose in a book, I shouldn't make the mistake of thinking you didn't care about people. Then he said"—she turned her head against the squabs to look at him in the gathering darkness within the hackney—" 'My brother decided years ago that the world is his responsibility. Every so often it proves a bit much even for him. He takes these lapses very hard.' "

Charles stared at a patch of damp on the hackney window. "Edgar's no fool, but I've never considered him a particularly good judge of character. Nor have you, if memory serves."

"No, but he has remarkably keen flashes of insight," Mélanie said. He could feel her gaze on the back of his head. "I don't know what happened between you, Charles. I don't need to know. But Edgar doesn't just love Colin. He loves you."

Charles swung his head round. "Damn it, Mel, you may be far more skilled at deception than I am, but I think I'm still a better judge of my own family."

She watched him with those damnably all-seeing eyes. "Darling, you've every right to push me away, but I hate to see you push everyone else away as well."

"Whatever the problems between my brother and me, they go back for years. As I recall, you and I were on remarkably intimate terms until this morning."

"Yes. But— No, I'm sorry, I'm being just the sort of meddling wife I loathe."

"Thank you." He folded his arms across his chest. "For once we're in agreement. As I thought we'd agreed that until we recover our son nothing else is of any moment."

He heard Mélanie's intake of breath. When she spoke her voice was tight with fear, but she merely said, "That goes without saying."

The hackney rattled on. Charles crossed his legs. The strong coffee and rough brandy, swallowed after a day with little food, had left a dull pain behind his temples and a nervous energy that thrummed through his veins. He glanced down at his hands, always the first part of his body to betray him. Even in the murky light, he noted a telltale tremor. Damnation.

"How much should we worry about Castlereagh?" Mélanie said.

Charles clasped his hands together. "We're safe for the moment. He thinks he has Edgar following us. He won't put anyone else on the matter."

Mélanie gnawed on her finger. "I'm surprised Castlereagh called Edgar in. I thought he had his own agents in London. Not as many as the Home Secretary, of course, but he used to have quite a tidy little network in England as well as abroad. I suppose it's closed down a good deal since the war."

The reality of what she had been, what she had done, what they had both done, hit Charles again like a punch to the gut. For a moment his brain was choked with images, fragments, heedless confidences, nighttime whispers, unthinking, unforgivable betrayals. How many of his friends had lost their lives because of his carelessness? How many people who thought they could trust him had been betrayed because he was so foolish as to trust his wife?

He thought of his friend Fitzroy Somerset, Wellington's military secretary, who had lost his right arm at Waterloo. He thought of the innkeeper near Salamanca who'd passed messages for him until the man was discovered by the French and shot. And then, unexpectedly, he thought of the family of *afrancesados*, French sympathizers, who'd sheltered him and dressed his wounds after he'd been caught in a skirmish. He'd told the family he was a French officer out of uniform, carrying dispatches to his commander. They'd believed him without question. The elder daughter was being courted by a French soldier, and by the time Charles left he'd learned some very interesting details about French troop deployment in the area.

He could still smell the scent of the hay in the barn where he'd slept and taste the fresh goat's milk the eight-year-old son of the family brought him to drink. He could still see the boy's bright, eager eyes as he knelt on Charles's pallet and drank in Charles's lies about life in the French army.

Mélanie's accusations about his intelligence work echoed in his head. In truth, he could not deny that his work had gone well beyond fetching and carrying. It had begun because he was good at ciphers, but before long he'd been asked to retrieve coded documents as well as decipher them. An odd collection of talents—a skill at playacting, a facility for languages, the ability to pick a lock and talk himself out of just about any situation—had drawn him deeper into the intelligence web.

But whatever paltry deceptions he had engaged in, whatever twinges of guilt he had felt, surely his own lies could not compare with what Mélanie had done. Surely deceiving strangers on the opposite side in wartime was different from deceiving the person with whom you shared your bed and body, your work and the raising of your children and the innermost recesses of your life.

He stared at his distorted reflection in the square of glass that was the hackney window. In the street beyond, a lamplighter on a ladder was battling the rain in an effort to light the oil in the blackened globe of a street lamp. The flame sputtered, puffed, and went out. "We can't risk letting Edgar know about your past," Charles said.

"No." Mélanie's voice sounded firmer than it had. "Edgar's definitely an Othello."

"What? Oh, I see." He remembered their conversation when they returned from the party at the Esterhazys'—another world in which they had loved and trusted each other and been deluded enough to think they could keep their children safe. " 'And when I love thee not, Chaos is come again.' "

"You know how I adore Edgar, but he does rather tend to see everything in extremes of good and bad. He's just the sort who would snap and turn violent if he learned his wife had betrayed him."

"If Edgar learned Lydia was a French spy, he'd probably drop dead of shock," Charles said. "I think I might as well. Espionage would be bound to violate her sense of decorum."

"Poor Lydia. I sometimes think her problem is boredom as much as anything. They'd both be so much happier if—"

She bit back the words. Charles said it for her. "If they had children."

"Yes."

Colin was a tangible presence in the carriage, so close Charles almost imagined he could hear his son's laugh or see the dark gleam of his hair. "Edgar would be a good father," Charles said.

"Yes. And Lydia might take to motherhood. Perhaps— It takes some couples years to conceive a child. I said as much to Lydia only last month. Of course, it would help if she and Edgar were actually sleeping together, and though she'd never discuss such things, I rather fear they stopped sharing a bed some time ago."

"So do I." Charles had more than once marveled at the difference between his own marriage, born of exigency, and the passionless union that had resulted from his brother's love match. Any such comparison had the bite of irony now, though whatever else could be said of his marriage to Mélanie, it could not be called passionless.

The silence was punctuated by the familiar rustle of Mélanie plucking at the skirt of her pelisse. After a moment she said, "Have you ever been to the Gilded Lily?"

"Don't be stupid, Mel. I've been a married man since I came back to Britain." In fact, his experience of brothels was limited to one visit in his Oxford days, which he had spent cooling his heels in the sitting room. Intimacy was difficult enough for him. He could never bring himself to pay for the substitute. But he was not about to go into that with the woman seated beside him, the woman with whom he had shared such intimacy that she almost might have coined him and from whom he had received nothing but lies in return.

"Then it's a lucky thing I have some experience to go on." Mélanie's voice was bright as cut glass. "Some brothels have a staff of girls to service clients. Some merely provide rooms to be used by courtesans and actresses, and even respectable married women who wish to meet their lovers. Some do both. I imagine the Gilded Lily is that sort. I shouldn't think it likely we'll meet any of your friends there, but some of the most discriminating gentlemen find a certain piquancy in going slumming. Or so I've been given to understand."

Her words brought the rest of her morning's revelations back to him. In the deluge of events, the fact that she had once been employed in a brothel had been swept aside as almost insignificant. Now he turned it over in his mind, another piece of the puzzle of the woman he had married.

The bits of information he'd gleaned during the day shifted in his head. She would have been an orphan of sixteen when Raoul O'Roarke found her in the brothel. Charles had always known she'd endured horrors before they met. What had happened to her in the brothel was probably not so very different from what he had thought she'd suffered at the hands of the French soldiers and Spanish bandits.

He stared at her, trying to see beyond the lies. "Mel—"

"What, Charles?"

What indeed? *If the memories are too painful, don't come with me?* She'd laugh, and he needed her help. *Tell me the whole of your past?* It wasn't the time.

She undid her pelisse at the throat and tugged off the muslin tippet at the neck of her gown. "No one will trust us if we look too fine." She unbuttoned her gloves, then slipped off her wedding band and put it in her reticule along with the tippet.

His throat tightened with a pang that might have been anger or loss or self-loathing. He'd only seen her remove that circle of gold a handful of times since he'd placed it on her finger. He looked at her face, the sweetness about the mouth, the fresh purity in the curve of the bones. Most men of his acquaintance would be horrified by the revelation that their wives had a past, let alone that they had sold their bodies anywhere but on the Marriage Mart (save for one or two who had actually married courtesans, but that was another matter).

Charles had always claimed that whose bed a woman had shared before her marriage was no more a man's business than it was a wife's business to ask the same about her husband. He recalled arguing as much in an after-dinner discussion fueled by plentiful port. "It's all very well to try to outrage us with your bohemian sensibilities, Fraser," one of the other men present had said, staggering to the sideboard, where their host kept a chamber pot. "You'd feel differently if it was your own wife we were talking about." And then everyone had laughed, because they all knew Mélanie and they thought Charles was the last husband in London who had to worry about his wife before or after their marriage.

It was always a challenge to have one's principles put to the test. With a detached part of his mind—a safe corner he retreated into all too often—Charles was relieved to find that he *didn't* feel differently when it was his own wife involved. Mélanie had never questioned his sexual past. He had no right to question hers. That she had no doubt slept with O'Roarke, not to mention God knew whom else, after their marriage was another matter entirely.

The bite of jealousy on his tongue was as unfamiliar as a draught of Blue Ruin after years of the smoothest whisky. Mélanie might tease him for his naïveté, but he knew the games many of their friends indulged in. He'd more than once wandered onto the terrace during a ball to hear a cry or a soft murmur from the shrubbery. Or stepped into a darkened antechamber only to have to withdraw with an averted gaze and a muttered apology. At those same entertainments he'd watched his wife glide about the room in a whisper of velvet, a rustle of silk, a stir of dark ringlets, exerting her charms with disarming insouciance and devastating accuracy. He'd been idiotically sure of her. What they had between them was too rich, too complex, too multilayered for her to risk it for transitory pleasure, any more than he would. Or so he had thought. But now he faced the fact that what he and Mélanie had was built on lies, while she and O'Roarke shared a past that was every bit as textured and complex as what he once thought they had had between them.

The memory of their wedding night thundered in his head. Every moment of it was etched in his memory. She'd looked at him with such perfect trust. Or so it had seemed. It had all been lies, that wordless vocabulary of touch they had constructed between them. Christ, she must have been laughing at him inwardly. Perhaps she had laughed about it later. Perhaps she'd told O'Roarke—

He slammed his fist into the leather of the carriage seat.

Damn her. She had tricked him into doing the one thing he had strenuously avoided since childhood. Baring his soul.

It was still raining when they pulled up in Villiers Street. Through the rain-streaked window Charles saw a faded sign, swinging wildly in the wind, bearing a painting of a lily in peeling gilt and beneath it a picture of a coffeepot, held in a beringed, lace-cuffed hand. He might not be experienced in such matters, but he knew the latter indicated a coffeehouse that doubled as a brothel.

The smell of damp and rot was thick in the air. He considered asking the hackney driver to wait for them but decided against it. It might draw undue attention, and in any case he wasn't sure the driver would comply. He handed his wife from the hackney and followed her into a piece of her past.

Chapter 16

The smell hit Mélanie like a fist in the face as she stepped over the threshold. Tobacco and sweat, cheap scent and cheaper liquor. And a sweet, cloying muskiness, a never-forgotten odor that took her back to hot hands and probing fingers, coarse linen sheets and groaning straw-filled mattresses and soul-destroying despair.

The tin lamps swayed with the opening of the door. The light jumped and wavered over the peeling walls, the stained tables, the rouged, sweating faces, lending a hellish aspect to an already hellish scene. She forced herself to note her surroundings, to anchor herself to the present. Smoke-blackened walls, floorboards that didn't appear to have been swept in a fortnight, bright, gaudy dresses, brightly colored hair. Her own hair had been hennaed once, until one of the older women had pointed out that her natural coloring was more dramatic.

She turned to Charles and pressed her face into his shoulder.

"Put your arm round me," she whispered against his collar. "We need to look as though we belong."

He hesitated only a fraction of a second before he draped his arm across her shoulders. She leaned into him, not with wifely, shoulder-brushing intimacy, but with a blatant, clinging sensuality.

Most of the customers were too absorbed in bottles, dice, and partners to take much notice of them, but as they moved past the brick fireplace, a hand shot out and gripped her skirt. "Here now, you're new." The speaker had an Oxbridge accent, and judging by his pimply face and squeaky voice, he was still at university. He ran a far from inexperienced gaze over her. Then he glanced at Charles. "Wouldn't mind having a turn when you're done with her, old boy."

The muscles in Charles's arm tightened. "Watch your tongue, lad. You'll never win a lady by talking behind her back."

He drew her away, but she turned back and ran her finger down the side of the boy's face. His skin was slick with oily sweat. "Sorry, love." She made her voice lower, rougher, throatier than usual, without a trace of a Continental accent. "He's got a hellish temper. Maybe some other time."

Charles steered her to a table in an alcove by the fire. She removed her bonnet and pulled some tendrils of hair loose about her face. A tired-looking waiter threaded his way through the tables to their side, surveyed her as though matter-of-factly totting up her monetary value, and asked what he could do for them. Charles ordered brandy, his Scots accent roughening the Mayfair edges out of his voice, and said they were looking for a woman named Susan Trevennen.

"Trevennen?" The waiter scratched his thin, greasy hair.

Mélanie leaned one elbow on the table. "She came from Cornwall originally. She'd be about thirty. She has red hair."

The waiter's face cleared. "Oh, you mean Copper Sue. Wait a tick, love, I'll send her over."

Charles looked at Mélanie. "My compliments."

"Practice." She unclasped her pelisse and let it slither down on the chair round her. If she kept her arm at her side, the rent in her gown wasn't too noticeable. The air felt clammy against her bare throat, though her gown covered far more of her than most of her evening dresses. Two men at a nearby table were staring at her, as was another from across the room. She'd forgotten how it felt to be raked with so blatant a gaze, as though you were stripped down to the sum of your body parts.

The waiter returned, plunked down two glasses of brandy, and said without embarrassment that Copper Sue was with a customer but would join them presently. Charles picked up the brandy and sniffed it. "Gin might have been safer."

"I think any sort of safety is a rare commodity here." She picked up the brandy and took a long swallow. It ranked several degrees lower than the liquor Charles had given her at the Marshalsea. They'd drunk raw red wine in the brothel in Léon. Sharp, sour, strong enough to blur the sharp edges of reality.

"Mel." Charles's hand moved across the table.

She looked from his hand into his gray eyes. The compassion in his gaze seared her. She summoned up the hard look she'd perfected at fifteen, when she needed all her defenses. "Don't worry, darling. It's not as if there's much left that can shock me."

A couple dropped down at the table next to them. Or rather the man dropped down, pulled the women into his lap, and began whispering a variety of suggestions into her ear in a voice that carried all too well. Crudeness combined with lack of imagination. A fatal mix.

Mélanie shifted her chair and transferred her gaze to the painting over the fireplace. It was smoke-darkened, but it seemed to depict Zeus, in a swan guise that was all too human, hovering over a recumbent Leda. Leda wore nothing beyond a thin strip of gauze about her waist, and Zeus was the only swan Mélanie had ever seen with an erect phallus.

Laughter drifted down the stairs, followed by an abrupt cry and the sound of a door being slammed shut. Upstairs there would be thin mattresses and stale sheets and cracked, cobweb-hung expanses of ceiling. And little one could do to control what happened once the door was closed and the money on the table.

At the center of the room, a woman with bright gold hair and a low-cut red dress started singing a bawdy song that was vaguely recognizable as a variant on "Là ci darem la mano." The undergraduate who had pawed Mélanie had pulled a fair-haired child who couldn't be more than fourteen onto his lap and was undoing the strings on her bodice.

"You wanted to see me?" A hard-eyed woman with hair the color of a copper skillet materialized out of the crowd and stood before their table.

Charles got to his feet. "Miss Trevennen?"

She laughed, a sound as harsh as the taste of the Gilded Lily's brandy. Her teeth were yellow and she was missing two of them. "It's a long time since anyone's called me that. Quite a novelty. Yes, that's me. What do you want?" Her gaze slid from Charles to Mélanie. "I don't do threesomes."

Charles didn't so much as blink. "It's about your sister."

"Helen?" A spark flashed in Susan Trevennen's eyes, like the glint of a knife blade. "She hasn't managed to get herself killed, has she? That's just about the only good news you could bring me about my bitch of a sister."

Susan could only be a few years Mélanie's senior, but beneath the layers of cheap powder and greasy rouge, her face was splotched and marked by deep furrows. A mark that might be a bruise showed beneath her left eye, but it was her eyes themselves that resonated for Mélanie. The wariness, the instinctive calculation, the knowledge that everyone wanted to use you one way or another and the only way to survive was to use him or her first. Her own eyes, Mélanie knew, had had that same look before her sixteenth birthday. It had taken all Raoul's training and all his patience in other ways to get rid of it.

"Your sister isn't dead, Miss Trevennen," Charles said. "At least not as far as we know."

"Nell always had the most godawful knack for self-preservation." Susan pushed limp strands of dyed red hair off her face. Beads of sweat had clotted the powder against her skin. "Why did she send you here?"

"She didn't send us," Charles said. "We're trying to find her."

Susan Trevennen gave a bark of dry laughter. "If you're looking for Nell, I'm the last person you should be talking to."

"You're just about the last person we've tried." Charles pulled out one of the rickety ladderback chairs at the table. "Won't you sit down, Miss Trevennen?" The Scots accent had faded again. It was his drawing room voice, the sort of voice Susan Trevennen must have been accustomed to as a girl in her father's vicarage.

Susan's eyes widened. She looked from the chair to Charles. "I can't talk long." Her gaze slid sideways. "I have customers waiting."

Mélanie took a handful of coins from her reticule and laid them on the table. Charles flagged down the waiter and ordered Susan a glass of gin.

Susan dropped into the chair Charles was holding out. "What do you want with Nell?"

Mélanie started to launch into the now-familiar story about the legacy, but thought better of it. Susan had no reason to want to help her sister to a fortune. Mélanie looked into Susan's blue-gray eyes. If she had seen an echo of herself in Helen Trevennen's sister, perhaps she could make Susan see the same in her. "Our son is in danger," she said. "And your sister may be able to help."

Something flickered in Susan's gaze. Surprise? Reassessment? Compassion, even? "In that case I'm sorry for you. Nell's not likely to help unless there's something in it for her."

"That's the least of our problems." Charles returned to his chair. "When we find her we'll make it more than worth her while."

Susan's gaze flickered between them, taking in Mélanie's ringless left hand. A gentleman and his whore, she'd think. So much the better. While Susan warmed to Charles's courteous treatment, she'd be more likely to talk to Mélanie if she thought they lived in the same world. "I haven't seen Nell in years."

Mélanie tugged at the neck of her gown. The gin-soaked air cloyed at her senses and made her skin crawl. "You know your sister left London?"

"I heard she had." Susan's own voice had grown more refined, as though she was falling back into the accents of her girlhood. "I hadn't seen her for some time before that. We quarreled."

"Over what?" Mélanie said.

"A man. What else? Nell always had her pick of men. She didn't need mine, too. I swear she did it just to be spiteful. Anyway, she didn't have him for long. He got a knife in his ribs in a brawl over a wager. Which cockroach could run across the table fastest. He always was a mad fool." An edge of regret flashed beneath the mockery.

"I'm sorry," Mélanie said.

Susan hunched a shoulder. "It was bound to happen sooner or later. He wasn't worth the heartache."

Mélanie rested her elbows on the table in an attitude that invited confidences. "When you first came to London you lived with your sister."

"I was more naïve then. About a lot of things." Susan tugged her spangled scarf closer round her bare shoulders.

The waiter plunked the gin down on the table. Susan took a long swallow from the chipped glass.

"Your sister's friend Violet Goddard told us Helen may have feared some sort of danger when she went away," Charles said. "Do you have any idea what that might have been?"

"Not in the least. Nell wasn't afraid of anything. I suspect she thought she was in trouble and she ran to get out of it. Or else she thought there was money to be made by disappearing."

"Where do you think she went?" Charles asked.

Susan shrugged. The spangled scarf slipped loose, revealing the tattered, lace-edged neck of her gown. A blue-black bruise spread across her collarbone, mottled by a dusting of powder. "Somewhere better than this. Nell has a knack for landing on her feet. And she likes nice things."

Charles sat watching her, intensity in his stillness. "Is that what she wanted most out of life? Nice things?"

"Yes. That is—" Susan picked at a grease spot on the table. Her voice and phrasing had echoes of the vicarage schoolroom. "In some ways I think what Nell wanted was respectability. Which is funny, because that's what our father wanted for us, and Nell ran away from it. Only she didn't want to be poor and respectable like Papa. She wanted people's respect and all the elegancies of life in the bargain. If anyone could manage it, perhaps Nell could. I haven't managed either one. It's funny—"

A fit of coughing seized her, a deep racking sound that came from the chest. She tugged a handkerchief from her bodice and put it over her mouth. "I haven't always been here, you know," she said when the coughs subsided. "I was an opera dancer and then I worked at a house in Marylebone. Not one of the grandest in the city, but quite nice. Gilt mirrors and velvet sofas and gentlemen in proper coats and neckcloths." She glanced about the room. A portly man was walking down the stairs, buttoning up his trousers. A couple were on their way upstairs, undressing each other as they went. "Not that it makes a lot of difference with the candle doused. Still, this wasn't quite what I had in mind."

Mélanie took a sip of the harsh brandy. In the past ten years she had known anger and fear and self-hatred. But since Raoul O'Roarke had taken her out of the door of the brothel in Léon she had rarely felt powerless. It was one of the reasons she would be forever grateful to him. "Did Helen ever talk about wanting to live anywhere besides London?" she said. "Did she ever mention starting over in America or the East Indies?"

"Nell in the wilds of the colonies? Oh no, that's the last place my sister would go. Paris, perhaps, or Italy."

A chorus of whistles carried across the room. A full-figured girl with dark ringlets was perched on the edge of a table, skirt drawn up well above her knees, making an elaborate show of unlacing the ribbons on her slippers. "Amy Graves," Susan said. "A posture moll. Toast of the Gilded Lily. She makes more money with her performances down here than the rest of us do upstairs. She's almost young enough to be my daughter." She turned back to Mélanie. "I wish I could help you. I'm sorry for whatever's happened to your son. But I don't have any idea where Nell might have gone."

Mélanie leaned forward. "You knew her once. Better than anyone. If she wrote to someone after she left, who might it have been?"

"Nell didn't have a soft spot for anyone. She didn't even tell our uncle she was leaving, and she wasn't talking to me at all by that time."

"Yes, but assuming she did write, to just one person, who might that have been?"

Susan frowned. The whistles from across the room grew louder. Amy Graves had removed her garters and was peeling off her stockings, sheer black silk embroidered in scarlet.

"I suppose—" Susan twisted the end of the scarf round her chapped fingers. "Jemmy. Jemmy Moore."

"He was one of her lovers?" Mélanie asked.

"He was her first lover. She ran off to London with him. She threw him over soon enough, but—" Susan turned her gaze toward the fireplace corner. The shadows were kind to her. Beneath the paint, her face had a delicate, heart-shaped sweetness. "Nell kept going back to Jemmy. Not for long, but consistently. If you were of a romantic turn, you'd call it love."

"Where is he now?" Charles asked.

"Probably picking someone's pocket or trying to break into a house, assuming he hasn't managed to get himself hanged in the past few months."

"He's a thief?" Mélanie said.

"Not a very good one, but he manages to scrape together a living." Another cough seized her. She brought the crumpled handkerchief up to her mouth. "Most of which he loses at the gaming tables."

"Where does he live?" Charles asked.

"I haven't the least idea." She folded the handkerchief. Bright red spots showed against the yellowed linen. "He changed lodgings half a dozen times in the years I knew him. But from sometime after midnight until the early hours of the morning, he can usually be found at Mannerling's gaming hell. A friend of mine saw him there just this past year."

Mélanie looked from the handkerchief to Susan's face. She should have read the signs in the fine-drawn translucence of Susan's skin sooner. She'd grown all too familiar with the inexorable ravages of consumption during her time in the brothel. "What does Jemmy Moore look like?" she asked.

Memory drifted across Susan's face. "Curly black hair. Blue eyes. Not too tall, but nicely made if he's taken care of himself. He had a fondness for yellow waistcoats."

Mélanie released her breath, though she hadn't realized she'd been holding it. "Thank you."

"It's little enough."

The whistles had given way to stomping feet. Amy Graves, now standing on the table, pulled her chemise over her head and tossed it into the crowd.

Susan swallowed the last of her gin. She looked at Mélanie for a moment over the rim of the glass. "Your little boy—is it dangerous?"

"Yes," Mélanie said.

Susan nodded. "I hope—I hope it turns out all right."

Two men were having a tug-of-war with Amy Graves's chemise. Amy was stretched out naked on the table. A full glass of claret rested on the curling thatch between her legs. The pimply young man who had pawed Mélanie was leaning forward and attempting to drink out of it, while onlookers shouted words of encouragement or mockery.

Charles leaned his arms on the table. He hadn't so much as

glanced in Amy Graves's direction. "Someone else may come asking questions about your sister. A dark-haired man with a Spanish accent. It would be convenient if you could lose your memory."

Susan smiled, a smile that curved her full mouth and lit her eyes and wiped the harshness from her face. "Faith, sir, my memory's not what it once was. It's a miracle I've remembered what I have tonight, it is."

Mélanie put some more coins on the table. "Do you think—"

"Here now—you've had your turn!" The crash of a chair hitting the floor echoed through the room. A man in a stained bottle-green coat grabbed the pimply young man by the shoulder and pulled him off Amy Graves.

The glass of claret tipped over and shattered on the table. Amy Graves sat up with a cry. The pimply man spun round and shoved the man in the green coat. The man in the green coat stumbled back and fell against a woman at the next table. The woman screamed. Her escort planted a fist in Green Coat's face.

"Oh, hell," Susan said, "now we're in for it."

She was right. Mélanie wasn't sure quite what happened next, but suddenly half those present seemed to be involved in the fight. Chairs splintered. Glasses shattered. A table was upended. Shouts and curses, cries of rage and pain and the sheer love of battle filled the air. A glass hit the painting and left a splash of red wine on one of Zeus's wings. Amy Graves scrambled up on the table, arms crossed over her breasts.

Charles glanced at the door. "I wouldn't try it," Susan said over the din round them. "Wait till it calms down."

Charles nodded and grabbed Mélanie's arm. Mélanie snatched up her bonnet and pelisse and they drew back into the corner by the fireplace.

"It's a while since we've had one of these," Susan said. "This one's worse than usual. Look out!" She ducked and Charles pulled Mélanie down just as a bottle went sailing across the room and shattered against the brick of the chimney.

The fight was eddying out into the farthest reaches of the

room. A man in his shirtsleeves vaulted over the stair rail and hurled himself into the fray.

Charles had gone still. He was staring across the room, as though he glimpsed something in the melee, though Mélanie couldn't imagine what he could make out in the sea of movement. She touched his arm. "Darling—"

He answered without looking at her. "Mel—"

She didn't hear the rest. Someone crashed into them. She dodged, but the next thing she knew a fist smashed into the side of her face. Pain slammed through her head and down her side. Her head swam blackly for a moment. She felt Charles's hands on her shoulders, heard his voice mutter, "Get under the table," saw a rush of movement as he sprang forward.

The fight engulfed them. Charles knocked a man to the ground. Someone else grabbed him from behind and gave his arm a vicious twist. Mélanie jumped on a chair and threw her pelisse over the attacker's head. Charles spun round and hit him through the enveloping folds of fabric.

Another man crashed into Charles from the side—the man in the bottle-green coat, who had started the brawl. His hands went straight for Charles's throat. Charles jerked and twisted. The first assailant struggled free of the folds of the pelisse and launched himself at Charles's legs.

Mélanie snatched up a glass from the table and brought it down on Green Coat's balding head with as much force as she could muster. White fire shot through the wound in her side, but Green Coat yelped and let go of Charles. Charles kicked the other man, grabbed her hand, and jumped over an overturned chair.

"There's a side door." Susan Trevennen spoke beside them, fighting to make herself heard over the shouts and screams and crashes that filled the air. "This way."

They dodged and elbowed their way past the fireplace and along the side of the room to a low wooden door. Their feet slithered on the liquor-soaked floorboards, and broken glass scrunched beneath their shoes. Susan had grabbed a spare bottle off a table as they moved past. She tossed the contents over two men who were grappling in front of the door. A temporary path cleared.

"Go now." She tugged the door open, letting in a blast of rain-soaked wind. "Good luck."

They stumbled out into a narrow, unlit alley. Charles pulled the door to behind them. The rain blew in their faces and the wind slapped against them, but the quiet was a blessed relief. Mélanie leaned against the rough stone wall long enough to draw a deep breath of the night air. "The man who started the fight was one of the ones who attacked you," she said. "The fight was a setup."

"Very likely." Charles stripped off his coat and put it round her shoulders. The umbrella had been abandoned inside, along with his greatcoat and hat and her pelisse and bonnet. He threw a sheltering arm over her shoulders and drew her toward the light at the near end of the alley. He walked quickly, but he wasn't quite steady on his feet.

"Did you break anything?" Mélanie asked.

"I don't think so, but not for want of their trying. The first man very definitely meant to break my arm."

"I noticed." They walked a few steps in silence. The wind howled through the alley. The rain felt like melted ice through the thin fabric of her gown.

Charles steered her round a puddle of water. "I saw a familiar face in the midst of the brawl. Victor Velasquez."

"From the Spanish embassy?" She lifted her face to the rain to look up at him. Victor Velasquez was an attaché at the embassy, a distant acquaintance from their days in the Peninsula, an occasional dancing partner. He was also a committed royalist, violently opposed to those like Carevalo who sought to change the Spanish government. It took her a moment to put the pieces together, probably because she was so cold. "You think he's Iago Lorano?"

"He fits the general description and it's a bit too much of a coincidence otherwise. His grandmother was a Carevalo, which would give him an added interest in the ring. We were saying that if the royalists wanted to make use of the ring they'd have to find a royalist Carevalo cousin to take possession of it. Velasquez would be the perfect choice."

They had reached the mouth of the alley. Villiers Street was empty in the immediate vicinity. Charles drew her forward into the yellow glow of a street lamp and glanced up and down the street. "Our best chance of a hackney is probably—"

A report ripped through the air. It was only when Charles collapsed against her and she smelled the cloying sweetness of blood that she realized the sound had been a gunshot.

Chapter 17

*I*nstinct took over, honed by years of dodging snipers' bullets in the Spanish mountains. Mélanie dragged her husband out of the telltale circle of lamplight, back into the concealing dark of the mouth of the alley, and pushed him against the support of a lime-washed wall. "Charles? Where are you hit?"

"My leg. Right. Upper thigh." His voice was hoarse. "Where did the shot come from?"

"I can't tell." She scanned the sliver of street behind them. Light shone behind several first-floor windows, but all the curtains seemed to be drawn. She glanced down at his leg. She could see a rent in the fabric, but not much more in the cloaking darkness of the alley. She put her hand over the wound and felt the sticky warmth of blood. Still flowing, but not spurting. He wasn't likely to pass out. She pulled up her skirt, tore a strip from her chemise, and bound it round his thigh. "Can you walk to the far end of the alley if I help you?"

"You're in no shape to support me, Mel. Look after yourself. I'll manage."

"You're a bloody awful liar, Charles. I got you this far, I can manage the rest. Put your arm across my shoulders."

He had the sense not to protest further. He walked, after a fashion, with his arm across her shoulders and hers about his waist and his right leg dragging awkwardly. Her side didn't seem to hurt as much as it had before. Perhaps the chill of the rain and wind was making her numb all over.

They passed the closed side door of the Gilded Lily and made their way agonizing step by step to the far end of the alley and the next street over. She got Charles into the shelter of the first doorway and scanned the street. No carriages. A cluster of brothels or taverns or gin mills to the right. The lights of what might be a lodging house to the left. A few women with shawls thrown over their low-cut gowns, leaning in darkened shop doorways, looking for custom despite the weather. A trio of boys trying to roast potatoes over a smoldering fire in a doorway on the opposite side of the street.

"Wait here," she said to Charles, and darted across the street before he could protest.

The boys looked up at her approach, wariness writ in their expressions. Mercifully, she had managed to hang onto her reticule. She fished out three half crowns. "One for each of you, and another for the first one who can bring me a hackney."

The boys stared at her for a moment in the light of their fire. Then all three grabbed the coins and were off like a shot.

"They may use the money to buy themselves a place by a warm fire instead of looking for a hackney," Charles said when she rejoined him. He was breathing erratically between the words.

"They'll come back. They're old enough to know that two half crowns can buy a lot more than one." She leaned against him for warmth, though they were both so frozen she doubted it would make any difference. Tremors wracked his body, but he wrapped his arms round her and rubbed her shoulders.

After an interval that was probably only ten minutes, though it felt like thirty, she was proved right. A mud-spattered hackney came trundling down the street with the smallest of the three boys running beside it. When she and Charles stepped out of the doorway, battered and bedraggled, the driver nearly took off again, but he stopped when she waved a pound note in his face. "Berkeley Square. As quickly as possible."

Charles made a protesting sound. "We have to have someone look at your leg," she said. "Besides, we can't hope to find Jemmy Moore until past midnight. And we should see if Addison and Blanca learned anything." She half pushed him into the carriage with the help of the young boy who had found the hackney. She pressed another pound note into the boy's hand, climbed into the carriage after Charles, pulled the door shut behind her, and collapsed on the dry seat.

"Has your wound started bleeding again?" Charles said from the opposite end of the seat.

"I can't tell. It doesn't hurt too badly." That wasn't strictly true, but it could have been a great deal worse. "Do you think the bullet broke a bone in your leg?"

"No."

She shot him a sideways glance. She couldn't make out his features in the dark, but his breathing sounded even more labored than before. "You'd say that anyway. I don't know why I bother asking." She folded her arms and realized she was shaking. Cold or delayed fear, she couldn't say which. Her gown was plastered to her skin and she thought her half-boots were soaked through, though she couldn't quite feel her toes. "If Victor Velasquez is Iago Lorano, how do you think he found us? I'd have sworn no one followed us from the Marshalsea. I thought we could trust Hugo Trevennen not to talk."

"Perhaps someone else at the Marshalsea told Velasquez about Susan. She visits her uncle. She must be known there."

She rubbed her arms. The trembling wouldn't stop. "Victor

Velasquez is no fool, but he's a soldier turned diplomat, not an intelligence agent. I wouldn't have thought he'd have the skills to organize all these attacks so quickly."

"Quite. Which is why I still wonder if O'Roarke's behind the attacks."

"Charles, I told you Raoul wouldn't—"

"Attack *you*." He drew a rasping breath. "You didn't say anything about me. Perhaps he wants you back."

She managed a laugh. "My darling Charles, if Raoul wanted me back, he wouldn't let anything as conventional as a marriage tie stand in his way. He also knows me well enough to realize he wouldn't have a prayer of getting me without my cooperation. Besides, Raoul rarely wastes energy on anything as mundane as personal relationships."

She felt Charles's gaze on her in the gloom of the carriage, hard and direct. "Mel, I may be blind to a lot of things, but it's obvious that the man's still in love with you."

She jerked and stared at him, but she could only make out the outline of his profile. "Don't be stupid, Charles. If Raoul's ever been in love, it wasn't with me. He keeps a lock of some woman's hair in a fob on his watch chain. But it's certainly not mine—he had it before I met him and anyway it's blond. That's the closest I've ever seen him come to showing any sentimentality."

Charles made no reply and said nothing further until they pulled up in Berkeley Square. The sight of the twin filigree lampposts spilling light onto their own portico was a blessed relief. She paid off the driver and helped Charles up the steps, arms shaking, half-boots squelching on the stone. The second footman, Michael, opened the door in answer to her ring, stared open-mouthed for an instant, then made haste to take Charles's weight from her shoulder.

"Thank you, Michael." She stepped into the welcome warmth of the entrance hall, dripping rainwater all over the black-and-white marble of the tiles. Her legs seemed to have turned to jelly. She gripped the console table for a moment. "Is Captain Fraser here?"

"Yes, madam, he's in the library."

"Good. Help Mr. Fraser in there. Then go to Dr. Blackwell in Hill Street. If he's out for the evening, find where he's gone and go after him. Tell him I'm sorry to disturb him, but Mr. Fraser's been shot and it's an emergency." Geoffrey Blackwell could be trusted to come quickly. He was an old friend, and his wife was Charles's cousin.

Mélanie ran ahead to open the library doors. Inside she found not only Edgar but the children's governess, Laura Dudley. Edgar was pacing before the fireplace, while Laura sat bolt upright in a chair, twisting something that looked like it had once been a piece of mending in her hands.

"Mélanie." Edgar came toward her. "I was starting to worry— Good God." He caught sight of Michael staggering under Charles's weight and ran to their side.

"It's not as bad as it looks." Charles's voice was remarkably steady, but now that they were inside Mélanie could see a sheen of sweat on his forehead. "Give me your arm, brother, so Michael can be off on his mercy mission."

"Warm water and clean cloths," Mélanie said to Laura. "And blankets and a dressing gown. Are Addison and Blanca back?"

"Blanca is. She didn't learn anything. She's in the nursery with Jessica. Addison's still out." Laura hurried from the room without further questions. Edgar helped Charles to a high-backed chair in front of the fire.

Mélanie dropped down beside him, unknotted the strip of linen—which took longer than it should have because her chilled fingers wouldn't cooperate—and got her first proper look at the wound. The bullet had entered the fleshy part of his thigh, thank God. He was probably right that no bones were broken. The wound was still bleeding, but not profusely. "Geoffrey will have to dig the bullet out, but I can clean it," she said. "Can you manage to get your trousers off or shall we cut them away?"

"I can manage if Edgar helps with my boots." His rib cage shook with each breath. "Intercept Laura and bring me my dressing gown."

Mélanie met Laura at the door and took the things from her. Between them, she and Edgar got Charles wrapped in the dressing gown. She cleaned the wound as best she could while Charles sipped from a large glass of whisky Edgar had pressed into his hand. Laura hovered in the background, managing to be near when necessary yet not violate decorum.

"Stop fussing at it, Mel." Charles tossed down the last of the whisky. "I won't die before Geoffrey gets here. Go up and see Jessica and put on a dry gown before you catch a chill."

The reminder of their daughter convinced her. Her gown was half dry and she had stopped shivering, so she went to Jessica's room first. She found Jessica curled up on the sofa beside Blanca, listening to a story. The moment Mélanie stepped into the room, Jessica jumped down, ran across the room, and hurled herself at her mother's legs.

Mélanie knelt beside Jessica and hugged her with a tightness that even she recognized as desperation.

Jessica wrapped her arms round Mélanie's neck and buried her face in Mélanie's shoulder, the way she did when she'd had a nightmare or when she'd been frightened by the guns at a military review or on a memorable occasion that involved smugglers, excisemen, and a particularly treacherous stretch of the Perthshire coast. Mélanie drew her daughter over to the window seat. She and Charles didn't exactly have a perfect record for keeping their children out of danger, but at least whatever happened they'd managed to protect Colin and Jessica. So far.

"Have you got Colin?" Jessica asked, her face squished against Mélanie's skirt.

"Not yet, *querida*." Mélanie sat down on the window seat and settled Jessica in her lap. How to offer reassurance without lying? "But we know what we need to do to get him back."

Jessica drew back and looked at her. "Your dress is wet and your hair's all crooked." She stared at Mélanie for a moment. Her eyes seemed bigger than usual and her face thinner. She picked at embroidery on the falling collar of Mélanie's gown. "I don't want to go away like Colin did."

Mélanie looked into her daughter's face. Charles's eyes and jaw, her own eyes and mouth, and something about the cheekbones that was pure Colin. "You won't, love." Her voice shook with the fierceness of it. "I promise." As she spoke the words, she heard an echo of a similar promise made to another little girl, a sister, not a daughter. The taste of bitter failure welled up on her tongue.

"Jessica—" She stroked Jessica's tousled hair. "What happened to Colin was very bad and it shouldn't have happened, but we're going to get him back and make sure it never happens again."

Jessica nodded with a simple, breathtaking trust that closed round Mélanie's heart like a fist. Eyes smarting, Mélanie reached for the storybook to finish reading the story Blanca had started. Jessica slithered down and sprawled against her, feet stretched out on the window seat, head flopped against Mélanie's arm, in that boneless way that made it difficult to tell where her body left off and one's own began. Her wide, sleep-tinged gray eyes were fixed on Mélanie's face with that same terrifying trust. When Mélanie finished the story, Jessica let her tuck her into bed. She did not even protest too vigorously when Mélanie said she had to go back downstairs. "Bring Colin," she murmured, her eyes drifting closed.

Mélanie shut the door of her daughter's room and leaned against the cool panels. Even if—when—they got Colin back, the children's lives would not return to normal. She could not imagine circumstances under which Charles would want to continue with their marriage. The best she could hope was that they could establish some sort of truce for Colin and Jessica's sake. A fiction of a marriage within which they led separate lives, as did many couples in the beau monde. The worst—

Charles had every right to throw her out of the household in which she had been living under false pretenses for seven years. It would not be in his character to do so. And yet she had never pushed him this far. They were on uncharted ground.

She drew a breath and walked down the corridor to the

room she and her husband shared, unlike most couples in their set. The bed where they had made love only two nights ago loomed before her. Their dressing gowns lay together in an untidy heap on the chaise longue. Berowne, whom she and Charles had rescued from the streets as an orphaned kitten, was curled up on top of some notes for a speech she was supposed to give on women's education.

She took a step forward and found her vision blurred and her cheeks damp. Tears were streaming down her face. A sob tore through her, squeezing her chest, pulling painfully on the wound in her side. She gripped the bedpost, her face pressed into the fluted wood, her body wracked by shudders.

Something soft brushed her leg. Berowne. He gave a mew, half plaintive, half concerned. She dropped to her knees and ran her fingers through his warm fur.

The tears still spilled down her face. She knew from experience that it would be a waste of much-needed energy to try to stop them. She sank down at her dressing table, slid her fingers into her hair, and pressed the palms of her hands over her eyes.

When she finally lifted her head, her splotched, tear-streaked face was reflected back at her in the looking glass panels. If one discounted the faint lines about her eyes, the plucked arch of her brows, the fashionably cropped curls falling over her forehead, it was the same face she had always had. The face of the girl who had known Shakespeare and Molière and Beaumarchais backwards and forwards but had understood nothing of the world; of the child whore whose life had been reduced to survival; of Raoul O'Roarke's most trusted agent; of Charles Fraser's wife and dearest friend; of Colin and Jessica's mother. Mélanie Fraser, who could speak to a reform society in the morning and take her children out for ices in the afternoon and give a dinner for fifty in the evening, without ever looking flustered or forgetting to wear the right shoes and earrings.

"I don't know how you do it," her friend Isobel Lydgate—

herself the enviably competent mother of three and wife of a rising young Member of Parliament—had said only last week. "I often feel like I'm failing on three fronts at once."

"Oh, darling, that's inevitable," Mélanie had replied with a laugh. "The trick is not minding when you *do* fail."

But that was only part of it, of course. Isobel was one of her closest friends, but she hadn't the least idea how truly precarious Mélanie's life was. The trick was bundling your life into neat, separate little boxes and believing your own deceptions. The trick was smiling and sipping champagne even though you knew the boxes might break apart and come tumbling down about your ears at any moment. The trick was acknowledging the inner scream of panic that welled up all too often but never, ever letting anyone else hear it.

She remembered waking the morning after her wedding and turning to look at the tousled oak-brown head on the pillow beside her. A knot of terror had closed her throat as she realized that her performance as Mrs. Charles Fraser would not be rounded by the span of a play or the length of a specific mission but would stretch for the foreseeable future.

If her life had taken a different turn, if she had made different choices, she might be preparing to open a new production of *Romeo and Juliet*, like Violet Goddard. Or dying of consumption in a brothel, like Susan Trevennen. Instead, she lived an aristocratic life that was at odds with the principles she claimed to believe in, whatever the comfortingly reformist politics of her husband. She was admired and sought after by a society that would shun her if they had the faintest idea of her origins. She was the wife of a man who would never believe she loved him, the mother of children whom she could never tell the truth about their heritage.

If she were honorable in the best British tradition, no doubt she would disappear onto the Continent and leave her husband and children to get on with their lives. But even in the guise of Mrs. Charles Fraser she had never fully embraced the values of her husband's world. Custody of the children would go to Charles if their marriage was legally ended. And yet Charles had no grounds for divorce or separation. He could not reveal her treachery without damaging his own reputation and career and hurting the children. He might risk himself, but he'd never risk Colin and Jessica. It was leverage of a sort.

Sacrebleu! That *she* should be thinking of leverage on Charles. But she wouldn't have survived this long if she hadn't learned to employ whatever means were necessary to win. Just as she would fight heart and soul to get Colin back from Carevalo, she would battle to the death to keep Charles from taking their children from her.

She looked down at Berowne, now curling himself into a ball beside her chair. "I won't leave," she promised, to the cat, to Colin and Jessica, to herself.

She poured water from the rose-patterned ewer into the matching basin and splashed her face. Her breathing was steadier, as though having acknowledged this decision eased the tumult inside her. She unhooked her gown, stripped off her ruined chemise, unlaced her sodden half-boots, and began to pull on fresh clothing.

Charles's makeshift bandage was still in place, and the wound hadn't started bleeding again, but it still hurt to move her arm, which made dressing an awkward business. She chose a gown with a waistcoat bodice that buttoned down the front, but she had still only managed two of the buttons when Blanca slipped into the room.

"Jessica's asleep." Blanca crossed the room and began to finish the buttons, without making any comment on Mélanie's tear-streaked face. "You told him, didn't you?" she said after a moment, as though they were discussing something perfectly ordinary, as though both their lives hadn't been turned upside down.

"I didn't have any choice." Mélanie swallowed. "I'm sorry, Blanca, I made the decision for both of us."

"*Dios*, Mélanie, of course you had no choice. I knew that when you told us about Colin." Blanca did up the last button. "I'll talk to Addison as soon as—I'll talk to him when we have Colin back. I don't think Mr. Fraser will say anything to him until then."

"I'm sure he won't." Mélanie looked at her friend, the one person who had known her secret all these years. "Addison can hardly accuse you of seducing him for information. I was already getting any information we could possibly need from Charles."

"Addison is a man of honor. He won't—" Blanca shook her head. Her inky hair slipped loose from its knot and fell about her face. "He wanted to marry me."

"Oh, Blanca." Mélanie checked the words of congratulation that sprang to her lips. They were hardly in order now. "Why didn't you tell me?"

Blanca made a wry face. "Addison was worried about what Mr. Fraser would think. It isn't usual for valets and ladies' maids to marry."

"*Sacrebleu!* As if Charles would care a rush for such things."

"I know." Blanca jabbed her hair behind her ears. "But Addison cares. He's very particular about the forms. At any rate, I don't suppose it matters now."

Mélanie squeezed the younger woman's hands. "*Querida*—"

Blanca shook her head. "We both went into this with our eyes open, Mélanie. We made our beds, and now we have to face the fact that our men may throw us out of them."

A desperate laugh escaped Mélanie's lips. She flung her arms round Blanca. They clung together for a moment while the reality of their situation washed over them. At last Blanca pulled back, sniffed, and rubbed the heels of her hands over her eyes. "No sense in crying over spilt tea."

"Milk," Mélanie said, dashing fresh tears from her face.

"Bah, what Englishman drinks milk?" Blanca pulled a handkerchief from her skirt pocket and blew her nose. "Are you going to tell me why you have a bandage wound round your ribs?"

Mélanie gave a brief account of the day's events. Blanca listened without comment. Her tendency to chatter disappeared when there were important matters at hand. She was even persuaded not to examine Mélanie's wound when Mélanie pointed out that the doctor was on his way. "Do you want me to help with Mr. Fraser?" Blanca asked.

"No, stay upstairs in case Jessica wakes." Mélanie gave Blanca a quick hug and went back down to the library.

Charles ran a sharp gaze over her face, but said nothing. He was sitting with his leg propped up on a footstool and another glass of whisky in his hand. He had apparently managed to recount the events at the Gilded Lily, because the normally unflappable Laura was white-faced with shock, and Edgar was pacing up and down in front of the fireplace, raging against the immorality of Victor Velasquez.

"Velasquez doesn't know about Colin," Mélanie pointed out. "Charles, don't you think—"

"We can talk about it later." Charles stared into his whisky instead of meeting her gaze.

"The library?" said a high, carrying voice from the hall. "No, no, I'll announce myself."

Dr. Geoffrey Blackwell swept into the room, black-haired, wiry, and intense, his evening cloak billowing about his shoulders, his medical bag clutched in one hand. His gaze went straight to Charles. "Here now, what have you been doing with yourself, my boy? Haven't I patched enough of you young men up on the battlefield?" He set down his bag, unclasped his cloak, and tossed it over a chair back. "Hullo, Mélanie. Glad you sent for me."

"Thank you for coming, Geoffrey. I'm sorry to disrupt your evening."

He waved his hand. "We were supposed to dine with the Whartons. Damned dull affair. I told Allie to go on without me." He nodded at Edgar and Laura, acknowledging their presence and dismissing them as irrelevant to the matter at hand in the same motion. "Let's have a look at you, lad." He picked up his bag and dropped down beside Charles's chair. "Dear heaven, what have you been up to? No, don't try to talk. Tell me later. Mélanie, civilian life hasn't turned you squeamish, has it? Good, I'm going to need your help."

Geoffrey Blackwell's brisk manner never varied, whether in the ballroom, on the battlefield, or on the nights he had delivered Colin and Jessica (on which occasions he had informed Charles that if he had the stomach for the business, he was welcome to stay, more power to him, and he could hold the hot water basin while he was at it). Geoffrey had been an army surgeon all through the war in the Peninsula, frequently bemoaning the fact that he stitched young men up only to see them cut to ribbons. After Waterloo he'd left the army and settled in London with his young wife and daughter. He claimed to be relieved to return to a more civilized practice, but Mélanie thought that he sometimes missed the excitement of the war.

He worked at Charles's wound in silence, except to ask Mélanie to hand him various implements, and at one point to suggest that Edgar pour Charles some more whisky. Mélanie had stood by on another occasion when Charles had a bullet dug out of him, after he'd returned to Lisbon from one of his "errands" for the embassy with his arm in a sling. She'd held his hand then. She didn't think he would welcome such a gesture tonight. He got very white and at one point she thought he might have fainted, but he made no sound beyond his labored breathing.

"There," Geoffrey said at last. "Neat enough stitching even my old nurse would approve."

"Good." Charles's clenched jaw relaxed a trifle. "Now you can take a look at Mélanie and see how badly I botched it patching her up."

Geoffrey cast a swift glance at Mélanie. His eyes narrowed. "Your side. I should have seen it sooner."

He drew in his breath at the sight of her wound, which was rare for Geoffrey, but he made no comment other than that if Charles must insist on dressing wounds himself, he hadn't done a bad job of it.

"Under normal circumstances, I'd tell you both to rest for the next few days," he said, when Laura was refastening Mélanie's gown. He snapped his medical bag shut. "Is whatever got you into this over and done with?"

"No," Charles said. "We have to go out again in a few hours. Tell us how best to go on. We'd as soon not collapse in the street."

Geoffrey's eyes narrowed. "It's not wise, but I've stitched up men in worse shape than both of you in the midst of battle and seen them hurl themselves back into the fray. Change the dressings twice a day. Get to a doctor—any doctor—if you see signs of infection. Elevate the leg when you can, even if it's only for a few minutes."

Charles's mouth lifted in a quick smile. "Thank you, Geoffrey. I—"

"Spare your breath, lad." Geoffrey clapped him on the shoulder, a rare gesture of intimacy. "If you haven't got time to recuperate from your injuries, you certainly don't have time to be talking to me." He glanced at the mantel clock. "Looks as if I'll make it to the Whartons' after all, more's the pity."

Mélanie brought him his cloak. "Give my love to Allie."

He took the cloak from her and laid his hand over her own for a moment. "Don't hesitate to send for me again if you need to, whatever the hour." He swung the cloak round his shoulders and fastened it. His gaze moved from her to Charles. "You've both always been quite good at taking care of each other. I trust you'll keep it up. No, don't bother to ring for the footman, this is no time for formality."

He nodded at Edgar and Laura and went out of the library, leaving silence in his wake.

"See here, Charles." Edgar crossed the room in three strides and dropped down in front of his brother. "You've got to rest. So does Mélanie. Let me go to Mannerling's and see this Jemmy Moore."

"No." Charles's voice was firm. "Edgar, I'm sorry. I don't discount your abilities and I know how much you love Colin, but I'm his father. And Mélanie's his mother."

Mélanie turned her head away for a moment. Her throat constricted and she felt a prickle behind her eyelids.

Edgar stared at his brother, face knotted with frustration. "You'll drop."

"I think not."

The two brothers regarded each other. Mélanie watched them, the sharp cheekbones, the strong noses, the finely molded mouths. So alike and so different. At thirty, Edgar still had an open, sunny countenance. Charles, she knew from a painting of the Fraser children, had had lines of experience etched in his face at fourteen.

Edgar got to his feet and turned to poke up the fire. "And to think I get accused of being the reckless one. You're a damned fool."

"Quite possibly," Charles said.

Edgar jammed the poker into the coals. "And you are too, Mélanie."

"Undoubtedly." Mélanie turned to Laura. "Could you see what Mrs. Erskine can manage for us in the kitchen? Something simple and nourishing and easy to get down, like soup. And plenty of coffee."

"Yes, of course." Laura slipped from the room.

Charles spoke to his brother's back. "Come with us tonight and make sure we don't take our foolery too far. You've been to Mannerling's before?"

Edgar spun round. "Confound it, Charles, can't I have any secrets from you?"

"Elder-brother intuition." Charles grinned, in the way he probably had when they were boys. Mélanie thought the grin was a sort of apology. "I know you've always been fond of roulette. There aren't that many places to play it in London. Will we have trouble getting in?"

"Not if the porter recognizes me." Edgar returned the poker to its stand. "I haven't been there all that often. It's run by a Julia Mannerling, a widow. Supposedly her husband was an army officer, though frankly I have doubts that he ever existed. It's a sight more raffish than Waitier's was." His gaze flickered in Mélanie's direction.

"Edgar," Mélanie said, "if you're going to say I can't go there—"

Edgar gave her a smile that made him look very like Charles. "At this point, I wouldn't dare tell you not to do anything, sister."

Charles shifted his leg on the footstool. "We'll leave at eleven-thirty. Depending on what we learn, at dawn one or more of us can start for Surrey to see Mrs. Jennings. How long until you have to report to Castlereagh, Edgar?"

"I sent him a message when I got here saying I hadn't been able to discover anything so far. That will do until tomorrow. Thank God Lydia's in the country with her parents. I couldn't silence her questions so easily."

Mélanie walked to the sideboard, poured herself a glass of whisky, and swallowed half of it in one gulp. Now that Charles's wound had been treated, the churning need to keep moving, to be doing *something*, anything, was back. She glanced at the mantel clock. Eight-thirty. Less than twenty-four hours since Colin had been taken.

"More than three hours before we can hope to find Jemmy Moore," Charles said behind her.

"Yes." She returned to the fireplace and dropped down in a chair across from him. He was still very pale, but he was no longer shaking and his breathing seemed more regular. "Darling, shouldn't we see if we can find Victor Velasquez and tell him about Colin? He might call off his hounds."

Charles's gaze had shifted to the fire. "No," he said without glancing at her.

"Why not?"

"Because I don't think it would persuade him to call off his hounds."

"I know he's a royalist to the bone and he hates Carevalo, but he always struck me as fundamentally decent. It's worth a try—"

"And because if Velasquez knew my son was in danger it might make him all the more eager to do whatever it takes to stop us."

She set her glass down on the table beside her. "Why, for heaven's sake?"

He continued to look into the fire. There was a set quality to his expression, as though he were holding pain at bay, but she wasn't sure the pain came from the bullet wound. Edgar, standing beside the fireplace, had gone very still.

"Why doesn't matter," Charles said.

"Doesn't matter?" Mélanie leaned forward. "Anything that may have a bearing on what's happened to Colin matters."

A muscle twitched beside Charles's jaw. "My history with Victor Velasquez doesn't. Trust me."

Edgar cleared his throat. "Mélanie, perhaps it would be best—"

"Stay out of this, Edgar." She sprang to her feet, leaned over the chair, and grabbed Charles by the shoulders. "Charles Kenneth Malcolm Fraser, our son's life is at stake."

He looked up at her, his eyes cold and hard. "I had grasped that fact."

Her grip on his shoulders tightened. "Then stop being so bloody high-handed."

"Mélanie, the least you can do is trust me when I say it's unimportant—"

"Goddamnit, Charles." Her face was inches from his. "Don't you dare try to tell me that anything is unimportant that may have the smallest chance of having anything to do with why Colin's been taken or with this damned ring that's the key to getting him back. You have no right to make that sort of decision for yourself."

His gaze locked with hers. His face was like a thing carved

from alabaster in the firelight. "Velasquez hates me. He has a right to hate me."

She held his gaze with her own. "Why?"

He released his breath, a sound harsher than when Geoffrey was digging the bullet out of leg. "Because I murdered his cousin."

Chapter 18

*M*élanie slackened her grip on Charles's shoulders and drew back.

Edgar stared down at his brother. "Charles, for God's sake, what are you talking about?"

"She has a point, Edgar." Charles kept his gaze on Mélanie. "Husbands and wives shouldn't have secrets from each other."

That last was a challenge. Mélanie took him up on it. "No, they shouldn't." She dropped back into her chair. "At least once the truth is out, it can be faced."

"An interesting way of putting it." They regarded each other for a moment. The day's revelations thrummed in the air between them, like pistol shots echoing across the green after a duel.

Edgar sat down on a cushioned bench between them. "Charles, I may not know your secrets as I did when we were boys, but I'd stake my life on it that you didn't murder anyone."

"There we're in agreement," Mélanie said. She leaned back

against the carved mahogany slats of the chair. "Charles? With-out the melodrama?"

"She's dead," Charles said. "If it wasn't for me she wouldn't be. You could call that murder."

Quiet settled over the library, an uneasy quiet that precedes a storm. The tension of words as yet unvoiced pressed against the oak wainscot. "Who?" Mélanie asked.

"Kitty—Katelina Ashford."

Edgar sucked in his breath. "Charles—" He looked at his brother, as though Charles was a man pushing himself beyond the limits of his endurance. "Are you sure you want to tell us this?"

"Not in the least, but I don't see an alternative."

"Kitty Ashford?" Mélanie sifted through her memories, try-ing to find an image to go with the half-remembered name. Her first days in Lisbon. A party at the embassy. Two officers' wives whispering behind the ivory sticks of their fans. "She was a Spanish noblewoman married to an English officer. She died. Not long before I came to Lisbon. Some sort of accident. I for-got she was Velasquez's cousin. So that means she was connected to Carevalo, too?"

"Aristocratic families are as intermarried in Spain as they are here. Kitty and Victor's grandmother was a Carevalo daughter who married a Velasquez. Their daughter was Kitty's mother and their son was Victor's father." Charles's voice sounded dis-tanced, as though he was speaking about events that had little meaning for him. Charles only spoke like that when his feelings were very near to the surface indeed. "Kitty and Velasquez were close as children. I think he was half in love with her. It's not sur-prising. She was quite lovely."

His voice had an odd quality to it as he said this last. For a moment his gaze was somewhere beyond the confines of the library. It occurred to Mélanie that she had never, in the seven years she had known him, heard him describe another woman as lovely. The word lingered in the air, with echoes that went beyond mere physical beauty. Her fingers closed on the *gros de Naples* folds of her gown. "She met her husband during the war?"

Charles's gaze moved over the mantel as though he could not bear to keep still—the invitations she'd stuck into the gilt frame of the chimney glass, the wax tapers burning in the silver candlesticks, the Meissen tinderbox they'd brought back from Vienna. "Edward Ashford went to Spain with Sir John Moore in '08. He and Kitty were betrothed before Corunna and married a few months later. Kitty stayed in Lisbon. I think she would have been happier following the drum, but Ashford was the sort who believed women—wives, at least—are meant to be sheltered. And I think he liked being free to pursue Spanish girls on the campaign."

Mélanie folded her hands. She could see where the story was going. Or where with most men one would think it was going. It did not fit what she knew of her husband. What she thought she knew. "Go on."

"We met at a party at the embassy in Christmas of '09. I'd taken refuge in the library."

"What a surprise," Mélanie murmured.

He smiled, a faint lift of his mouth that didn't reach his eyes. "Not really. The surprise was that Kitty slipped into the room, claimed she was bored to tears, and asked if I minded if she joined me."

"And?"

"We played chess. She won."

No wonder she had caught Charles's interest. Mélanie's gaze flickered toward the table that held the chess game she and Charles had begun—was it only yesterday? Charles had had her in check when they left off, though she'd seen a way out of it. She could imagine the scene at that Christmas party in 1809. She knew the library in the British embassy well—she'd gone into the room often enough in search of her errant husband at some embassy function. She could imagine Charles—a younger Charles, he would have been only twenty-two—shoulders sunk into one of the burgundy leather chairs, head bent over Adam Smith or John Donne or the latest London papers. She could imagine Kitty Ashford slipping into the room.

Unusual coloring for a Spaniard. The words of the officers' wives came back to her with sudden clarity. *Hair like honey and the prettiest green eyes.* Charles would have been startled at the interruption, embarrassed perhaps, and then—

"You were so delighted to find someone who could give you a good game that you began to play chess a great deal?" Mélanie said. The words came out sounding more arch than she intended.

Charles looked into the fire, as though scenes from the past flickered between the griffons' heads on the andirons. "We played chess. She borrowed books from me. She convinced me to take her riding outside the city, places an officer's wife wouldn't normally go. Kit had a restless intellect and a rebellious streak. I think that was what had drawn her to Ashford in the first place. An English soldier was the most daring and adventurous husband she could choose. Or so it seemed. She couldn't have picked anyone more rigidly conventional than Ashford."

Mélanie willed her shoulders to relax. *Don't let yourself get locked into a pattern.* Raoul's cool, steady voice echoed unexpectedly in her head. *It can be fatal. Always be ready to shift the facts, to look at them in a new way.* She studied her husband, the tension about his mouth, the shadows round his eyes and in their depths. She forced herself to let her image of the man he had been when they met break apart in her mind. "The Ashfords' marriage was a disaster," she said. "To all intents and purposes it was over before you met Kitty. You wouldn't have let what seems to have happened between you happen if it had been otherwise."

His mouth twisted. "Two steps ahead of me as usual, Mel. You're right on both counts. Though it didn't . . . happen for some time. Oh, I'll admit that from the first I—"

"Wanted her," Mélanie said.

He looked into her eyes. "Crude but true."

"Dear God." Edgar pushed himself to his feet. "Mélanie, you shouldn't have to listen—"

"It's all right, Edgar. I know Charles wasn't a virgin when he married me."

Edgar regarded her with that puzzled expression he always wore when she said something particularly blunt.

Charles looked at his brother. "Did you know? About Kitty and me? I always wondered."

"Not then." Edgar ran his hand through his hair, the way Charles often did. "I wasn't in Lisbon much in those days. Though I was at that reception the night she—the night she had her accident. Christ, it was awful. But I had no idea that she was your— A few weeks later, I heard some gossip in the officers' mess." He drew a breath. Beneath the embarrassment, his face ached with regret. "I wish you could have confided in me, Charles."

"You think you could have saved me from my folly?"

"I wouldn't presume. But after she died—you shouldn't have had to bear your burdens alone."

Charles's gaze went bleak. "One could argue that that was the least I deserved."

Edgar turned away, as though he had glimpsed something he didn't want to face. He crossed to the table where the decanters were kept. "She'd have been a hard woman for any man to resist. She— Oh, God, Mélanie, I keep putting my foot in it."

Mélanie smiled at him over her shoulder. "I'd already heard her described as beautiful."

"There was a brightness about her." Edgar rejoined them, carrying a glass and the whisky decanter. He stared down at the cut glass, shot through by the light of the fire. "A sort of reckless brilliance."

"Yes." Charles spoke without looking at his brother. "She met life head-on instead of shying away from it. Which was why sitting cooped up with the other officers' wives in Lisbon was exactly the wrong place for her."

Edgar refilled Charles's and Mélanie's glasses, splashed whisky into a glass for himself, and returned to the bench.

Charles took a quick swallow of whisky, tented his fingers together, and said, as if reciting a date from a history book, "By early 1812 we were lovers."

Mélanie realized her hands were gripped tight in her lap. She knew Charles had had mistresses of course. Though he was no rake, he'd been far from inexperienced when they married. She'd never questioned him about those liaisons, but she'd always assumed he'd chosen women with whom there was no risk of emotional intimacy. He'd retreated into the safer realms of the intellect long before he reached adulthood. Detachment had been a survival mechanism, a way of coping with his father's cutting tongue and his mother's violent moods, and then later with his mother's death and his own estrangement from his brother. He hadn't let his guard down with anyone until he met Mélanie.

Or so she had always thought. So he had led her to believe. But there was no mistaking what lay beneath his bone-dry, factual statement. Despite the overlay of bitterness and pain, his face held an echo of what he had felt for Kitty Ashford. An echo not of lust but of an unbearable longing.

"There was no hope for it, of course." Charles spoke with the clinical detachment she had heard Geoffrey Blackwell use when he amputated a gangrenous limb. "I did try to convince her to run off to Italy with me, but she wouldn't leave her husband. Kit could rebel, but she took the family honor seriously. She told me once that her debt to her family went back generations. How could a love of a few months hope to compete?" He drew a breath. The wine-colored silk of his dressing gown shimmered in the firelight. "In April I was sent to retrieve some papers from Valencia. While I was gone, Kitty realized she was pregnant."

Edgar made a strangled sound. "Good God."

"Quite," Charles said.

Mélanie's nails pressed into her palms. She began to have a

sickening sense of where the story was headed. "Her husband was away as well?"

"Oh, yes. Ashford hadn't been home in two months and wasn't expected to return until after the campaigning season. Her options were not pleasant."

"Charles," Edgar said in a hoarse voice.

Charles glanced at his brother with something between defiance and apology. "It's an ugly story, Edgar. But it's got to be finished. I'm sorry for the associations."

Edgar made no reply. Rain pattered against the long library windows. Mélanie felt the heat of the fire, the hardness of the chair at her back, the dull ache of her wound. "Kitty's death wasn't an accident."

"No. She threw herself off a footbridge in the garden during a reception at the embassy."

The silence was broken by the sound of crystal shattering. Edgar's whisky glass had fallen from his fingers, hit the leg of the bench, and broken into shards on the chestnut and gold of the carpet. Without speaking, he got to his feet and strode from the room.

The pungent smell of whisky filled the air. Mélanie closed her eyes for a moment. "How do you know?"

"Velasquez. He was the only person in whom she'd confided about her predicament. When I returned to Lisbon, he came to see me, told me the truth of her death, and challenged me to a duel."

"You fought him?" Charles was a crack shot, but he abhorred dueling as an archaic way of settling differences.

"I fought him. At the time I rather hoped he'd put a bullet through me, but he was drunk and only grazed my arm. I deloped." He looked up at her with a gaze from which he had forced all emotion. "So you see, it wouldn't necessarily help if Victor Velasquez knew we want the ring to get Colin back. Kitty wasn't the only one who took the family honor seriously. I think Velasquez feels he has yet to avenge her. He might weigh Colin in the scale against the baby who died with Kitty."

Mélanie got to her feet and walked to the fireplace without knowing what she meant to do. She stared down into the fire, the leaping flame, the wrought-metal grate, the sticks of pine with their sweet, clean smell, redolent of her first memories of Britain when she came here as Charles's wife. With a few words, an illusion that had been at the heart of her marriage had shattered like the crystal of Edgar's glass. "You already did that," she said.

"Did what?"

"Weighed Colin in the scale against Kitty's baby." She turned, leaned against the mantel, looked at her husband, the father of her children. For a moment, she wondered if she'd ever really understood him at all. "It was only—what? seven months?—after Kitty died that you were sent after the ring. And you found me, a woman without protection, with a fatherless child on the way. I know you're not one to believe in fate, darling, but it must have seemed the perfect opportunity to make up for failing Kitty and your own baby."

He shook his head. "If you think that's why I asked you to marry me, you aren't as good a judge of character as I always thought."

"No?" She studied the face she knew so well, the eyes that mirrored so many of her memories. His head was tilted down in that way that gave him the unexpected look of a vulnerable schoolboy. It hit her, with the force of a blow, the full horror this would have been for Charles. Charles, who planned, who foresaw consequences, who seldom—if ever—let his passions rule his head, who took his responsibilities seriously, who loved his children without condition. "It wasn't your fault she killed herself, Charles."

"It was my fault she was pregnant."

"Both your faults. I assume the affair was mutual."

"Yes. It was that." Something shifted in his eyes. For a moment she realized he was speaking to her not as a woman who had betrayed him, not even as his wife, but as his closest friend. She hadn't thought he would ever speak to her in that way again.

He leaned forward. "But Kit had more to lose, so I was the one who should have been careful. Don't try to tell me I'm blameless, Mel. Not you, of all people."

"Of course you aren't blameless, darling. No one should bring children into the world without being in a position to care for them. I know that better than anyone. I also know it's far easier said than done. Once the mistake had been made, there were other options. She could have waited until you came back and told you about the baby."

"And given me the chance to do what pathetically little I might to help?"

"If she knew you at all, she must have realized you wouldn't abandon her. She could have gone to Italy with you. You could have taken her to Scotland. It wouldn't have been easy. You'd have been ostracized by polite society—or at least she would—but none of you would have starved and she and the child would have been sure of your love. That's more than most children have."

"Then my failure is all the greater. Perhaps if she'd had more faith in my love she would have waited."

"It was your baby, too. You deserved to know about it."

He held her gaze for a moment. "Did you tell O'Roarke about Colin?"

"Yes. But I told you first. I didn't realize I was pregnant until Blanca and I were in the mountains waiting to intercept you." She saw his face twist at the memory. "I wasn't trying to play on your sympathies that morning you found me being sick by the stream, darling. I swear it. I was honestly trying to decide what to do about the child I was carrying. I'd realized I wanted to keep the baby no matter what, you see. I wanted him, Charles. I didn't do it to trap you. Acquit me of that at least. I was shocked when you asked me to marry you."

"You hadn't bargained on the extent of my idiocy, I suppose."

"I didn't know your mistress had just killed herself while pregnant with your child. If I'd known that, not to mention that you had questions about your own paternity—"

"You think *that's* why I married you? To replay the farce of my own childhood?"

"No, but I think you were determined to be a better father to Colin than Kenneth Fraser was to you."

"That goes without saying. But it wasn't until later—after Father died—that I realized he probably wasn't my father at all."

"Darling, you'd wondered for years, perhaps without even admitting it to yourself."

"Perhaps." Charles glanced into the fire. "O'Roarke didn't want his child?"

"Raoul lived his life as though he might be killed at any moment. He still does. He couldn't afford to think about his own future, let alone a family."

"And he couldn't have married you in any case. Last I heard, he had a wife in Ireland."

"Yes, though they haven't lived together for years. He offered to send me to France and provide for me and the child. I couldn't—" She grimaced, a rank taste in her mouth. "I told myself I couldn't turn my back on my work and my comrades and my cause. But to be brutally honest, darling, I also couldn't bear the thought of being shunted off out of the fray. If I'd truly put Colin first, I suppose I'd have taken Raoul up on his offer. And yet Colin would have been immeasurably poorer, not having you for a father."

"But that wasn't why you agreed to be my wife." His fingers curled round the brocade arms of his chair. "You consulted with O'Roarke before you gave me an answer, didn't you? That's why it took you three days to decide."

"I couldn't very well have made such a decision without consulting him."

"No. I don't suppose you could." Anger leapt in his eyes. "How the devil did you think it would end? You couldn't have expected to stay married to me forever. You couldn't have wanted to."

She twisted her hands together, but she didn't let herself flinch from his gaze. "I'd scarcely known you a month when we were married. I knew you were a remarkable man, but I didn't understand in the least why you'd proposed to me. You didn't exactly wear your heart on your sleeve, dearest. You still don't. I thought your proposal was some sort of quixotic, chivalrous gesture. I didn't realize—"

"That I have feelings just like a normal person?"

"I didn't realize how deep your feelings ran. I didn't realize how completely you gave your loyalty. I didn't realize how much I could hurt you." She swallowed, remembering the quiet conviction in his voice as he spoke his wedding vows. It had been like a shock of cold fire, the realization that whyever he was marrying her, this man took those vows as a solemn promise. What she hadn't known until now was that that promise was more than half a debt he felt he owed to another woman. That the loyalty he gave to her was the loyalty that belonged to Kitty Ashford. "I'm not saying I'd have acted differently if I had known," she said. "I can't be sure. But when I agreed to be your wife, I hadn't the least idea what marriage meant to you." *Or to me.*

"And Colin?" Charles's voice was harsh. "What was supposed to happen to Colin when the marriage had served its purpose?"

Her fingers locked together. "I was used to thinking of immediate objectives and not giving much thought to the future. I hadn't yet realized one can't do that when one has children. But to the extent I considered the future at all—I thought I could walk away from the marriage and take Colin with me. Until I saw how much you loved Colin. And how much Colin loved you."

"And then?"

"Does it matter?"

"Yes."

"I was actually mad enough to tell Raoul that we'd made a horrible mistake and we had to tell you the truth. Raoul told me not to be a bloody idiot. He said if you knew the truth the marriage would certainly be over and I'd either have to leave and take Colin with me or give Colin up to you. Not to mention the fact that I might be arrested as a spy. He said if I really couldn't handle it any longer, he'd send Colin and me to France. I took that as a challenge. Like you, I don't care to admit there's any challenge I can't meet, dearest."

"And O'Roarke knew that challenging you was the best way to keep you at your post."

"Oh, yes, Raoul's fiendishly good at getting people to do what he wants. Besides, by then it was late 1813 and Wellington had pushed his way into France. Raoul asked me if I wanted to turn my back on the cause I'd worked for so long just when things were desperate." His voice echoed in her head, at once caustic and impassioned. She looked at Charles. "And the truth is, my darling, I didn't want to turn my back on it."

"So our farce of a marriage continued. A marriage born of your duplicity."

"And your guilt."

He started to protest. Then he looked away. When he spoke the words seemed to be dragged out of him. "Oh, Christ. Can we ever really be sure of why we do anything? I'd failed Kitty when she needed me most. If you're asking if I thought of that when I saw you in trouble, then of course I did. If you're asking if I thought of my own unborn child when I learned you were pregnant, then of course that's true as well. I told you the truth when I said I'd never expected to marry. I didn't think I'd be much of a prize as a husband, and my parents had given me a singularly low opinion of the institution. If it hadn't been for your predicament and my guilty conscience, I might never have found the courage to offer for you. But— I didn't need guilt or duty to make me want you for my wife or love your child."

Her fingers ached to smooth the shadows from his eyes. She wondered if she'd had this same urge to ease hurts before she was a mother. She couldn't remember. "I've tainted it for you, haven't I?" she said. "Whatever your reasons for marrying me, you gave your love to Colin freely, without condition. Now you feel as though I manipulated you into it. If you think everything between you and me was false, what does that do to what's between you and Colin?"

His eyes went cold. "I'd never," he said with precision, "let what's happened between you and me affect how I feel about Colin."

"But Colin's inextricably bound up in everything that's happened between us, from that moment you found me being sick by the stream. I didn't mean to use him to trap you, but I did drag him into the deception with me. That's probably the most unforgivable thing I've ever done."

He stared at her, his gaze steady, appraising. "If I'd known the truth," he said, "I'd never have let myself become Colin's father. But that doesn't change the fact that I *am* his father."

And he always would be. But what did that mean for their future life when he couldn't bear to live with Colin's mother?

The fire gusted behind her and let loose a puff of smoke that prickled her eyes. She unhooked the brass dustpan and broom from the stand beside the fireplace and stared down at the wreckage of the glass Edgar had dropped. "At least now that I know about Kitty, I have an idea of what went wrong between you and Edgar."

"What?" Charles turned his head.

"Why you aren't as close as you once were." She dropped down on the carpet. A jolt of pain reminded her of the wound in her side. She swept the sparkling shards of crystal into the dustpan. "It can't have been easy for him to learn you'd been the lover of the woman he loved himself."

In seven years, she could count the times she had taken her quick-witted husband completely by surprise. This was one of them. "My brother broke his share of hearts in the Peninsula," Charles said, "but he wasn't in love with Kit. He scarcely knew her."

"He may have loved her from afar, but there's no doubt he loved her." She stood and emptied the dustpan into the fire. The fragments of crystal sparkled diamond-bright in the flame. "Didn't you see his face when you were talking, darling? He couldn't even bear to hear the whole story."

"Of course he couldn't. A story about a woman killing herself cuts a bit too close to the bone. Not because he loved Kitty. Because her fate is rather too much like Mother's."

Which must have burned Charles all the more. Mélanie returned the broom and dustpan to their stand. "There is that, of course. But it was more than the painful associations that drove him from the room. You could see it in his eyes."

Charles picked up his whisky glass and stared at it. "I'd have noticed."

"Under normal circumstances I don't doubt it, but you can scarcely have been yourself at the time, dearest. You never talked to him about Kitty. And Edgar was away with his regiment most of the time in those days."

Charles tossed off the last of the whisky. "Even if it were true, whatever went wrong between Edgar and me started long before either of us met Kitty, when I was still at Oxford. When Mother died."

"Then perhaps what happened with Kitty merely made it worse."

He twisted his empty glass between his hands. She could see him turning the possibility over in his mind. Then he shook his head. "We've scarcely time to dwell on it at the moment. If this sordid story has convinced you there's no good to be had from talking to Velasquez, it's served its purpose. There's no point in discussing it further."

Mélanie hesitated, but instinct said she had pushed him as far as she could. She moved to the door. "Edgar must have forestalled Laura. I'll see if the food's ready."

Charles pulled his dressing gown closed at the neck. He looked more weary than she had ever seen him. "You're unfailingly practical."

She gave a bleak smile. "I'm a mother."

Colin shifted his position on the bed. His leg jerked. He sat up and disentangled the chain that ran from the metal cuff round his ankle to a similar cuff on the bedpost. It didn't hurt, really, except when he pulled on it. But it felt very undignified.

He'd managed to sleep when they first brought him here, once his heart stopped pounding so loud he could hear it. But now he felt as though he'd been sleeping for hours and he didn't think he could anymore, even if it was the only way to pass the time.

He hitched himself up against the thin pillow and kicked off the scratchy blanket. The air clogged his throat and tickled his nose. Maybe that was because of the dust motes dancing in the glow from the rush light beside the bed. The air had a sour smell, too, like his stuffed duck when he'd left it outside for days and it had got rained on.

He'd only been in a place like this once before, last year just before Christmas, when Mummy took him with her to give toys to children whose parents didn't have enough money to buy them presents. Some of the places they'd gone then had been even dirtier and damper than this, but Mummy had told him it wasn't polite to stare or make comments about people who were less fortunate than you were. He wasn't sure if that still applied if the people were holding you prisoner. He thought maybe it didn't.

A door opened and closed with a thud in the room outside. The man, Jack, coming back. Colin wondered if he'd brought food. They'd given him some bread and smelly cheese when he woke up, but he'd only been able to swallow a few mouthfuls.

"Christ, you took long enough." Meg's voice came from the other room. Colin squirmed against the pillow. He could see shadows on the wall through the crack in the door.

"I stopped at a tavern. Got to pass the time somehow. Didn't think there'd be another message since he told us to sit tight this morning. Turns out I was wrong."

"There was a message? Why didn't you say so to begin with? Let me see."

"Pipe down, woman, ten to one he's just telling us to be patient. There's no money with it. I checked."

Colin heard the sound of a paper being ripped open. "There's a card enclosed," Meg said. " 'Just in case you think I don't mean what I say.' What the bloody hell— The rest is in that damned code. Got a pencil?"

"What the hell would I be doing with a pencil?"

"What indeed? It's a bloody good thing for you I went to the parish school for a spell. His lordship wouldn't've hired us unless one of us could read. Here we are." The scratch of a pencil on paper followed.

"How's the brat been?" Jack asked.

"Quiet. Someone taught him manners. Christ, Jack, you've had one too many pints."

"You like me when I'm drunk."

"No, I don't. Damn it, Jack!" Meg gave a yelp of protest.

"Why not?" Jack said, in a funny, thick-sounding voice. "You must be bored out of your wits."

"Your breath smells like stout." A thud followed, as though Jack had fallen into a chair. "Anyway, the kid's right next door."

"So what?"

"You know I don't like having an audience."

"You turning into a mum?"

"Don't be stupid, Jack." Her voice was harsh, like sandpaper.

"Oh, hell, Meggie, I forgot about your own kid. I'm sorry."

She was quiet for so long Colin thought she wasn't going to answer. She drew in her breath with an odd sort of hitch, but when she spoke her voice sounded flat and ordinary. "I forget myself half the time."

They fell silent. Then the sound of the pencil on paper stopped. "Oh, Christ." Meg sounded as though she'd lost her breath for a moment. "God, he's a sick bastard."

"What?" Jack said.

She muttered something in a voice too low for Colin to hear. Jack let out a low whistle. "Not turning squeamish, are you?"

"Course not. But I don't see the point—"

"That's his lookout." Jack's heavy boots thudded on the floorboards. "Come on, let's get it done."

"I've a good mind not to."

"Don't be daft, Meg. He'd find out soon enough. We won't get the blunt we were promised, let alone more, if we turn soft. Get a move on, will you, woman?"

"This wasn't part of the agreement." Her voice faded, as though she'd crossed the room.

"Damn it, Meg, we do what it takes to finish the job, same as always."

"No!" Her voice bounced off the thin walls. Something in it sent a prickle of fear down Colin's back.

"Jesus." The boots thudded again. "I'll do it myself, then."

"Wait a minute, Jack." Meg's lighter footsteps hurried after him. "Hell. Bloody, bloody hell." She drew a rasping breath. "All right, if it's got to be done, let's make sure it's done proper-like. Do we have any more laudanum? No? Then where's the brandy?"

They appeared in the doorway a moment later. Jack had his hands behind his back, as though he was hiding something. Meg's gaze moved over Colin's face. She didn't look angry, but something in her eyes made Colin want to crawl under the bed. He would have, if it wasn't for the leg shackle. As it was, he inched back as far as he could against the spiky iron headboard.

Meg stood there for a long moment, long enough for his heart to start pounding again. Then she walked toward him. She had a bottle in her hand. She pulled out the cork. It had a strong, raw sort of smell. "Drink, brat. Bottoms up. Trust me, love, it'll make what's coming that much easier."

Colin took a sip and gagged. It didn't taste like the stuff they'd given him in the cart. It burned his throat like hot coals.

Meg tipped the bottle up and forced the rest down his throat. Then she looked over her shoulder at Jack. "Don't stand there with your mouth hanging open. Let's get the bleeding thing over with."

Chapter 19

"Colin is a sensible boy," Blanca said. "He'll know you and Mr. Fraser will come for him." She was doing up the strings on Mélanie's evening gown with trembling fingers that pulled at the silk.

"He's always had such faith in his parents. I hope—" Mélanie swallowed, her throat dry, the supper she had forced herself to eat roiling in her stomach. "I hope his faith proves warranted."

"Don't be foolish, Mélanie. You and Mr. Fraser are ten times more clever than Señor Carevalo. I never thought he had much wit for all his—how do you say it?—for all his swagger. Oh, *Dios*." This last was because one of the strings had snapped off in Blanca's hand.

Mélanie shut her mind to images of failure while Blanca stitched the string back onto the frock and finished doing up the ties. Ridiculous to be fussing with evening dress at this of all times. But though Mannerling's gaming hell might be raffish, proper attire would be expected. She had left Edgar downstairs in the library to help Charles dress, after the three of them and Laura Dudley had choked down mouthfuls of soup and coffee in uneasy silence. Edgar had made no further reference to Charles's revelations about Kitty Ashford or to his own abrupt exit. Mélanie doubted that he would have even had Laura not been present, but the memory of Charles's story had reverberated through the room nonetheless.

Blanca did up the last string and gave Mélanie's shoulders a quick squeeze, then picked up the curling tongs and plunged them into the chimney of the Agrand lamp. Mélanie sat at her dressing table and began to brush French rouge, ordered every month from the best parfumerie in Paris, onto her cheeks and lips. The actions were mechanical. Her thoughts were on the revelations in the library. How could she have lived with Charles, have been his wife, scarce seven months after Kitty Ashford's death and never caught a hint of his torment? She had known he battled his own demons, but she had put it down to his troubled relationship with his parents. Surely she should have been able to see it was something more recent.

She reached for her eye-blacking with fingers that were not quite steady. She'd never thought of herself as a romantic, but the truth was, she had fallen victim to her own fairy-tale version of what she had meant to Charles, as florid as any lending-library novel. She had let herself be seduced by the belief that he had opened his heart to her as he had to no one else before or since. She had deceived him, but she had thought that she knew every corner of his soul, that she had broken down every barrier, that he was wholly hers. She was well served for her folly.

The truth was that she was jealous. She had no right to Charles's love, but she was jealous of what he had felt for a woman who had been dead before she met him.

Her hand jerked, smearing the blacking beneath her eye. She wiped it away, more viciously than was necessary, dusted a light film of powder over her face and décolletage, and forced herself to sit still while Blanca set to work on her hair.

A memory shimmered in her mind, sweet as hedgerow brambleberries, painful as a knife beneath her nails. She and Charles had been married less than two years and were visiting the Fraser estate in Scotland for the first time before going to the peace congress in Vienna. The French had been driven out of Spain. Napoleon had abdicated and been sent to Elba, but already plans to help him escape were brewing. Once they got to the congress, she would be in the thick of the plotting, but on that trip to Scotland, far removed from the world of politics, she had shut her mind to all thoughts of intrigue and luxuriated in the simple pleasures of a holiday.

Charles had woken her and Colin early to give them their first sight of the beach. They walked side by side along the sand, Charles carrying Colin on his shoulders. Colin laughed with glee, as though he knew he was home. She took off her stockings and half-boots and let the sand squish round her toes. She could still remember the shimmer of the sun striking gray stone and clear blue water and ivory sand. A sight so intense it hurt.

The quote she'd had engraved on the watch she gave Charles their second Christmas together echoed in her mind.

My bounty is as boundless as the sea,
My love as deep; the more I give to thee,
The more I have, for both are infinite.

She'd chosen the quote because she knew he loved the sea. But until that moment on the beach she hadn't realized how much it meant to him.

Charles had been watching her watch the ocean. She turned her head and met his gaze. His eyes were steady, intent, a little questioning, more interested in gauging her reaction than imposing thoughts of his own. Something in his gaze pierced through the layers of lies and deceptions to an inner core she had almost forgotten existed. In that moment she realized that though he might not know her true name or any of the details of her life, he understood her as no one else ever had, not even

Raoul. In a world gone mad, he was a constant she would never doubt.

Too early seen unknown, and known too late! But she couldn't claim Juliet's girlish naïveté. She'd walked into this with her eyes open. And it wasn't his name she'd known too late, it was how she felt about him.

"Sorry." Blanca unwound a curl from the tongs. "Too hot?"

"No." Mélanie folded her hands in her lap. "It's me. I can't make my thoughts be still."

Blanca pinned another coil of hair high on the crown of Mélanie's head. "I know— Oh, the devil, as Addison would say, of course I don't know, not really, not until—unless—I have little ones of my own. I can only imagine—" She coaxed a last ringlet to fall over Mélanie's shoulder. "There. A bit wild, but that's the sort of place you're going."

"Just the thing for a gaming hell." Mélanie reached for her gloves.

Blanca set the curling tongs down on their stand and tidied the extra hairpins away in their porcelain box. Her lips trembled. "Oh, Mélanie, why can't I—"

Mélanie got to her feet and gripped Blanca's hands. "Waiting's the hardest part. But there's no sense in all of us going, and you need to be here to talk to Addison when he gets back."

Blanca nodded, straightened her shoulders, and handed Melanie her scarf and cloak.

Mélanie walked down the stairs, white gloves in hand, velvet cloak over her arm, skirt trailing behind her. On that first visit to Britain she'd been overwhelmed by the sheer scale on which Charles lived. She had always known that he was the grandson of a duke, that he was connected to half the British peerage, that he was the heir to estates in Scotland, England, and Ireland, a London town house, and an Italian villa. But in the relative simplicity of their lodgings in Lisbon—listening to Charles's disparaging comments on rank and inherited privilege—his heritage had seemed more an abstract concept than the reality of who he was. Seeing him on his ancestral estate, surrounded by servants and tenants who had known him since he was a boy, there was no ignoring the world he had been born into. Whatever causes he espoused, that world would always be a part of him.

She paused at the base of the stairs. Michael, who was on duty in the hall, went to open the library doors for her. She smiled at him and he smiled back, concerned, yet mindful of his place. The servants knew she and Charles were looking for Colin, but only Addison, Blanca, and Laura Dudley knew about Carevalo and the ring.

When she and Charles came to live in Britain after Waterloo, learning to manage a large household—several large households—had been a challenge in and of itself. For the first year, she'd had to bite her tongue to keep from apologizing to the servants for the charade of the roles society forced them all to play. Even today, she was sometimes brought up short by the realization of how her marriage to Charles had catapulted her neatly over an artificial and unconscionable social divide. Yet the longer one played a role, the more natural it became. She had grown all too comfortable with the privileges she had married into.

Because she had married Charles, her children had been born into that same world of privilege. Even now, thank God, Colin had the elite of British law enforcement searching for him. Most children were more likely to encounter Bow Street Runners because they were hauled before a magistrate. Only last month, Charles had had to use all his influence to intervene when their housemaid Morag's nine-year-old cousin was sentenced to transportation for stealing a lace cap and two silk handkerchiefs. And for all the horror Mélanie had seen in Spain, nothing had quite prepared her for the story she'd heard one evening round a London dinner table, an account of a little boy who'd been sent to the gallows by good British justice and had gone to his death screaming for his mother. The boy had been six. Colin's age.

Images of Colin and that unknown boy and her own sister chased themselves across her mind as she crossed the hall and stepped into the library. It was just past eleven, thirty maddening minutes more before they were to leave for Mannerling's. Charles was sitting by the fireplace once again, but he had shaved and changed into a black evening coat, a waistcoat of ivory silk brocade, and black trousers, rather than the knee breeches he would have worn on a more formal occasion. Charles had little interest in fashion in the general run of things, but he had a keen eye for detail when playing a part. He had even stuck a diamond pin, which he rarely wore, in the folds of his cravat.

He turned his head at her entrance. "Edgar went up to the nursery to sit with Laura, though I think it was an excuse to avoid my company. He could scarcely look me in the eye while he was helping me dress." Charles frowned into the shaving basin on the table beside him. "I can't believe he was in love with Kitty. I can't believe I wouldn't have seen it. But I can't deny the story unsettled him. Damn it, I shouldn't have—"

"You couldn't have avoided telling the story, Charles." Mélanie set her cloak and gloves over a chair back, then walked to the mantel and realigned the silver candlesticks. She couldn't bear to be still. "If he did love Kitty, the pain must be there all the time whether it's forced into the open or not."

"Edgar always tended to dally with women of the demi-monde or pay court to virginal debutantes. I wouldn't have thought Kitty—"

"Was in his usual style?" She rested her forehead against the chimney glass. The mirror felt cool against the pulse pounding in her brow. "We can't choose whom we fall in love with, Charles. Or when we fall in love with them." She turned from the mirror. "I remember the moment I knew I loved you. I couldn't believe I hadn't seen it sooner."

She expected him to turn her words aside, as he had every other time today when she'd claimed to love him. Instead he watched her with a steady gaze that neither accepted her statement nor gave it the lie. "When was this?"

"On our first visit to Scotland."

"And yet you went on working for O'Roarke for another year."

"Yes, I—" She moved away from the fireplace in three impatient strides. "Oh, God, what does it matter beside what's happening to Colin? The details don't change the picture."

"We can't do anything for Colin until we leave and we can't leave for another half hour. I hate the waiting as much as you do. Tell me."

She turned to him, fingers biting into the flesh of her arms. She'd trained herself so well never to speak of such things that it was difficult to find the words. "For the rest of that trip I was determined to stop spying. I even thought of telling you the truth."

"But—?"

"What could I have said? I married you because I was an enemy agent, but now I love you? You'd have laughed in my face."

"Probably. And then? When we went to the congress? You didn't stop spying."

"No." She turned and began to pace the carpet. The control that was second nature to her had cracked in pieces, leaving her throat raw, her voice unsteady. "Loving you didn't change what I believed in. When we got to Vienna for the Congress it was clear how things stood. Castlereagh—your Foreign Secretary, the man you worked for—wanted to turn the clock back on every reform made in Europe for thirty years. He and Metternich and most of the other men at the congress thought stability meant a world in which any dissent was stifled for fear of revolution. That isn't the world I want my children to grow up in."

"A world run by people like me."

"If you're going to define people by birth and fortune, yes. I don't think that's the future you want either, Charles."

"Very true. I argued the point with Castlereagh on more than one occasion."

"And where did it get you? What the hell's the use of a lone voice arguing a point over a glass of port?" She stopped and turned to face him, breathing hard. "I'm sorry, Charles. But—"

"You thought putting Napoleon back in power would get you further than quiet diplomacy."

"Yes." A single word that summed up endless hours of inner turmoil. "And so I went on doing what I could. At the congress, and after Napoleon escaped and returned to France, and then when we went to Brussels with the allied army."

"Where you watched Edgar and Fitzroy Somerset and the rest of our friends prepare to fight your countrymen at Waterloo."

"What do you want me to say? That I felt guilty every time I smiled at a fresh-faced young ensign? I did, as it happens, but I'd never have survived if I hadn't learned how to live with guilt long since. I had friends who fought on the French side who died as well."

To her surprise, Charles drew in his breath. "I wasn't thinking," he said. "Of course you would have." He pushed his fingers through his hair. "It was when we were in Brussels that you got so thin. I was afraid you were ill. I should have known—" He gave a mirthless smile. "That seems to be a dirge tonight, doesn't it?"

Her heart twisted because it was so like Charles, when he must be choked with anger, to try to push past that anger and understand what had happened and why. She could not find the words to explain what the days surrounding the Battle of Waterloo had been like. The fear, the hope, the despair, the sense that her divided loyalties would finally tear her in two. *Are you going to be all right,* querida? Raoul had asked a week before the battle. He'd been leaning against her carriage under cover of a seemingly chance meeting at a military review. She had just given him some information about troop movements gleaned from two careless young staff officers at her dinner table.

Afraid I'll crack? She could hear her brittle tones even now.

No, he'd replied. *I know you too well.* He'd gripped her hand where it lay on the carriage door, as though he could feel the sharp bones through the thread-net of her glove. *But I think you might break your health.*

But in truth, there'd been no time for any sort of breakdown, mental or physical. During the battle, their house in Brussels had been filled with wounded soldiers for whom just taking their next breath was a struggle. She had dressed wounds and mopped burning foreheads and closed the eyes of the dead, and all the while wondered how she and Charles could possibly go on, whatever the outcome of the battle.

Charles was watching her closely. "After Waterloo when we went to Paris—it can't have been easy for you."

She remembered the horror of seeing the city her father had loved, the cradle of revolution, occupied by foreign troops. She thought of the men like Marshal Ney, who had died in the White Terror as the French royalists wreaked vengeance on those who had been loyal to Napoleon. She remembered walking with Charles beneath the Porte Saint-Martin. Someone had tried to obliterate the inscription from the stone but she'd been able to make out the words *Liberté* and *Egalité*. The ideals of the revolution might have been twisted and trampled on, but those words could still fire her heart. The sight of them scraped from the stone had brought home to her, as nothing else had, what the loss at Waterloo meant.

"No," she said, "it wasn't easy. But I knew then that whatever I did in the future, I'd have to find a way to do it without deceiving you. I know I can't make you believe that, darling—"

"I believe that much." His gaze was still trained on her face. "Why?"

"Because it was in Paris after Waterloo that you told me you wanted to have another child. You weren't going to risk anything that tied you to me before then, were you?"

She looked into his clear gray eyes and thought of all the times she might have told him the truth. She wondered if anything would have been different if she had. "I was already tied to you in a hundred ways, darling. But I wasn't going to risk making the tie stronger, no."

"Until you decided your cause was lost."

"No cause is ever completely lost, Charles. I'll still fight for what I believe in. But I won't lie to you."

Charles stared at her as though he were trying to see beneath her skin. "And yet you thought you could spend the rest of your life playing a role."

"I wasn't playing a role. Not always. Not when I was with you."

"Damn it, of course you were." He leaned forward, gripping the arms of his chair. "You turned yourself into a pattern card of the perfect wife for Charles Fraser. *Didn't you?*"

"Of course not."

He gave her a withering look. "Everything was calculated to perfection from the moment we met. Did O'Roarke tell you I liked Shakespeare?"

"No. Yes. But I've been quoting Shakespeare since I was a child. I didn't put that on for your benefit."

"But you made yourself into the perfect political hostess for my benefit. The perfect house, the perfect parties, the perfectly run nursery—"

"Don't you dare, Charles. Don't you dare imply the children have anything to do with my playing a part."

"Even without the children, it's a brilliant performance. For God's sake, Mélanie, you were a revolutionary who was trying to turn the world upside down. This can't be the life you wanted."

"I'd look like a bloody hypocrite if I said it was, wouldn't I?" She tugged the sheer fabric of her scarf about her shoulders.

"I know you, Mel." He gave a brief laugh. "God, that's rich, isn't it? But I know you well enough to know that at times you must have been ready to scream with the longing to speak your mind. To box my ears and tell me what you really thought of me."

"Of course I wanted to box your ears at times, Charles. I'm your wife. And if memory serves, I tell you what I think of you quite often."

"But you could never talk freely. Not even to me. How could

you, when you had to pretend to be the daughter of a man who fled France because he opposed the same revolution you were actually trying to defend?"

"What do you want me to say?" The words were ripped from somewhere beneath the bright veneer she had learned to wear like a second skin. "Of course I hated not being able to speak my mind—when I wasn't buried so deeply in the part I was playing that I lost track of who I was entirely. Of course I sometimes think I'll go mad if I have to fuss over one more seating arrangement or pay one more round of calls or pour out one more damned pot of tea." She drew a breath. She hadn't realized until now just how maddening the incessant round of such activities could be.

Charles regarded her, arms folded across his chest. "I can't believe I didn't see it. I suppose I assumed you enjoyed such activities because it was the life you'd been brought up to. If I thought about it at all, which I have a lowering feeling I didn't. I was arrogant enough to think that the fact that I'd read Mary Wollstonecraft made me an egalitarian husband. I don't know what's more humiliating. The fact that all the time I thought our marriage was a model of equality and intellectual understanding, you were biting your tongue and catering to my every whim. Or the fact that I didn't realize you were doing it."

"I do a lot more than pour tea, Charles, in case you hadn't noticed."

"Acquit me of blindness, at least. You play the social game to perfection and you still manage to speak to reform societies and organize committees and write pamphlets. Not to mention writing half my speeches. That's the woman I fell—" He glanced away. "You were wrong. You didn't need to be some ideal of a perfect wife to hold me."

She settled the folds of her scarf over her elbows, searching for the right words. Speaking the unvarnished truth was like picking her way through a foreign tongue. "It's true, I tried to be what I thought you wanted in the beginning, because that was the way to succeed in my part and because that was the least I thought I owed you. But I'd never have stayed, I'd never have wanted to stay, if you'd wanted the sort of wife most men want. If I'd thought for one minute that all you cared about was having someone to plan your dinner parties and charm the opposition, if you hadn't believed in so many of the things I believe in, I'd never have been able to survive for seven years if I hadn't been able to be myself with you."

He looked at her for a long moment, his gaze dark and opaque. "My God, Mel. After seven years of lies, how can you have the least idea of whether or not you can be yourself with me? How can you know yourself at all?"

Her fingers clenched on the gauzy folds of her scarf. She stared back at him, unable to find an answer.

He reached for the walking stick that was leaning against his chair and pushed himself to his feet. "It's nearly eleven-thirty. Let's find Edgar."

Chapter 20

The street door of Mannerling's gaming hell was half open, spilling lamplight onto the rain-black steps, a sign that play was in progress within. Charles swung down from the hackney after Edgar and Mélanie, leaning on his walking stick.

"It looks as though we gave our watchers the slip," Mélanie said at his shoulder.

"Yes." They had taken three hackneys and traversed two back alleys to reach Mannerling's.

They went through the half-open outer door into a dank, narrow passageway. The lamplight revealed a second door at the end of the passage, solid oak, with a lighter patch in the middle that looked as if it might cover an eyehole. Edgar rapped at the door. A few moments later, the lighter piece of wood slid back. Wary eyes stared out at Edgar. After the first glance, the wariness eased a trifle. "It's Captain Fraser, isn't it?" The voice had a rough cast, like the scrape of the wood. The dark eyes peered beyond Edgar at Mélanie and Charles.

"Good evening, Simpson." Edgar spoke with easy familiarity, as though he had been to the club regularly rather than once or twice. "I've brought my brother with me this evening. And—ah—a lady of our acquaintance. They aren't Bow Street Runners in disguise, I promise you."

Simpson gave a grunt that might have been a chuckle and slid the eyehole shut. After a few more moments, a bolt rolled back and he pulled open the door.

They stepped into an entrance hall dominated by a large gilt mirror and a red and black carpet that was a good imitation of an Axminster. Voices and footsteps and the smell of tobacco and brandy came from the rooms opening off the hall and drifted down the stairs.

Simpson proved to be a barrel-chested man with graying hair. He wore an evening coat and a showy pin in his cravat, but judging by the breadth of his shoulders and the bend in his nose, Charles suspected he had once been quite at home in the boxing ring.

Simpson took Charles's and Edgar's greatcoats and hats with an impassive face, but when he lifted Mélanie's black velvet cloak from her shoulders, his eyes widened, like a pawnbroker who has stumbled upon a black pearl in a box of glass beads.

Mélanie was wearing a low-cut claret-colored silk that clung to her body. It was one of Charles's favorites of her gowns, but normally she wore it with pearls and a black lace mantilla. Tonight she had draped a spangled scarf over her elbows. The pendant he had given her for their first anniversary nestled in the hollow of her throat, the diamond at the center of the gold knotwork twinkling provocatively. Diamond earrings swung beside her cheeks, twining with loose tendrils of hair. More diamonds sparkled on her white-gloved wrists and the combs in her hair. She had applied her rouge and eye-blacking with a heavy hand and splashed on twice as much scent as usual.

Charles had an impulse to take off his coat and throw it

round his wife's shoulders. Not so much to protect her from the knowing appraisal in Simpson's eyes, as to protect her from the associations of their visit to the Gilded Lily and the horrors of a time before he had known her. Which was ironic, because any woman who had done what Mélanie admitted to doing in her years as a spy didn't need any sort of protection.

Edgar led the way up the gilt-railed staircase. They could hear the rattle of dice, the whir of a roulette wheel, the whiffle of cards being shuffled. Through one doorway a linen-covered table was visible with a supper buffet, through another the corner of a gleaming mahogany billiard table. A waiter passed by with a tray of glasses. Pipe and cigar smoke hung thick in the air.

They went into the largest of the rooms, which had a faro bank at one end and smaller tables for games such as whist and hazard and écarté scattered about. The walls were hung with a pale green paper that was textured to resemble watered silk. A handsome chandelier hung from the ceiling, though the glint of the wax tapers showed that the silver gilt was peeling to reveal the brass beneath. The mantel, beneath which a log fire blazed, was papier-mâché painted to give the appearance of Siena marble. The overall effect was of the clever illusion and slightly tawdry glamour of a stage set.

Edgar glanced round the room. "That's Julia Mannerling." He nodded toward an auburn-haired woman in a green velvet gown. She was moving about the room, stopping to speak to various members of the company and to murmur instructions to the waiters, very much as Mélanie would be doing if they were entertaining at home. "The man presiding over the faro bank is Ralph Seton, her current lover."

Seton was an angular, elegant young man with carefully combed light brown hair and an unexpected scar slashing across his cheek. "A soldier?" Charles asked.

Edgar nodded. "Sold out after Waterloo. Country squire's son. Went to Winchester, though he's not received in the best houses anymore."

"See anyone you know, darling?" Mélanie asked.

Charles scanned the throng at the gaming tables, which ranged from obvious cardsharps to a number of gentlemen who looked as if they'd just come from the House of Commons or an evening at the opera and more than a handful of ladies, though most of the latter would not be found in Mayfair drawing rooms. "No, but I couldn't swear there's no one who'll recognize us. I don't see any yellow waistcoats, either."

"The only ladies present definitely seem to be of a certain kind," Mélanie said. "What a good thing I dressed for the part."

Charles glanced at her for a moment. The glint in her eyes was as hard as the diamonds she wore. He cleared his throat. "Right. We're clear on the plan. Look sharp, troops."

They separated according to prior arrangement. Edgar went into another room to play roulette. Mélanie circulated about the various apartments. Charles sat down to play faro.

Ralph Seton greeted his arrival with a careless nod and a gaze that took in rather more than he let on. Charles played automatically, one eye peeled for yellow waistcoats. Waiters moved among the tables with bottles of claret and brandy. Someone sneezed, letting loose a cloud of snuff. Two of the men at the faro bank had their coats turned inside out for good luck, in imitation of Charles James Fox. Charles doubted it would do them any more good than it had done Fox. At a nearby écarté table a well-dressed young man of little more than one-and-twenty appeared to be doing his best to run through his entire fortune in the course of the night. A hot-eyed man in a thread-bare coat was frantically scribbling his vowels.

Charles had seen similar scenes in a half-dozen London clubs, not to mention the card rooms at just about any ball. Yet beneath the showy elegance, he could feel an uneasy edge to the atmosphere, like a piece of glass run along his skin. Gazes were sharper than one would expect of mere gamesters. He suspected a number of the gamers had knives and pistols hidden beneath their flashy coats.

He hadn't played cards much lately, but in Lisbon, cooped

up for the winter, they'd all whiled away hours with games of chance. Kitty's ghost hovered at the edge of his consciousness tonight. She had had quite a knack for faro and been quite brilliant at écarté. She'd liked the risk of it. He could see her bright eyes just beyond the green baize, hear her brittle laugh over the clatter of tokens, feel the texture of her honey-colored hair between his fingers as he calculated the odds of which card the dealer would turn up next.

He felt as though a scab had been stripped raw somewhere inside him, yet it had been a strange sort of relief to confide the story to Mélanie. She had given him, if not absolution, at least understanding. He hadn't realized how much he craved it.

Mélanie had claimed to know the moment she'd realized she loved him. He couldn't be sure he believed her—given how long she'd been playing a part, he wondered if she could be sure of what she felt at all or if she had merely begun to believe her own deception. On the other hand, while he had no doubt that he had loved her, he realized he could not pinpoint the moment he had first known it. He hadn't let himself think in those terms when he married her, nor for a long time afterwards.

He remembered watching her sleep the morning after their wedding, the dark tumble of her hair, the sleep-softened line of her profile, the curl of her hand against the sheet. He had felt as though he was standing on the edge of a cliff, exposed to the scouring of the wind and the rain. It had been easy enough to pledge his fidelity, his fortune, the protection of his name. But what else did marriage mean? In binding his life irrevocably to someone else's, had he also pledged a part of his soul? And was he capable of giving it even if he had?

In the end he had given it to her, of course, and much more besides. Though it was not until after his father's death that the last of the barriers had given way.

Mélanie's accusations this evening had had a kernel of truth. On some level, without ever articulating it, he had felt he was paying a debt to Kitty by doing what he could for Mélanie and her child. And Mélanie's other accusation? That he had been thinking of his own relationship with his father when he offered to raise another man's child?

The faro game ended and another began. Charles pulled in his tokens automatically. Gaming had been one of his father's passions. He had a clear image of Kenneth Fraser at a baize-covered table, a glass of brandy at his elbow, cards held negligently in his hand.

He recalled, with uncompromising clarity, a fragment of conversation overheard in the card room during one of his parents' evening parties. He'd been fourteen, paying a rare visit to his parents in London after winning a history prize at Harrow. *You must be proud of the boy,* one of the other cardplayers had said. And Charles had frozen, telling himself the answer didn't matter, even as a treacherous hope squeezed his chest.

Kenneth Fraser had glanced over at Charles, and Charles had been sure his father knew he could hear. For a moment there had been something sharp and deadly in his father's gaze. *Oh, my dear fellow,* Kenneth had said, turning back to his friend. *I know better than to take credit for any of my heir's achievements.*

Charles hadn't admitted it to himself at the time, but looking back now he knew that that was the first moment he'd questioned whether Kenneth Fraser truly was his father.

Charles smiled automatically at a joke one of the other gamers had made. Was Mélanie right? When he married her, had he wanted to prove it was possible to love another man's child as one's own? Had he seen a certain justice in leaving the inheritance that might not be rightfully his to a child who was not his by blood? Because in the world he had been born into, blood was the only thing that mattered in defining a son and heir. With one step, he had made a measure of atonement for failing Kitty and at the same time struck a blow against everything his father stood for.

He stared unseeing at the green baize before him, his thoughts like a slap to the face or a shock of icy rainwater. A few hours ago he would have said it was Mélanie who had entered their marriage under false pretenses. And yet in his own way he had been less than honest about his reasons for asking her to be his wife.

A moment later an unmistakable scent washed over him, and his wife draped herself over the back of his chair. "Nothing," she murmured into his ear. "Of course we're a bit early." She glanced at the mother-of-pearl counters lying on the green baize cloth by his elbow. "Pity you aren't fonder of games of chance, Charles. You could have made a second fortune." She squeezed his shoulder as though in flirtation. "I'm going to circulate again."

Her pendant swung against him. He remembered fastening it about her throat on their first anniversary. She'd been nursing Colin, then five months old. He turned his head and reached up to pull her closer, half for the illusion of dalliance, half so he could speak in a lower voice. "Be careful."

"I'm armed, remember?" She had a pistol in her beaded reticule. He had one in the pocket beneath his coattails.

"I say, Fraser," a voice called as Mélanie moved away.

Charles looked up to see a tall man with untidy brown hair making his way toward him.

Mélanie whisked herself off. Charles smiled and bowed to the inevitable. "Hullo, Bertie."

Bertram Vance, Viscount Tilbury, came to a stop beside Charles's chair. He was wearing an impeccably cut dark blue evening coat with an ash stain on one of the cuffs. "Must say, I wouldn't have expected to find you in a place like this." Bertram had always, from their days at Harrow, been superb at blundering into the middle of the wrong situation.

"Can't spend all my hours in Westminster," Charles said.

"Suppose not." Bertram pulled up a spare chair and glanced at Charles's winnings. "Doing rather well, aren't you? Makes sense. You always were damnably good at figures and such. Suppose that comes in handy at the table. Maybe it explains my rotten luck, now that I think of it. Is your game finished? Care to have a drink with me?"

Charles hesitated, but he could keep an eye out for yellow waistcoats as well in Bertram's company as at the faro bank, and it would keep Bertram from stumbling across Mélanie. He cashed in his winnings and they moved to a table against the wall.

Bertram signaled to a passing waiter. "What are you drinking? Whisky? Scotsman to the core, aren't you? Think I'll stick to brandy." He glanced round the room and spoke in a lowered voice. "I say, old boy, who was the dusky beauty you were talking to?"

Charles achieved a creditable look of embarrassment. "Oh, did you notice her?"

"Caught a glimpse out of the corner of my eye. Very fetching. But I must say I never thought—not one to judge, of course. But if I were married to your wife—"

Charles drummed his fingers on the tabletop. "If you were married to my wife, you'd understand very well."

Bertram's brows drew together. "That way, is it? Always took you two to be unfashionably devoted, for all you don't make a show of it."

Charles could just glimpse the flash of Mélanie's scarf through the archway into the supper room. Her back was safely to them for the moment. "Devotion can prove tiresome, Bertie." He sent a mental apology to Mélanie as he spoke. Then he swallowed a mouthful of whisky to wash the bite of self-derision from his tongue.

Bertram stared into the brandy the waiter had brought him. "Wouldn't know about that myself. Never tried it. Always rather wanted to, if I could find the right girl."

Through the archway, Charles glimpsed his wife again. She was leaning seductively on another man's arm. A dark-haired man wearing a yellow waistcoat.

Mélanie had caught the gleam of yellow satin across the crystal and candlelight of the supper room. He was sitting alone at a table in the corner. She threaded her way toward him, warding off the attentions of a portly man with claret on his breath who managed to get his hand beneath the neck of her gown. When she was a half-dozen feet away, she collided with a waiter carrying a tray with a decanter of port and a half-dozen glasses. The glasses clattered. The decanter sloshed. The waiter staggered and clutched the tray. Her foot caught in the hem of her gown.

An old trick, but it worked. The man in the yellow waistcoat sprang to his feet and steadied her. "Thank you," she said, making her voice go soft. She smiled up at him. He had coal-black hair that curled over his forehead and a face that retained a sort of youthful optimism, despite the lines of dissipation set into his features.

The man removed his hand, somewhat later than was necessary. "Always happy to oblige a lady. No damage to you? Or to your gown?"

"None, thanks to your quick thinking." She let her scarf slither lower on her arms.

"Good, good." He glared at the waiter. "Fetch the lady a glass of champagne, man. And a brandy for me." He held out a chair. "Won't you join me, Miss—?"

"West. Mary West."

He swept her a bow. "James Morningham, at your service."

Mélanie sank into the proffered chair at an angle that gave him a good view of her décolletage. "You're sure I'm not keeping you from the faro table or the roulette wheel?"

"On the contrary. There's more than one sort of game to be played at Mannerling's."

"You look like a man who knows his way round"—she paused, just long enough to offer a suggestive hint—"a gaming table."

"I've had some experience." His voice was suggestive as well, but his eyes had a friendly, likeable sort of glint.

She leaned forward, her arm resting on the table. All the old instincts came back, though it was a long time since she'd played this particular game. Or perhaps that wasn't true. She'd used much the same technique to charm a number of politicians and

foreign diplomats; she'd merely employed the tactics less bla-
tantly. "Do you come here often?" she asked.

"Fairly often." He seated himself and stretched his legs out
in front of him. "Shockingly shabby of your escort to neglect
you for the tables." He ran his gaze over her. "What can the man
be thinking of?"

Mélanie looked into his good-natured face and lied cheerfully. "Oh, no, I came alone."

Morningham leaned back in his chair and gave her a lazy
smile. "Did you now?"

The waiter returned with their drinks. Mélanie took advantage of the pause to study Morningham. His fine yellow waistcoat was snagged in spots and one of the buttons did not quite
match the others. His cravat was frayed about the edges, but the
linen was spotless and well starched. He carried a few pounds
more than were necessary, but the curling hair, the bright eyes,
and the playful smile had an undoubted appeal. Fifteen years ago
he must have been a very handsome man indeed. He fit Susan
Trevennen's description of Jemmy Moore to a nicety. One could
see why Helen Trevennen would have turned her back on her
father and Cornwall and run off to London with him. And one
could see why she would have decided he would never give her
what she wanted from life, and turned her back on him as well.

Out of the corner of her eye, Mélanie saw a tall, vaguely
familiar man talking to Charles. She shifted her chair so her face
wasn't visible through the archway. Perhaps it would be best to
question Morningham directly before someone recognized her.

"What brought you to Mannerling's?" Morningham asked.

Mélanie took a sip of champagne. Dry and yeasty and chilled
to perfection. Mannerling's didn't stint its guests. She smiled
over the rim of the glass. "To tell the truth, Mr. Morningham, I
was a bit duplicitous. I meant to seek you out."

"Oh?" He looked flattered, not suspicious. Poor man. It was
a wonder he'd lasted in the underworld as long as he had.

Mélanie pushed her glass round on the crisp linen of the

table. "I think you may know something about a friend of mine." She looked up at him from beneath her darkened lashes. "Helen Trevennen."

Morningham's eyes went wide. He cast a quick glance round, like a trapped animal. Before she had time to move, he sprang to his feet and ran full tilt across the room. A knot of people stood round the door to the hall. He veered round them—careening into a supper table and tipping plates of cold salmon and glasses of champagne into the occupants' laps—and ran through the archway to the room beyond.

If it hadn't been for the upturned table, Mélanie might have been able to catch him. By the time she'd waded through the wreckage, dodged the angry crowd, and made it to the archway, James Morningham was across the faro room at the door to the hall.

Charles was on his feet but was not, Mélanie was relieved to see, attempting to give chase.

Morningham pulled on the door, which seemed to be sticking. It opened with a wrench, but before he could bolt, there was a rushing sound, followed by a thud. Morningham fell to the ground. Charles lowered his arm in the completion of a throwing motion.

Morningham struggled to his feet just as Edgar came running through the door from the hall. He grabbed Morningham by the arm, but Morningham struck him a blow to the jaw that sent him careening into the open door. Edgar grabbed Morningham by the shoulders as he charged through the doorway, and the two men tumbled to the ground in the hall beyond.

Mrs. Mannerling's lover, Ralph Seton, jumped up from the faro table and ran for the door. Mélanie ran as well, ignoring shouts and cries and one or two hastily made bets on the nature of the altercation.

Ralph Seton got to the door first. By the time Mélanie reached the hall, Edgar and Morningham were on their feet grappling, both their noses streaming blood. Seton strode toward them, but before he could reach them, Edgar tightened his grip on Morningham, Morningham's feet slipped out from under him, and they both slammed into the balustrade. The slender gilded railing gave way, and Edgar and Morningham crashed down into the stairwell.

Chapter 21

The sound of wood splintering and metal snapping and bodies slamming into carpeted stairs echoed up to the gilded ceiling. Ralph Seton ran down the stairs, with Mélanie at his heels. Edgar and Morningham were sprawled on the steps, the wreckage of the balustrade strewn about them. Edgar had his hands round Morningham's throat. Morningham wrenched his elbow free and jabbed Edgar in the eye. Seton grasped the combatants by the backs of their coats and hauled them to their feet. The broken balustrade tumbled end over end to the floor below.

"You seem to have forgotten you're in a lady's house. No, don't try to run." Seton tightened his grip on Morningham. "If any accusations are going to be made, we want the air cleared here."

"Oh, please, Mr. Seton." Mélanie ran down the stairs. "I'm afraid I was the cause of the argument. Oh, Mr. Morningham, you're hurt." She flung her arms round him. The force of her action jerked him out of Seton's grip. He fell against the stair wall, held there by the press of her body. "I wouldn't try to leave, Mr. Moore," she murmured, her lips against his ear. "I have a pistol in my reticule and I never miss at this range."

The sound of a walking stick came from the landing above, followed by Charles's voice. "Edgar, what the devil are you—Mr. Seton, you must allow me to apologize for my brother. He's always been hotheaded." Charles walked down six steps to stand just above them and surveyed his brother with weary disgust.

"I'm not hotheaded." Edgar spoke in the aggrieved tone of a man who has downed one too many brandies. Mélanie had never realized how much he shared Charles's talent for playacting. He gestured toward Morningham. "He started it."

"I—" Morningham opened his mouth, then glanced at Mélanie and closed it.

"What's the trouble?" Julia Mannerling appeared at the head of the stairs, green velvet gown falling in regal folds round her, green eyes calm and serene.

"I'm sorry, Ju." Seton cast a wary glance from Morningham to Edgar. "I wish I could have stopped it before the damage to the stairs." He wiped at the blood that had spattered onto his own coat.

"Mrs. Mannerling, I take it?" Charles inclined his head. "I'm afraid my brother and his friend have had an unfortunate altercation. I will of course compensate you for the damage. I have some words to say to both of them. Perhaps there is someplace we could be private?"

Julia Mannerling ran her gaze over Charles. "I don't believe I—"

Charles smiled, the sort of melting smile he rarely employed but that invariably got results. "My name is Fraser. Charles Fraser."

"Ah, yes. And your brother is Captain Fraser, though he looks a bit worse for wear at the moment. Could someone give both those gentlemen handkerchiefs before we have blood all over the carpet?"

Edgar pulled a handkerchief from his pocket and pressed it to his bleeding nose. Mélanie tugged her handkerchief from her reticule and gave it to Morningham, keeping his body blocked with her own.

Julia Mannerling turned her gaze back to Charles. "Mr. Fraser, you look like a sensible man, but I have strict rules against brawling. Pray remove your brother and his friend."

Morningham edged his foot down the stairs. Mélanie flung her arms round him and cracked open the clasp on her reticule.

"I'll vouch for Fraser, Mrs. Mannerling." An untidy nut-brown head peered down from where the balustrade had been. Mélanie found herself looking into a familiar pair of hazel eyes. Lord Tilbury. She turned her face away, but there was nowhere to hide. He hadn't recognized her. Yet. "There's not a more honorable man in London," Tilbury said. "If he says he needs to talk to them here, he must have his reasons."

Mrs. Mannerling hesitated. Seton stepped forward, ready to push Edgar and Morningham down the stairs. Mélanie tightened her grip on Morningham. She could almost feel him debating the wisdom of making a run for it.

The silence was broken by Tilbury's quick intake of breath. "I say—Mrs. Fraser?"

"Hullo, Lord Tilbury." Still clinging to Morningham, Mélanie looked up and gave him the most ladylike smile she could muster.

"But—" Tilbury stared at her, then cast a glance round the room, as though trying to reconcile her with the setting.

"Don't ask," Mélanie told him. "You'd never believe the lengths Charles will go to for a wager."

"I say." Tilbury turned to Charles.

"Shocking, isn't it," Charles said.

Mrs. Mannerling burst into laughter. "Mr. Fraser, I believe you are the first gentleman ever to have brought his wife to my establishment." She looked from Charles to Mélanie for a moment. "Very well. If you are willing to break the rules of your world, I will break mine. There's a sitting room at the back of the hall. You may have the use of it for half an hour. If there is any more hint of disturbance, Ralph and Simpson will throw the lot of you from the house."

Mélanie turned to Mrs. Mannerling, still keeping her hold on Morningham. "Perhaps we could have some ice and towels? And a bottle of your best brandy?"

Mrs. Mannerling looked at her for a moment, woman to woman, a smile playing about her lips. "Very wise, Mrs. Fraser. I'll see to it. Ralph, could you show them to the sitting room? It's all right," she said to the crowd of spectators who had gathered on the landing. "The misunderstanding has been cleared up."

When Mélanie shifted her weight, Morningham gathered himself, as though to bolt, but Mélanie had eased her pistol out of her reticule. It was a small gun, which she could nearly hide within the palm of her hand. She pressed it against Morningham's side under cover of taking his arm. "Mr. Morningham? Shall we?"

Tilbury was lingering on the landing when they reached it. Charles clapped him on the shoulder. "Thank you, Bertie. I'll explain later, I really will." He hesitated a moment, then added, "It's more important than you can guess."

Tilbury nodded, with the air of one let in on a state secret. He suddenly looked less awkward and untidy than usual.

Ralph Seton led them down the hall, past a number of open doorways and interested gazes. Mélanie kept her arm tucked through Morningham's and the pistol pressed against his side. Edgar and Charles walked behind, guarding against flight.

Seton opened the door onto a small, surprisingly cheerful room hung with cherry-striped paper. There was a fire burning in the grate and a lamp lit on the Pembroke table. "Make yourselves comfortable," he said. He regarded them for a moment, as though he more than a little regretted not being in on the coming scene. Then he inclined his head and left the room.

Mélanie took a step away from Morningham as the door closed. Edgar released his breath. "Glad you finally saw sense, Moore. I half expected you to try to bolt again— Oh, I see." He noted the pistol in Mélanie's hand. "Wise man. She's a capital shot."

James Morningham—or, rather, Jemmy Moore—stood stock-still in the middle of the room, Mélanie's handkerchief pressed to his bleeding nose. His gaze darted from Edgar to Mélanie to Charles, who was leaning against the door panels. "Who the hell are you working for?" he said in a hoarse voice.

Mélanie lowered the pistol. "Mr. Morningham—Mr. Moore— we owe you an apology. Had I realized how my question would distress you I'd have phrased it differently and we all might have been spared a great deal of bother. Please sit down."

When he continued to stand motionless, she took him by the arm and steered him to a chintz-covered armchair. "No, don't tilt your head back, lean it forward, that stops a nosebleed faster." She set the pistol down on the table. "Trust me, I have cause to know, I have two children."

Jemmy Moore dropped his head in his hands, then winced as he touched his forehead. "Which one of you hit me? With what?"

"I did." Charles moved away from the door. "With a dice box. It was the nearest thing to hand. Sorry for the bruises. We weren't prepared for you to run." He walked to the table, leaned his hand on it, and stood looking down at Moore in the glow of the single lamp. "Miss Trevennen told you she'd be in danger if anyone knew where she was. Caring for her as you do, you took that very seriously."

"Yes, I—" Moore dropped his head forward as his nose started to drip blood again. "Don't suppose it would do much good now to say I've never heard of a Helen Trevennen?"

"None at all." Charles walked to the fireplace, took a brimstone match from a jasperware jar on the mantel, and held it to the fire. "I don't know what this lady told you, but her name is Mélanie Fraser, and she's my wife." He lit the tapers in the brass candlesticks on the mantel. "Our six-year-old son was taken from our house last night and we think Miss Trevennen may— quite unwittingly—hold the key to getting him back."

Moore gave a bark of laughter. "You expect me to believe a story like that?"

"Not really," Mélanie said. "That's why I didn't try it to begin with. But it happens to be the truth."

Moore looked at her for a moment, from an awkward angle, his head still tilted down. "It's mad."

"It most certainly is." Charles tossed the match into the fire and turned to face Moore. "And this madness could cost our son's life."

Moore swallowed. "But—"

He was interrupted by a scratching at the door, followed by the entrance of one of the waiters with a decanter of brandy, glasses, a champagne bucket full of ice, and plentiful towels. Charles poured the brandy. Mélanie supplied Edgar and Moore with ice wrapped in towels to apply to their various bruises.

"How do you know my name?" Moore asked, as Mélanie handed him the towel.

"Helen's sister Susan told us."

His mouth quirked. "Susy. I haven't seen her in years." He pressed the ice-filled towel to his forehead. "What do you really want with Nelly?"

Mélanie sank into one of the painted beech chairs clustered round the table. "What we've told you is true. We'd never invent something so fantastic." As quickly as possible, she sketched the story of the ring and why they believed it was in Helen Trevennen's possession.

Moore listened in patent disbelief, which changed to amazement and then, just possibly, to the faintest stirrings of acceptance. By the time she finished, he was slumped back in his chair. His nose had stopped bleeding, but he looked as if he had just received another blow to the face. "If that's true," he said at last, "it's monstrous. But—"

Mélanie leaned forward, hands spread palms-down on the table to still their trembling. "Mr. Moore, you're our last hope."

Moore sloshed the brandy in his glass. "I knew when I brought Nelly to London that I wouldn't be able to keep her to myself for long. Still, I thought there'd always be something between us . . ."

Charles had moved to a chair beside Mélanie. "Susan said her sister kept coming back to you."

"Every now and again."

"I can't believe she'd have left London without saying good-bye to you."

"Oh, she said good-bye. Nelly was good at saying good-bye. She came to see me the night before she left London. She said she had to go away, she was going to be all right—more than all right—but she couldn't come back. It wouldn't be safe. I didn't really believe her." He shook his head. "She'd always come back before."

"Did she say why she had to go away?" Charles asked.

"I assumed she was going off with a man. I didn't want to humiliate myself by asking. I half thought the secrecy was just Nelly giving herself airs. But there was a note in her voice— She was afraid of something, and Nelly didn't frighten easily. When the months went by and I didn't hear a word from her, I—I worried. It would take a lot to keep Nelly away from London."

Charles held Moore with the steadiness of his gaze. "And then you did hear?"

Moore released his breath in a long sigh of capitulation. "Four years ago. I had a letter. She said she was well and I mustn't worry about her, but that it still wasn't safe to tell me more."

Mélanie heard a gasp of relief and realized it came from Edgar. She drew a breath. Her necklace felt cold and hard round her throat. "Did she say where she was?"

"No. Nothing so specific."

"Did she mention friends?" Charles asked. "Landlords, employers?"

Moore shook his head. "She didn't mention anyone, by name or by implication."

"Activities?" Charles drilled him with his gaze. "The climate, the surroundings—"

Something flashed in Moore's eyes. He hesitated, then spoke

in a rush. "She said she was growing to like the sea air. And then she added that the Prince Regent's taste in architecture was as garish as one heard."

Mélanie looked at Charles. She felt as though a crushing weight had just been lifted from her chest. "The Pavilion. Brighton."

"Very likely." Moore took another swallow of brandy. "If Nelly did leave London, it's like her to pick somewhere stylish."

Mélanie took a piece of paper and a pencil from her reticule and began to sketch in quick, broad strokes. "Did she say anything else?"

Moore screwed up his face as though in an effort to remember. "That she might not be able to write again, but I should know she'd be thinking of me. That she"—he turned his head toward the fire—"that she treasured her memories of our time together." This last seemed to be a quote committed to memory. "Damned sentimental language for Nelly."

Charles picked up the decanter and refilled the glasses. "What sort of paper was the letter written on?"

"Paper?"

"Was it foolscap, pressed paper, scented—"

"Oh, I see what you mean." Moore closed his eyes. "Nice cream laid paper. Smelled like lavender. Not the sort of scent Nelly wore when I knew her. I suppose—that sounds as though she's doing rather well for herself, doesn't it?"

"Yes," Charles said. "It does."

Mélanie set down her pencil and pushed her sketch across the table to him. "Does that resemble Miss Trevennen at all?"

"Good lord." Moore stared at the sketch. "I thought you said you'd never met Nelly."

"I haven't. I based it on Susan Trevennen. Does it look like her?"

"Quite a bit. Her eyes are a trifle wider set and her mouth curls up a bit more. And—" His fingers drifted over the drawing. "Her brows arch more," he said, as though only just realizing it.

Mélanie pulled the paper back, smudged out some lines, redrew them, and returned the sketch to Moore.

He studied it for a long moment. "Yes, that's Nelly. To the life." His eyes misted. He put an impatient hand to his face. "Sorry. But it's rather nice to look upon her face again."

Edgar rested his head against the greasy squabs of the hackney. "Christ." His voice trembled, roughly equivalent to the way Mélanie's insides were behaving. "I didn't think we'd pull it off. I forgot you could throw like that, Charles."

"I've had a fair amount of practice of late." Tossing a ball to Colin, but Charles didn't add this last.

The cracked leather of the squabs creaked as Edgar turned his head. "I had no idea you had a talent for portraits of people you'd never met, Mélanie."

"Parlor tricks." Mélanie folded her hands round her reticule. The drawing was tucked safely inside along with her pistol. "Someone showed me once, a long time ago." She felt Charles looking at her. He would realize, as clearly as if she had said the name, that she was referring to Raoul O'Roarke.

"So we go to Brighton," Edgar said into the silence.

"As soon as we can pack." Charles's voice was matter-of-fact, conversational even, as though they hadn't just been pulled back from the yawning precipice of failure.

"Four years since Miss Trevennen wrote the letter to Moore." Edgar drew a breath. "You sound so confident."

Charles turned his head. "My dear Edgar." Mélanie could feel the force of the gaze her husband turned on his brother. "We can't afford to be anything else."

"I'm coming to Brighton with you. You need at least one person who isn't a member of the walking wounded."

Charles was silent for a moment. "You certainly won your spurs in that brawl tonight."

"Look, Charles, if you don't want me—"

"On the contrary." Charles's tone was warmer, the vocal equivalent of a hand clapped on the shoulder. "We'll be glad of your help. Addison can go to Surrey and talk to Mrs. Jennings."

They pulled up in Berkeley Square, paid off the hackney, and climbed the steps. "Nothing definite," Mélanie told Michael, who greeted them at the door, "but we have a promising lead. We're leaving for Brighton as soon as possible." She unfastened her cloak. "Ask Randall to ready the traveling chaise."

"I'll send word to the stable at once, madam." Michael lifted her cloak from her shoulders. "There's a parcel on the table that came for you while you were out." He gestured toward the console table beneath the hall mirror. A paper-wrapped parcel lay on its polished surface, beside the silver filigree basket for calling cards.

"Who brought it?" Charles asked.

"Scruffy-looking lad of no more than ten." Michael took Charles's hat and greatcoat. "He said a gentleman paid him a shilling to deliver it."

Mélanie walked to the table. Nothing was written on the parcel. It looked innocuous enough, yet she hesitated. Charles moved to her side, leaning on his stick. "Want me to open it?"

"No, I will." She tugged at the string wrapping. It got tangled, perhaps because her fingers weren't steady. Edgar gave her his penknife. She sliced through the string and it fell away. The paper rustled as she unwrapped it. Inside was a box, a plain wooden box, about four inches high and six deep.

A chill seemed to rise up from the marble floor and seep beneath the folds of her gown. She was vaguely conscious that Charles had moved closer to her. She opened the lid of the box, hands trembling.

Inside was her son's severed finger.

Chapter 22

Mélanie choked, turned her head, and vomited onto the scoured marble tiles.

Charles gripped his wife's shoulders. A sour taste clogged his own throat. He held Mélanie, one hand on her shoulder, the other wrapped round her waist, until the retching stopped. In his years in the Peninsula he had seen shattered skulls, entrails spilling onto the ground, heads cut from the body with the mouths still twitching and grimacing. Mélanie had seen as much. He had never known her to react like this, nor had he reacted so himself.

"My God." Edgar's voice came from behind him. "Are you sure—"

Mélanie wrenched herself away from Charles, wiped her hand across her mouth, turned back to the open box. "It's Colin's."

Charles forced himself to follow her gaze. The branch of

candles on the table cast all too much light on the contents of the box. It was a child's pinkie finger, severed just below the second knuckle. Beneath the smears of blood, the skin was pale and creamy. Like Mélanie's. Like Colin's. But— "Are you certain?" he said. His voice didn't sound like his own.

"It's the little finger of his right hand." Mélanie's voice was without expression. "There's a scratch by the second knuckle from where he fell down playing knights with Jessica yes—" Her voice caught as though she suddenly couldn't breathe. "Yesterday."

A cloud of rage darkened his vision. He ran his gaze over the box with deliberation. For the first time he noticed a white card tucked into the side. He picked it up by the corner. The writing on the card matched Carevalo's letter this morning.

Just in case you think I don't mean what I say.

He dropped the card on the table and snapped the lid of the box shut. "Michael. Go round to Mr. Roth at number Forty-two Wardour Street. If he's not at home, try the Bow Street Public Office. Ask him to come to Berkeley Square as soon as possible. Tell Randall to ready the traveling chaise. We'll leave for Brighton as soon as we've seen Roth. Is Addison back? Good. Have him and Blanca pack valises for Mrs. Fraser and me. Enough for a day or two. And tell Addison to pack some things for Captain Fraser as well." He put his hand on the back of Mélanie's neck. "Library."

"We'd better bring the box," she said in the same expressionless voice. "And the note. Roth should see them. Edgar, perhaps you could—"

"Yes, of course." Edgar reached for the box, paused for a moment, then gathered up both it and the card.

They walked the few steps to the library without speaking, Charles still with his hand on the back of Mélanie's neck. Inside the room, she pulled away from him and dropped down on the sofa, hugging her arms round her.

Edgar set the box and card on the table nearest the door and began to pace the carpet. "The bastard. The goddamned lily-livered, spineless, immoral—"

"Edgar." Charles tugged his handkerchief from his pocket and splashed it with water from the pitcher on the drinks table. "That's not helping."

"I don't think—" Mélanie spoke in a low, rough voice, her gaze on the carpet. "Part of me didn't believe he'd go through with it until now."

"Yes." Charles dropped down in front of her and wiped her face with the damp handkerchief.

She jerked away from him. "Charles, we can't—we don't have time to wait for Roth," she said, as though his words in the hall had only just registered with her.

"We can afford an hour." He sat back on his heels, ignoring the twinge in his leg. "Roth should know about this. It may affect the search for the people who are holding Colin. And we should tell him we're going to Brighton and what we've learned and how to reach us."

She retched again. She was shuddering, hunched over, as if fighting some private war with herself.

"Do you want some tea?" Charles said. "Or—"

"I'm all right, Charles." The words slapped against his skin. "I don't need cosseting. Colin does."

In two swift motions he was off the floor and on the sofa beside her. "Christ, Mel. You don't have to do this alone." He gathered her against him.

"Goddamnit, Charles, what are we doing?" She flung his arms off her and sprang to her feet. "We've been running round London all day sipping tea and swilling brandy and all the time Colin was—"

"Colin's alive. We're doing what we have to do to get him back. That's all that matters."

"We're not doing a very good job of it, are we?" She paced the length of the room, her hands pressed against her sides, as though she would either shatter from the force of her feelings or break her bones in the effort to contain them. "You can't control this, Charles. You can't think your way out of it. *Sacrebleu!* Those jagged cuts— He's always so brave about inoculations, but a knife—"

"He needs you, Mel."

"*Dios*, Charles, that's just the point." She whirled round, claret silk skirts snapping about her legs. Her eyes glittered with rage, but tears shimmered on her cheeks. "He needs us and we—"

Charles crossed to her side. "I need you."

The pain that filled her eyes was more than anyone should have to bear. "Don't, Charles." Her voice slashed at him. "Don't try to manage me."

"I'm not." He wrapped his arms round her stiff body. "I meant it."

For a moment she held herself rigid; then she made a choking sound and buried her face in his throat.

"I'm sorry," he said, his voice muffled by her hair. "I'm fussing over you because I can't fuss over Colin."

Her fingers gripped the cloth of his coat, tight with desperation. On the edge of his consciousness, he was aware of Edgar slipping from the room. He rested his chin on Mélanie's head. Her ribs shook. He could feel the bandage beneath her gown. Something jabbed him in the shoulder. Her pendant. His anniversary gift to her.

She felt the same in his arms tonight as she had yesterday. Every line and angle of her body was familiar. The scent of her skin, the silky texture of her hair, the hitch in her breathing as she struggled for self-command.

Marriage was supposed to endow one with knowledge of one's spouse, carnal and otherwise. So much about Mélanie was still alien to him, and yet he knew her in a host of ways. The exact amount of boiled milk she put in her coffee; the way she curled her fingers to hide the ink stains on her nails when she'd been at her writing desk; the precise chord in the "Moonlight Sonata" that always brought tears to her eyes.

Whatever else she had been, whatever she had done, whatever the reasons for their marriage, she was his wife. He knew now that she always would be, though he could not say with any certainty what those words meant for the shape of their future life.

"Why?" She spoke at last, her face still pressed into his cravat. "Why did he think he needed to do it?"

"To convince us he was in earnest." He smoothed her damp hair back from her temples. "It worked, too, damn his soul to hell."

"He—" She lifted her head to look at him. Her eye-blacking had smeared below her lashes. Beneath the stains were blue shadows of fear and exhaustion. "Charles, I've been deluding myself that we could fix this. That if we could only get Colin back we could somehow make everything right, at least for him. But we'll never be able to do that—to put everything back the way it was before."

He put his hand against the side of her face and stroked her cheek. "He can learn to live without a finger, Mel."

She shook her head. "That's going to be the least of the damage."

"Colin's tough. He can learn to live with the other hurts as well." He tucked her hair behind her ear. "You and I both did."

"Did we?" she said. He saw the scars of his own past reflected back at him in her gaze. "Haven't we faced the fact over and over today that we really haven't?"

Before he could answer, the door swung open. Edgar came back into the room, carrying a tea tray. "Nursery lessons never fade." His voice was as bright as the gleaming silver of the tea service. "When in a crisis, brew a pot of tea." He set the tray down on the library table and began to pour. "Oh, damn," he added in a different voice, as tea spattered into the saucer and sloshed onto the table. "I'm afraid my hands aren't very steady."

"None of ours are." Mélanie moved back to the sofa and peeled off her gloves.

Edgar pressed cups of sweet, scalding tea into both their

hands. The three of them sat in silence until Michael ushered Jeremy Roth into the room.

Charles got to his feet. "Thank you for coming, Roth. I know it's late."

Roth waved aside the apology. His coat was rumpled and his neckcloth looked even more hastily tied than usual. He scanned Charles's face, then looked at Mélanie. "What's happened?" His voice had a new sharpness.

"Carevalo decided to show us he meant business. He sent us that box on the table by the door. It—" Charles swallowed and found his throat raw. "Colin's finger is inside."

"His . . . Dear God." Roth snapped open the lid of the box, snapped it shut, and put his hand to his mouth. "I see a lot of horror in the course of my job," he said after a moment, "but . . . Not a pleasant man, this Carevalo."

"No." Charles gestured Roth to a chair. "But we already knew that."

Roth dropped into the chair and fixed his gaze on Mélanie. "Carevalo still has every reason to keep the boy alive."

Mélanie nodded. Her face had the set pallor of wax. "Unless we fail to produce the ring by Saturday. We have less than four days."

Roth didn't try to offer false reassurance, as he might have this morning. He was coming to know Mélanie. "True, I'm afraid." He accepted the cup of tea Edgar was holding out to him. "You've learned more?"

Charles returned to the sofa and told him of their visit to Susan Trevennen—glossing over the details of the gunshot, but mentioning his glimpse of Carevalo's royalist cousin Victor Velasquez—and then recounted the news they'd received from Jemmy Moore.

"Impressive." Roth scribbled in his notebook, then flipped to an earlier page. "We've made a bit of progress ourselves. One of my men brought me a report not two hours ago. Harry Rogers was in full view of half of St. Giles at the Pig and Whistle from nine o'clock last night until well into the morning. A man who sounds astonishingly like Bill Trelawny held up a mail coach on Hounslow Heath at eleven last night. That means the man Polly saw is probably Jack Evans or Stephen Watkins. We haven't been able to find any word of Watkins. Someone thinks they glimpsed Evans drinking in a tavern in Wapping earlier this afternoon."

Mélanie stirred her tea for the third time without drinking it. "Then it's most likely Watkins who has Colin?"

"Most likely, but it's possible Evans has your son and was foolish enough to go out in public. He may not realize we have a description of him. I've got a patrol making inquiries in the vicinity of the tavern." Roth reached for his cup and took a quick swallow of tea. "I'll get a description from your footman of the boy who brought the parcel, see if we can trace him and the man who gave it to him. Though if they have any brains at all, the parcel changed hands several times before it got here."

Charles tossed down a mouthful of tea. It had grown lukewarm, but it eased the rawness in his throat. "Michael said Addison's back, but we haven't talked to him yet."

"I have." Roth set down his cup without looking up from his notebook. The cup tilted at a precarious angle against the side of the saucer. "He stopped by Bow Street on his way home. He got no news of the ring from his inquiries with the jewelers, and neither did Miss Mendoza. He gave me a list of the places they visited. They're a very capable pair. I told Mr. Addison if they ever tire of working for you and Mrs. Fraser, I'd be happy to employ them. Two of my men talked with various fences this afternoon. Nothing there either."

"That doesn't prove she didn't sell the ring," Charles said, "but it does make it less likely."

Roth nodded. "Quite. We've had no luck so far tracing Carevalo himself. For such a gregarious man, he played his cards close to his chest. He had a number of acquaintances, but no friends intimate enough to have any idea where he might have gone to earth." He spun his pencil between his fingers. "This Victor Velasquez. You say you don't believe any good would come of talking to him?"

"None." Charles eased his right leg straight. It had begun to throb.

"I'll take your word for it. But there's no reason I can't have one of my lads keep an eye on him. Make sure he doesn't follow you to Brighton. Do you know where he lodges?"

"The Albany."

Roth jotted down a note, then looked up at them. "Miss Trevennen is no doubt living under an assumed name in Brighton. You have a plan for trying to trace her?"

Charles exchanged a look with Mélanie. They hadn't discussed it, but the solution was obvious. "Aunt Frances."

"Oh, God." Edgar, who had dropped his head into his hands, looked up with a groan.

"She's the logical choice." Mélanie sounded almost like herself again. "Lady Frances has ruled Brighton society for years," she said to Roth. "She knows everyone."

Charles got up and went to stir the fire, though it was blazing briskly. "She's also my mother's younger sister and my godmother. She has a sharp tongue, but she'll help. You can contact us at her house on the Steyne, though there'll always be someone here to relay messages."

Roth picked up his cup again and stared at it for a moment. The firelight shone through the porcelain, turning the ecru a molten orange. "Why do you think Miss Trevennen left London just after she got Jennings's letter and the ring?" He looked up at Mélanie with the glint of a chess player puzzling over a new gambit. "Coincidence?"

"I doubt it." Mélanie unfastened her heavy earrings and rubbed her earlobes. The jerky shimmer of the diamonds betrayed her shaking fingers. "I suspect she was blackmailing someone."

Charles replaced the poker and gave her a sharp look.

"Don't tell me you haven't thought of it, darling," she said.

"No, it occurred to me during our talk with Susan Trevennen." He rested his arm on the mantel. His hand closed on the marble, so hard that he felt the imprint of the carved oak leaves on his palm. "I'd have said something, but—"

"We got distracted."

"Here now." Edgar set down his teacup with a clatter. "Mind telling us mere mortals why this blackmail business is so obvious?"

Mélanie plucked at the spangled fabric of her scarf. "I wouldn't call it obvious. But if you think about it . . . She told Violet Goddard and Jemmy Moore that her fortune had been made but she'd be in danger if anyone knew where she was. That would make sense if she was blackmailing someone but was afraid of what might happen to her if that person found her."

"Well, yes—I suppose so." Edgar shook his head. "Couldn't Moore's first idea be right? That she was going off with a man—perhaps even eloping—and wanted to cut herself off from her past?"

"Possibly." Charles took a turn about the room, but movement couldn't hold at bay the images that kept tugging at his mind, images of his son under a stranger's knife. Had Colin screamed? He was a brave lad, but— "That doesn't explain why she ran off right after Jennings's death. If she'd found a wealthy lover or potential husband, I can't see her letting Jennings' stand in her way."

He stopped and stared down at the onyx and alabaster of the chess set. A single pawn stood between the white king and checkmate. His fingers clenched with the impulse to sweep the pieces onto the carpet. The screams of men suffering amputations in field hospitals echoed in his head. Had they drugged Colin, tied him— "The night she received Jennings's letter she told Violet Goddard that her fortune had been made. The next day she disappeared from the face of London. As Roth pointed out, it's a stretch for the timing to be coincidence."

Roth sat forward in his chair. "So the blackmail was based on something in Lieutenant Jennings's letter? I admit it's by far the neatest explanation. Any idea what that something might be?"

"None." Charles moved behind the sofa and drummed his fingers on the coffee-colored velvet.

"A military scandal?" Mélanie said. "Was there anything Jennings was involved in or might have known about? You knew him a bit, didn't you, Edgar?"

"We were nodding acquaintances. I wish— There were scandals enough among the officers. Duels that had to be hushed up. Liaisons with Spanish and Portuguese women." Edgar avoided so much as a flicker of a glance at Charles as he said this last. "Jennings could have learned someone's secrets, but I know of nothing definite."

Roth slumped back in his chair and frowned up at the heavily molded ribs of the ceiling. "If someone's been paying her to keep this secret for seven years, it must be something fairly explosive. She'd need some sort of proof. Love letters? Possible, I suppose."

"Perhaps Jennings stumbled upon a procurement fraud," Mélanie said, in the crisp voice she used when she was trying desperately to focus her mind. "There was a shocking amount of that sort of thing going on. Suppose Jennings found some incriminating papers?"

"Yes." Roth blew the steam from his cup. "Perhaps I'm a cynic, but I find it easier to imagine a man paying money for seven years to cover up fraud than to cover up a love affair." He sipped the tea. "Or suppose Jennings had uncovered proof that someone was involved in espionage?"

He said this last casually. Charles thought he meant it casually. Probably. Mélanie did not react with so much as the tremor of a finger.

"Fraud and espionage are both possibilities." Charles perched on the arm of the sofa beside his wife. "Jennings could have stumbled upon all sorts of secrets—his game with the ring certainly proves he was devious and had an eye for the main chance."

"Or suppose—" Mélanie broke off and stared up at him. Her face had gone white. "My God, we're sitting here speculating, while Colin—"

"We're speculating so we can get him back," Charles said. The words came out with a harsh rasp he hadn't intended. He had a sudden impulse to fling his Sèvres teacup into the fireplace, as though destroying something would ease the knot of frustration in his chest.

Roth's gaze moved from Charles to Mélanie, missing little. "Quite a pair, Jennings and Miss Trevennen. A gift for survival, though in the end it seems to have failed Jennings." Roth stared at the chewed end of his pencil. "I stopped at Raoul O'Roarke's hotel this afternoon, but he was out. You're sure he can't tell us more?"

"As sure as we can be," Charles said.

"Because from what you've described, the ring would benefit his cause as much as Carevalo's." Roth doodled on the blank page before him. "You think he'd cavil at using a child where Carevalo would not?"

"I don't know about that," Charles said. "But he knew I'd break his neck this morning if he didn't tell us the truth. More to the point, Carevalo would know it. He'd never have let O'Roarke meet us if O'Roarke had been able to betray him."

"Sound reasoning." Roth closed the notebook and looked up at Charles. His gaze was mild, pleasant, and as sharp as a knife. "So why did O'Roarke come to see you this morning so soon after you called on him?"

"My dear Roth, have you been having us followed?" Charles said.

"Hardly." Roth smiled, but the sharpness didn't leave his eyes. "I made some inquires about O'Roarke while I was at his hotel. One of the clerks heard him direct a hackney here an hour or so after you left the hotel this morning."

"Yes, he did." Mélanie's voice was the most normal it had been in the entire interview. "He wanted to assure us again that he would do whatever was in his power to help."

Roth leaned forward, hands between his knees. "Mr. Fraser. Mrs. Fraser. It would be redundant to say that this is a serious matter. Carevalo has made sure we know that. I've seen enough today to realize that you love your son as much as any parents could and that you know full well the jeopardy he's in. Is there anything you haven't told me?"

"I say, Roth," Edgar said, "that's a damned—"

"It's all right, Edgar. Roth's just doing his job thoroughly." Charles looked at Roth, aware of Mélanie's stillness beside him. "We'd have to be fools to hold anything back, Roth. Whatever else my wife and I are, neither of us is a fool."

Roth regarded him for a moment. "No. You certainly aren't that." He got to his feet. "I won't keep you. I know you're eager to be on your way to Brighton. Thank you for the tea."

At the door, he turned back, one hand resting against the polished panels. "I hope you realize how seriously I take this. No harm will come to your son if it is within my power to prevent it." He inclined his head and left the room.

Edgar shook his head. "What the devil was that about?"

"Roth questions everything." Charles got up from the sofa. "It's what makes him a good investigator."

"I suppose so. Still, to be questioning you, of all people— You *have* told him everything, haven't you?"

"As Charles said, we'd be fools not to." Mélanie picked up her gloves and earrings. "I'm going up to change."

Charles accompanied her upstairs. Addison and Blanca were both waiting in the bedchamber, with valises packed, traveling clothes laid out, and a multitude of questions that they heroically did not voice. But explanations were the very least they deserved, so while they helped him and Mélanie into traveling clothes, he and Mélanie recounted the most recent events.

Addison and Blanca listened without comment until it came to Colin's severed finger. At that, Addison went very white and dropped one of Charles's top boots, and Blanca launched into a tirade in furious Spanish.

"What do you want us to do?" Addison said at last, gripping Blanca's arm. "Make more inquiries about the ring?"

Charles shook his head. "I think we've done what we can. Go to Surrey and call on Mrs. Jennings. Find out if Victor Velasquez has been to see her and what if anything she knew about Helen Trevennen. And sound her out about any possible information her husband may have had that Miss Trevennen could be using for blackmail."

Addison and Blanca both nodded. They were standing side by side. For the first time, Charles noticed that their hands were clasped. Addison had been in Charles's employ since Charles was at Oxford, and in all those years, Blanca was his first serious love—or at least, the first Charles had known of. Addison still didn't know that the woman he loved had been in the employ of French Intelligence. Poor devil. For a moment, Charles found himself wishing that Addison and Blanca, at least, could be left free of this hell. But now that the truth was out, they could none of them hide from it.

Blanca and Addison took the luggage downstairs. Charles picked up his walking stick. "Do you think we can look in on Jessica without waking her?"

"Let's risk it." Mélanie picked up a pair of doeskin gloves from her dressing table. "He's right, you know, Charles."

"He?" Charles was at the door.

"Roth." Mélanie pulled on the gloves, tugging each finger smooth. "How can we justify keeping anything secret in the face of what's happening to Colin?"

Charles strode across the room, dropped the walking stick, and took her by the shoulders. "For God's sake, Mel, are you losing your grip? It would hardly help Colin if you and O'Roarke were hauled into Bow Street and questioned as foreign spies." He released her and took a step back. "They'd probably decide I was one, too. They'd never believe I could have been married to you for so long and not have known the truth."

Something flinched in the depths of her eyes. "If they thought that, they'd be woefully underestimating my abilities, darling."

"Or overestimating mine."

Mélanie picked up her bonnet by its gray silk ribbons. "You're right, of course. I was being silly. But Roth suspects something. And he doesn't strike me as a man who'll abandon his suspicions."

"Even if he could guess at the truth—which I doubt—I don't see how he could possibly prove it."

"Oh, darling, he wouldn't have to prove it. He'd just have to drop a word of his suspicions in the Home Secretary's ear. Can you imagine the kick-up? I don't—" She unwound the ribbons, which had twisted round her fingers. "I don't want your parliamentary career to be hurt, Charles."

"You might have thought of that before you started this farce. If you'd been caught during the war, we both could have been shot as spies."

Denial flashed in her eyes. "I'd never have let them accuse you."

"How? Do you imagine your word would have meant anything? You can control a lot, Mel, but you couldn't control that. It was an implicit risk from the moment you married me."

She swallowed, but she didn't try to deny it. She was too honest. "It was a risk," she admitted.

"But probably a small risk. Without proof, they'd have hesitated to execute the Duke of Rannoch's grandson as a spy. I'd never have been trusted again, of course. At best I'd have been branded a fool. At worst a man who destroyed his honor. One could make a good argument that both are true."

She shook her head. "The gentleman's code again. 'What is honor? A word.' "

"Words can have a lot of power."

"And they can mask the truth. My God, Charles, you know better than to think honor has any chance of surviving in the midst of a war. It gets drowned in blood in the first battle."

"One can still live by one's own code, even then. Especially then." He looked into her eyes, feeling the slash of her earlier accusations. "But I suppose you'd claim that my own actions in the war violated my code long before I met you."

"Only if you make that code so simple that everything's reduced to clear-cut choices," Mélanie said. "And you're not a man to do that. You see all sides of a question better than anyone I know. But ultimately you had to make a choice or let all your thoughts 'be nothing worth.' You had a loyalty to your country and your allies and that loyalty came first. So you swallowed your scruples and deceived people for the information they could give you, information which your side could turn against theirs."

"Are you saying I shouldn't have?" he demanded.

"I'm saying you didn't have any choice, given where your loyalty lay. Any more than I did."

"Damn it, Mélanie—"

"Tell me you don't know what it is to look into the eyes of the deceived and see trust, Charles. To draw innocent confidences from people, knowing all the while that you're going to use those confidences against them."

Her clear gaze cut through to a painful welter of memories. The family of *afrancesados* who had given him shelter and the boy with hero worship in his eyes. A Jesuit priest who had confided his hopes for Spain under Joseph Bonaparte to the disguised Charles and had quite unwittingly betrayed the disposition of the local French garrison. A young French sentry who had shared a flask of brandy with Charles and confessed his fear of battle, until the laudanum Charles had put into the brandy knocked him out, and Charles was able to steal the dispatches from his coat. "You're saying I forced others to betray their friends even as you forced me to betray mine?" he said.

"You picked up military secrets from drunken soldiers in taverns. You gave out false information about British troop movements. You stole documents from people whose trust you'd won. If the people you deceived knew how you used them, I expect they'd be just as sick with self-disgust at what they'd colluded in as you are at the things you confided to me."

The impulse to give the lie to everything she had said choked his throat, but he could not speak the words. She had thrown a glass up to his face. As ugly as the reflection was, he could not look away from it.

"So we're equally tainted by our actions?" he said. His voice was harsh, but he couldn't have said whether the anger was directed more at her or at himself.

"I don't think anyone could have emerged from the hell of the war untainted. But equally? Oh, no, my darling. In my case I deceived and betrayed the man to whom I'd sworn vows of fidelity, which makes the betrayal a hundredfold worse."

But did it change the nature of the betrayal? He looked into her eyes and found he could not answer his own question. Every qualm, every doubt, every twinge of guilt he'd ever felt, turned aside at the time by the exigencies of the moment, now echoed through his mind and senses.

Mélanie tugged at the stiff lace of her collar. "I suspect Roth's remark about Jennings stumbling across espionage was just a random shot, but I couldn't swear to it."

"Nor could I." He regarded her for a moment, his keen-eyed stranger of a wife. "Do you think it's possible?"

"That Helen Trevennen is blackmailing someone who was a French spy? Of course it's possible. I can vouch that it's not the sort of thing one likes to have bandied about." She stared at him. "*Sacrebleu!* Charles, did you think she was blackmailing me?"

He looked back at her without flinching. "At this point, nothing would surprise me."

She swallowed. "I deserved that. She wasn't blackmailing me. Any chance you'll believe me?"

He let his gaze move over her face. "Yes, as a matter of fact. Once you knew she had the ring, I think you'd have admitted the truth."

She released her breath, a faint, harsh scrape of sound. "Thank you."

Charles retrieved his walking stick which he'd leaned against her dressing table. "If not you, who else?"

"I didn't know the identity of every French agent in the British army, darling."

"Does O'Roarke know?"

"He'd know more than I do."

"Good. When we come back from Brighton I'll have a talk with him." He moved to the door. "Ready?"

They walked down the corridor and eased open the door of Jessica's room. She was curled up beneath her rose-patterned quilt. The cat, Berowne, had settled himself next to her on the pillow. Her cheek was pressed against his gray fur. Her left hand rested on the white spot on his stomach, as though she had fallen asleep stroking him.

Charles looked down at his daughter. Her porcelain skin, the short curve of her nose, the long lashes veiling her cheeks. The delicate fingers resting against the cat's fur. The rage he had held in check throughout the scenes in the library and bedchamber slammed against every cell of his body, like a storm striking the rocky Perthshire coast.

Mélanie bent down, smoothed the quilt, brushed her lips across Jessica's brow, touched her fingers to Berowne's head. Charles did the same, committing the moment to memory. Jessica's brow furrowed, then relaxed. Berowne purred softly. After a long moment, without looking at each other, he and Mélanie left the room.

"Charles." Mélanie stopped midway down the empty, candlelit corridor. Her gaze was fixed on a watercolor on the wall opposite. "If you want a divorce, I'll give you grounds as long as you don't keep the children from me. Or the cat."

The words were like a fistful of snow down his back. "When did I say I wanted a divorce?"

"You said you never wanted to see me again." She turned her head. The light from the candle sconces fell at a sharp angle across her drawn face. "The least I owe you is the right to start over again."

"Christ, Mel. After all you've been through, haven't you learned that we can't any of us start again? I may have been a fool to marry you, but I can't erase the past seven years." He looked at the watercolor, a painting Mélanie had done of the stream on their Perthshire estate. The cool grays and mossy greens always brought an ache of longing to his throat. "What were you proposing to do? Hire some half-pay officer to get caught in bed with you?"

She regarded him with that unblinking courage he knew so well. "If that's what it takes."

His hand clenched with the impulse to wipe that look from her face. "You may be willing to put the children through that. I'm not."

She swallowed. She was either too brave or not brave enough to leave it there. "Then—"

The image of the watercolor wavered before his eyes. He had a vivid memory of Mélanie picking her way over the mossy stones of the stream bank with Colin while he followed with Jessica on his shoulders. He looked into her eyes and said what he hadn't yet articulated even to himself. "I don't know if I can go on living with you, Mel. A marriage based on preserving appearances would drive us both mad. But if you think I'd keep you from the children, you know me even less than I knew you. Shall we go? The carriage awaits."

Chapter 23

Colin sat hunched against the iron headboard, his right hand cradled in his left. He wasn't sure how long he had sat thus, without moving. His right hand throbbed, as if it had been slammed in a door, only much, much worse. The bandage Meg had put over it was stiff with dried blood. The room had a sour smell. He'd been sick when they cut him. Meg had changed the sheets, but the smell wouldn't go away.

No one had ever hurt him before. Not on purpose. Well, Billy Lydgate had punched him in the arm once, but he'd been mad because Colin had eaten the last custard tart, so Colin could sort of understand it. Meg and Jack hadn't been mad. They'd stood there so calmly. Colin had been scared when Jack pulled out the knife, but even then he hadn't understood. When Meg held his hand down and Jack slashed the knife across his skin, he'd been so shocked he hadn't felt the pain. Not at first. Then it had hurt awfully.

He'd screamed and fought and kicked. Jack had held him down while Meg bandaged his hand. She'd kept saying she was sorry, that they'd had to do it. When someone said they were sorry, you were supposed to forgive them, but there must be a limit, mustn't there? Colin wasn't sure he'd ever be able to forgive Meg and Jack.

"Christ." Jack's voice came from the other room. It made Colin jump. "I'm going to the tavern."

"You bloody idiot," Meg said. "You'll get us caught."

"Better than watching you mope. You'd think you'd never seen a knife turned on anyone."

"Not on a kid, I haven't."

"Jesus." The wall shook as though Jack had struck it with his fist. Colin's heart leapt into his throat. "You think I liked hacking up the brat? Damned ugly work. But we knew it might come to worse than that when we started. Still could."

"It's different—"

"When the smell of blood gets up your nose?"

"When the kid's right there in front of you." The boards creaked as though Meg was pacing. "I always wondered how far I could go. Now I'm not bloody sure I want to find out."

"Look, Meggie—"

"Get out of here, before I hit you myself."

"Like to see you try."

"Don't tempt me."

The door slammed shut.

Colin retched again, but there was nothing left in his stomach to come out. The remnants of the brandy scratched his throat. His face screwed up as though he was crying, but no tears came. They seemed to be bottled up somewhere inside him. He was shaking, so badly he thought he'd fall into pieces. He curled into a ball and hugged his hand against his chest. A single word came from his throat, muffled by the pillow.

"Mummy."

The familiar low moan of distress jerked Charles from slumber. He sat up, reached for Mélanie, and tumbled onto a hard, swaying floor. He caught himself on one elbow. Pain shot through his leg. The vibration of wheels rumbled through the floorboards. The traveling chaise. Colin. Helen Trevennen. Brighton. He'd been sprawled on the backward-facing seat beside Edgar.

Mélanie moaned again, a quiet sound but one to which his senses had long been tuned. Moonlight slanted through the carriage windows. He could see the outline of her body twisting beneath the carriage rug on the seat opposite. In another minute, she'd awaken with a scream. He crawled across the floor, bumping his knee against the charcoal brazier. "Mel." He reached up and gripped her shoulder. "Sweetheart, you're dreaming."

She started and sat up, though he knew from experience that she wasn't awake yet. He pulled himself onto the seat and put his arm round her to keep her from falling. Her shoulders shook and her chest heaved. "Wake up, Mel." He put his mouth against her temple. Her forehead was damp with sweat. "I'm here. You're safe."

Her stillness told him that she had woken. He could almost hear the stifled scream that caught in her throat.

He slid his hand to the familiar place at the nape of her neck. The carriage jolted over the rutted road. Charcoal smoke from the brazier drifted through the damp air. Edgar snored softly on the seat opposite, but then his brother had always been able to sleep through anything. In boyhood Charles had had to resort to pitchers of cold water to wake him.

Mélanie sucked in deep drafts of air. "I'm sorry. I'm all right now." She started to pull away.

He wrapped his arms round her and sank back into the corner of the carriage. "It's bad." He peeled strands of sweat-soaked hair from her neck. "But not as bad as whatever you were dreaming."

She lifted her head. "Charles—"

"There's nothing we can do until we get there." He let his fingers drift through her hair, heedless of the pins. "Sleep if you can."

Her head fell into the hollow of his shoulder. He pulled the folds of his greatcoat round her and shifted his arm, settling her against him. It was a scene they had played out dozens of times, in their bed at home, in inns and lodgings and camps, even once or twice in carriages. He remembered the first time, in the Cantabrian Mountains, the night after the ambush. He hadn't known the warning signs then. He'd been wakened by a full-throated scream. He'd crawled across the rocky ground and gathered her terror-wracked body into his arms, feeling stiff and unsuited to such an action. He could still recall the desperation in the way her fingers had clenched his shirt.

He'd never asked her to describe the nightmares and she'd never talked about them. He'd thought he knew their substance well enough. Anyone who'd been through what Mélanie had been through had more than enough demons to face in the night.

Only she hadn't been through it, at least not what he'd thought she'd been through. The French soldiers who killed her parents and the bandits who attacked her and Blanca in the mountains had been merely part of her cover story, designed to rouse his chivalrous instincts. And yet he'd stake his life that the nightmares were real, all of them. In that small corner of their marriage, at least, she had not been pretending.

He kept sifting through what he had learned about her, as though if he could just put the pieces in the right order, he could find the key to deciphering who she was, this woman he had given himself to, this woman he'd believed he had known intimately. But whenever he thought he had begun to grasp the pattern, some new discovery would shake it to pieces.

He looked down at her, but the moon must have gone behind a cloud. He couldn't see her face. Instead he put his lips against her hair, and stared into the dark silence of the night.

He thought she slept again. He dozed off himself for a bit.

He came awake with a start as they pulled into the yard of the Star in Alfriston. Dawn was turning the inky sky a pale charcoal. The cobbled yard was congested—a mail coach, two post-chaises, three private carriages, and a farm cart laden with cabbages. Randall opened the carriage door and poked his head in. It would be a good half hour before a fresh team was ready.

Mélanie sat up, jabbed the pins into her hair, and reached for her bonnet. "We might as well go in. We need to tend to our cuts and bruises."

The timbered entrance hall was thronged with serving maids with jugs of hot water, post boys with tankards, and mail coach travelers gulping down mugs of milk and rum, but Mélanie had a way of drawing attention in a crowd. They were shown to a whitewashed parlor with a sturdy brick fireplace and a gateleg table, supplied with hot coffee, and promised a hearty breakfast as well as plentiful warm water.

Mélanie stripped off her gloves and untied the ribbons on her bonnet, then let out a groan. "*Sacrebleu!* My wits are deserting me. I forgot to ask them for some brandy or sherry to clean the cuts." She dropped her bonnet on a chair and hurried from the room.

Edgar went to pour himself a cup of coffee. "I never thought we'd find ourselves visiting Aunt Frances in the midst of all this. I expect she'll be as sharp-tongued as ever."

"I expect she will," Charles said. "But if there's news of Helen Trevennen to be found in Brighton, she'll make sure we find it." He moved to the fireplace. "Just ignore Aunt Frances when she tries to shock you. It's the most effective way to shut her up."

Edgar grimaced. He took a sip of coffee, then glanced at the door. "I say, is Mélanie all right? I thought I heard something in the carriage."

"She had a bad dream." Charles held his hands out to the fire. "Not surprising in the circumstances."

Edgar frowned into his coffee. "Is everything all right between the two of you?"

Charles turned his head to look his brother full in the face.

"Considering that our son is missing, hacked with a knife, and threatened with worse—oh, yes, Mélanie and I are right as rain."

Edgar met his gaze. "That isn't what I meant. It's just—I know I'm not good at reading such things and God knows we're none of us acting normally, but something seems—well—*different*—between you."

"What's happened to Colin makes everything different."

Edgar continued to look at him with a piercing gaze that held an unexpected echo of their mother in her rare moments of insight. "Perhaps I've no right to ask. But you do realize how lucky you are, don't you, Charles? What you and Mélanie have—" He shook his head. "When you were first married, I couldn't make sense of it. Half the time you don't even act as one expects lovers to act. But every so often I'll catch you looking at each other—just *looking*—and I feel like a voyeur for watching something so intimate. Most people never find what you and Mélanie have. And for those who do, it often doesn't last."

Charles stared into his brother's clear, unshadowed blue eyes. "Thank you, Edgar." He forced his voice to soften, though he could not quite keep the irony from it. "I'm well aware of my wife's worth."

Edgar set down his coffee cup and began to stir far more milk and sugar into it than he usually took. "I was convinced I was in love with Lydia when I married her. She was so lovely, so pure, so removed from all the horrors I'd seen in the war. So comfortingly sure of herself and her place in the world. She seemed to—well, to represent everything that was good about Britain."

"Everything you'd been fighting for?"

"I suppose so. Yes. And then I looked at you . . . I think I thought—I hoped—I could find what you and Mélanie have. Laughable, isn't it?"

"Not at all."

"It didn't last, of course. Or perhaps I only dreamed it into existence in the first place. We hadn't been married six months before I realized we hadn't two thoughts in common. What I thought was purity was coldness. What I thought was modesty was pride. Lydia decided it was time she was married and it suited her to be an officer's wife. I was almost irrelevant to the equation."

The puzzled frustration on Edgar's face and in his voice was all too familiar. When they were boys, when Edgar still confided in his elder brother, Edgar routinely spilled his heart out to Charles about some girl he was convinced was the embodiment of all womanly perfection. Invariably, he would prove to be seeing the object of his affections more as he wished her to be than as she really was. When the first flush of infatuation faded and he woke up to the fact that the girl didn't match his idealized image, he would fall out of love as quickly as he had fallen into it.

Was Mélanie right? Had Edgar ever put Kitty on a pedestal as he later had Lydia? Given the chance, would his chivalrous brother have taken Kitty to his bed, as Charles had done, or would he only have worshipped her from afar?

"Mother and Father didn't set the best example of wedded bliss," Charles said.

Edgar tensed at the mention of their parents. "That's not—"

"Mother was bored and miserable with her life and found attractive men the best distraction. Father was addicted to winning and seduction was his favorite game. If there was a moment when they didn't hate each other, it ended long before my earliest memories." Charles had the familiar sensation of looking at his parents through the wrong end of a telescope. A bitter taste like a mouthful of burned coffee scalded his throat. "I'm sorry, Edgar, it's not much of a heritage, but at least we survived after a fashion."

Edgar grimaced and turned back to the window. "It didn't exactly fit us for marriage, you mean? You've done well enough."

Charles bit back a shout of bitter laughter. He remembered his father's look of amazement on first meeting Mélanie. *My compliments, my boy*, he had said to Charles later, in the cool voice that rarely showed any emotion beyond boredom. *A diamond of the first water. I wouldn't have thought you had such taste. And she seems genuinely devoted to you. Though I understand from amateur theatricals that she's proved herself an excellent actress.*

Even Kenneth Fraser couldn't have known how devastatingly accurate his assessment had been. And yet, Charles realized, for all the deceptions, he had known Mélanie's strength and her courage and her intelligence from the first. One could argue that when they married he'd had a clearer image of the woman she was than Edgar had had of Lydia.

The opening of the door ended the silence that stretched between him and Edgar. Mélanie came into the room carrying a tray with a steaming bowl of water and a bottle of sherry. A serving maid followed, bearing a second tray laden with a nauseating amount of food.

"You two stay here," Edgar said when the maid had withdrawn. "I think I'll have something to eat in the coffee room."

"But . . . Oh, I see." Mélanie touched his arm. "Don't you think it's a little late to worry about my modesty? You can always turn your back when Charles changes the dressing."

Edgar hesitated, then gave a crooked grin and squeezed her hand. "It won't hurt for you to have a bit of time together."

"What was that about?" Mélanie asked when the door closed behind him.

"He's worried something's wrong between us."

"I told you he had flashes of perception."

"Yes, but why he had to pick this of all times to display them—" Charles passed a hand over his eyes. They ached, possibly from lack of sleep, though he suspected there were other reasons. "We'd been talking about our parents and about Lydia."

Mélanie began to unhook her pelisse. "Oh, dear. Not the most comfortable topics."

"No." He dropped his hand and blinked to recover his focus. "Edgar's always fallen in and out of love with great ease. But marriage is damnably irrevocable."

Mélanie's fingers stilled on the bands of ruby velvet that ran down the front of her pelisse. "Yes, it is, isn't it?"

He looked into her eyes. Wisps of dark hair clung to her cheeks and neck. Her high-standing velvet collar was crushed on one side where he'd held her in the carriage.

Mélanie returned his gaze, then shrugged out of the pelisse and laid it over a chair back. She opened her valise and took out a roll of lint. "Do we tend to your injuries first or mine?"

She changed the dressing on his wound first. Blood had seeped through the stitches and matted the dressing to his skin, which made the process of taking the bandage off tiresome and more than a little uncomfortable. But the blood, Mélanie reported as she cleaned the wound with sherry, was bright red, with no sign of infection.

Other than that, she said little as she fitted a fresh bandage over the stitches and fastened it in place. Neither of them referred to her nightmare nor to the mutilation Colin had suffered and the risk of infection their son ran if his own wound was not being tended to properly.

The cut in Mélanie's side was still raw and red, but there was no sign of swelling. She sat on the settle before the fire, her gaze on the flames, while he removed the bandage. And then, without looking at him, she broke the silence with a single word. "Lescaut."

He turned from the table, a length of lint in his hands. "What?"

"My real name. Mélanie Suzanne Lescaut."

Charles looked at his wife. Her profile was outlined against the firelight, stripped down to the essentials of flesh and bone. The features he could mold from memory, which could glow with innocence or sensuality or piercing intelligence. The smooth skin, the soft, ironic lips, the changeable eyes. "How did your father and sister die?" he said.

She turned to look at him. Her eyes had the turbulent emptiness of the sea after a storm.

"The nightmares weren't part of the deception," he said.

"No. The nightmares weren't part of the deception." She turned back to the fire. She had taken off her gown and chemise so he could tend to the wound. He'd draped a blanket round her, but her right shoulder was exposed, a bare, vulnerable curve. "I used to be able to control them," she said. "The nightmares. I only had them when I slept alone, or sometimes with Blanca or—"

"With O'Roarke."

"Yes." She pleated the rough blue wool of the blanket between her fingers. "I never had a nightmare when I was playing a role until that night in the mountains with you."

A few hours ago he might have said, *What a clever way to add to the deception.* Now he merely walked back to the settle, folded the lint into a pad, and placed it over the wound in her side.

She held the bandage in place while he fastened it with a length of lint bound round her ribs. "*Papá* was an actor—an actor-manager, though not nearly so grand as Kemble. He had a small troupe that traveled in the provinces on both sides of the French-Spanish border. He met *Mamá* when he was performing in Barcelona. Her parents were landowners—what you'd call 'country gentry' here. I never met them. They disowned her when she eloped with *Papá*—an actor, a Frenchman, and a Jew to boot." She looked up at him. "Do you remember the pearl cross Edgar and Lydia gave me last Christmas? That's why I don't like to wear it."

"Understandable." He knotted the lint and clipped off the ends.

"A silly sort of weakness. Just the sort of thing that betrays you, Raoul would say."

She stood, arms raised. He took a fresh chemise from her valise and dropped it over her head in place of the sweat-soaked one she'd been wearing. "Your father's favorite writer was Beaumarchais?" he said.

"Next to Shakespeare." Her head emerged from the folds of linen and lace. "How did you guess?"

"Suzanne."

She gave a brief smile. "I never got to play Figaro's Suzanne. *Papá* said I could when I was sixteen."

"I take it he was an ardent supporter of the revolution."

"Dear God, yes." She gave a dry laugh. "Poor word choice again. *Papá* didn't believe in God. I wish I could have seen him in the early days of the revolution. By the time I was born the Terror had begun and one couldn't be an idealist without a healthy dose of cynicism. Still, his beliefs never died. He passed his love of liberty on to me, along with his love of theater."

"Did your mother act as well?"

"She was back onstage a fortnight after I was born." Mélanie stepped into her gown and slid her arms into the long sleeves. "I'm not sure which she fell in love with first, *Papá* or the theater, but she was mad for both. They put me onstage before I could walk. I grew up traveling from town to town, falling asleep in dressing rooms, helping actors practice their lines, experimenting with greasepaint." She tugged the pale gray fabric over her shoulders. "It was a happy childhood."

"So that's how you learned Shakespeare backwards and forwards."

She dropped onto the settle. "I knew the plays in French and Spanish before I read the English. I was the changeling boy in *Midsummer Night's Dream* when I was three, one of the princes in the Tower when I was five, Ariel when I was ten. *Mamá* never got to see that. She died when Rosie was born."

"Rosie?" He stared down at the row of hooks and eyes on her gown. "Rosine?"

"Rosalind. I told you *Papá* liked Shakespeare even better than Beaumarchais. He wanted to call me Beatrice, but *Mamá* said it was too much of a mouthful for a child. They compromised on Mélanie. She convinced him it was after the Dark Lady of the Sonnets."

He fastened the first of the hooks, his gaze fixed on the flattened copper and the shiny gray fabric. "How much younger was Rosie?"

"Seven years."

"So you mothered her."

"In a sense." She fingered the bands of charcoal satin on her cuffs. "There were a great many people to take care of us, but not having a mother made us that much closer."

"It was much the same for Edgar and Gisèle and me. We had a mother, of course, but we often didn't see her for months at a time." He did up the last hook and straightened the narrow lace ruff at her throat. "Being the eldest takes on an added weight."

She bent her head, her gaze on her hands. "Colin reminds me of Rosie, more than Jessica. The dark hair, the pale skin, the strong brows. She had a stubborn streak. Colin and Jessica are easier to cope with. Or perhaps I'm the one who's improved." She leaned toward the fire, hands between her knees. "We were in Spain in December of 1808. I was playing Juliet for the first time."

Charles moved to the fireplace and looked at her vivid face. Despite the shadows round her eyes, a clear, fresh, heartbreaking sweetness shone through. She would have been an enchanting Juliet. "I'd give a great deal to have seen you."

Her mouth curved in a bleak smile. "I'm sure I didn't grasp all the nuances—though I felt terribly sophisticated—but people thought it a great novelty to have Juliet played by a girl who was almost as young as the character's meant to be."

Charles dug his shoulder into the pine mantel. The year 1808 had been the early days of the war in the Peninsula. The French, who had occupied the country, had been temporarily driven back by the Spanish resistance. Napoleon had come to Spain himself with reinforcements to retake the country. A British expeditionary force under Sir John Moore was supposed to be assisting the increasingly fragmented Spanish resistance, but Moore had been forced into an inglorious retreat to the coast by the victorious French. "Did your father have any idea how dangerous it was?"

"We were actors. There were people in the company who

supported both sides. He thought we'd be all right as long as we stayed out of the path of the various armies." Her fingers twisted in the delicate fabric of her skirt. "One of the company had family in a village not too far from Léon. We spent Christmas there. Sir John Moore's army came through the village on their retreat."

A knot of cold closed round Charles's throat. He'd heard stories of Moore's retreat. The British army had been angry at retreating without a proper fight, and the commissary could not keep them adequately provisioned. Discipline had almost completely collapsed. Pillage and wholesale slaughter had been visited on more than one Spanish village in their path.

"The house we were staying in was on the edge of the town square," Mélanie said. "It was afternoon. The people we were visiting had gone out. *Papá* and Rosie and I were alone in the house with two of the other actors. Rosie and I were fighting. She was pestering me to play dolls and I was trying to mend a rent in my costume. We heard horses' hooves and then screams from the square. *Papá* and the actors ran outside. He told us to hide, but I looked through the window." She drew a quick breath. "I saw the bullet that struck him. It went through his head."

Charles stared at her bent dark head for a moment, then walked to the table. He looked down at the flaky game pie, the wedge of Stilton, the congealing dish of eggs. A coppery taste welled up on his tongue. "And then?"

She didn't look at him. Her voice was level in a way that only came with a massive effort at control. " 'Liberty of bloody hand . . . With conscience wide as hell.' You've heard Edgar talk about what happened after Badajoz, darling. It was much the same, though on a smaller scale."

The blue and white dishes wavered before his eyes. After the siege of Badajoz, the British army had indulged in an orgy of plunder and rape and destruction. His brother's voice echoed in his head. *The things I saw men do, Charles. Men I knew. Good men. Honorable men. It was as if they were in the grip of a collective mad-*

ness. Even Wellington knew he couldn't stop it. And Sir John Moore had had far less control over his army than Wellington later did.

He poured a cup of coffee, filling the cup to an exact mark just below the lusterware rim. He carried the coffee over to her and put it in her hand, curling her fingers round the cup. She gulped down a sip and sat holding the cup between her hands like a talisman.

"They . . . well, you can imagine what they did to every female they could get their hands on. Four soldiers burst into the house where Rosie and I were hiding. There's no point in going into the details and I don't remember very much of it, which is a mercy, I suppose. The ceiling was white plaster with oak beams. One of the beams had a crack in it, and there was a cobweb in the corner. I don't think I'll ever forget the sight of that ceiling."

Charles's fingers curled inward, until his nails cut into his palms.

"It's difficult to separate the reality from my nightmares," she said. "At some point they dragged us outside. I remember crawling through the square afterwards looking for Rosie." A spasm crossed her face, swiftly subdued. "The smell of blood. It seemed to choke the air. The cobblestones were sticky with it."

He dropped down beside the settle. "Did you find Rosie?"

"Yes." She put the cup on the settle beside her. The coffee sloshed over the rim and dripped unheeded onto the floorboards. "They'd thrown her against some sacks in an alley. She was only eight years old. She—" For a moment Mélanie's voice cracked and her face crumpled. "I tried to stop the bleeding but it just kept coming. So much of it."

He took her hand and clasped it between his own. She didn't look at him, but her fingers tightened round his. "She wasn't unconscious at first. She looked at me as if I could make her better. Such trust. I kept telling her she was going to be all right. I could lie very convincingly, even then."

"Mel—"

"It's her face I usually see in the nightmares. Tonight her face kept changing into Colin's. She was only two years older than he is. Just a little girl."

He sat back on his heels, still holding her hand, and watched her in the cool predawn light and the warm glow of the fire. "So were you."

"No. By the end of that day I wasn't a child anymore."

He stroked his thumb over her fingers. For the moment, her story left no room in him for anything but tenderness. "It was my countrymen who did this."

Her shoulders curled inward, pulling at the seams of her gown. "It was war. I saw every side, every faction of every side, commit atrocities just as vile. And yet— I admit I still can't look at a British uniform without seeing my father with his brains spilling onto the cobblestones and my sister violated and bleeding to death. Without remembering how it felt to have my own body invaded and torn asunder. It was British soldiers who first taught me the meaning of fear and hatred."

He turned her wrist over. In the gap where a corded loop fastened the button on her cuff, he could see the corner of a scar, a scar that he had known was there but had never asked her about. He looked up at her, a question in his eyes.

She shook her head. "No, that was later. I was posing as a Spanish peasant girl to try to infiltrate a group of *guerrilleros*, but they saw through my ruse. They had some interesting ways of trying to get me to talk before Raoul managed to get me out."

Her words were calm. The images that went with them were not. Charles looked into the fire, contemplating the leap from orphaned fifteen-year-old to French agent. "What did you do after Rosie died?"

She picked up the coffee with her free hand and blew on the steam. "Half the people in the village were killed, and nearly all the houses burned to the ground. At least five of the theater company were killed. Two were too badly wounded to be moved. The rest fled. After the dead were buried, most of the villagers left to find shelter with friends or relations. A family who were going into the mountains took me with them as far as Léon. My parents had friends in the city. I found their house but it was empty. Later I learned that they'd fled to the north. The people I'd traveled with were already gone."

"And you were left alone in a strange city. A fifteen-year-old child."

A tremor ran through her. The firelight made bands of light and shadow out of the satin piping on her skirt. "I survived on the streets for a while. If you can call it surviving. I was lucky if I ate two days out of the week. I got passably good at picking pockets, but one day I was caught. My victim said I was too pretty for prison and he might be able to find me employment. I knew what he meant. To own the truth, I was relieved."

He looked down at the hand clasped in his, the smooth rounded nails, the delicate fingers, the porcelain skin that smelled of roses and vanilla. He thought of his own childhood. His parents had been only erratic presences, and tutors and governesses had come and gone with depressing regularity. But he and his brother and sister had taken it for granted that they would always have their rambling, centuries-old house to live in, with a fire and wax candles in the schoolroom in the bargain. Whatever emotional deprivations they had suffered, they had never questioned that ample meals would be set before them each day on the second-best Spode china. "Food and a roof over your head must have seemed a promise of heaven," he said.

"Yes." She tried to slide her hand out of his, but he kept hold of it. "It could have been worse," she said after a moment. "I think it was a bit cleaner than the Gilded Lily. But I'd been a better pickpocket than I was a whore. My acting skills had a tiresome tendency to desert me in the bedchamber. At least then. I was too young."

She fell silent, her gaze frozen, as though to look at him was too great a risk, even for her. He remembered his words that morning in the Cantabrian Mountains. *I'd like to kill them for you.* Even that seemed inadequate now.

He lifted her hand to his lips and held it there for a moment. She turned her gaze to him and read his thoughts as she so often did. "Many women face as much and more."

"Most of the world lives in squalor. That doesn't lessen the horror. Or it shouldn't." He laced his fingers through her own. "No wonder you jumped at the chance when O'Roarke found you."

"He was the first man in all the months I'd been in the brothel who looked at me like I was a person. It was amazingly seductive. He asked me questions about myself. He learned I'd been an actress. He talked to me about the war. After a few visits, he too offered me employment."

"A chance at vengeance."

"In part." Her brows drew together, sooty smudges against her parchment-white skin. "But it's too simple to reduce it to that. He gave me something to believe in beyond survival. He reminded me of Rousseau and Thomas Paine and William God-win—all the ideas I'd been raised on."

"He could hardly have turned you loose as a spy with noth-ing but Rousseau and Paine and Godwin to guide you."

"Hardly. He showed me how to wield a knife and fire a gun and pick a lock. He taught me to create a cover story and stick with it. He made sure I could manage the right accent to pass myself off as a native of any part of Spain or France. He drilled me on army ranks and court protocol." She paused a moment. "And after he took me out of the brothel, he didn't touch me again until I asked him to."

"If he cared a scrap for you, why the hell didn't he—"

"Send me off somewhere safe? I'd have gone mad, darling. I didn't want to be safe. I wanted to fight."

"You could have been killed."

"So could you, any number of times during the war." She

touched her fingers to his hair. "Raoul and I saw a chance to remake the world. You may disagree with our methods, but you of all people should agree that it needs remaking."

"Oh, yes. The question is, into what?"

She was silent for a moment. "My father never forgave Napoleon for crowning himself emperor. But when the French moved into Spain, he thought Joseph Bonaparte's regime offered all sorts of promise." She scanned his face with a familiar challenge. "Can you really claim Spain wouldn't be better off now if we'd won?"

"No. You've heard me say as much. And yet many Spaniards hated the monarchy but also wanted the French the hell out of their country."

"A palpable hit, dearest. Those same Spaniards were naïve enough to think Britain would support their bid for freedom when the French were gone."

"A far more palpable hit, wife." He realized, belatedly, what he had called her. He looked down at their intertwined hands. "That was what kept you going all those years? A dream of freedom?"

"Oh, no, darling." An edge hardened her voice. "I'm neither so naïve nor so saintly. Part of it was the pure love of the game— the challenge of a new gambit, the thrill of becoming another character, the sheer bloody exhilaration of being able to pull off a deception. You must have felt that yourself."

He started to voice a denial, then forced his mind back to his days in the Peninsula and later in Vienna and Brussels. He could taste the wine-sweet rush of triumph on his tongue even now. Triumph at passing himself off as a French staff officer, at breaking a code that was supposed to be unbreakable, at rescuing two of his men from a mud hut that was an excuse for a prison without a shot being fired. "Yes," he said. "Far more often than I'd like to admit."

Her gaze moved over his face, as though it was important that she make him understand. "You build up a shell. You become so caught up in the rules of the game that you quite lose track of the outer edges. You forget that you were playing the game for a reason. And then suddenly you remember and you wonder if that reason can survive when you've worn your own integrity to shreds."

He thought of her reasons for playing the game and wondered how his own held up in comparison. "Can it?" he said.

She shook her head. Her gaze at once held rueful regret and stark torment. "Oh, darling, if I knew the answer to that—"

They sat in silence. A curious peace had settled over the room, the peace of an unexpected, tentative balance. Still holding his wife's hand, Charles looked into the leaping flames and tried to recast their past yet again in the light of her revelations. Those revelations certainly made clearer the steps that had brought her to the moment she agreed to be his wife. Did they excuse her actions? Mélanie wouldn't thank him for saying so. He could almost hear her telling him not to dare deny her the free will to be responsible for her own actions. Beneath the dazzling charm, she was every bit as uncompromising as he was himself. And yet— With her words echoing in his head, he could not feel the anger he had before.

Her fingers stirred in his own. "Charles?"

"Yes?"

"Whatever happens, don't let Jessica be stifled. Give her an education, let her travel, give her an independent income. Make her as free as a woman can be."

The speech at first seemed a complete non sequitur. But in light of their whole conversation, perhaps it was not. "Of course." He squeezed her hand. "We've always agreed about that."

"If I'm not there." She stared at the smoke-blackened iron of the hob grate. "Promise."

The intensity in her voice shook him as much as her words. "I told you I wouldn't take the children away from you."

"Yes. But—"

He gripped her hand tightly, as though he could anchor both of them to safety. "Nothing's going to happen to you, Mel."

She turned her gaze to him. Her eyes held visions of a future he would not let himself contemplate. "You can't possibly know that, Charles. We were both almost killed today." Her voice turned low and urgent. *"Promise."*

A pain closed round his chest that was not rage but fear. He looked into her eyes and inclined his head. "I promise."

Chapter 24

Mélanie drew a steadying breath and forced her hands to unclench for the third time since she and Charles and Edgar had been shown into the blue parlor of Frances Dacre-Hammond's house in Brighton. Edgar was staring at the fire grate, as though if he looked hard enough he could find answers in the gleaming brass. Charles was pacing, his walking stick thudding against the Savonnerie carpet.

Her revelations to Charles in the inn parlor in Alfriston were a thing of the past. She felt the echoes sometimes when Charles's gaze rested upon her, but their world had shrunk to the next few hours and the task of finding Helen Trevennen.

They had been waiting for Lady Frances for a nerve-scraping ten minutes. It was just past nine-thirty on Wednesday morning—more than twenty-four hours since Colin's disappearance, less than four days until Carevalo's Saturday-night deadline. If Lady Frances could not help them, searching for Helen Trevennen in Brighton would indeed be like looking for a needle in a haystack.

Just when Mélanie was ready to run up to Lady Frances's boudoir and drag her husband's aunt downstairs, the door opened. Lady Frances swept into the room and surveyed them like a queen regarding a trio of upstarts who have invaded her audience chamber. As usual, she was dressed in shades of purple, in this case a morning dress of twilled lilac sarcenet that turned her eyes the same color. Her hair—which had only turned a brighter gold with the years—had been hastily dressed, but she wore a full suite of cameo jewelry.

"What on earth are you doing here?" she said in the low silk-velvet voice that could command the attention of every drawing room in London (and, rumor had it, had whispered across the pillows of half the cabinet, two royal dukes, and possibly the Prince of Wales). "The only one in the family who's up at such an ungodly hour is Chloe and she's at the park with her governess." Chloe was Lady Frances's youngest child, a girl of ten. "I know London has become horridly modern, but I wasn't aware that it was the custom to pay calls before noon there any more than it is here."

Charles moved forward, leaning on his walking stick, took her hand, and kissed her cheek. "Our apologies, Godmama. We wouldn't have come if it wasn't very serious indeed."

A smile broke across her angular features. "You haven't called me 'Godmama' since you were at Harrow. You must want something." She drew back and looked up at him. "Good God, Charles, what have you been doing to yourself? You look dreadful." She touched his cheek, an uncharacteristically maternal gesture. "You'd better tell me about it. I'm having chocolate sent in, since I didn't have a chance to finish my morning cup in my boudoir."

She walked forward, the folds of her gown clinging to the long line of her legs. "Mélanie, you're looking indecently beautiful as usual, despite the fact that you obviously haven't had enough sleep in the last twenty-four hours. You must be careful, my dear, even a complexion like yours needs tending. Edgar, I'm glad to see you in company with your brother." She sank down on a chair covered in cerulean blue satin, positioned so the light fell at a flattering angle across her face. "Now, tell me what's happened."

Charles returned to the settee. "It's about Colin," he said, and gave as concise an account of Colin's disappearance as was possible.

Each time, Mélanie found it harder to sit still while the story was told. Each time, the precious minutes spent going over already familiar ground grated more on her strained nerves. She forced herself to watch her husband's aunt as Charles spoke. Lady Frances's shrewd eyes went wide. Her face paled, so that despite the angle of the light, lines stood out against her carefully tended skin. She did not interrupt with questions, though a footman came in with a chocolate pot in the midst of the story. Lady Frances poured with hands that were not quite steady. When Charles finished, she sat in silence for a long moment. The rich, sweet aroma of chocolate and the musky scent of her perfume drifted through the air. Frances Dacre-Hammond had been privy to half the political secrets in London and had broken up more than one marriage, but Mélanie had never seen her so completely shocked.

"Good God." Lady Frances put her hand to her throat, fingering her necklace. The sunlight flickered over the carved alabaster of the cameos. "I met that man Carevalo. He came to Brighton on a visit two years ago. Emily Cowper introduced us. At a card party at the Assembly Rooms. He seemed—"

"Crude. Charming." A chill rang along Mélanie's skin at the memory of that charm, exercised on her herself so recently. "Amusing. Harmless." Her lips curled over the last word. She opened her reticule and took out the picture she'd drawn of Helen Trevennen. "Do you recognize this woman?"

Lady Frances held the sketch out at arm's length, frowned, and at last reached into the pocket of her skirt for a pair of gilt-rimmed spectacles. She hooked the delicate wires over her ears.

Her penciled brows drew into an unaccustomed frown. "There's something familiar about the face, though I can't quite place her. No, let me think." She held up a hand before any of them could voice their disappointment.

Charles sat perfectly still, one white-knuckled hand gripping the Grecian arm of the settee. "Someone you've seen here? Recently?"

"No, not recently. But I think it was here."

Mélanie wound the strap of her reticule through her shaking fingers. "Could you have seen her on the stage?"

"No. It was a social occasion, I'm sure of it. She was a lady. At least she lived like a lady, which is all any of us can say." Lady Frances lifted her cup and took a sip of chocolate, her gaze still on the picture. Mélanie swallowed a scream of frustration and suppressed the impulse to dash her own chocolate cup against the Chinese wallpaper.

"Thanks to the prince, the world flocks to Brighton these days," Lady Frances continued. "One sees people at the shops and the lending library and the Promenade without ever actually being introduced."

"Perhaps she altered her appearance when she came here." The steel links of the strap cut against Mélanie's hands. "Her hair or—"

"That's it." Lady Frances snapped her fingers. "Her hair was quite dark, even darker than yours, Mélanie. Very dramatic and well done—you couldn't tell it was dye. Not someone who moved in my set, but I must have seen her a handful of times."

Charles leaned forward. "Where?"

"Not the Old Ship or the Castle Inn or the Assembly Rooms. Somewhere outdoors. The Promenade? That doesn't quite seem right."

"She was fond of horse races," Charles said.

Lady Frances tapped her fingers against the picture. "Of course, the races. Excellent taste in clothes, dressed with propriety but never looked dowdy."

"What was her name?" Charles asked.

"I haven't the least idea, I'm afraid. I don't believe we were ever formally introduced."

Disappointment robbed Mélanie of speech for a moment. It was Charles who spoke. "When did you last see her?"

Lady Frances frowned and took another sip of chocolate. "The years have a way of running together. I do remember catching a glimpse of her when your cousin Cedric and Maria were paying their annual visit. One of the children was a baby. Ronald? No, I think it was Algernon, so that would make it four years ago. Cedric kept turning his field glasses her way. It was more life than I'd seen in him since he was a boy."

"She's not in Brighton anymore?" Charles said.

"I couldn't swear to having seen her since that time with Cedric and I know I haven't in the last year or two. People are always coming and going at Brighton."

She got to her feet with a decisive sweep of her skirts. "I fear I can tell you no more, but I believe I know someone who can. Give me ten minutes to make myself presentable." She swept from the room without waiting for an answer.

"Good God." Edgar broke the silence in a soft, low voice. "Miss Trevennen actually was here."

Mélanie unwound the strap of her reticule from her chafed hand and spread her sketch of Helen Trevennen out on the marquetry table beside the settee. "It sounds as though she lived in a rather different style here than she had in London." She took a pencil from her reticule and darkened Helen's hair.

Charles righted his chocolate cup, which was tilting toward the carpet. "The blackmail theory seems more and more likely."

Mélanie lifted her pencil and studied the drawing. "We may actually—"

"Yes." Charles was staring at a Turner seascape on the wall opposite. His voice shook with suppressed hope. "I know."

In two minutes less than the promised ten—Mélanie tracked the time on the Staffordshire mantel clock—Lady Frances returned to the room, swathed in a violet pelisse trimmed in sable, a violet satin bonnet adorned with ostrich feathers, and an enormous sable muff and tippet. Her crested amethyst barouche awaited them in the street below.

She didn't speak until they were settled in the silk damask interior. "Billy Hopkins," she said, twitching her skirt smooth. "Runs Lord Hodge's racing stable just outside of town. He knows all the comings and goings of the racing set. If anyone remembers this Helen Trevennen or whatever she was calling herself here, he will."

"You know him well?" Charles asked.

A smile played about her lips. "Well enough. I am confident he can be trusted."

Mélanie gripped the carriage strap to steady her nerves as much as her person. "Good. We can't afford any mistakes."

Lady Frances put a lilac-kid-gloved hand over Mélanie's own. "I know what you must be feeling, my dear. I confess I grow quite alarmed when Chloe catches a simple chill, and I worry over the older children far more than I'd ever admit to them. Even Cedric. He may grate on my nerves after a three-day visit, but he is still my son."

Mélanie looked beneath the ruched gauze brim of Lady Frances's bonnet and saw genuine sympathy in the cool eyes. "One's children always are," she said.

"Quite." Lady Frances nodded, then glanced across the carriage at Charles and Edgar. "It's a mystery to me how my sister managed to raise the pair of you, while I produced Cedric. He's entirely too like his father. That's what I get for giving my husband a legitimate heir."

Edgar flushed. "Aunt Frances—"

"Don't you turn into a prude too, boy. Anyone who knew Dacre-Hammond would be relieved to claim just about anyone else as a sire."

Mélanie met Charles's gaze without meaning to. His expression gave nothing away, but surely he could not help but think of Colin, who was his son in every way but the biological. And of his own father, who might not be his father at all. Mélanie wondered, not for the first time, if Lady Frances knew the truth of

Charles's parentage. She knew Charles would never be brought to ask his aunt.

Lady Frances settled her muff and reticule on the seat beside her. "A sense of humor is an invaluable asset. If your mother had been able to laugh at the world more she'd have had an easier time of it."

"Very true." Charles's voice was cool and level. "She took everything intensely."

"She was the cleverest child." Lady Frances traced a pattern in the mist-filmed window glass. "She could run rings about me when we did lessons—when she hadn't taken to her bed with one of her fits of the blue devils. Too much brains to know what to do with. Marrying your father was about the worst thing she could have done with herself. You must have realized that by now, you always were intelligent boys."

"It had occurred to me," Charles said.

Lady Frances studied them. "She'd be pleased to see the two of you working together. Do I gather that this unfortunate business has made you friends again?"

Edgar, who had been staring at his hands, looked up at her, robbed of speech.

"Aunt Frances," Charles said in a tightly clenched voice, "this is hardly the time—"

"On the contrary. We have another quarter hour before we get to the stables and silence will drive us all mad. I've been waiting for the right time since your mother died. If it hasn't come in the past thirteen years, I have no faith in it coming in the next."

"There are some matters," Charles said, "about which there is nothing to say."

"Perhaps." Lady Frances tucked a strand of gold hair beneath her bonnet. "This isn't one of them. I know Elizabeth wasn't the best of mothers—she was rather poorer at it than I am, and God knows I'm no prize—but she was always very proud of how close her two sons were."

"No doubt." Charles sat back and folded his arms across his chest. "It eased her conscience for not being close to us herself."

Edgar shot him a glance. "It's true," Charles said.

Lady Frances surveyed them like a governess searching for the right way to drive home the point of a lesson. "It's never easy to lose a parent, and it must have been particularly beastly for you to lose her as you did. But it's foolish and self-indulgent to let it govern your lives over a decade later. It isn't as though you saw her that much when she was alive, after all."

"Very true," Charles said.

Lady Frances was treading on ground that Mélanie had not dared explore in seven years of marriage. Mélanie studied her husband. His face was closed, but the tension about his mouth was one step short of an explosion.

"And it's sheer folly," Lady Frances continued, "to let Elizabeth's death interfere with what you have between you."

"Who says it did?" Edgar demanded.

"No one," said their aunt. "But I can't think what else went wrong between the pair of you. And it's plain something did."

Charles said nothing, a trick of his when he couldn't think of an appropriate retort.

Edgar rose to the bait. "Who says it's plain?"

Lady Frances lifted her brows. "Anyone with eyes in her head, boy." She gripped the strap as they rounded a corner. "At the risk of sounding appallingly sentimental, surely if a crisis such as this teaches us anything, it is that we cannot afford to waste time on petty quarrels."

Charles smiled into her eyes with a sweetness that was as deadly as absinthe. "Or on idle speculation."

That silenced even Lady Frances. But she had forced the Fraser brothers into presenting a more unified front than Mélanie had seen in seven years.

Which, Mélanie thought, might have been Lady Frances's intention from the first.

Chapter 25

Mélanie caught the smell of horses as she descended the carriage steps to a brick-paved yard. A thick mist eddied in the breeze, like a muslin undercurtain, affording glimpses of low gray-stone buildings, slate roofs, leaded-glass windows.

A ferocious bark sounded. A streak of black and white came hurtling out of the mist, resolved itself into a border collie, and put its muddy paws up on Lady Frances's pelisse.

"Down, Jasper." Lady Frances patted the dog's head. The dog subsided, danced round her in a circle, and went over to sniff Charles's boots.

A towheaded young man of about twenty followed the border collie through the mist. "Your ladyship. I didn't realize you were coming to the stables today. Is Mr. Hopkins expecting you?"

"Hullo, Giles." Lady Frances gave him the same smile she

would give to a young diplomat in her drawing room. "No, this is an unexpected visit. Is Mr. Hopkins in?"

"Out on a training gallop, but he should be back any minute now."

As if on cue, the thud of horses' hooves on damp ground echoed through the mist. Two men galloped into the yard, sending up a spray of muddy water.

"Fanny." A lean, bearded man with silvery hair swung down off a sleek chestnut mare. A piercing smile crossed his face. Then he took in the others standing round her. His shoulders straightened, as though he had shrugged into a formal coat instead of his tweed riding jacket. "Lady Frances."

"Hullo, Billy." Lady Frances gave him an answering smile that spoke volumes about their intimacy, then introduced her nephews and Mélanie. "We're in rather desperate need of information."

Billy Hopkins's bushy steel-gray brows rose, but he asked no questions, an action that went a long way toward winning Mélanie's heart. "Best come in out of the damp, then." He patted the chestnut mare's neck and glanced up at the dark-haired young man who rode the other horse. "See them stabled and then take out Lightning. But be sure to lock Jasper up first.

"New horse," he explained as he led them across the mud and straw of the yard. "Magnificent animal, speed like I've never seen. But he must have had a bad experience with a dog. He goes berserk round poor Jasper. Danger to himself, and not exactly safe for anyone else who happens to be in the area."

He opened a door onto a stone-floored kitchen with gleaming copper pans on the wall and the smell of bacon and coffee lingering in the air. He waved them to seats at the long deal table, tossed his damp coat over a chair back, and went to the range. "Something to drive out the chill." He lifted the lid from an iron pot, releasing the pungent, winey scent of spiced cider. "Have to admit I feel the damp more than I used to."

Mélanie willed herself to more time spent sitting with what grace she could muster, drawing out information, nursing a cup of whatever hot beverage was served, clutching the remnants of her sanity.

Lady Frances sank into one of the ladderback deal chairs as though it were gilded brocade and began to unbutton her gloves. "We're looking for a woman who used to frequent the races. Dark-haired, striking. Her name, at least at one time, was Helen Trevennen."

"Trevennen? Never heard of it." Hopkins took a mug from a hook on the wall.

Mélanie opened her reticule. "She almost certainly used another name here. Mr. Hopkins, have you ever seen this lady?" She held out the sketch as he set a mug of cider in front of her.

Hopkins held the sketch to the circle of light cast by the tin lamp on the table. His blue eyes crinkled up at the corners. "Good lord. Elinor Somersby."

A name. An innocuous name that washed over Mélanie in a deluge of relief that left her trembling like a spent racehorse.

Hopkins smoothed the curling edges of the picture. "She was a war widow, or so she said. Lived quietly but loved the races." He turned back to the counter and picked up the remaining mugs of cider. "Bet lavishly and with fair success. Used to stop by the stables every now and again to see the horses put through their paces. A good judge of horseflesh. Haven't thought of her in years."

"How many years?" Charles asked.

Hopkins hooked his foot round a chair leg, pulled the chair over, and sank down on it. "She was here the season Equinox won at Newmarket. And when Fenton's Pride won at York. But not when Bellevigne pulled off the upset at Pontefract. So that would be—" He paused, doing sums in his head. "Three years ago."

Charles leaned forward, elbows on the table, fingers clenched beneath his chin. "Do you have any idea why she left Brighton? Or where she went?"

"Always fancied her leaving had something to do with a man."

Lady Frances gave a most unladylike snort. "Just because a

woman is attractive and cares for her appearance, men think her life revolves round them."

Hopkins's gaze slid to her. "I'd never assume something so cork-brained, Fanny. But Elinor Somersby was the sort who finds men useful to get her what she wants." He pushed himself to his feet and flung open the door on the chill air of the yard. "Giles!" He looked back at the group at the table. "Giles has a memory like an encyclopedia. And he was more than a bit fond of Mrs. Somersby. All the lads were."

Mélanie met Charles's gaze for a moment. So close. Somehow that made the waiting worse.

A few moments later the towheaded young man scraped his boots on the rush mat and stepped into the kitchen. "You remember Mrs. Somersby," Hopkins said without preamble, waving the picture at him. "Why the devil did she leave Brighton?"

Giles blinked, surveyed the picture, and let out a low whistle. "Sorry. But she was a stunner." He looked up at Charles and Mélanie. "Is she a friend of yours?"

"In a manner of speaking," Charles said. "We're trying to find her. Do you have any idea why she left Brighton?"

Giles hitched himself up on the edge of the table, all the chairs being taken. "She got married again."

And acquired another name, damn it all to hell. "To whom?" Mélanie asked in an even voice.

"Hmm?" Giles was looking at the sketch. "Oh, one of those respectable-looking chaps who hang about the track. Can't remember his name. Fred might. He was quite taken with Mrs. Somersby. Well, we all were, but she had more time for him." He shifted the sketch in his hands. "The glamour of being a jockey, I suppose."

Charles's fingers tightened. Mélanie almost fancied she could hear the scrape of bone against bone. "When will Fred be back?" he asked.

"In an hour or so." Hopkins was pouring cider for Giles.

"He's just gone to give Lightning a brief gallop." He paused, the mug clutched in one hand, and stared at Charles from beneath lowered brows. "Here now. This is more serious than I realized."

"Yes." Charles gave him and Giles the same version of the story that he had given Lady Frances.

Hopkins knocked over his mug. Giles let out another whistle, this one lower and sharper. "But that's monstrous."

"Yes," Charles said. "It is."

Hopkins righted the mug and mopped up the spilled cider with his handkerchief. "Is there anything else we can tell you? Before Fred comes back?"

Charles picked up his mug and turned it between his fingers. "You said she was a war widow. Did she talk about her past?"

Hopkins flicked a glance at his groom. "Giles?"

"Not really." Giles took an apple from a basket on the table and tossed it in the air, as though it would aid his memory. "That is— It doesn't do to ask a lady about her late husband, and she almost never mentioned him. But I remember once—she'd come to watch a training gallop and I brought her a flask of tea. It looked as though she'd been crying, so I asked her if anything was the matter. She said this was the time of year her husband had died."

"What time of year was it?" Charles asked.

"Autumn. November, I think."

The month Jennings had died. Charles met Mélanie's gaze for a moment, then looked back at Giles. "Did she say anything else?"

Giles turned the apple over in his hand. "I said she must miss her husband. And she got an odd sort of smile—as though she had a secret, but then she always had a bit that sort of a look." Giles tossed the apple again. "Then she said he'd given her more than she'd ever thought possible, but sometimes a gift could also be a burden."

"Do you remember her ever wearing a ring?" Charles said. "A heavy gold ring with rubies? Shaped like a lion's head?"

"Good lord, no. She never wore anything that flashy. A wedding band and maybe a pearl here and there."

"What about money?" Mélanie asked. "Did she seem in want of it?"

"No," Hopkins said. "She didn't live lavishly, but she wasn't dependent on her winnings at the track. She could snap her fingers at a loss." He stared at his sodden handkerchief. "She obviously was living off more than an army pension. I don't much care for gossip, but I know some people speculated that her husband's family were paying her to stay out of their way. Or that he hadn't been her husband at all."

Charles sat back in his chair and folded his arms over his chest. "Do you think it's possible she was blackmailing someone?"

The apple Giles had been tossing thudded to the floor. "Why should she need to blackmail anyone?" he asked.

"In order to have a steady income," Mélanie said.

Hopkins frowned. "There's no way to prove it, but I suppose that could explain where her income came from."

Giles stooped to retrieve the fallen apple. "She was so beautiful."

"The most treacherous ones always are, lad," Hopkins said.

"Thank you," Lady Frances murmured.

Giles put the apple back in the basket. "There is one other thing. It may have nothing to do with all this, but—"

"What?" Mélanie could not keep the impatience from her voice.

"She'd give me a few pence sometimes when I fetched her a glass of lemonade or placed a bet for her. Sometimes I'd catch a glimpse inside her reticule when she took the coins out. Along with her handkerchief and scent bottle and coin purse, she always carried a pistol."

"Good God," Hopkins said.

Lady Frances raised her brows. "She sounds a decidedly interesting woman. I'm sorry we were never formally introduced."

Mélanie met Charles's gaze again. Whatever Helen Trevennen had been afraid of, apparently she'd feared it would follow her to Brighton.

There was little more to be said and over half an hour left before Fred, the jockey, could be expected back. Hopkins offered to show Charles and Edgar the yard. Lady Frances said she was staying in the warmth of the kitchen and advised Mélanie to do the same. Mélanie welcomed the excuse. With the need for immediate action over, she was aware of a dull pain behind her eyes and a quivery feeling in her muscles.

"He's a nice man," she said as the door closed behind the gentlemen.

"Billy Hopkins? Oh, yes, he's far and away the best man I've ever called mine. I haven't spent so much time round the stables since my sister Elizabeth died. She loved horses." Lady Frances picked up the mug of cider Mélanie had been nursing for the past half hour, dumped the contents in the basin, and refilled it. "Drink that down, my dear. And it wouldn't hurt to eat an apple. You'll never get through this if you don't keep your strength up."

The briskly maternal words were so out of character that Mélanie nearly smiled despite everything. She lifted the warm earthenware mug and took a sip of the fragrant cider. Apples and cloves. Harvest dances in the country. Colin and Jessica holding hands with the tenants' children—"I've been saying much the same thing to Charles for the last twenty-four hours."

"You've always had a healthy sense of self-preservation." Lady Frances returned to her chair. "Charles is the one who'll suppress everything until he cracks. It's a good thing he has you to look after him."

Mélanie glanced down at her hands, curled round the mug. Her wedding band glinted with golden warmth. Perhaps it was a trick of imagination, but she thought she could feel the date inscribed in the metal against her skin. "It's at least as much the other way round."

"Hmm. Yes, I suppose that's true. Charles is more nurturing than most men, though one wouldn't think it to look at him." Lady Frances traced a knot in the worn wood of the table. "Was

I wrong to talk to him and Edgar about their mother? I kept thinking they'd sort the matter out between themselves, but they don't seem to manage it."

Mélanie blew on the steaming drink. "I don't doubt they care deeply for each other. You should have seen Charles after Waterloo when he went out to the field to look for Edgar. I've never known him so frantic. Until now."

"Being Charles, he's no doubt got himself convinced he should have foreseen what happened to Colin and prevented it."

"Of course. I'm sure he thinks he should be able to mend matters with Edgar, but he doesn't understand what went wrong himself. They don't seem to have quarreled about anything in particular. It's as if a curtain dropped between them. And apparently it was Edgar who dropped it."

"Which is odd. Edgar was always the one who wore his heart on his sleeve, while Charles buried everything so deep I doubt even he knew what he was feeling."

"But it was Edgar who saw their mother kill herself."

A spasm crossed Lady Frances's face, anger as much as distress. "Damn Elizabeth. Oh, I was very fond of her, but if she had to take her own life why the devil did she have to do it in such a way as to inflict this legacy on her children?"

Despite the warmth of the range, Mélanie hunched her shoulders to fight off a shiver. However she and Charles resolved matters, the legacy she had inflicted on her own children would not be an easy one. And it could be argued that she had had more control over her actions than Lady Elizabeth Fraser had done.

Mélanie looked at Lady Frances. She had probably been as close to Elizabeth Fraser as anyone. She had also, Mélanie knew, shared Kenneth Fraser's bed on more than one occasion. Apparently the affair hadn't troubled Elizabeth, but then both the Frasers had been unfaithful to each other on a regular basis. "Why did Lady Elizabeth marry Kenneth Fraser?" Mélanie said. "Charles almost never talks about his parents' marriage, except to say it was a disaster."

"It was certainly that." Lady Frances stared into her mug, as though she was trying to get the past into focus. "Father was worried by her choice from the first. He doted on Elizabeth, though he didn't understand her any more than the rest of us did. With her looks and her fortune and the family name, she could have had any man she wanted. A lot of people were surprised when she chose a plain Mr. Fraser. Of course, Kenneth was an attractive man."

"Was it infatuation, then?"

"Not romantic infatuation. I think she saw Kenneth as a sort of anchor of stability. Unfortunately, what she took as stability was lack of feeling."

"And Mr. Fraser? Did he love Lady Elizabeth?"

Lady Frances snorted. "You knew Kenneth. I don't think he was capable of loving anything, except possibly himself. He saw women as a challenge. Mastering a woman reinforced his sense of power."

She frowned, as though of all her love affairs, the memory of this liaison with her sister's husband still disturbed her. "Kenneth was proud of having won Elizabeth," she said. "The way he was proud of a Renaissance masterpiece or a fine piece of porcelain or a prize thoroughbred. Though any good horseman has more feeling for his cattle than Kenneth displayed for his wife. He enjoyed parading her about for the first year or so. By the time Charles was born they cordially disliked each other. Elizabeth took to spending most of her time raising horses on Father's Irish estates. Kenneth kept to London and Perthshire."

Mélanie studied her husband's godmother. "I think sometimes Charles wonders if Kenneth Fraser was really—"

Lady Frances's face closed. "Oh, no, Mélanie." Her voice was gentle but firm as iron. "I don't doubt that he wonders, but some questions are best left just that. For everyone's sake."

"Charles is still trying to make sense of his relationship with his parents."

"And always will be, I daresay, like most of us. For better or worse, Kenneth Fraser stood in the position of father to him. Nothing can change that." Lady Frances fingered the pointed edge of the pelerine at the neck of her gown. "I've heard people say Charles is like Kenneth, but in truth he's just the opposite. Kenneth didn't care for anything but his own comfort and consequence. Charles feels things deeply—perhaps too deeply. In his case the coldness is an effort to keep all that passion under control. Quite understandable. Anyone who was Elizabeth's son would be afraid of giving way to his emotions. He's lucky to have you, my dear. Without you, I'm afraid, he'd have buried his feelings so deep he'd never have been able to bring them to the surface."

"But that's just the trouble." The words burst from Mélanie's lips with unintended force. "He's got to find a way to care about things without filtering it all through me. Or he'll never—" *Or he'll never manage without me.* She bit the words back just in time.

She pressed her hands over her face. She had, she realized, considered what the ruin of her marriage meant for the children and for herself, but not for Charles.

However much she cared for Charles, she had begun by using him. She had taken advantage of his loyalty and trust for her own ends. The revelations about Kitty Ashford made the picture even more grim. She had taken unwitting advantage of what he felt for another woman and used it to bind him to her. Yet whatever their reasons for entering into the marriage, for better or worse they had come to depend on each other. She could scarcely imagine not waking up with his arm flung across her, not turning her head to find his gaze there to meet her own in unspoken understanding, not sitting beside him amid a litter of ink-stained papers and arguing over the way to frame a speech or the best approach to a cipher.

But she had learned through the years that the unimaginable came to pass entirely too often. What that might mean for her was something to be faced later, on her own terms. But whatever else happened, she owed it to Charles to see that he came through this as unscathed as possible. Even if that meant making sure he found a way to go on without her.

"Mélanie?" Lady Frances's voice softened. "My dear, I'm

the last person to advise anyone on marriage. But I can guess what a strain this must be on both of you. It would be only natural for you to take that strain out on each other. Natural and quite disastrous."

Mélanie dragged her hands away from her face. "I know. Trust me, Aunt Frances, we're doing our best."

She was spared further speech by the sound of a horse's hooves. They snatched up their pelisses and went back into the yard. Hopkins, Charles, Edgar, and Giles emerged from one of the buildings. The mist had lifted a bit, though the sky was still low and gray. Fred rode into the yard on a magnificent dapple gray, prancing and tossing its head after the gallop.

"He did well, Mr. Hopkins." Fred swung out of the saddle. "More biddable than he was, though still plenty of spirit."

Hopkins walked forward. "Good, good. Come into the kitchen for a bit, Fred. Fan—Lady Frances's friends want a word about—"

An ecstasy of barking interrupted his words. A blur of black and white hurtled round the side of one of the buildings. The dapple gray let out a whinny of pure, shrieking terror, jerked out of Fred's hold, and tore forward.

Mud sprayed in the air. Mélanie had an image of flailing gray legs and slashing hooves. The horse's terrified shrieks and the barking of the dog pierced the air. Edgar and Charles both reached for her. They got tangled up, and Charles slipped to the ground. Edgar pulled her out of harm's way. She saw the hooves flash over Charles. She screamed.

Giles flung himself over Charles. The thud of hoof striking skull and bone echoed through the yard.

Chapter 26

The shrieks stopped, leaving an eerie silence. Mélanie pushed herself up against the straw-covered stone. She was lying against a barrel, with Edgar's arm over her face and the folds of her pelisse tangled up with his booted legs. Hopkins and Fred were both holding Lightning's bridle, murmuring to the horse. The horse's sides heaved and breath puffed from his nostrils, but he was standing still. Lady Frances had a squirming Jasper in her arms. A thin boy younger than Giles and a girl in a white apron had run up as well. Everyone was staring at the middle of the yard where Charles was bending over Giles, who was sprawled on the ground, legs and arms splayed.

Charles put his fingers to the base of Giles's neck, picked up his wrist, pressed his ear against the younger man's chest. He looked up at Hopkins. "I'm afraid—"

"My God." Hopkins started, then stroked Lightning's neck as the horse jerked. "He's not—"

"I can't feel a pulse. Mel, do you have a mirror?"

Mélanie scrambled to her feet without help from Edgar. She took a small silver-backed mirror from her reticule and went to kneel beside Charles. Giles's face was peaceful but unnaturally still. His skin had the ruddy glow of a country boy. Beneath his tangle of white-blond hair, a hoofprint was imbedded in his smooth, young forehead, leaking blood round the edges. She held the mirror over his mouth, while Charles studied the glass. Despite the damp air it was clear, the clear, smooth emptiness of the absence of life.

Charles looked at the others. "I'm sorry."

A stillness settled over the yard, as tangible as the shrieks and barking had been—death forcing its icy presence among the living. Mélanie had felt it in the mountains and valleys of Spain, in the streets of Léon, in their house in Brussels after Waterloo. But it did not belong there, in the tranquillity of the English countryside, in a world of strong animals and bustling activity and healthy young people.

The silence was broken by a sharp cry from the girl in the apron. She turned her head away. The young man put his arm round her.

"Jesus." Fred dragged his gaze from the sprawled body and stared at Lightning. The horse was standing with his head lowered, almost as if he understood.

Charles closed Giles's eyes. "Don't blame the horse. He was driven to it. If I'd been quicker on my own feet, the boy wouldn't have had to get in the way." He looked down at Giles. A muscle tightened along his jaw.

Mélanie closed her hand round his arm.

Lady Frances's crisp voice cut across the yard. "There's nothing to be gained from the lot of us standing out in the cold. Edgar, perhaps you could help Christopher carry Giles inside. Fred, Lightning should be stabled. Lottie, my dear, perhaps you could make us all some tea?"

Her words jolted them back into the world of the living. A quarter hour later Giles had been laid out on the sitting room sofa beneath a blanket, Lightning was rubbed down and secure in his stall, and the company were gathered round the kitchen table, with steaming mugs in their hands, and a subdued Jasper lying on the stone floor. Mélanie stared at the corner of the table. Little more than an hour ago Giles had sat there swinging his booted foot against the table leg, tossing a russet apple in the air.

Hopkins took a long draught from his mug, which contained something stronger than tea. "Who the *hell* let Jasper loose?"

"I don't know, sir." Fred was slumped in his chair, chin tucked onto the sweat-soaked linen of his shirt, eyes glazed and vacant. "I shut him up safe in his pen before I took Lightning out. I checked the latch twice."

Lottie, the maid, tucked a cinnamon-colored curl beneath her cap. "The gate to his pen is ajar." She sounded almost apologetic, as though by discovering it she had made it so. "I checked before I came in to make the tea."

Charles looked from Lottie to Christopher, the youngest of the stable lads. "Have you seen anyone about the stable today who doesn't belong here?"

Hopkins thunked his mug on the tabletop. "Good God. Surely you don't think this was deliberate."

Charles met his gaze. "I'm not sure. It wouldn't even occur to me if my wife and I hadn't been the victims of so many accidents in the past twenty-four hours."

Christopher tugged off his tweed cap, as though he had only just realized he was still wearing it. "We got a grain delivery while you were touring the yard."

"An expected delivery?"

"Oh, yes." Christopher turned his cap in his hands. "But it wasn't the usual deliveryman. He said the regular chap was home with a chill. I didn't think twice about it, it's happened before. But—"

Charles flicked a glance at Mélanie.

Mélanie pressed the fabric of her skirt over her lap. Her limbs felt not quite steady. She kept looking at Charles and imagining Lightning's hoof imprinted on his forehead. Despite the injuries they had both suffered in the past twenty-four hours, this was the first time death had intruded with full force. "I suppose it's possible we were followed here," she said. "But even if we were, it would have been very chancy."

"Did you talk to this deliveryman?" Charles asked Christopher. "Did you say anything about Lightning?"

Christopher fingered the brim of the cap. "Not about Lightning by name. But he did ask why the dog was penned up—Jasper was lying there with his best woebegone look—and I said one of the horses that was out now went berserk round the dog." The full realization of what his words might have meant registered in the young man's dark eyes.

Charles clapped him on the shoulder. "You couldn't have known, lad. When did this man leave?"

"Twenty minutes or so ago."

Charles shifted his gaze to Hopkins. "What would Jasper do if he was let out of the pen? Would he run out into the yard immediately?"

"What?" Hopkins ran a hand over his hair. "Oh, I see what you're driving at. No, not necessarily. He might have sniffed round until he heard the horse's hooves. Jasper loves the horses. Whenever there's anything doing he wants to be in the middle of it. He—" Hopkins put a hand over his eyes. "My God, I can't believe it's happened."

Lady Frances laid her hand over his own on the tabletop.

Edgar took a sip from his mug. "So Jasper could have been let loose sometime before Fred came back with the horse and then came running into the yard when he heard Lightning. Hard to see how this deliveryman could have counted on it all working, though."

Fred looked up as though struck by a sudden thought. "I'm sorry—perhaps it's none of my business—but why the devil would anyone want to hurt any of you, even assuming they could count on the ploy working?"

"No, actually it is your business." Charles sat forward in his chair. "We were waiting to talk to you when the tragedy occurred." Once again, he gave a brief outline of the story of Colin's disappearance.

Lottie gasped, and Christopher's eyes went wide. Fred shook his head, as though he was beyond shock. He stared at the sketch Mélanie held out to him. "Yes, that's Mrs. Somersby." His gaze drifted over the picture, the past intruding on the present horror. "Lovely, wasn't she? We all—Giles was as taken with her as any of us." He put his fist against his mouth. "Christ."

"I know," Charles said. "Giles was a brave and generous lad, and he had no business being mixed up in any of this."

"Do you remember the man Mrs. Somersby married?" Mélanie asked. Such a simple question, on which so much rested.

"Oh, yes." Fred's hands curled round his mug. He had the graceful fingers of a man used to giving the subtlest commands with the reins. "When a woman you admire marries, you notice the man she chooses, even if you haven't a prayer with her yourself."

"London barrister, wasn't he?" Christopher said.

"Yes. Started with a *C*, I think. Constant? No, Constable, that was it. We used to joke about him being as poker-faced as a constable. I told her outright once she was throwing herself away on him. She laughed and told me she'd always wanted to go back to London and he'd bought her the most charming house in Bedford Place. She said she'd marry me if I could do as much."

A street. A house. A name. Mélanie saw the realization break over Charles's face, like the sweat that signals the end of a fever. "Thank you." He drew a long breath. Beneath the table she could see his hands trembling. "Thank you very much."

Charles stared at the oil painting that hung on the wall of his aunt's library, between bookcases filled with French novels, parliamentary registers, and just about every volume of erotic poetry written from ancient times to the present.

The painting, in the soft, sensuous style of Sir Joshua Reynolds, showed two girls sitting on a blue blanket beneath the glistening leaves of a copper beach, a picnic basket beside them. Both girls had fair hair dressed in a profusion of loose curls. Both wore white frocks in the full-skirted, tight-waisted fashion that had been in vogue thirty-five years ago, one sashed in blue, the other in purple.

The girl with the purple sash had bright, buttery hair and the angular features, sharp eyes, and sardonic mouth that were characteristic of Lady Frances today. The girl in the blue sash was paler, her features more delicate. She might have been merely pretty in an insipid sort of way, were it not for the restless fever that burned in her eyes. As though she had a great thirst for life and knew, even at sixteen, that it could never be satisfied.

"She was ill, you know," Charles said.

"Who?" Edgar's voice came from the sofa behind him. They were alone in the room. Mélanie had gone upstairs to change her gown before their return to London.

"Mama. Mother." Beneath the smells of ink and leather and beeswax, Charles almost fancied he could catch a hint of jasmine. A teasing scent that always made him tense with wariness. In Lady Elizabeth Fraser's presence one had had to be braced for anything. "Aunt Frances was right. Mother had a brilliant mind and she didn't know what to do with it—much like Kitty. But it went beyond that. The black moods that confined her to bed for weeks on end. The reckless giddiness that had her staying up all hours and running crazy risks and flitting from one man's bed to another—"

Edgar looked up from a contemplation of the carpet. "For God's sake, Charles." A pulse pounded beneath the pale skin of his jaw. "You're saying Mother's—indiscretions—were an illness?"

"Not exactly." Charles walked to a Queen Anne chair by the fireplace. The fresh bandage Mélanie had put on his leg felt stiff against his skin. "Aunt Frances told me once that when Mother was in one of her frenetic states she'd be convinced anything was possible. And then the depression would set in and she'd think that nothing was." He stood behind the chair and rested his arms on its high back. "I didn't understand until I saw the same symptoms in a friend in my college at Oxford. He wrote poetry. Quite good poetry, I thought. At times he'd stay up writing through the night convinced he was producing a work of genius. And then for a fortnight he'd scarcely leave his bed."

Edgar turned his gaze toward the fire. "I don't see what this—"

"I talked about it with Geoffrey Blackwell. He has an interest in illnesses of the brain." Charles looked his brother full in the face. "Geoffrey says there are a number of people who show symptoms similar to those of Mother and my friend at Oxford. He thinks it's something organic that goes on in the mind. She was probably born with it."

Edgar looked back at him, his eyes wary. "And if she was?"

"We'll never understand the demons she battled. We'll never understand what finally pushed her over the edge. But it isn't your fault she put that gun to her temple."

Edgar pushed himself to his feet. "Who says I think it is?"

"You do, brother. By your very silence."

Edgar moved to the table where the coffee and cold collation Lady Frances had insisted on serving were laid out. "You're being unusually melodramatic, Charles." His voice had the bite of sleety air. "I admit being there when Mother killed herself was particularly unpleasant. I admit to thinking I should have been able to stop it, especially in those first hellish days. Later I realized no one could control Mother when she set her mind to something. It hasn't warped my life, I assure you."

"It's warped your relations with me."

"Has it?" Edgar poured a cup of coffee, picked up a fork, and stared down at the plate of cold beef and sliced Double Gloucester. "Perhaps I haven't the imagination to see it properly, but I think you and Aunt Frances exaggerate. We've grown apart as we grew older. It happens to most siblings. We get on better than a score of brothers I could name."

"Oh, yes, we ride together, we play catch with Colin and Jessica, you and Lydia dine with Mélanie and me. But when was the last time the two of us had a talk that was more than superficial?"

Edgar speared a piece of beef. "You like chess, I like roulette. You loved Oxford, I couldn't wait to be gone from the place. You have a perfect marriage, I—made rather a mull of mine." He added three pieces of cheese to the plate and picked up a jar of chutney. "I'm a soldier in the British army. Half the time you don't even seem to be sure what country you belong to."

The last was like a fist to the face in the midst of a fencing match. "What?" Charles said.

Edgar frowned down at the plate of food he'd assembled, then lifted his gaze to Charles. "I know Carevalo's blackmailing you to find the ring, but you'd go against British policy in Spain in a heartbeat, don't deny it."

"I won't." Charles fell back on the even voice he'd use to answer such questions in the House of Commons. "Just because I disagree with our current government's foreign policy doesn't make me less British. We live in a parliamentary system, or had you forgotten?"

Edgar fixed him with a gaze as hot and hard as the coals burning in the fireplace. "Only last month you said you thought France might be better off today if we hadn't won at Waterloo."

Charles pushed his fingers through his hair. "Did I? When?"

"One night at Brooks's when you'd drunk enough whisky that it even went to your head."

"Well, I don't deny I've thought it." On more than one occasion. But the words had a strange resonance now that he knew his wife had been working to bring about just that outcome.

"My God, Charles, our whole way of life was at stake."

"I seriously doubt that. Though it might have been a very good thing if it had been."

"Men fought and died—"

Charles looked at his brother and found himself answering as he knew Mélanie would have done. "Men fought and died on both sides, Edgar."

Edgar shook his head. "I can't even begin to understand how you could think that way. But that's the difference between us." He turned from the table without touching the food and paced the carpet, hands clasped behind his back. "You like pulling ideas apart and twisting them and looking at them upside down. I can't imagine anything more uncomfortable. I like to know where I stand. I need to know where I stand."

"And if it turns out you're standing in a mire?"

"You see?" Edgar whirled round and faced him down the book-lined length of the library. "That's exactly what I mean. Sometimes I'm not sure you'd admit there's such a thing as good and evil."

"I'm not sure I would."

"Even after what's happened to Colin?"

Fear squeezed Charles's chest, but he held his gaze steady. "Even then."

Dust motes danced in the gray light between them. "Do you even believe in God?" Edgar demanded.

"Not even before I witnessed war firsthand."

Something flared in Edgar's clear blue eyes. One might have called it a sense of betrayal. "Damn it, Charles, do you believe in anything at all?"

"Humanity," Charles said after a moment. "Though I must confess to being disappointed more often than I would care to admit."

Edgar shook his head and turned away. Charles realized how far they had moved from the original conversation. Belatedly, he recognized Edgar's gambit as the smokescreen it was. "You're better at this than I credited, brother."

Edgar walked back to the table and picked up his coffee. "Better at what?"

"Diverting the conversation." Charles spread his fingers on the blue velvet of the chair back. "Mélanie thinks you were in love with Kitty."

Edgar laughed, but the five-second pause before he spoke told volumes. "Women, even Mélanie, like to romanticize things."

"I'm sorry," Charles said. "I didn't realize."

Edgar stared at him. "Hell, Charles, don't you ever miss anything?"

"In this case I was singularly blind. It was Mélanie who noticed and even then I wasn't sure." He hesitated, searching for the right words. "It can't have been easy learning I was her lover. I'm sorry."

"Most men were a little in love with Kitty Ashford. Truth to tell, I didn't have the faintest idea you'd been more than a friend to her until the gossip after her death." Edgar's mouth twisted. "She seemed to me to be the purest of women."

"I don't excuse my own behavior, but you can hardly blame Kitty. Ashford had forfeited any right to fidelity."

"He was her husband."

"He was a rutting bastard who couldn't keep his hands off the local women."

Edgar thunked the coffee cup back onto the table. "It wasn't Kitty who changed things between us. It goes back far longer."

Charles fixed his gaze on the cream-and-gold patch of carpet in front of him. "When I got word of Mother's death, I wanted nothing so much as to talk to you. By the time I got home the house was full of relatives and mourning rituals and there was no chance for private conversation. I got through it knowing that as soon as the house settled down for the night we could have one of our midnight conferences."

The late-night conferences in one or the other of their bed-chambers had been a tradition from the time they left the nursery. They would sit talking half the night on the hearth rug, toasting slices of bread with the poker and warming pans of chocolate over the spirit lamp. "But when I knocked at your room, you didn't answer. You'd bolted the door. We never had a midnight conference again." Charles looked up at his brother. "You can't tell me that was because you'd suddenly discovered we view the world through different lenses."

Edgar walked to the window that overlooked the back garden. He stared at the silvery trunk of a birch tree, though he seemed to be seeing beyond it. "Why does it matter to you so much?"

Charles crossed to the window and put his hands on Edgar's shoulders. "Because I love you, brother mine. As it happens, there are only a handful of people on this planet I would say that to." One of whom was held hostage and in danger of losing his life. Another of whom had lied to him from the moment he met her.

Edgar stared down at Charles's hands on the blue cloth of his coat. A look crossed his face that seemed to Charles to echo his own sense of loss. "Charles—"

"We saw a boy killed today, Edgar. If Giles hadn't flung himself into the fray, it would have been me. If we'd got tangled up differently, it easily could have been you. God knows what we have facing us when we get back to London. It's no time to let things fester."

Edgar looked up at him. The armor cracked open. For a moment Charles was looking into the blue eyes of the companion of his boyhood. Then Edgar wrenched himself from Charles's hold and hurled his coffee cup into the fireplace. "Christ, Charles. How many ways do I have to tell you that there's nothing *to* fester?" He stared at the wreckage of snow-white porcelain amid the coals in the grate. "You're the one who keeps saying we can't afford to think of anything but Colin."

He flung across the room and nearly collided with Mélanie as she came through the door, clad in a dove-colored gown, her hair neatly pinned. She put a hand on his arm to steady them both. Her gaze slid from him to Charles and lingered for a moment.

"The carriage is ready," she said, in the silver-toned voice she used to smooth over diplomatic contretemps. "Shall we go? With luck we can be in London by eight o'clock."

Chapter 27

ou were right. Edgar was in love with Kitty."

Mélanie turned from the mullioned panes of the inn parlor window to look at her husband. They were at the King's Head in Cuckfield, waiting for a fresh team of horses. Edgar had been silent on the first stage of their journey and had once again taken himself off to the coffee room when they reached the inn. "He admitted it?" she said.

"When backed into a corner. That seems to be the only way my brother confides in me anymore." Charles paced the narrow length of the room. "Perhaps I shouldn't be surprised that I misread Carevalo, considering how blind I've been to those closest to me."

Mélanie leaned against the casement. Her body ached with exhaustion and at the same time thrummed with the need for action. She felt naked and vulnerable, as though the layers of goffered linen and pin-tucked sarcenet and ruched velvet had been stripped from her body. Layers that constrained her but also defined who she was, who she had been for seven years.

That day on the Perthshire beach, when she realized what Charles meant to her, she had been sure he could see through to the truth of who she was. Perhaps he still could. The question now was whether she could see that inner core herself. Charles had accused her of lying for so long that she couldn't know herself anymore, and he'd been more accurate than she cared to admit. Even with the lies stripped away, she wasn't the woman she'd been seven years ago, before she met him.

"My father used to tell actors you can never get a character truly, definitively right," she said. "You can only get *your* version of the character right, because you have to make choices and fill in the gaps the playwright leaves. Surely that's even more the case with another person than a character in a play. You can never really know what another person is thinking or feeling. You have to make guesses and assumptions. The picture keeps changing with new evidence." She studied her husband, thinking of all she had learned about him in the past two days. "Like looking at a faceted glass from different angles. Or stripping away layers of paint."

"Except that with a character in a play there can be more than one interpretation," Charles said. "With another person there is some core of truth, buried beneath all those layers."

She looked into his eyes. It was a strange relief and an unexpected terror to be able to do so without trying to hide any part of herself. "But it's difficult enough to know the truth buried within ourselves, let alone someone else."

He returned her gaze for a moment. Then he crossed the room in a burst of restlessness. He'd left his walking stick leaning against the wall. "Edgar says we grew apart inevitably as we grew older. Perhaps he's right. Perhaps he was always more important to me than I was to him. God knows he's always been able to form bonds more easily than I have."

Tenderness washed over her, like the familiarity of a well-worn cloak. "Oh, darling, Edgar's been measuring himself against you his whole life. In a lot of ways he must be fearfully jealous."

"Edgar? Jealous of me?" Charles stared at her. "Try again, Mel, or I'll start thinking you're as lacking in perception as I am."

"How could he not be jealous? His brilliant elder brother who thinks he can handle anything and who's very nearly right. Who's always known who he is and has never craved acceptance. Who's maddeningly, infuriatingly self-assured. Because I expect Edgar sees the self-assurance but not the scars underneath. You don't let very many people see the scars, Charles."

"Don't talk twaddle, Mel. All Edgar saw in me was a bookish elder brother who was all right when he was the only companion available but was a dead bore next to his school friends. Although he did admit he was jealous of our marriage."

She fought the urge to look away from his eyes. "As I said, we can all form a picture that's incorrect."

Charles stood watching her, his expression unreadable. The pressure of his gaze was suddenly more than she could bear, like a wound ripped open. She crossed to the fireplace, blinded by a betraying onslaught of tears.

"Mel?" Charles said behind her.

She knew that voice. It was the tone he used when he thought she might need him but didn't want to press her. To hear it now, when she had forfeited all right to his care, was like a knife cut.

She forced back the tears and turned to him with an attempt at a smile. His face held the bone-deep tenderness of her husband who loved her, who had forgotten for the moment everything that lay between them.

"We know where to find Helen Trevennen," Charles said. "She has the ring or at least she had it once—Violet Goddard saw it. We'll make her give us the ring or tell us what she did with it. We're going to get Colin back."

She nodded, because she couldn't let herself believe anything else. It occurred to her that once they had Colin back, once the crisis was past, the enforced intimacy between herself and Charles would be at an end. The future was still uncertain terrain, set with mines. This might be her last chance to reach him.

She sought for the right words. She felt strangely unsteady, as though she'd been forced to abandon the script and improvise in the middle of a performance. She was still unaccustomed to talking to Charles without the ever-present voice at the back of her head critiquing everything she said lest she unwittingly give herself away. She almost missed the clear boundaries of her role. "After Waterloo, I had no faith left in anything," she said, looking into his eyes, willing him not to turn away from her. "All those years of fighting and compromising and twisting ideals to meet necessity and what was the point? We'd lost. The monarchies I hated were restored in France and in Spain, foreign troops overran Paris, the very symbols of the revolution were obliterated. The one thing that kept me going was you."

His brows rose. "Doing it much too brown, Mel. Don't pretend—"

"Because no matter what, you still believed you were bound up in mankind. You still believed in the future. You still believed you could make something better of the world than what you'd found."

Charles gave a shout of bitter laughter. "Irony of ironies. Good God, we're a pretty pair. Don't turn me into a false ideal, Mel. If I believed in anything then—if I believe in anything now—it's only because you helped me find that belief, my enemy agent of a wife."

"That's not true. When you were at Oxford—"

"I was filled with high-sounding ideals." The bitterness was in his voice now, sharp as acid. "I wrote reams about the rights of the individual and the evils of inherited privilege and the horrors of the workhouse. I even made speeches when I had an audience who'd listen, which usually meant a tavern full of drunken undergraduates. But what did I do when I left university? Did I stand for Parliament or join a radical society or start a reformist newspaper? No. I ran away."

"I'd hardly call joining the diplomatic service running away, darling."

"I became a diplomat at least as much to get away from my family and everything in Britain as because I thought I could do any sort of good."

"Your mother had killed herself, your father had made it clear he didn't love you and never had, your brother had turned into a stranger. Of course you wanted to get away. But you can't tell me you didn't think what you were doing made a difference."

"At first. I thought the French had no business in Spain, it's true. I met Spaniards who didn't support Bonaparte but who saw the war as a chance to change their country for the good. For a long time, I was fool enough to think our government would support them. But when I saw the brutality on all sides, when I saw the contempt many of our soldiers had for their Spanish allies, the goddamned reactionary entrenchment of the Foreign Office—" He shook his head. "You said you could become so caught up in the game you forgot the reason you were playing it in the first place. I realized, when you said that, how truly hollow my own reasons for playing the game had been. Like you, I could be caught up in the sheer challenge, but it was harder and harder to believe any good could come of the war. For a long time I told myself that as long as I had some sort of belief in myself, I could make a difference, at least on an individual level. After Kitty's death—"

He turned his head, as though whatever his face might reveal was too intimate to share with her. She suppressed the impulse to take him in her arms. Kitty's death was a scar too private for her to touch.

He looked back at her, his gaze a wasteland. "After Kitty killed herself, life seemed a farce without meaning. If I was destined to make any difference in the world, it seemed to be only to bring destruction on those I loved. I was going through the motions when I was sent after the ring. Then I found you."

"And you couldn't give up because you were needed. I know you, Charles. You'd never let down someone who needed you. If I hadn't reminded you of it, something else would have."

"Christ, Mel." He took a quick step toward her, then checked himself. His eyes were angry. "Don't cheapen what was between us. It may have been lies, but you can't reduce it to something I could have found with anyone." He scraped his hand through his hair. "I loved Kitty, but loving her scarcely brought out the best in me. You did. With you I found something in myself I thought I'd lost. How could I back away from life when you attacked it with every fiber of your being? How could I turn away from the future when the future was a legacy we'd bequeath to our child? Besides—" He paused for a heartbeat, his gaze steady on her face. "In a world where I could feel what I came to feel for you, anything seemed possible."

For a moment she was robbed of speech or even breath. This was Charles talking, Charles who had not said "I love you" to her until they'd been married more than a year, whose feelings were more often expressed with a look or a touch than with words, who was more likely to quote someone else's impassioned declaration than to frame one for himself. That he should make such a declaration now, when she had destroyed his trust, when the revelations about Kitty had made her question the very nature of his feeling for her, was at once so sweet and so painful it tore her in two.

He glanced into the fire. "You weren't the only one who was disillusioned after Waterloo. I didn't like the future Castlereagh and the others were shaping any more than you did. Even I eventually saw how futile it was to be—how did you put it? A lone voice arguing over a glass of port?"

"Charles, I didn't mean—"

"No, you were right. That's why I left the diplomatic service."

"And you came home and you did stand for Parliament."

"Where at least my lone voice is heard by the entire House of Commons, which gives me the illusion that my arguments might make a difference." He looked up at her. The firelight sparked in his eyes. "But I'd never have had the courage to come home without you beside me."

She closed the distance between them in one move and took his face between her hands. "You're the best person I know, Charles. If I have any understanding of love or trust or compassion, I learnt it from you. I'm sorry I'm not the woman you thought I was. But however tainted your view of me has become, don't let it taint the rest of life for you." Her fingers trembled. She looked deep into his eyes. "I have no right to ask anything of you. But for God's sake, try to love yourself."

For a long moment he said nothing. Then he reached up and covered one of her hands with his own. "That's a bit much to ask of anyone, don't you think?" He squeezed her fingers. "I'm all right, Mel. Like you, I know how to survive. Colin's the one who's going to need us both."

She said nothing, because to that there could be no answer.

Colin's heart slammed into his throat at the approaching footsteps. He flung himself to the edge of the bed farthest from the door.

The door creaked open. "Brat? Are you awake? I've brought your supper."

Meg came into the room, carrying a splintery wooden tray. No sign of Jack or of a knife. Colin was tempted to put his arm over his eyes, but that seemed cowardly, so instead he sat very still. If they grabbed him again, he'd bite.

"I got Jack to bring a meat pie and some lemonade back from the tavern," Meg said. She set the tray down on the rickety, three-legged table by the bed.

The smell of the meat pie made him gag, but even if his stomach hadn't been twisted in knots he wasn't going to eat anything they gave him. "I don't want it," he said.

"See here, brat." Meg folded her arms over the stained linen of her shirt. "You've got to eat something or you'll make yourself sick."

Colin pulled his hurt hand closer against his chest.

Meg grimaced. "Oh, poison." She dropped down on the edge of the bed. The straw in the mattress crackled. Colin flinched. Fear shot up his spine like lightning.

Meg sat watching him. "Look, lad, I know it must hurt like the devil. But it'll get better, I promise you. You're lucky to still have the rest of your fingers. I know lots of children lost two or three fingers or even a whole hand to those new machines in the cotton mills. They learn to get on, one way or another."

Colin drew his knees up to his chest. He wasn't inclined to believe anything Meg said, but he'd heard Mummy and Daddy and their friends talk about how bad things were for children who worked in the mills. One evening when the grown-ups didn't realize he was listening, he'd overheard a story about a little boy who'd got his scalp pulled off. So perhaps Meg was telling the truth. Daddy's friend Fitzroy Somerset had lost his arm at the Battle of Waterloo, and he could do all sorts of things and even still be a soldier. Colin wondered how long it had been before Uncle Fitzroy's shoulder stopped hurting where his arm had been.

" 'Least you don't need your hands to make a living," Meg went on. "You can still hold a fork and ride a horse and fire a gun and all the sorts of things a gentleman does."

She smiled at him, a real smile that made her eyes crinkle up and her mouth look less sour. Colin inched back against the iron headboard. She'd done something really beastly, like a bad fairy in a storybook, but when she smiled like that she didn't look evil at all. And she sounded as though she was trying to be nice. It was very confusing. How was he supposed to know when he could trust her and when to be afraid?

"Anyways," Meg said, "better eat up or you won't grow. That's what I used to tell my little boy."

Colin was startled into speech, in spite of his determination not to talk to her. "You have a little boy?"

Meg's face went pinched. "I had a little boy once."

He stared at her in the flickering glow of the rush light. She looked like she was the one who'd just been stabbed. "What happened to him?"

Meg plucked at a thread in the frayed calico coverlet. "He died."

"Was he sick?" Colin asked.

"He caught a chill."

"Couldn't the doctors make him better?"

"Doctors?" Her laugh was like sandpaper. "Christ, brat, do you think we could afford—" She shook her head. "No, no one could make him better."

"How old was he?"

"Just past three."

"I'm sorry." It was true. Whatever he thought of her, he was sorry for her little boy.

Meg shrugged her shoulders. "I had ten brothers and sisters. There's only two of us left and I can't be sure about my sister. She went to work in a mill in Yorkshire and it's close on two years since I've had word of her. Life's cheap where I come from."

Colin frowned, puzzled by this last. "But—"

"What the hell are you doing, Meggie?" Jack yelled from the other room. "Get back out here."

"In a minute." Meg stood and looked down at Colin. She started to lift her hand, then let it fall to her side when he jerked back against the headboard. "Eat your supper, brat. You don't know how lucky you are to have it."

She turned on her heel and left the room. Colin looked after her, mulling over the things she had said. He wasn't sure how life could be cheap or expensive, since it didn't cost anything to be born. He wasn't sure why she was so worried about him eating when she'd helped cut his finger off. She looked as though she really missed her own little boy. So why didn't she understand that he wanted his mummy and daddy back?

"Jesus, Meg," Jack said. He clunked down something heavy, like a tankard. "What're you doing talking to the brat? You trying to make this harder than it is?"

"We'll be in a right mess if he stops eating and makes himself sick, won't we?" Meg's voice sounded harder than it had when she'd been talking to Colin.

"It's only been a day," Jack said. "Plenty of kids go two or three without a meal."

"Not his sort. He won't be used to it."

"All right, have it your own way. But you're making it that much harder for yourself if—"

"If what?" Meg said. Something in her tone made Colin's stomach take a dip.

"Well, hell, we still don't know how this is going to end, do we?" Jack said.

There was a long silence. A shivery sort of silence. Colin grabbed the coverlet and clutched it round him.

"No," Meg said at last. "But then that's always true, isn't it? Don't worry, Jack, I haven't gone soft. If it comes to it, I'll do what needs doing. Let's eat."

The sand-scoured steps and polished front door glowed in the lamplight, no different from the countless other front steps and doors in the row of brick town houses with white-framed sash windows and neat area railings that lined Bedford Place.

"It looks as if Helen Trevennen got the respectability she craved," Charles said, turning up the collar of his greatcoat.

"Not the sort of place one would think the summit of her ambitions," Mélanie said. "But perhaps by the time she came here she was looking for a haven."

Charles glanced at his wife, wondering if there were undertones to the statement. Beneath the green satin brim of the fresh hat she'd put on when they returned to Berkeley Square, her face was unreadable. Difficult to believe it was only Wednesday night. Their trip to Brighton had taken less than twenty-four hours. Three more days remained until Carevalo's deadline, though that time seemed scant enough, even with Helen Trevennen's house before them.

Edgar moved to stand beside them on the pavement. Charles glanced up and down the street. It was empty, dark save for the yellow blurs of lamplight in the soot-sticky air and quiet save for the distant rumble of wheels and clop of hooves. They'd left their hackney three streets over and walked the rest of the way.

Charles's gaze drifted toward Russell Square, where Addison was waiting. He and Blanca had returned from their visit to Lieutenant Jennings's widow shortly before Charles, Mélanie, and Edgar reached Berkeley Square. Mrs. Jennings had apparently been all too willing to vent her frustrations with her late husband. She had known a great deal more about him than Jennings realized, including his affair with Helen Trevennen of the Drury Lane. She admitted to talking about Miss Trevennen to a man calling himself Iago Lorano, who had called on her a fortnight before. But any secrets Jennings had shared with his mistress in his last letter, he had seemingly not confided to his wife.

Edgar stared at the house. "What if she's out for the evening?"

Charles started up the steps. He'd left his walking stick in Berkeley Square, though the stiff soreness in his leg told him this had perhaps been more wishful thinking than wisdom. "We'll find out where she's gone."

"What if she refuses to see us?"

He rang the bell. "She won't."

A manservant with a stiff shirt collar and an air of self-importance opened the door.

"We're here to see Mrs. Constable," Charles told him.

The manservant's eyes widened. "But—"

"We apologize for the late hour. If you take her my card, I think she will agree to see us."

The manservant glanced at the card, blinked in recognition, then cleared his throat. "If you'll wait in the hall a moment," he said in a voice several degrees warmer, "I'll inquire if Mrs. Constable is at home."

His footsteps faded up the polished stairs. Charles glanced about, seeking clues in the surroundings. The table against the wall was mahogany, and a handsome Turkey carpet covered the floorboards. The vase of dried flowers on the table had the sparkle of crystal, and the silver salver for cards did not appear to be plated. He met Mélanie's gaze in silent acknowledgment. Either Mr. Constable's legal practice was doing very well or the former Helen Trevennen still had an outside source of income.

Edgar paced the carpet. "What do we do if she won't come down?"

"Go up," Charles said.

"Oh, Christ." His brother stared at him. "You mean it, don't you?"

"Can you think of an alternative?"

But the manservant returned with the news that Mrs. Constable would be happy to receive them. He conducted them up the stairs and opened a door onto yellow-striped wallpaper, a gleaming pianoforte, and chintz furniture. A world of secure respectability.

"Thank you, George. That will be all." A dark-haired woman set her tambour frame on the settee beside her and got to her feet. She wore an apricot-colored evening gown, with a demure, ruffled neck and a skirt that did not cling too close. An amber cross hung from a black velvet ribbon round her throat. Beneath her curling fringe of dark hair, she was Mélanie's sketch come to life. The heart-shaped face, the wide, light eyes, the finely arched brows, the full, soft lips.

But what Mélanie's sketch had not caught, what none of those with whom they had spoken about Helen Trevennen had conveyed, was the sweetness that shone behind her eyes, in the curve of her mouth, in the tilt of her brows. Helen Trevennen, or Elinor Constable, radiated simple, artless charm. But then, if Charles had ever doubted that looks could be deceiving, his own wife had given him cause to know his folly.

"Mrs. Fraser? Mr. Fraser? Captain Fraser?" Her gaze drifted politely from one of them to the other. She smiled, a gentle smile that held no hint of the hard brilliance Charles had expected to find in Helen Trevennen. "Your names are familiar to me, of course, though I don't believe we have ever met. Perhaps you have business with my husband? I'm afraid he isn't in. He's dining with a colleague in the Temple."

Charles smiled at her, as though she was any lady in her drawing room, as though it was not past ten o'clock at night and his son's life did not depend upon the outcome of the interview. "As it happens, our business is with you, Mrs. Constable."

"Oh?" Her brows lifted, but she was too polite to blurt out a question. "Please sit down." She gestured to chairs, returned to the settee, and bent down to retrieve something peeking out from beneath her worktable. A doll, Charles realized, with yellow yarn hair. "My daughter's," she explained with a smile. "My children like to play in the drawing room after dinner and I'm afraid we haven't managed to teach them tidiness."

Charles leaned forward in his chair. "I'll come to the point, Mrs. Constable. We're looking for a ring we believe you have in your possession. We'll pay handsomely for it."

The blue-gray eyes widened. The delicate brows rose in what Charles would have sworn was genuine puzzlement. "A ring?" She glanced down at her hands. On her left, she wore only a simple gold wedding band. On the second finger of her right hand was an aquamarine set in seed pearls. "I'm afraid I don't understand, Mr. Fraser. I don't have a great deal of jewelry."

"This is a gold ring, a heavy gold band, wrought in the shape of a lion with ruby eyes."

Charles could detect no false note in the bewilderment in her eyes. "I have no ring like that at all, Mr. Fraser. No rubies and nothing of such an old-fashioned design."

"We believe it was sent to you by Lieutenant William Jennings."

This time her face tensed beneath the look of confusion. "I don't know a Lieutenant Jennings."

"Not anymore perhaps. But you did once, Miss Trevennen."

The words registered on her face like a slap. The blood drained from her skin, but she held her head high. "It's a long time since I've heard that name." She smoothed her hands over her lap, pulling the sheer fabric of her dress taut. "I think you'd better tell me the whole story, Mr. Fraser."

Charles summoned a smile from his inner reserves. "You were born Helen Trevennen in Cornwall, near Truro. You came to London about fifteen years ago. You worked as an actress at the Theatre Royal, Drury Lane. I should say, Mrs. Constable, that we realize this is not quite the version of events you gave to your husband when you met him. We have no wish to disabuse him of the facts. That is a matter between you and him." His voice was steady. He did not so much as glance at his own wife. "We are only interested in the ring that you received from Lieutenant Jennings in January of 1813."

Helen Trevennen folded her hands in her lap with the grace of a trained performer. "It's true I knew a Lieutenant Jennings once, a long time ago. I was—I was very fond of him. He was killed in the Peninsula."

"And shortly before he died he wrote you a letter that you received after his death."

She lowered her gaze to her hands. "Yes."

"And enclosed in the letter was a ring. Come now, Mrs. Constable, your friend Violet Goddard saw it."

She looked up at him, her eyes wide and compelling. "Mr. Fraser, I assure you—"

"We will pay whatever you ask for it."

"Believe me, Mr. Fraser, when it comes to William Jennings it is not a question of money."

"I understand the ring must have great sentimental value."

Her hands clenched. "Mr. Fraser, *he didn't send me a ring*."

"Miss Goddard saw—"

"I'll show you what Violet saw." She sprang to her feet and ran from the room.

Edgar groaned. "She sounds as though she's telling the truth."

Charles stood and took a turn about the room. "She's a very good actress."

"Because she worked at the Drury Lane?"

"Because she sounds as though she's telling the truth."

"We're threatening everything she has," Mélanie said. "She'll work hard to defend it."

Charles looked at her, ignoring the echoes of their own life that reverberated through the room. "Then her defenses have to be broken."

Helen Trevennen hurried back into the room, her color high and her breathing rapid, as though she had been running. "This is what Will—Lieutenant Jennings—sent to me with his final letter." She extended her hand. In her palm lay a garnet brooch set in gold of a Spanish design. "Not very valuable, I believe, but I treasure it."

Gold with a red stone. It fit Violet Goddard's description. Charles could feel Mélanie's certainty waver, as did his own. "Mrs. Constable, you don't—you can't—realize how important this is," he said. He told the story of Colin's kidnapping in the brisk outlines he now had memorized.

"Dear heaven." Helen Trevennen put her hand to the cross at her throat.

"You have children of your own," Mélanie said.

"Yes." She picked up the yarn-haired doll that lay beside her on the settee. "Jane will be three in March and Benjamin's just turned one."

Mélanie leaned forward, in that attitude that could win confidences from anyone. "Mrs. Constable, as a mother—"

Helen Trevennen looked into her eyes. "I wish I could help you, Mrs. Fraser. I can't." She smoothed the doll's yarn hair. "I've never seen this ring. If Will had it, he said nothing about it."

"What was in the letter?" Charles asked.

The knots of gold ribbon on her sleeves snapped as she drew herself up. "Mr. Fraser. It was a letter from my—from the man I loved. It was not meant to be read by anyone else. Nor did it contain anything that others could find of interest. Nothing about a ring or a Marqués de Carevalo or even about Spain."

"Sergeant Baxter said it was a long letter."

A faint smile drifted through her eyes. "Will could be very ardent."

"Do you still have the letter?"

"No, I—" She glanced at her hands, then looked back at him. "I'm embarrassed to say so, but I burned it before my marriage. I did not want to risk my husband finding it. My husband is the best of men, Mr. Fraser, but I don't think he'd understand about Will."

Charles leaned back in his chair and crossed his legs. "Violet Goddard and Jemmy Moore said you were frightened when you left London seven years ago. Why?"

She drew a breath. He thought she might be sorting through her story, but he couldn't be sure. "I'm not proud of my actions," she said. "I was going to begin a new life. It is difficult to escape one's past—particularly so for a woman. I knew that the only way to do so was to cut myself off from . . . from my former friends and associates. I thought saying I was afraid was the best way to assure this."

"Where did you get the money to begin this new life in Brighton?" Charles asked.

"Will sent it in his letter. He said he'd recently come into a windfall and he wanted to share it with me. He didn't explain further."

Charles folded his arms across his chest and watched her for a long moment. "It's a good story, Mrs. Constable. Now please tell us the truth."

Her eyes widened with a perfect look of wounded outrage. She was almost as good an actress as Mélanie. "I have told you the truth, Mr. Fraser."

"I think not, though you've told the lies brilliantly."

"Mr. Fraser—"

"Mrs. Constable, I said we had no intention of telling your husband what we've learned of your past. That is true in and of itself. But if you persist in these denials, I fear we shall have no choice but to lay the whole matter before him."

"That is blackmail, Mr. Fraser."

"Call it what you will. The ring, Mrs. Constable?"

"Mr. Fraser." In the light from the branch of candles beside the settee, her eyes were luminous with tears. "If I had this ring it would take no threats to make me give it to you. I would do so happily for the sake of your child." She stood in one swift, fluid motion, hesitated, then moved about the room, adjusting the shade of a lamp, realigning the score on the piano. Mélanie had done much the same in the library last night. Laying claim to the home she feared losing?

"It goes without saying that you could do great—I fear irreparable—harm to my marriage." Helen Trevennen stared at a framed silhouette on the wall with a faint, wistful smile. "I'm afraid my husband's view of me is sadly idealized. I perhaps deserve that he should know the truth, but he does not deserve the pain it would cause him."

"There is a simple way to spare him such pain," Charles said.

Helen Trevennen turned to face him, with the tragic dignity of Desdemona refuting Othello's accusations of infidelity. "All I can do is beg you not to speak to him of the past, for it will avail you nothing. I do not have the ring."

Her eyes held a compelling plea, yet thanks to his wife, Charles knew something about resisting the pull of a pair of beautiful eyes. He stared at her for a long moment. He did not glance at Mélanie, but he felt her making the same calculations he made himself. "You're a parent, Mrs. Constable. If you can understand my fear for my son, you must believe I will use this." He reached inside his coat and drew out a pistol. "The ring."

Helen Trevennen went very still. Her gaze fastened on the barrel of the gun. Fear radiated off her like waves of heat.

Charles pulled back the hammer. He heard Edgar gasp, felt Mélanie go tense.

Helen Trevennen lifted her gaze to his face. The flutter of the lace at her throat betrayed her trembling. "Mr. Fraser, I cannot help you. I don't have it."

Charles held the gun steady and measured the look in her

eyes. The metal was cold and heavy in his hand. It would be so easy to pull the trigger and give vent to the scream of frustration that had been building inside him for almost forty-eight hours. So easy, so deadly, and so completely useless. If he shot, even a warning shot, the servants would come running into the room. Helen Trevennen, no doubt, would continue to deny she had the ring. And just possibly, she was telling the truth.

He lowered the pistol and got to his feet. Helen Trevennen let out a rough, gasping sigh.

Charles held out his hand to Mélanie. "You have my card, Mrs. Constable. If by any chance you discover you are mistaken and have the ring after all, send word to us at once. You can have whatever you ask for it. Otherwise, there seems to be nothing more to be said."

Chapter 28

As they descended the front steps of the Constable house, Mélanie could feel the weight of failure pressing on her husband, as heavy as the soot-laden night air that seeped through their outer garments. When they reached the pavement, she put a hand on his arm. "You couldn't have done anything else. All other considerations aside, shooting her wouldn't have got us anywhere."

Edgar stopped and looked up at his brother. The lamplight glowed in his wide eyes. "You really might have shot her, mightn't you?"

"Possibly." Charles scowled into the dark street.

"I don't suppose it's occurred to you that she might be telling the truth?"

"It could hardly fail to occur to me." Charles started along the pavement toward Russell Square. "It was one of the most compelling performances I've ever witnessed." He didn't glance at Mélanie, but she felt him add, *Though no more so than the one you gave for seven years*, as surely as if he had said it. "But if Jennings didn't put the ring in his letter to her, what the hell happened to it?"

Edgar's boots clicked on the pavement. "Perhaps Jennings never had it at all."

"One of the soldiers did, or at least told the bandits he did when he employed them. Jennings is the only one who had anything removed from his body."

Edgar frowned at the paving stones. "Suppose Sergeant Baxter's lying and he had the ring himself?"

"If Baxter had the ring, why didn't he try to sell it again after the debacle with the French?" Mélanie said. "He had nothing to gain from hanging on to it." She tried to sound as though she was analyzing chess moves, but the words came out with a tight strained sound, perhaps because her chest and throat felt as if they were being squeezed raw. "Helen Trevennen's performance may have been grounded in truth, as all good performances are, but I think she has the ring. And what I want to know is why she's so determined to keep it rather than sell it to us."

"Perhaps she sold it already," Edgar said.

"Then one would think she'd have admitted it when Charles held the pistol on her."

"So what now?" Edgar asked.

Charles stopped walking and turned back to scan the street. "We burgle the house."

His brother stared at him, digesting this statement.

Addison detached himself from the shadows by the square railing. His gaze flickered from Charles's face to Mélanie's to Edgar's. "You didn't get it?"

"No," Charles said.

Addison gave a curt nod. "The kitchen door is locked but not bolted. The ground-floor windows round the back are sash windows with a simple latch. They open onto the breakfast parlor and Mr. Constable's study, respectively. I knocked on the area door—I said I was a groom who'd got lost delivering a message—and had a brief word with the kitchenmaid. Mr. and Mrs. Constable's bedchamber is at the front of the house on the second floor. The cook and kitchenmaid sleep off the kitchen. The rest of the servants sleep in the attics and the nursery is there as well. The manservant locks up at midnight. Mr. Constable is expected to stay in his chambers in the Temple tonight rather than return home."

"Thank you, Addison. Well done."

Edgar was still staring at Charles. "You were planning to break in even before we spoke to Mrs. Constable?"

"No, but I knew it might come to that. Which it has. We should return to Berkeley Square to make our plans. Addison, stay here. If Mrs. Constable or anyone else in the household goes out, follow him or her and send word as soon as you can. We'll be back just after midnight."

"Right, sir." Addison said nothing more, but the gaze he exchanged with Charles had the warmth of a hand clapped on the shoulder.

In silence they cut through a mews, rounded two street corners, flagged down a hackney, and directed it to Berkeley Square.

"How would you do it, Mel?" Charles said when they were settled in the carriage.

"The back windows. There's more chance of being spotted at the kitchen door and more chance of waking someone at the front of the house."

"My thoughts exactly."

"You sound as though you've done this before," Edgar said.

"I have," Charles replied.

"But— Oh, I see. In Spain."

"And Portugal. And once or twice in Vienna. Ask Castlereagh to tell you the story sometime. He was grateful for my somewhat unorthodox talents on that occasion."

"Charles picked the lock on a wine cave the night I met him," Mélanie said. "Of course, it wasn't until later that I learned what an expert he was."

"You mean you were there when he— Do you mean he dragged you along on these adventures?" Edgar asked.

"Oh, yes," Mélanie said. It was quite true. She neglected to add that she had also done more than her share of breaking and entering on her own.

"Good God." Edgar shook his head and looked at his brother. "Your 'fetching and carrying' went even further than I realized."

"A great deal further," Charles said. He flicked a glance at Mélanie. "Might as well call a spade a spade, brother. I was a spy."

Mélanie opened the door of her and Charles's bedchamber, carrying a bowl of warm water and a roll of lint. She found her husband alone in the room, unfastening the cuffs of his shirt. "Edgar's changing in the guest suite," he said. "He ducks out of sight whenever he realizes I have to change your bandages."

"Poor Edgar. He has a delicacy of mind neither of us can appreciate." She set the water and lint on her dressing table. "I sent Blanca to make coffee. She's itching to be doing something. I had a hard time convincing her it would only complicate matters if she came with us. Are you going to be able to climb through a window with your leg in that state?"

Charles pulled his shirt over his head and reached for his dressing gown. "I'm going to have to."

In truth, both his bullet wound and her knife cut had begun to heal, as was revealed when they changed the dressings. They didn't speak of what lay ahead until the fresh bandages were in place and they had begun to don clothing appropriate for a burglary.

"If she has the ring hidden in the house, it's probably in her bedchamber," Charles said, buttoning a black waistcoat over a fresh shirt. "Have you ever broken into a room while someone was sleeping in it?"

"Once or twice." Mélanie dropped a gown of jet-colored merino over her head. Most of the time she had managed to already be in a gentleman's bedchamber before he fell asleep. She saw this realization dawn in Charles's eyes as she thrust her arms into the long, tight sleeves. "Difficult and dangerous, but not impossible," she continued, pulling the fabric over her shoulders with more force than was necessary. A stitch snapped in one of the shoulder seams. "But there's a good chance she keeps the ring in a dressing room rather than the bedchamber itself. A lady's boudoir is the one room she can keep inviolate."

"She may have moved it after our visit." Charles crossed to her side and began to do up her buttons. "She must guess we won't give up."

"Addison's there if she tries to leave the house or send anyone away with the ring. Charles." She forced herself to voice a suspicion that had been tugging painfully at the corners of her mind. "Suppose Victor Velasquez got to her before we did? If she sold him the ring, she might have promised not to reveal the truth to us."

Charles did up the last button. "Not at the risk of her own life. She knew how close I came to pulling the trigger. I could see it in her eyes. Which means she was afraid of something— or someone—if she gave us the ring or told us what she'd done with it."

"If she doesn't have it—"

He squeezed her shoulders. "We'll deal with that possibility after we've established it's not in her house." He went to his chest of drawers and rummaged beneath a stack of cravats. "When did you last see my picklocks?"

"A couple of months ago when Jessica locked Colin in the garden shed." The memory tugged at her throat. She opened the doors of her wardrobe and forced herself to debate between a black velvet cloak and a slate-colored wool. "Try your handkerchief drawer, darling."

She decided on the black velvet—camouflage was more important than warmth—and turned from the wardrobe. Charles, normally far more tidy than she was herself, had tossed half the cravats on the floor and was doing the same with his handkerchiefs. She went to her dressing table and opened the central drawer. She lifted out a box with rosewood cranes inlaid in the lid, pressed one of the cranes to release the false bottom, and took out the set of picklocks Raoul had given her so many years ago. She crossed back to her husband, who was now riffling through a box of sleeve-links, and held out her hand.

Charles stared at the shiny instruments held together with green satin ribbon rather than a metal ring like his own set. "Of course. Any self-respecting agent would need her own." He pushed the drawer shut. The sleeve-links rattled like ammunition. "Handy for all sorts of things. Including opening your husband's dispatch box, I imagine."

She received his gaze as a duelist might receive a bullet. "Among other things."

The brief, hard flare in his eyes made her bleed inwardly. "I always wondered why you took to picking locks with such natural ability. But then there are any number of things you pretended to learn from me that you were already expert at."

They stared at each other. Every paper she had stolen, every secret she had gleaned from him and passed on to Raoul hung between them, as impenetrable as the wall of any fortress.

Mélanie drew a breath. "If you're wondering exactly when—"

"No." Charles folded his arms across his chest. "As it happens, I'm trying to remember how many dispatch boxes I've broken into myself through the years."

He watched her a moment longer, his gaze steady and unreadable on her own. Then he shrugged into a black coat, wound a black silk scarf over the white gleam of his shirt, and walked to the door. Mélanie put the picklocks in the pocket of her gown and picked up the black cloak.

After seven years, her husband could still surprise her.

The back of the Constable house was as Addison had described, two ground-floor windows with simple latches. The curtains were drawn, but the fringed chintz at one and the velvet drapes at the other easily differentiated the breakfast parlor and study.

Mélanie glanced at Charles. They had left Addison and Edgar to keep watch at the front of the house, with orders for one of them to follow anyone who left.

Charles jerked his head at the study window. Mélanie took out her picklocks and opened the window of this London house as easily as she had any in Lisbon or Vienna. Charles boosted her up and she pulled herself over the sill, ignoring a twinge in her side. She stretched down a hand to Charles and he pulled himself up, using the strength in his arms to make up for the weakness in his leg. He sucked in his breath as he dragged his wounded leg over the sill.

A faint smell of ink washed over them in the darkness. *Don't rush at things headlong, whatever your instincts.* Raoul's advice echoed in her memory. *Wait a moment to let your eyes adjust to the dark. Look for clues to orient yourself.* She held back the curtains so that enough light from the three-quarter moon spilled through the window to show the outline of the door. Charles seized her hand in his own and they picked their way across the floor, which proved to be covered with a thick, soft carpet. Thank goodness Helen Trevennen was able to afford luxuries.

Charles eased open the door. The hall to which they had been admitted a few hours before stretched before them. A smell of scented beeswax lingered in the air. A half-moon of gray light indicated the fanlight over the front door. After a few moments, she could make out the mass of the stairs and the outline of the hall table.

They tiptoed over a few feet of polished floor to the muffling pile of the Turkey rug. Space seemed to expand in the dark. It felt as though the relatively compact hall took as long to traverse as a palatial gallery. The trick was not to panic and move too quickly, not to rely on one's faulty memory rather than the evidence of one's senses. At last Charles stopped, and she heard the faint stir of his hand closing round the newel post.

Mercifully, thanks perhaps to the house's newness, none of the treads squeaked. Her foot nearly collided with the balustrade as they rounded the first-floor landing, but Charles steadied her. On the second floor, they paused at the head of the stairs. A window at the end of the corridor let in a faint glow of moonlight. The white-painted doors stood out as pale blurs against the dark wallpaper. No light shone beneath the doors.

The door directly across from the stairhead was wider than the others, with a carved doorcase. Charles jerked his head at her and moved to the door to the left of it. It opened on the smell of camphor and lavender. Standing behind Charles, Mélanie could make out the bulk of a four-poster. A spare bedchamber. They moved to the door to the right of the carved doorcase. A faint smell of perfume and face powder seeped round the door as Charles reached for the handle. He pushed the door open.

The curtains had been thrown back from the windows. A scene of chaos shimmered in the moonlight. The wardrobe doors gaped open. Gowns and shawls and hats were strewn about. The dressing table drawers hung from their slots. Powder and jewels and scent spilled across the top of the dressing table. A small oil painting had been pulled from the wall, the canvas slashed.

Charles made a quick circuit of the room. Mélanie moved to the door to the adjoining bedchamber and put her ear to the panels. No sound, not even the stir of bedclothes. She turned to Charles and shook her head. He moved to her side and exchanged a look with her. She nodded and turned the door handle, a fraction of an inch at a time, so it made only the softest of clicks. She put her shoulder to the door and eased it open.

The curtains were thrown back in this room as well. The moonlight fell over the rumpled, empty bed. The room was marked with the same signs of chaos as the boudoir, but her gaze skimmed past them. For on the hearth rug, before the cold, banked fire, was the sprawled figure of Helen Trevennen, the woman who now called herself Elinor Constable.

A pistol gleamed silver on the carpet beside her, and a red stain spread over the front of her nightdress. But Mélanie still hurried forward, dropped to her knees, and put her fingers to the woman's cold neck. She was dead.

Chapter 29

Mélanie looked up at Charles, who had knelt beside her. Rage flared in his eyes, then was quickly banked.

He looked from the pistol to the wound in Helen Trevennen's chest. Scorch marks showed on the embroidered linen of her nightdress. "The bullet went in at an upward angle," he said, "at close range."

Mélanie glanced at the bed with its thrown-back covers, then looked at Helen. Her sheer nightdress was lavish with lace, but she wore no dressing gown and her feet were bare. The pistol was small and elegant, a lady's weapon. "He was searching the room, she woke and jumped out of bed and grabbed her pistol—she must sleep with it beside her bed, which fits with Giles saying she kept a pistol in her reticule. They struggled and the gun went off."

"Yes, that's how it looks. The question is, did he find the ring?" Charles put out his hand as though to close Helen's eyes, then drew it back. "Best not to disturb things more than we have to. But I think we can risk lighting a lamp." He pushed himself to his feet and held out his hand to her.

Mélanie stood and glanced once more at the still face of the woman they had spent the past thirty-six hours searching for. Violet Goddard's friend, Hugo Trevennen's niece, Susan Trevennen's sister, Jemmy Moore's lover. A different woman to all of them, but in all their eyes she had been a creature of life and vitality. With a single bullet, all that life and vitality had been extinguished. Put out the light indeed.

Further speech was a dangerous luxury. They found a tinderbox on the mantel and lit a single lamp, then moved about the disordered room in silence, unscrewing finials, rummaging through already opened drawers, turning back the pastel carpets, glancing in vases and jewel boxes, under the mattress, inside the coal scuttle. It seemed obvious that the murderer had begun in the boudoir and only risked the bedroom when his search of the first room proved fruitless, but Charles checked the boudoir again while Mélanie inspected the porcelain on the bedroom mantel.

He came back into the bedchamber, shook his head, then went still. Mélanie heard it a fraction of a second later. A faint thud outside the door that was different from the normal stirrings and creakings of the house. She barely had time to call herself a fool before the door from the corridor was pushed open.

"Darling?" A man's voice, questioning, not suspicious. More candlelight spilled into the room. "Are you awake? I decided to—"

He broke off and looked across the room at Mélanie. He looked to be in his mid-forties, a slight man with pleasant, unremarkable features, rumpled brown hair, and a rumpled black evening coat. His face twisted with bewilderment. He glanced down at the carpet, stiffened, and stared transfixed at his wife's body. He opened his mouth, but before he could let out a scream, Charles's fist connected with his jaw.

Charles lowered Mr. Constable's crumpled form to the carpet. He moved to the door, cracked it open, and nodded at Mélanie. She extinguished the lamp and followed him into the corridor. His hand closed round her own. His fingers were cold and she could feel the pounding of his pulse, but he led the way back downstairs with a silent, measured tread. Down the corridor, into the study, out the window. Cold night air and the blessed relief of moonlight.

Edgar was waiting for them at the back of the house. "Are you all right?" he demanded in a low voice. "We saw someone go in the front door. We weren't sure what to do."

"Later." Charles clapped a hand on his brother's shoulder and pushed him toward the garden gate. They returned to where Addison was waiting, but Charles merely said, "We can't stop here," and led them two streets over. Then he stopped and slammed his hand against a lamppost, so hard Mélanie thought she could hear the bones rattle.

"Darling." She gripped his arm. "Not now."

He jerked away from her and pressed his white-knuckled hand to his face. "Sweet bloody Christ, how could I have been such a fool?"

"Because your options were limited. We were both fools, though I don't honestly see what we could have done differently and in any case it doesn't matter. It's done." She put her hands on his shoulders. "We have to decide what to do next."

"What happened?" Edgar asked.

She released her husband and turned to her brother-in-law. "Someone broke into the house before we did, and searched for the ring and killed Helen Trevennen."

"Dear God." Edgar blanched in the lamplight. His eyes seemed to jump from his face. "But who—"

"Who's been dogging our heels since yesterday?" Charles's voice was as sharp as a knife turned inward. "Victor Velasquez."

Edgar looked as though he was going to be sick. "But how—"

"I don't know." Charles's hand curled into a fist. "Damn it, I don't know."

"Does he have the ring?" Addison asked.

"We can't be sure. Helen Trevennen seems to have awakened and interrupted him in the midst of his search." Charles glanced at Mélanie. "He entered and left through the boudoir window. When I went back in I found that the latch was ajar, and there were traces of rope caught on the windowsill."

He turned back to Addison and Edgar and gave the rest of the details of their discovery of Helen Trevennen's body, their search of the rooms, and their encounter with her husband. "Addison, go see Roth. Try Bow Street first, then his house. Tell him what's happened and what we suspect. Someone should get to the Constable house at once. I trust they will convey my apologies to Constable, though in the circumstances it's likely to be the least of the poor devil's concerns."

"Right, sir." Addison handed them their shoes and cloaks, which they had removed before they broke into the house. "You're going to see Mr. Velasquez?"

"To begin with."

Mélanie and Charles put their shoes back on and wrapped their cloaks round their shoulders, and then they and Edgar found a hackney and directed it to the Albany, where Velasquez had rooms. When they were settled inside the carriage, it was Edgar who broke the thick silence. "Did Constable see your face?"

"He saw Mélanie's. I'm not sure about me."

"He'll think—"

"It can't be helped. Roth will sort things out. Poor bastard. First his wife died. Now he's going to have to learn far more about her than he ever wanted to know."

Mélanie tried to read her husband's expression in the dark of the carriage. His features were armored to reveal nothing. She wondered what would be worse for Mr. Constable, losing his wife or learning she had lied to him about everything in her past.

They turned off Piccadilly and pulled up in the forecourt of the Albany, a Palladian building of brown stone, once the home of the Duke of York, now transformed into bachelor's chambers.

Lord Byron had lodged there, as had Charles himself in a brief interval between Oxford and Lisbon. The porter, who remembered Charles, directed them to Velasquez's flat, where they were greeted by a manservant in dressing gown and cap who said that his master had not been home since morning.

Charles seized the manservant's arm. "Where is he?"

The manservant stared at him out of sleep-flushed eyes. "I don't know, sir. But he'll have to return before morning. There are papers here that are needed at the embassy."

Charles slackened his hold. "We'll wait."

The manservant started to protest.

"You can go back to bed," Charles told him. "We require no attention."

The manservant hesitated, but Charles's ducal voice won out. The manservant fussed about the fire, made an offer of tea, which they refused, and returned to his own chamber.

They were left alone in a small sitting room where Spanish silver candlesticks and a tooled leather chest jostled side by side with English walnut furniture. Mélanie glanced at the mantel clock. Ten minutes past one in the morning. It was already Thursday. Less than three days until Carevalo's deadline. She perched on the edge of a ruby velvet chair and rubbed her arms. The image of the doll with yellow yarn hair danced before her eyes. Beneath the numb aftermath of the crisis, reality gnawed at her insides. "Two children lost their mother tonight."

Edgar turned to look at her. He had found the decanters and was helping himself to a large brandy. "Because of us, you mean?"

"No." Charles was prowling about the room. "Because Helen Trevennen was playing a dangerous and foolish game. Though what exactly that game was—" He brought his fist down on the mantel.

Edgar downed a quarter of the brandy. "We can't be sure Velasquez has the ring."

"On the contrary." Charles drummed his fingers on the plaster. "There's a good chance he doesn't have it. He tore those rooms apart. If he found it, it must have been in the last place he searched."

"Charles." Edgar looked at his brother across the room. His gaze had an intensity that took Mélanie by surprise. "Are you sure Raoul O'Roarke is merely an innocent emissary in all of this?"

Charles rested his foot on the fender. "I'm sure of nothing, especially not where O'Roarke is concerned. Why?"

Edgar scowled, swallowed the rest of his brandy, refilled the glass, and took a turn about the room. "It oughtn't to have anything to do with this. I can't see how it could possibly have anything to do with this. I've been telling myself that since yesterday. But—"

"Edgar." Charles crossed the room in two strides and seized his brother by the shoulders. "This is no time to be making judgments on your own. If there's the remotest connection to Colin, you have to tell us."

Edgar's brows contracted. "It's not that simple, brother."

"It's just that simple, as Mélanie said to me last night." Charles's fingers bit into the black cassimere of Edgar's borrowed coat. "Scruples are nothing next to Colin's safety."

"It's not just scruples, it's—"

Charles slackened his grip. His mouth lifted in one of his warming half-smiles. "All I'm asking for is the truth of whatever it is."

"The truth. Jesus." Edgar tore away from Charles and stared at the dark red folds of the curtains. The lamplight shimmered against the velvet. "Be careful what you ask for, Charles."

Charles's gaze drilled into the back of his brother's head. "Edgar, I haven't got the least idea what you're getting at, but after everything else that's happened, I don't see what you could possibly have to say that I couldn't take in stride."

Edgar crossed to the table where he had left his brandy glass. "You were right. The talk about Kitty—Mrs. Ashford. About her death. It did remind me of Mother."

Mélanie, who had been doing her best to fade into the chair, stared at her brother-in-law at this non sequitur. So did Charles, but he made no comment other than a neutral "Go on."

Edgar took a swallow of brandy. "And you were right that I've avoided talking about Mother's death. I didn't . . . She talked to me before, you see."

"Before she killed herself?"

"Yes. I'd got to Scotland a few days earlier. You were still at Oxford and Father was in London—you know that. Gisèle was in the schoolroom, of course, she was only eight. Mother was in one of her black moods. I'd scarcely seen her since I'd arrived. But that evening she sought me out after dinner. In the billiard room. She said she had to talk to me."

His face twisted. Mélanie understood. She knew all too well the horror of the moment when you opened the door onto the ugliness of the past and forced yourself to go through. The first step over the threshold was always the hardest.

Charles stood absolutely still, yet his body hummed with intensity. "And?"

"We went into the library. She poured us both—brandy." Edgar looked down at the glass in his hand and set it on the nearest table, as though it burned him. "She said she had to tell someone and you weren't there and Gisèle was too young so it would have to be me. She said it was important that we understand."

The words trailed off. Mélanie had the sense that they'd got stuck somewhere between his brain and his lips.

"Understand what?" Charles said.

"She and Father . . ." Edgar's gaze fastened on the plaster garlands on the mantel, as though they were a refuge. "You said it yourself this afternoon. Neither of them was faithful. I'm not sure which of them strayed first or how soon—"

Charles's brows lifted. "From the moment of the betrothal, I should think, at least in Father's case."

"Yes. And Mother . . . she must have followed suit not long after the marriage, because she told me—" Edgar walked forward and gripped the mantel with both hands.

Silence stretched through the room, punctuated by the rattle of wheels in the forecourt outside and the crackle of the coal in the grate. "Edgar, are you trying to tell me I'm a bastard?" Charles said.

Edgar whirled round and stared at him. "Doesn't it bother you?"

Charles ran his fingers through his hair. "Not a great deal. To own the truth, I've wondered for years, and I've been fairly certain since Father died. It explains much of his attitude toward me. I take it he knew?"

"Suspected, I think, the way Mother described it."

"Of course he didn't treat you much better. Unless—no, you've got the Fraser profile." Charles studied his brother. "Why didn't you tell me years ago?"

Edgar straightened his shoulders, as though facing up to an accusation. "I didn't see any reason to burden you with it."

"That was thoughtful if misguided." Charles's voice had that rare, stripped-to-the-bone gentleness it sometimes took on. "And no doubt a strain. No wonder you pulled away from me. In your place I'd have felt a share of jealousy. Everything I inherited—the estates, the Berkeley Square house, the Italian villa—should have been yours."

Edgar flushed. "Charles—"

Charles moved to a chair and perched on its arm. "If you didn't feel jealous, you're more of a saint than I am."

"I'm no saint. I— Yes, all right, I was jealous. A bit." Edgar glanced at his top boots. "Maybe more than a bit at times."

Charles's eyes narrowed. "Did Mother tell you all this because she'd decided to kill herself?"

"I think so, yes, though of course I didn't know it at the time. I was shocked. How could I have been otherwise? I ran from the room. I heard a shot behind me. When I went back—"

He turned his head away. The firelight caught the sparkle of tears on his cheeks. Charles got to his feet, walked forward, and clapped a hand on his brother's shoulder. "Did it ever occur to you that learning Kenneth Fraser wasn't my father would hurt me much less than losing my brother?"

Edgar looked at him with the pained expression of one struggling to find a clear path across shifting sands. "I never meant for you to . . . You'll always be my brother, Charles."

"I'm relieved to hear it." Charles's fingers tightened on Edgar's shoulder for a moment. Then he pulled Edgar to him and put his hand behind Edgar's head, the way he did with Colin. He held his brother for a long moment before he stood back. Mélanie felt the prickle of tears on her own cheeks. "It shouldn't really matter," Charles said, "but did she happen to tell you who my father is?"

Edgar's face drained of color, but Mélanie was ahead of him. A second or so before, an idle part of her brain had linked up his story with the seemingly incongruous questions that had prefaced it. A horrid suspicion she could not quite articulate, even to herself, grew in her mind. She gripped the arms of her chair to keep from leaping out of it.

"That's just it." Edgar stared into Charles's eyes, as though seeking a humane way to deliver a killing blow. "Why I had to tell you. Can't you guess like you guess everything else? Mother spent half her time in Ireland in those days. He was a handsome devil. Still is, come to that."

"He?" Charles said.

"Raoul O'Roarke."

Chapter 30

The words reverberated in Charles's head. He looked at his brother for a long moment. Then he turned on his wife. All the blood had drained from her face. He stared into the broken glass of her eyes while the pieces of his life once more disintegrated and re-formed round him.

He grabbed Mélanie by the wrist. "Edgar, wait for Velasquez. Use whatever threats it takes."

"But—"

"If Velasquez gets back before we do, wait here for us. If some emergency forces you to depart, leave word with the porter."

"Where are you going?"

Charles jerked open the door. "To act on your information and find out what the hell else O'Roarke is hiding."

He pulled Mélanie into the corridor, down the stairs, across the columned portico, and into the forecourt. Two young men in evening cloaks and silk hats were staggering out of a hackney. Charles bundled Mélanie into the hackney, directed the driver to Raoul O'Roarke's hotel, and sat back against the squabs. "Did you know about this?"

"No." A single word, low and numb.

"*Mélanie.*"

"I'm not that good an actress, Charles." Her voice shook like a sail battered by a storm. "I can't believe it's true."

"I fail to see why Edgar would have made it up." He stared into the gloom of the hackney, his vision filled with memories. A cold, chill morning, horses stamping their feet, liveried servants with sherry, ladies in velvet habits, gentlemen in hunting jackets and riding boots. His mother, eyes brilliant with life, tossed into the saddle by O'Roarke. An evening party, hanging over the stair rail with Edgar, his mother and O'Roarke crossing the hall below, his dark head bent close to her golden hair. Coming upon them once, walking together by the lake, her gloved fingers curled round O'Roarke's arm.

Innocent enough memories. She had flirted as much or more with a score of men. But the images were suggestive seen through the glass of Edgar's revelations. "It has a certain internal logic," he said. "Mother spent a great deal of time on Grandfather's Irish estates and O'Roarke would have been at university in Dublin about the time I was conceived. She had a fondness for dark intense types."

He felt Mélanie's gaze fasten on him. "The eyes. I should have seen it."

"What?"

"You have Raoul's eyes. When you were pacing yesterday you reminded me of him, but I never guessed—"

"It would have been rather beyond even your powers of gathering information, *mo chridh.*"

"He lied to me." The words contained a raw pain that Charles knew all too well. "Even when—"

"Even when you were intimate? Yes, it's rather a nasty realization, isn't it?"

She sucked in her breath. "I already knew how despicable such lies are, darling."

"Do you still think O'Roarke knows nothing more about Colin's disappearance?"

"At the moment I can't be sure what I think about anything. All of this may have nothing to do with Colin." Her breath caught, as though she had been dealt a fresh blow. "Except that it means Colin is—"

"My brother."

"Charles— Dearest—"

"I always told Edgar our family are a direct descendant of the House of Atreus. I never realized how spot on I was. No, I'm wrong." His voice cracked. It seemed to have slipped beyond his control. "Clytemnestra slept with a pair of brothers."

"Cousins." Mélanie's own voice was harsh and unsteady. "Aegisthus was Agamemnon's cousin."

"So he was. There must be some mythological heroine who slept with a father and son. Damnable how a classical education deserts one just when it would come in handy."

"Phèdre. But she didn't sleep with the son, she only lusted after him. And no, I never played her. I was too young, and my father didn't care for Racine."

"Pity. You'd have been good at it." He put his hands over his face. "Jesus. Sweet, bloody Jesus. I don't know—" He drew a breath. His chest hurt as though it had been pummeled black and blue. "Colin will always be my son, before anything else. Nothing can change that."

He said nothing more for the rest of the drive, and she followed suit. They went straight to O'Roarke's suite. Charles shouldered past O'Roarke's manservant even more roughly than he had Velasquez's. They waited in the sitting room by the light of a single lamp. A few moments later O'Roarke came in, carelessly wrapped in his dressing gown, with no shirt beneath it, his hair standing on end.

He cast one quick look from Mélanie to Charles. "What's happened? Is it the boy?"

Charles heard Mélanie draw in her breath, then deliberately check herself and cede the reply to him. "Not directly," he said. "That is, we're here to find out how it concerns Colin. My brother just told me that you're my father."

O'Roarke's eyes widened in rare surprise. He swallowed once, started to speak, bit back the words. He smoothed his hand over his hair, scraping it back from his temples. "I didn't realize Captain Fraser knew."

Charles studied the bony, ascetic face, searching for an echo of himself. "It's true, then?"

"Oh, yes." O'Roarke moved to the fireplace and stirred the banked coals. "At least your mother led me to believe so. And I've always fancied I could see something of myself in you."

Charles crossed the room in two strides, seized O'Roarke by the arm, and pushed him into a wing chair. "You sick bastard, how long had you been planning this?"

O'Roarke met his gaze without shying away. "I didn't plan it at all."

"No? You just happened to get Mélanie pregnant and then married her off to your son?" Charles gripped the arms of the chair and leaned over O'Roarke. "I don't give a damn about my own birth, but I want to know what this means for Colin."

"Believe it or not it has nothing to do with Colin. Save that—" O'Roarke drew a breath. "Having watched over you from your birth—albeit often from a distance—I knew I could trust you with Mélanie and her baby."

"Don't." Charles tightened his grip on the chair arms until he could feel the damask give way beneath his fingers. "I may be the most gullible fool since Malvolio, but don't expect me to believe you wasted one minute thinking about Mélanie and the baby."

"I don't expect you to believe anything, Fraser. But it happens to be the truth."

"You set Mélanie to spy on me."

"Loyalty is always a matter of choices. Surely a career in diplomacy and politics has taught you that."

"Your only loyalty is to yourself, O'Roarke." Charles drew back and stared into the gray eyes Mélanie had said were like his own, seeking answers. Throttling the man would be satisfying but would get him nowhere.

Mélanie was staring at O'Roarke. "How could you?" Her sterling and crystal tones gave way to the scrape of iron and rock. "I was carrying your child. Our child. How could you marry me off to your son and not tell me?"

O'Roarke looked past Charles at her. "It would have created unnecessary complications."

She walked up to him and slapped him hard across the face. "My God, Raoul, you were playing games with all of us from the first."

He took the slap without flinching. "But of course. I never pretended otherwise, *querida*. Though the stakes in this particular game were the future of a country." He regarded her for a moment, then got to his feet, walked to a table where decanters were set out, and filled three glasses half full of whisky.

Charles watched him, noting the telltale tremor in his hand, the rattle of the decanter jerking against the glasses. It seemed there were ways in which he took after O'Roarke. "You're saying it's purely coincidence that Carevalo is holding my son and using you for an emissary and that you happen to have . . . fathered both me and Colin?"

"I wouldn't quite call it coincidence." O'Roarke walked across the room and set two of the whiskies down where Charles and Mélanie could reach them. "I had nothing to do with your being sent to retrieve the ring seven years ago, but if you hadn't been my son—if I hadn't known all I know about you—I doubt I'd have been so quick to urge Mélanie to accept your offer of marriage."

Mélanie looked at him as though he had stripped the skin from his face to reveal another person beneath. "For the past two days I've been telling Charles that I knew your limits, that there were certain things you wouldn't do. I don't believe that anymore." She glanced at the whisky. "And getting me drunk won't change things."

"It takes more than half a glass of whisky to get you drunk, Mélanie." O'Roarke returned to the table, picked up the third whisky, and took a swallow. "I'm not claiming to be proud of my actions. I don't know that I'd do what I did again. But then I rarely play a hand the same way twice."

"Is that what we are to you?" Mélanie said. "Charles, Colin, me? Playing cards?"

"No." O'Roarke looked into her eyes. "You were pregnant. I couldn't marry you myself, you didn't want me to send you back to France, you wanted to keep the baby. Charles offered you marriage."

"And as his wife I was ideally positioned to spy for you. Don't deny that that was why you leapt at the opportunity."

"Of course. But as I said, I'd had knowledge of Fraser from the time he was a child. When he was a boy, I knew him rather well." He glanced at Charles. "I don't know that you . . ."

A hand offering ices, advice about how to hold a fishing pole, the treasured copy of *The Rights of Man* with O'Roarke's signature on the flyleaf. Seemingly chance encounters when Charles was out riding or walking, casually begun conversations that touched on ideas Charles barely grasped at the time, but which he drank in with youthful hunger. "I remember," Charles said.

For an instant, the same memories seemed to flicker in O'Roarke's eyes. "I'm glad to hear it." He looked back at Mélanie. "I felt—rightly, I think—that I knew the sort of man Charles was. If I hadn't, I'd have argued against the marriage."

Mélanie watched him with drawn brows and an angry mouth. "So the fact that he was your son made it easier? Sleeping with a father and son is—"

"A sin in the eyes of a church you have no use for."

Mélanie drew a sharp breath and turned her head away. O'Roarke reached out his hand to her, then let it fall.

"And my mother?" Charles said. His voice shook despite his best efforts.

"Your mother was a fascinating and troubled woman, Charles. When I was young I would have said I—" O'Roarke shook his head. "That's neither here nor there. We were lovers off and on for a decade or so, though the affair was at its most intense in the year before you were born." He cleared his throat. "There was no question of not pretending you were Kenneth Fraser's son, of course. Your mother was reckless, but there were certain risks she wasn't prepared to run."

"She told my brother the truth of my birth just before she put a bullet through her brain," Charles said.

O'Roarke's cool gaze wavered, like ice under a hammer blow. "Poor Elizabeth," he said, in a voice so low Charles wasn't sure he had heard correctly. "Poor, stubborn, brave, tormented Elizabeth." He looked at Charles. "She would have wanted you to know the truth. But I'd stake my life on it that her killing herself had nothing to do with you or with your brother or sister."

"No," Charles said. "We weren't important enough to her."

O'Roarke was silent for a moment, but he didn't try to contradict him, which was just as well because Charles would have thrown the words back in his face. "I was always afraid— She couldn't bear being out of control, and she was out of control far too often. I suspect that's what finally drove her to pull the trigger."

"For what it's worth," Charles said, "so do I."

They regarded each other for a moment. Even in death, his mother exerted enough power to hold the attention of two men who should have been at each other's throats. "I don't know that I understand her looking back with thirty-some years' perspective," O'Roarke said. "I certainly didn't understand her at the time. But she meant—a great deal to me. Though not as much, incidentally, as Mélanie later did."

Mélanie turned her gaze from a contemplation of the pastoral print on the wall. "We've had enough of your gambits, Raoul."

"That last was no gambit, *querida*."

"No," Charles said, "that I believe."

O'Roarke met his gaze in silent acknowledgment. "Then surely you realize that Mélanie and the boy—and you yourself, I might add—are the last people on this earth that I'd hurt."

"That doesn't mean you *wouldn't* hurt us." Without pause or inflection, Charles added, "Someone's been trying to kill Mélanie and me."

O'Roarke's gaze skimmed between them. "Hadn't you better tell me about it?"

As succinctly as possible, Charles recounted the events of the past thirty-six hours—the search for Helen Trevennen, the attacks, their meeting with Helen, and their discovery of her body.

O'Roarke's mouth hardened and his hands clenched at the mention of Colin's severed finger, but he bit back whatever he had been going to say. When Charles finished, he went right to the point. "You think Velasquez is behind the attacks on you and Mélanie?"

"It seems most likely. Though it did occur to me that you'd find it inconvenient if Mélanie or I told anyone of your past activities for the French."

"My dear Charles, I assure you I have faced the risk of discovery more than once. I have never resorted to anything as inelegant as murder to protect myself."

"You just said you rarely play a hand the same way twice."

Something glinted in O'Roarke's eyes that might have been appreciation. "If I wanted you dead, Fraser, you would be."

"That's distinctly insulting, Raoul." Mélanie picked up her whisky and took a sip. "And not necessarily true."

"You really think I'd be capable of killing you?"

"A number of people have taught me not to trust, but you certainly made your contribution."

O'Roarke whirled away, then spun round to face them again. "Use your heads, both of you. You have two of the finest brains I've ever encountered. If I thought Mélanie was a liability, I'd have had to worry about her at any time in the past seven years. I convinced you both yesterday morning that I wasn't working with Carevalo. Surely these revelations about Fraser's parentage make that possibility less likely rather than more so. I think you'll understand that, Mélanie, when you stop being outraged because I didn't tell you everything seven years ago."

"Don't push me too hard, Raoul," Mélanie said. "I admit you have a point."

"Progress at least. Charles?"

"Yesterday I decided you were a safer bet than Carevalo. That hasn't changed."

"Good. You both have a right to demand explanations. I'll answer any questions you wish, though perhaps some of them would better wait until after you have the boy back. Now do you want to know what I've learned from Carevalo?"

Mélanie started. "You didn't say—"

"You didn't give me a chance, *querida*. I've received one message from Carevalo. He said he'd been called away by pressing business but he hoped to be back shortly with good news." O'Roarke's mouth curled round this last with cold contempt. "The message was given to an hotel porter by a young street urchin. I managed to trace the lad but he claimed that he'd received the message from a man in a brown coat, and no amount of threats or bribes could produce more information from him or anyone in the vicinity. I also tracked down two of Carevalo's mistresses today, a Covent Garden flower seller and an equestrienne from Astley's Amphitheatre. The flower seller claims not to have seen Carevalo for a fortnight and the equestrienne insists she broke with him a month ago when her husband caught them in her dressing room. But I have some other feelers out and I'll make more inquiries tomorrow. Knowing Carevalo, there were more than two women in his life." He frowned into his whisky glass. "It's difficult to make sense of the facts, isn't it?"

Mélanie rubbed her hands over her face. "Distinctly. Helen

Trevennen made sense up to a certain point, but I can't think why she was so determined to hang on to the ring."

"It obviously had some sort of value to her, greater than anything she thought you and Charles could offer. You aren't sure if Velasquez found the ring?"

"I doubt it," Charles said. "But questioning him is the next step."

O'Roarke nodded. "I suggest you try the Rose and Crown in Haymarket. It's his favorite place to drown his sorrows."

Little remained to be said, and they had already wasted too much time dwelling on personal revelations. He and Mélanie took their leave, engaged another hackney, and made for Haymarket.

They sat in silence. In the past hour, their images of each other had been stripped one level deeper. Charles rubbed his hand across his eyes. His body ached with the weariness that follows extreme exertion. Just when he had begun to feel he might make sense of his life again, the ground had been cut out from under him. For years he had wondered who his father was. Why had it never occurred to him that knowing might be infinitely worse than not knowing?

Raoul O'Roarke was his father. What the hell did that mean? O'Roarke had never been a father to him in the sense that Charles was a father to Colin. And yet, when he was a boy, O'Roarke had attempted to maintain some sort of bond with him. And that, perhaps, was more unsettling than anything.

"The term 'fortune's fool' seems fairly accurate just about now," he said. "It doesn't really matter. Who went between my mother's legs and left the spark of a child behind. It *shouldn't* matter."

"But it does?" Mélanie said.

"I suppose so. Yes. More than I'd care to admit." He pressed his fingers against his temples and breathed in the damp, close air of the hackney, as musty as memories. Without looking at her, he said, "Did you love him?"

It was a long moment before she answered. "He took me out

of the brothel. He gave me a sense of purpose. He taught me that physical intimacy can be more than violence or commerce. How could I not love him?"

Charles had an image of O'Roarke's gaze fixed on her face. For a moment, O'Roarke's eyes had held a bone-deep longing that he knew all too well. "And after tonight?"

"I don't know that tonight changed things. Living with you did."

He twisted his head toward her, though he couldn't make out her expression in the shadows. "Don't insult my intelligence by pretending you married me for love, Mel. I could no more believe that than you could believe O'Roarke wanted you to marry me merely for your own protection."

A flash of lamplight outside the hackney window illumined her eyes. "I didn't say I married you for love, Charles. I said I stayed with you because of it."

He stared into her eyes. It would be so easy to believe, and he wasn't sure he could bear it. " 'Truth is truth / To the end of reckoning,' " he said. "The question would seem to be how to recognize it."

"Please let me know if you ever figure out how, darling."

"My dear wife, haven't I proved that I'm the last person on earth who can recognize anything of the sort?"

They rattled over the cobblestones in silence. Then Mélanie spoke in a voice so low he had to strain to hear her. "I loved Raoul. But I never let myself become lost in that love. I had to protect myself by keeping some part of myself separate. But you." She shook her head. The folds of her cloak rustled. "In the end you held nothing back. So I couldn't either."

"Except for that damnable truth we were just mentioning."

"Except for one part of the truth. Yes. But then you held back the truth about Kitty."

Charles stared at her for a long moment, but made no response. Too soon and too late they pulled up in Haymarket. Lamplight issued forth from the Rose & Crown.

Stale, ale-soaked air greeted them inside. Not one of the roughest taverns in the city, but far from one of the most respectable. They threaded their way among scarred, blackened tables, through eye-stinging smoke, hearty laughter, and over-turned tankards. Fortunately at this hour most of the customers were too cheerful, too morose, or too deep in their cups to pay them much heed.

Mélanie's hand closed on Charles's arm. "There. In the chimney alcove."

Charles followed her gaze. The man's face was half in shadow, but the finely chiseled profile, the heavy line of the brows, the uncompromising set of the shoulders were unmistak-able. He was slumped forward, elbows on the ale-stained table, gaze buried in the depths of his pewter tankard. He did not stir at their approach. They came to a stop before the table, effec-tively blocking any rush to the door.

"Did you think we were dead, Velasquez?" Charles said.

"Fraser." Velasquez dragged his hands from his face and stared up at them. His eyes were red-rimmed. "Mrs. Fraser." He pushed himself to his feet, staggered, and had to grip the table with both hands to keep from falling.

Charles put out a hand to steady him. "You haven't answered my question."

"Why on earth should I think you were dead?" Even from a man in his cups, the words sounded forced.

"Possibly because you've been trying to kill us." Charles pushed Velasquez back into his chair, pulled out a chair for Mélanie, and sat down himself.

Velasquez collapsed backwards with a thud. His gaze was unfocused, but there was wariness in its depths. "Don't know what you're talking about, Fraser."

"Come now, Velasquez, surely the accidents can't have slipped your mind already. The incident with the horse was really very clever. My compliments."

Velasquez rubbed his hand over his eyes. "Fraser—"

"Of course, if you'd been really successful, we'd be as dead as Helen Trevennen."

At the name, Velasquez leapt from his chair and nearly fell across the table. Charles grabbed his arm. "Sit down, Velasquez. You aren't going anywhere. Surely knowing what you do, you can't be surprised that Mélanie and I were in the Constable house shortly after you left it. We found Mrs. Constable's body."

Velasquez drew a breath, as though he was trying to gather his broken defenses. "Who's Mrs. Constable?"

"The woman also known as Helen Trevennen whom you murdered a few hours ago. I'm sure it can't have slipped your mind, however many pints you've downed in an effort to forget."

Velasquez straightened his shoulders and jerked his head up. "I've never heard of either of them."

"Or was it an accident?" Charles continued as though the man hadn't spoken.

Velasquez stared at a point over Charles's shoulder. "I don't know what you're talking about, Fraser."

"Mr. Velasquez." Mélanie gave him one of her sweetest smiles. Her voice rang with sterling truth. "We saw you leaving the Constable house. Edgar Fraser and Charles's valet saw you as well."

Her words had the effect of a chisel applied to faulty plaster. The denial in Velasquez's eyes cracked open to reveal a sick, dark guilt. "But—"

"She woke up while you were searching, didn't she?" Mélanie's gaze was steady, sympathetic, implacable. "The pistol was hers. Was there a struggle? I'm sure you didn't mean to kill her."

Velasquez seemed to have forgotten that there was any question that he'd been in the Constable house. The bravado drained from his soldier's shoulders. His spine curled against the chair back. "I don't know why she woke—I'd swear I was being quiet. She kept a pistol in her bedside drawer. I've never known a woman to do that. She didn't scream. She just told me to get out. It was almost as though she wasn't surprised to find someone searching her bedchamber." He shook his head in disbelief. "I didn't believe she'd shoot. I asked her where the ring was. The woman pretended she didn't know what I was talking about. She jumped out of the bed and aimed the pistol at me. I tried to wrest it away from her and—" He put his hands over his face, as though he would scrape away the memory.

"And the ring?" Charles said.

Velasquez dragged his hands from his face. "Fraser, would I be here if I'd found it? When I realized she was dead, all I could think of was to get away from there as quickly as possible." He stared down at his hands. The guttering candlelight flickered over the smears of dried blood. "I cut my hands to pieces on that damned rope. Oh, God, her face."

"You're a soldier, Velasquez. You've killed before."

"Not a woman." He looked up at Charles. His cousin Kitty's name echoed between them for a moment.

"Why the hell can't you leave our country alone?" Velasquez demanded. "The ring was forged in Spain. It came back from the Crusades, it was spared the Armada, it survived the Inquisition and the endless War of Succession. It belongs in Spain."

"Carevalo is Spanish. The ring belongs to the Carevalo family. You of all people should respect that. You and Kitty had a Carevalo grandmother."

Velasquez's eyes sparked at the mention of his cousin. "Carevalo would turn our country over to the rabble. He fought bravely in the war, but now he's turned traitor to his heritage. And you're helping him. But then betrayal's something you know all about, isn't it, Fraser?"

It was an allusion to Kitty. Velasquez couldn't know what other weight the words carried. "It's true my sympathies are with the liberals rather than the royalists," Charles said. "But that isn't why we're helping Carevalo." He looked at Velasquez and calculated that the truth would serve him better than deception. "Carevalo took our son hostage. He's threatened to kill Colin if we don't produce the ring."

Velasquez stared at him as though he couldn't believe he'd heard correctly. Two men at the table next to them began to argue with the waiter about the reckoning, claiming the wine had been watered.

"Good God, Fraser," Velasquez said. "Why didn't you tell me sooner?"

"I didn't think you'd have much sympathy for a child of mine."

"I'd have sympathy for a child, whoever fathered it. I'm a parent myself now. Christ, if things had been different your son might also have been—"

He couldn't put it into words. Charles could. "Kitty's child."

Velasquez swallowed. "You haven't found the ring?"

"We haven't found it. I suspect it isn't in the house at all." Charles sat back in his chair. "How did you track Helen Trevennen? Did you follow us?"

"Yes, though it was only with the devil's own luck." Velasquez frowned. "It's a bit strong to say I tried to have you killed. Did you say something about an attack with a horse?"

"You needn't try to deny it now, Velasquez. It's hardly worse than what you've admitted doing to Helen Trevennen."

Velasquez reached for his tankard, but seemed too exhausted to lift it to his lips. "Fraser, I'm in no fit state to deny anything or I wouldn't have admitted what I have. I engaged one of the stagehands at the Drury Lane to let me know if anyone came asking questions about Helen Trevennen."

"So you followed us to the Marshalsea and stuck a knife in Mélanie's ribs."

"Knife?" Velasquez thunked his tankard down on the table. A horror that appeared genuine filled his eyes. "See here, Fraser, I wasn't at the Marshalsea until well after you left. That rascal Trevennen wouldn't tell me anything, but the porter remembered that Miss Trevennen had a sister who worked at the Gilded Lily."

"Where you did see us," Charles said. "And paid someone to start a fight and try to break my arm."

Velasquez flushed. "I didn't tell him to break your arm. But I had to do something to get you away from Susan Trevennen."

"And when you had got us away from her?" Mélanie said. "Wasn't it a bit excessive to have a sniper shoot Charles in the street outside?"

"A sniper?" Velasquez blinked, as though he had lost his ability to focus. "Why would I do that? I wanted you as far away from the Gilded Lily as possible."

Charles folded his arms across his chest. It was precisely what he had wondered at the time. "And then?" he said.

Velasquez picked up the tankard. It tilted in his hands as though he'd lost the ability to command his fingers. "After the brawl died down I managed to speak to Susan Trevennen, but she claimed she hadn't seen her sister in ten years. Was she how you found Mrs.—" He took a long swallow from the tankard and choked. Ale dribbled out of his mouth. "Mrs. Constable?"

"In a roundabout manner. What did you do after you left the Gilded Lily?"

"Tried to pick up your trail, but I couldn't discover where you'd gone."

"I'm relieved to hear it."

Velasquez returned the tankard to the table, sloshing the ale over the side. "So I hired a lad to watch Berkeley Square until you returned. He sent word to me this evening. I followed you when you left the house, but I lost you when you changed hackneys the second time. I was just wandering about when I caught a glimpse of you on foot crossing Russell Street. I couldn't believe my luck."

"Nor can I."

"I could tell from your demeanor when you came out that you didn't have the ring. I assumed it was no use my trying to buy it from her if you'd failed. So I went round to the back, waited till the house quieted down, and—" He stared at the table. "You know the rest."

Charles sat back and studied him. The difficulty, as he had said to Mélanie, was to recognize the truth when you saw it. Velasquez was not good at dissimulation, particularly not when he was in his cups. His eyes were bloodshot, his face raw with shame and guilt, his skin slack with drink and exhaustion. "Bow Street know we suspect you in Mrs. Constable's death. We'll have to tell them the whole story when we talk to them, but you should have an hour or so to decide what you're going to do."

Velasquez straightened his shoulders, as though with an effort. "That's more courtesy than I'd have afforded you, Fraser."

Charles looked into Velasquez's eyes. They were the same unexpected green as Kitty's. "For what it's worth, I know something about how it feels to have a death on one's conscience."

Velasquez's eyes narrowed. The past reverberated against the smoke-blackened tavern walls. "You didn't kill anyone."

"Not directly. But if it wasn't for me, Kitty would still be alive." Charles pushed back his chair.

"Fraser," Velasquez said, as Charles helped Mélanie to her feet.

"Yes?"

Velasquez drew a breath. "I don't know why the hell I'm telling you this. I called you a lot of names in our last private conversation. I still believe most of them are true. I still think that if it wasn't for you, Kitty would be alive today. But perhaps she shouldn't be quite as much on your conscience as she is."

The room seemed to rush away round him. He felt Mélanie go still. "Why?" he said.

Velasquez stared at the tabletop for a moment. Then he pushed himself to his feet and looked Charles in the eye. "I was the one who found Kitty in the stream. When I first pulled her body out, all I could think was that she must have thrown herself off the footbridge. I knew the despair she'd been in. I knew I had to make it look like an accident to protect her honor. But later, thinking back—the way her dress was torn, the marks on her neck—" He gripped the edge of the table with both hands. "I think it's possible she didn't jump from the bridge, Fraser. I think she may have been pushed."

Chapter 31

Mélanie saw a tumult of feeling rush across her husband's face. The slosh of ale and the clatter of cutlery drifted through the tavern. Someone was tossing dice. Someone else hummed a fragment of "Over the Hills and Far Away."

"That doesn't make any sense," Charles said at last.

"I know." Velasquez stood still and alert despite the weariness in his face. "I'd have sworn Kitty didn't have any enemies. Of course, I'd also have sworn she didn't have a lover." He drew a breath, then glanced down at the table. "Her husband was away. You weren't there. When I challenged you, I still half believed it was suicide because I couldn't make sense of any other scenario. And because I wanted you to believe it. Because I wanted you to suffer. I thought you deserved to suffer." He looked up at Charles again, his bloodshot eyes hard as a musket barrel. "You did deserve to suffer."

"Granted." Charles's face was set with intensity. "You're sure it isn't just that you couldn't face that she'd killed herself?"

"Every moment of that night is etched into my memory. I don't see how she could have come by those marks or the damage to her gown without another person being involved." Velasquez's hand curled into a fist. "I'd give a great deal to know whom."

"So would I," Charles said.

The two men looked at each other for a moment, a whiff of understanding between them. "Thank you, Velasquez," Charles said. "I appreciate your confidence."

Velasquez inclined his head, a stiff, soldier's nod. Then he frowned. "It's odd, you know. He was there that night. The night Kitty died."

"Who?"

"Lieutenant Jennings. But I daresay it's just coincidence. He scarcely knew Kitty."

"It's still possible the ring is in the Constable house," Charles said when he and Mélanie had left the smoky warmth of the tavern for the crisp bite of the street. "We could find Roth and arrange a search of the house."

"But by the time we explain the story and Mr. Constable is persuaded to go along with the search, it could take hours."

"My thoughts exactly. And my instinct says the ring isn't in the house."

"Mine, too." Mélanie fingered the silk braid that edged her cloak. "Charles, suppose she didn't take it to Brighton with her at all?"

Two young men in coats with absurdly padded shoulders staggered out of the tavern, shouting for a hackney. Charles took Mélanie's arm and began to walk along the pavement. "What makes you think she didn't take the ring with her?"

"Her departure for Brighton seems to have been triggered by the arrival of Jennings's letter and the ring. When she left she seemed to think she could be in danger if she stayed in London. As you pointed out, her refusal to give up the ring today implies that she feared grave consequences if she did so. The woman used to carry a pistol in her reticule. Perhaps she still did. We know she slept with a gun in her nightstand—either she had it there always or she put it there tonight because she feared we'd come after the ring. Whatever the truth of it, she was frightened, and she wasn't a woman who frightened easily. It looks to me as though her fear was connected with the ring, though I can't begin to think how. But if the ring was important yet potentially dangerous, I think I'd have hidden it rather than taking it to Brighton with me."

"Well reasoned, Mel." Charles swung round to look at her in the glow of a street lamp. His face was still drawn, but his eyes had the light of the chase. "She had little more than twenty-four hours between the arrival of Jennings's letter and her own departure. She performed at the Drury Lane, she went to a tavern with Violet Goddard, she—"

"Sought out Jemmy Moore."

"Who seems to have meant more to her than anyone." Charles glanced up and down the street and flagged down a passing hackney before the inebriated young men by the tavern could commandeer it. "Jemmy Moore should be at Mannerling's at this hour. We can collect Edgar from the Albany on the way. If we can't learn anything from Moore, we'll see what progress Roth has made at the Constable house."

It was only when they were in the hackney that she said, "Velasquez was quite convincing when he claimed not to have been behind the attacks."

"Quite."

Without looking at him, she continued, "Raoul was convincing as well, but he's a better actor."

Charles turned his head toward her. "An admission. I'm impressed."

"Raoul always said I'd make a better agent if I was quicker to admit I was wrong." The threat of betraying tears pulled at her face. Raoul O'Roarke and their cause had been the center of her life. She had always known his greatest loyalty wasn't to her and never would be. But she had trusted him far more than she would admit, even to herself. Yet another weakness. "I don't trust my judgment of anyone anymore," she said.

"I know the feeling." To her surprise, Charles's voice was more gentle than bitter. He was silent for a moment. "Oddly enough, after that last scene I'm less inclined to suspect O'Roarke."

His words eased the knot of fear inside her. "Then you think Velasquez is lying about not being behind the attacks?"

"I'm not sure."

She reached for the carriage strap as they rounded a corner. "The incident with the horse might have been an accident, but the rifle shot and the knife in my ribs certainly weren't."

"I know."

"You don't suppose someone else could be after the ring?"

She couldn't see Charles's face, but she could imagine him scowling in frustrated concentration. "It's mad, but it's the only alternative I can see to O'Roarke or Velasquez."

"Charles." She hesitated. She wasn't sure if she should ask, but this would be their last chance to talk alone for God knew how long. "Can you think of anyone who might have killed Kitty?"

For a moment she thought he wasn't going to answer. "No." His voice was rougher than it had been.

"What about the rest of her family? Suppose they'd found out about the pregnancy and couldn't bear the scandal?"

"None of them were in Lisbon. Her mother had died a few years before. Her father was in the country. Both her brothers were off fighting."

"A fellow officer of her husband's who'd learned the truth?"

"Possibly, but I can't imagine how anyone would have learned it. Velasquez only knew because Kitty told him."

Mélanie pictured the winding paths in the embassy garden where Kitty Ashford had met her death, the curving footbridge, the rushing stream below. "Perhaps she stumbled across something in the garden that she wasn't supposed to see?"

"You think someone killed her because she witnessed an amorous intrigue?"

"If the stakes were high enough, I suppose it's possible. But there were a lot of intrigues in Lisbon that weren't amorous."

"Espionage?" Charles reached across the carriage and gripped her wrist. "What have you heard?"

"Nothing, darling, I swear it. I'm only speculating. I don't know much about what was happening in Lisbon before I came there."

He slackened his grip on her wrist. To her surprise, he laced his fingers through her own and let their clasped hands rest on the worn leather of the seat. "I admit I'd very much like to find out. But it's of little urgency beside the ring."

"No. Unless—" The pieces of information sifted through her brain. "Unless it's not coincidence that Jennings was at the embassy that night."

"Jennings would have had no reason to kill Kitty. Velasquez was right, he scarcely knew her. Oh, I see." She felt his sudden alertness. "The blackmail."

"Suppose Jennings witnessed Kitty's murder. Murder's a secret a lot of people would pay to conceal."

"And Jennings wrote to Helen Trevennen about it and she took up the blackmail. Possible, I suppose. I wonder—" His fingers tensed round her own, then relaxed. "Even if that were true, it still doesn't take us to the ring. Which at present is all that matters."

They had the hackney wait while they went into the Albany. They found Edgar pacing the carpet in Velasquez's sitting room. On the drive to Mannerling's, Charles gave the details of their talk with Velasquez and their conclusions about the ring. He made no mention of Velasquez's revelations about Kitty's death, and he glossed over the visit to Raoul. Edgar didn't press him for details.

Mélanie could feel her brother-in-law trying to sort through the morass of new information. "It doesn't make any sense that she'd be afraid of the ring," he said.

"No sense at all," Mélanie agreed. "Except that it's the only theory that makes sense of her actions."

Charles was sitting very still. "We can't tell Jemmy Moore she's dead."

"Good God, Charles." Edgar straightened up with a jerk. "Don't you think he deserves to know?"

"Undoubtedly. I suspect the news will hit him as hard as it did Mr. Constable. But he'd want to run off and take his revenge. We wouldn't get anything coherent out of him." Charles paused a moment, glanced at Mélanie, then added, "Lying's not pleasant, but at times it's necessary."

At Mannerling's, the porter frowned at them through the eyehole, then slid the bolt back with a grudging scrape. "Mr. Morningham," Charles said, handing over his cloak and hat. "Is he here tonight?"

The porter's scowl deepened. He cast a pointed glance up the stairs at the broken section of balustrade. It had been closed off with a red velvet rope.

"We merely have a question to put to him," Charles said. "We promise not to brawl."

The porter moved to Mélanie and took her cloak from her shoulders. His hands were stiff. "Upstairs. Try the faro bank."

Jemmy Moore spotted them as they came into the long room with the faro table. Instead of running away, he came toward them. "Did you find her?" he asked as they met in the center of the room. He made no attempt to keep the eagerness from his voice.

"Not yet, I'm afraid." When called upon to do so, Charles could lie with as much conviction as Mélanie herself could. "Could you spare us a moment? Perhaps we could go into the supper room?"

"Of course." Moore squared his shoulders and offered his arm to Mélanie.

"Mr. Moore," Mélanie said when they were clustered round one of the small tables near the supper buffet, "the last time you saw Miss Trevennen, did she give you anything to keep for her?"

"What?" Moore scratched his head. "Oh, you think she might have given me this ring you're looking for? Sorry. I doubt Nelly had so much trust in me."

"Did she say anything else about where she'd been that day?" Charles asked.

Moore frowned into his glass of champagne. "She'd obviously been to the theater—she still had some of her makeup on. We—ah—we didn't actually do that much talking."

"Of course." Mélanie smiled at him. "How else does one say farewell to a lover?"

Moore returned the smile. It was, it seemed, a happy memory. She was glad he had some of them. "In the morning she told me she was leaving and I— Well, I told you about the conversation. I wasn't thinking very clearly, I'm afraid, because it was so damned early. She said she had to get up so she could be at the Marshalsea to visit her uncle when the gates opened."

Mélanie felt her shoulders jerk. "She was going to visit her uncle before she left?"

"Yes. Wanted to say good-bye, I suppose. More consideration than she usually gave the old boy."

Edgar glanced from Mélanie to Charles. "Nothing so very odd in that."

"Except that according to Trevennen she never actually did say goodbye. She asked Violet Goddard to tell him she'd left London." Charles looked at Mélanie, eyes alight.

Moore frowned. "You mean Nelly didn't visit him after all? She seemed quite set on it when she left my rooms."

Charles tapped his fingers on the damask tablecloth. "I suspect she went to see him but didn't tell him she was leaving London. Because she wanted the visit to appear perfectly ordinary."

Edgar leaned forward. "I say, Charles."

"What better hiding place than a debtor's prison?" Charles

said. "She knew there was little chance of her uncle leaving." He pushed back his chair. "Mr. Moore, thank you. This may prove invaluable."

"Oh, of course. Glad to help." Moore seemed to have quite forgotten his earlier mistrust of them. But then this was a man who had been able to forgive and forget all too easily with Helen Trevennen.

"Is there anything else?" Mélanie asked, looking into his eyes. "Any other detail you can remember about the last time you saw her, even if it seems insignificant?"

Moore ran his fingers down the stem of his champagne glass. "No. I'm afraid not. Except . . ." He scratched his head. "I told you I didn't ask if she was going off with another man. That's not strictly true, though I don't like to remember it. I did ask in the end. Couldn't help myself. Nelly just laughed and said, 'Not exactly. But I'll be well taken care of, thanks to poor Tom.'"

"Tom? Do you know who that was?"

"Haven't the faintest idea. Probably just one of Nelly's jokes. I never knew when she was being serious or when she was funning."

Mélanie pressed his hand. "Thank you, Mr. Moore. My husband is right. Your help has been invaluable."

"We can't get into the Marshalsea at this hour," Edgar said as they descended the stairs. "The gates will be locked until morning."

"The gates will be locked, but we'll manage to get in."

"Christ, Charles, you aren't going to break into a prison?"

"Only as a last resort. I'm going to pull rank as I never have before."

They had reached the street. "Should we travel separately?" Edgar asked as Charles hailed a hackney.

"Now?" Charles said. "Velasquez is in no fit state to follow us. I admit it's possible there's someone else after the ring, but I'm more concerned with not wasting time."

The streets round the docks were relatively free of traffic at this hour, but the drive to Southwark still seemed to take far too long. The porter at the Marshalsea was disinclined to let anyone in or even listen to their story. It took a quarter hour to persuade him to show them into a small, airless sitting room and summon the jailer and another quarter hour for the jailer to appear. Charles, in his most biting tones, proceeded to invoke the names of his ducal grandfather, the Foreign Secretary, the Prime Minister, and the Leader of the Opposition. Mélanie contributed the most winning smile she could muster and a discreet display of the clocks embroidered on her silk-stockinged ankles.

At length, they were escorted down a passageway to another room, given a lantern, and set free to seek out Hugo Trevennen.

"I say," the jailer exclaimed. "What's become of the other gentleman?"

What indeed. Mélanie realized she hadn't seen Edgar since they'd left the sitting room.

"I daresay we'll find him," Charles said. "Very enterprising of Edgar," he murmured to her as they started down the walkway. "He's either learning from us or being corrupted by us, depending on one's view."

The walkways that had been full of activity yesterday afternoon were dark and still. Light shone behind a few windows and occasionally voices drifted through the glass, but for the most part the Marshalsea had settled down for the night.

Charles knocked once on Hugo Trevennen's door, turned the knob, and walked in without waiting for a reply. "Trevennen? Edgar?"

The smell of tallow candles hung in the air. The wavering light made shadows out of the cracks in the wallpaper and bounced off the grimy glass that covered the theatrical prints. Trevennen stood in the center of the room, wrapped in a brocade dressing gown, eyes wide with amazement. Edgar was in front of the fireplace. He held one of the fireplace tiles in his left hand. With his right hand, he was reaching into a gap where the tile had stood.

Mélanie froze and felt Charles do the same. Trevennen started, turned round, gave a smile, and broke the wax-thick silence. " 'But soft, the fair Ophelia.' "

Edgar swung his head round.

"For God's sake, Edgar." Charles strode across the room. "What have you found?"

Edgar withdrew his hand from the aperture, clutching a handful of papers. Mélanie hurried after Charles. Edgar glanced up at them, then unwrapped the papers without speaking. The tallow light caught the glint of gold. Mélanie felt a film of sweat break out on her forehead.

Charles reached into the paper wrappings. He lifted out an oval pendant set with carnelians. No lion, no rubies, no ring. Disappointment rushed through her, leaving her dizzy.

Charles had gone completely still. For a moment, his gaze met Edgar's. Some sort of silent communication passed between them that she could not begin to fathom.

Charles turned the pendant in his hand. Mélanie started to speak, then checked herself. Charles ran his fingers over the pendant and pressed two of the carnelians. The front of the pendant fell open, revealing a small pocket. Nestled within that pocket was the gleam of darker gold and a bloodred glow that could only be rubies.

Charles lifted it out. A circle of gold and a lion's head with ruby eyes.

Chapter 32

For a moment, all Mélanie could do was stare. The ring shimmered before her. The ring Princess Aysha had commissioned for her husband or her secret lover. The ring Ramón de Carevalo had taken as plunder or received as a gift of love. The ring that had been the cause of victory and betrayal and murder. The gold had a luminous sheen, perhaps because of its age or the fineness of the metalwork or perhaps because one saw it through layers of history.

Mélanie put her fingers to the cold metal to be sure it was really there. She looked into Charles's eyes and saw a relief so profound it could not be put into words. For all that the ring had been coveted throughout the centuries, surely no one could have valued it as much as they did in this moment.

Edgar wadded up the paper wrappings and tossed them onto the fire.

"I take it you've found what you needed?" Trevennen said.

"Yes," Charles said. "Oh, yes."

"And to think I never knew it was there. Extraordinary. But why on earth did she think it necessary to hide it? The necklace is a pretty thing and the ring might have fetched her a tidy sum."

"We may never know." Charles unhooked his watch chain, strung the ring on it, and rehooked it.

Trevennen shook his head. "Nelly always was one for freakish starts. But I would never expect her to hide away something of value. She didn't exactly agree with the Bard that 'The purest treasure mortal times afford / Is spotless reputation.' Quite the reverse, in fact."

Edgar didn't speak until they were back in the hackney. "I don't believe it," he said then. His voice was faint, as though he was still in shock. "To own the truth, I don't think I really believed you'd find it."

"You found it, brother," Charles said.

"Only because I was there first." Edgar's voice shook with the remnants of disbelief. "So we now have to wait until morning to place an advertisement in the *Morning Chronicle* and then wait on Carevalo?"

"Damnable, I know. But I don't think Carevalo will want to wait any more than we do. We should hear from him early tomorrow."

"Will he give Colin back?"

Charles was silent for the distance between two street lamps. "He'll agree to meet us. We'll make sure he gives Colin back."

Mélanie rubbed her hands over the velvet of her cloak. Her palms were damp. The first euphoric rush of the ring's discovery had faded. The constant need to think and plan was gone, leaving a hollow void inside her. All the fears she had forced herself to hold at bay during the search crowded into that void.

Her legs felt unsteady beneath her as they climbed the front steps in Berkeley Square. Her arms quivered, as they did after she'd carried Jessica back from a long walk. She was conscious of aches in her muscles that she hadn't been aware of before.

"Mr. O'Roarke arrived a short time ago," Michael told them as he took their cloaks. "He's in the library."

They hurried into the library. Raoul was standing over the chessboard, a pawn in one hand. "Mélanie. Fraser. You'll forgive me, but—" He scanned their faces. "You've found it?"

Charles paused just beyond the threshold. One gray gaze met another. In that moment, Mélanie thought that she was a fool not to have seen long since that they were father and son. Charles unhooked his watch chain and held out the ring.

Raoul stared at it. "My compliments."

"It was Mélanie who steered us in the right direction, and Edgar who actually found it. You remember my brother?"

"Captain Fraser." Raoul inclined his head.

Edgar returned the gesture with a stiff nod. "O'Roarke."

Raoul's gaze turned back to the ring. "I always thought all the fuss about a bit of gold and gems was foolish. Yet it does have a certain power, if only because so many generations have endowed it with that power. Where was it?"

Charles returned the ring to his watch chain. "In her uncle's rooms in the Marshalsea."

Raoul lifted his brows. "Remarkable. But why hide it?"

"Insurance against a bleak future, perhaps?" Charles said. "The truth is, we don't know and perhaps never will."

Mélanie walked into the room. "Why are you here, Raoul?" Belatedly, she remembered Edgar's presence and realized she should have said "Mr. O'Roarke."

Raoul set the pawn back on its black square on the chessboard. "I know where Carevalo is."

Mélanie was at his side in an instant. "What?"

Raoul squeezed her fingers and detached her hand from his sleeve, a warning in his eyes. "Earlier today—yesterday, strictly speaking—I attempted to trace a lady of Carevalo's acquaintance who plies her wares in Soho. She goes by the name of Corinthian Nan. She has no permanent address, so it was difficult to track her down, but I left numerous messages with offers of a generous reward. She arrived at my hotel shortly after you left tonight."

Charles closed the distance between them. "She'd seen Carevalo?"

"Not for several days. But apparently he talks to her more than to anyone else—perhaps he feels free to do so because she's so far removed from the circles in which any of us move. He seems to have enjoyed boasting to her about his other conquests, which is about the level of finesse one could expect from Carevalo in the bedchamber. According to Corinthian Nan, Carevalo's been much preoccupied with a Mrs. Grafton, who possesses a convenient Thames-side villa in Chiswick to which she can escape while business keeps her husband in town. The villa is kept shut up, except when the family go there in the summer. Mrs. Grafton even gave Carevalo a set of keys—he showed them to Corinthian Nan as a boast of his powers."

Charles frowned. "That doesn't prove—"

"No. But after Nan left, I turned to last week's editions of the *Morning Chronicle*—I had sent out for them earlier, thinking they might be of help. Which they were. According to that estimable paper, Mr. and Mrs. Grafton departed for Paris on Friday last. Leaving a conveniently empty house in Chiswick to which Carevalo possesses keys. I was going to wait for you another quarter hour, then set off for Chiswick myself."

Charles nodded. "It's not conclusive, but it's definitely worth investigating."

Edgar stared at Raoul from beneath drawn brows. "You're being very generous with your help, O'Roarke."

Raoul turned his gaze to him. "My dear Captain Fraser." His voice was gentle. "The boy is my grandson."

Edgar flushed and lowered his gaze.

Charles paced the carpet. "If you involve yourself, Carevalo will know you're working with us."

Raoul's mouth tightened. "At the moment that seems of little concern. I find I'm rather averse to the idea of Carevalo surviving this business."

Charles met his gaze with the force of one sword striking another. "We get Colin back before we even think of vengeance."

"That goes without saying. I think we can safely take one of your carriages. There seems little risk of being followed."

Mélanie saw Charles bridle at the word "we," consider the value of help, and come to a decision. "I'll order the carriage. We can leave in a quarter hour."

"We'll need to reload the pistols," Edgar said. "I'll fetch dry powder. You still keep it in your study?"

The Fraser brothers strode from the room. The heavy doors closed. For the first time in years, Mélanie found herself alone with her former lover.

She felt his gaze on her. He could read her like no one else—except Charles, which was odd, as she'd kept so much from Charles. "Are you going to be all right, *querida*?" His voice had that cashmere softness that was so rare and so devastating.

She walked to the fireplace, arms wrapped round herself. "If we get Colin back, the rest of it doesn't matter."

He followed her with his gaze. "I don't think even you believe that's true, Mélanie. Getting Colin back of course comes before everything else, but I think your life with Charles matters very much to you."

"Thank you, Raoul." Her voice was so dry it cut. "I must be getting very slow. I keep forgetting that you know me better than I know myself."

"Never that. But I may on occasion see things you miss." He regarded her, his head tilted to one side. "It strikes me that Charles's capacity for forgiveness and understanding is remarkable."

Charles's face, when the full realization of her betrayal had broken on him, was imprinted on her memory like a battle scar. "Some things are beyond forgiveness, Raoul."

He wandered back to the chessboard and stared down at it. "Like marrying your mistress to your son?"

She watched him, the graceful hands, the loose, elegant

limbs, the face that could hide more than that of any man she knew. "Among other things."

"Most of which, no doubt, I've done in my life." He picked up a knight and moved it. "Who was playing white, you or Charles?"

"I was."

He reached for a rook and paused with the crenellated top between his fingers. "He had you quite neatly boxed in. You saw a way out?"

She stared at the board. Memory of that two-day-old game returned like the plot of some long-forgotten play. "I was going to use the pawn on the far left to block his bishop, then bring up the rook to put him in check."

"Yes, that's what I would have done myself. He could protect his king, but you'd have him on the run."

She watched his elegant fingers hover over the board. Memories coursed through her with unexpected strength. Fingers brushing her cheek as she drifted into sleep. A steady hand teaching her how to fire a pistol and wield a knife. The glow of cannon fire reflected in his eyes. The feel of his hands tossing her into the saddle. The knowledge that only he could understand the way their work corroded the soul. The rush of one mind meeting another, as sweet as a caress, as intoxicating as champagne. "I knew you used me," she said, "like you used everyone else. But I thought you were honest about it."

He moved her rook to the attack, then moved one of Charles's knights to protect his king. "If I'd told you Charles is my son, would you have made a different choice?"

She bit back an angry retort and forced herself to consider. "I don't know. But I should have been able to decide for myself."

He turned from the chessboard and looked her in the face. "Are you sorry you're married to him?"

"Not for myself. But we did an unforgivable thing to him, Raoul. I don't expect him ever to trust me again. I only hope he doesn't lose his ability to trust at all."

"Charles is too sensible a man to do that."

"He has as many scars as the rest of us. Perhaps more. He's just adept at hiding them." She looked into his steady gray eyes. A painful truth burst from her lips. "Oh, God, Raoul, I probably would have married him even if I'd known he was your son. Part of me couldn't resist the opportunity. Not just for liberty or the future of Spain. For the sheer challenge of it. What could be more difficult? To deceive my own husband." And not just any husband. A man with whom she seemed to share her soul. With whom she did share her soul. "It was my greatest role."

"And you played it superbly."

"Because, as in all good performances, I found the truth within it. I learned to love Charles and that made it easier to betray him. You taught me well."

Instead of meeting the challenge in her eyes, his gaze softened, most unfairly. "Even if Charles can forgive you, can you ever forgive yourself?"

"I don't know." She swallowed, aware of a bitter, empty place deep inside her. "I've long since faced the fact that much of what we did was unforgivable."

He looked down at the chessboard again, the pieces frozen in the midst of plot and counterplot. "Betrayal has such a black-and-white sound, doesn't it?" His fingers drifted over the squares of the chessboard. "But like most things, it really isn't anything of the sort. Betrayal of a country, an ideal, a lover, a spouse, a friend. It's often impossible to be loyal to all. Which loyalty comes first?"

She glanced at the Siena marble table, the Aubusson carpet, the silver candlesticks, the intricate fretwork on the walls. "I claim to believe in liberty, equality, and fraternity. And I live here."

"A point. Though judging by those of Charles's speeches I've read, his political ideals are remarkably similar to yours. Or mine, for that matter."

"That's true. And he wouldn't let them be compromised by the challenge of a game."

"He moves in a different world than we did. He plays within

the system, which can be damnably difficult when the system itself is corrupt."

"But at least it doesn't force him to hide in the shadows."

"You've hardly been hiding in the shadows these past years, *querida*." Raoul watched her with a faint smile. "You help write his speeches, don't you?"

"Is my style so obvious?"

"Only to someone who knows you."

"Charles helps me when I address a public meeting or write a pamphlet. We—work well together." The words seemed pathetically inadequate to describe the melding of minds that their marriage could be. "I've never tried to influence him to say anything he didn't believe in. Nor has he with me."

"No, that would be out of character for both of you." Raoul was still watching her steadily.

She looked into his smiling, unreadable gaze. "You've followed Charles's career more closely than I realized."

"I could hardly fail to be interested." He paused a moment. "I must admit that when I read his speeches I'm conscious of a pride I have no right to feel."

"How could you bear it?" she said, thinking of Charles and Colin and what he had and hadn't been to both of them. "You gave up both your sons."

The smile faded from his eyes, replaced by the blankness of emotion held in check. "I was scarcely in a position to do much for either one of them."

"Did it never occur to you that they might need you?"

His mouth twisted. "I don't think I'd have made much of a father, *querida*. Colin has a far better one."

"Charles didn't."

"No. Charles's childhood was—unfortunate. I did try— When he was a boy, when I was still in Ireland, I spent time with him when I could, without rousing suspicions. But then after the Irish uprising it was a long time before I could comfortably go back to Britain." He paused and drew a breath that did not sound entirely even. "His mother would send me news of him from time to time. I confess—I missed him more than I would have expected."

Mélanie stared at him. At nineteen, she had been arrogantly confident that she understood him. Now she wondered if she had known him at all. "The lock of hair," she said. "The lock of blond hair you keep in your watch fob. For a moment I thought it might be Elizabeth Fraser's. But it isn't a woman's at all, is it? It's Charles's baby hair."

Raoul returned her gaze, though she sensed he wanted nothing so much as to look away from her. "What a dreadfully sentimental thought."

She took a step toward him. "If you owe me nothing else, you owe me an honest answer. We're talking about my husband. It's Charles's, isn't it?"

Raoul drew another harsh breath, then released it. "Elizabeth sent the lock of hair to me just after his first birthday. It's hardly the sort of thing I could fail to keep."

"You could have tucked it away in a drawer somewhere. Instead you carried it with you. Because—"

He continued to watch her. She would swear his color had deepened. "I may not have your parental instincts, Mélanie, but I'm not wholly devoid of them."

She remembered, in a moment of foolishness after Colin's birth, asking Raoul if he wanted to see the baby. Raoul had said *No, I think I'd better not* in the sort of detached voice that, now she thought about it, was just like Charles's when he most wanted to hide his feelings. Later Raoul had seen Colin at a reception she and Charles gave in Lisbon. He looked at the child with the same carefully blank expression she had seen on his face a few moments ago. "That's why you never wanted to see Colin, isn't it? Not because you didn't care, but because you were afraid of caring too much. Because in your own way you'd done your damnedest to be a parent to Charles and you knew how much loving a child can hurt."

"Colin didn't need another parent. Charles did."

"And yet when you saw Charles again in Lisbon—"

A shade closed over the pain in his eyes. "He was a grown man and we were on opposite sides."

She held him with her gaze, refusing to have her questions turned away. "You sent me after the ring knowing I'd meet your son. Did you expect me to seduce him?"

"I never asked you how you got your information. Though seduction would have been at odds with the role you were playing on that mission."

"*Damn* you." She whirled away from him, then turned back and said with reckless defiance, "Charles is mad enough to think you're in love with me."

Raoul went still for the length of a musket shot. "I told you he was a sensible man."

She tried to swallow and found her throat constricted. "You never said it."

"Don't you go sentimental on me, *querida*. You never needed words to know what I was thinking or feeling."

Her fingers closed on her arms, pressing through the merino of her gown. "I never had time to pay much attention to my own feelings, let alone anyone else's."

"Precisely." He moved toward her, then checked himself a few feet off. She knew only one other pair of eyes that could be at once so cool and so intense. "Long before I met you I'd decided where my greatest loyalty lay. I consider regrets a singular waste of time. That doesn't mean I don't have them. But any good chess player knows one can't change one's mind after a piece is moved." His gaze moved over her face. She felt it like a caress. "I remember when I realized I'd lost you. No, that's melodramatic and unfair. You were never mine to lose. But I remember when I realized things would never be the same between us. You hadn't been married long. We met in a park in Lisbon on a miserably cold January afternoon. You said—"

"That it wasn't at all like I expected and I couldn't control him." It was what she had lain in bed thinking on her wedding night, while Charles slept in her arms. She'd known that he had a quick wit she admired, a keen mind that could prove dangerous, an integrity that put her to shame. But she hadn't guessed at the emotional depths that lay beneath the cool, controlled façade.

Raoul moved to the fireplace and stood looking down at the coals. "Mélanie, if worst does come to worst—"

"You'd take me back?" She gave the words a bitter twist.

He looked at her over his shoulder. "I won't insult either you or myself by taking that seriously. But I would make sure you and your children were never in want. I owe you that, at least."

"Easing your conscience?"

"Say, rather, settling an old debt. Before today I'd have said that under the same circumstances you'd do as much for me."

"That might still be true." She watched his face in the firelight. She wondered how such a tumult of conflicting feelings could coexist inside her. "Raoul? Do you ever wonder if we were wrong?"

He smiled. "Oh, my darling girl. I rarely sleep well. As you know better than anyone."

"Did you ever think about—"

"Giving it up? Walking away from the game? Yes, as a matter of fact. When you told me you were pregnant."

She sucked in her breath and put a hand on a chair back to steady herself.

He continued to regard her with a steady gaze. "But in the end my love of the game was too strong. Or my belief in the cause. Or both."

"Perhaps we never should have begun the game in the first place."

"I rate my powers rather high, *querida*, but I didn't begin the war. Would any purpose have been better served if I'd joined the French army and spent the war in straightforward butchery? If you'd remained in the brothel and sold your body to whichever army controlled the city?"

"We didn't do very well as it was, Raoul. We lost."

"We tried. That's the most one can ask of one's self."

"That," Mélanie said, "sounds exactly like something

Charles might say. Only underneath he'd be cursing himself for his inability to win the war single-handed."

Raoul's mouth lifted in the ghost of a smile. "Then in some ways, he's remarkably like me."

The door opened on his last words to admit Charles and Edgar. Charles paused on the threshold and surveyed her and Raoul for a moment, then continued pulling on his gloves as though he had noticed nothing. "The carriage is ready. Shall we go?"

Chapter 33

On a warm spring afternoon, in an open carriage, bound for a breakfast or a fête champêtre with a basket from Fortnum & Mason tucked under the seat, the drive to Chiswick seemed to take no time. On this chill November night, in the stale air of the traveling carriage, with the prospect of seeing Carevalo at the end of it, each length of road pulled at Mélanie's worn nerves.

Edgar settled back in his corner of the carriage. "If Carevalo's alone in the house and we take him unawares, we might not have to give him the ring."

"We play by the rules until we have Colin back," Charles said. His voice left no room for discussion.

"Carevalo may not play by the rules."

"I know. But he wants the ring. I won't employ our bargaining chip lightly."

"Charles, there are four of us and one of him—"

"And if we start brandishing guns about, someone's likely to get shot. Possibly even Carevalo. He's the only one who can take us to Colin. Until he does so, his life is more precious than our own."

That silenced Edgar. Raoul had the sense to say nothing at all.

They stopped at an inn in the village to inquire about the exact location of the Graftons' villa. A groom who appeared to have been dozing at his post gave them the direction willingly enough and confirmed that the Graftons had indeed departed for France and the villa was closed up.

They resumed their journey and at last pulled up at a pair of locked iron gates. One of Mélanie's picklocks made short work of the bolts, and they wound down the oak-shaded drive. On Charles's orders, Randall pulled up out of view of the house. They left the carriage and walked along the gravel drive on foot, by the light of the three-quarter moon and a vast scattering of stars. The villa was serene and classical in the moonlight. The walls were a brick that was probably red in the light of day, the windows framed in white. No light shone behind them.

When they reached the circular drive in front of the house, Raoul stopped and peered at the ground, still muddy from yesterday's rain. "Fresh footprints. A man's. And by the look of it, he wasn't wearing laborer's boots."

"The two of you wait here," Charles told Raoul and Edgar. "Keep an eye out for any unexpected arrivals. If we don't come out in half an hour, follow us."

Edgar made a stir of protest, but Raoul's hand closed on his arm. "Right."

Mélanie and Charles paused in front of the Corinthian portico, a miniaturized version of Palladian splendor. They stared up at the dark mass of the door, exchanged glances, and with one accord made their way round the side of the house. A faint light glowed in the chink between the heavy curtains of one of the ground-floor rooms. Yet more evidence that Carevalo was probably within. Her senses quickened. They stopped and studied the windows for a moment, then continued round to the back of the house.

A stirring of wind brought the damp air of the river. The moonlight shone off the smooth flagstones of the terrace. The French windows opened with the simplest pressure from one of her picklocks. They stepped onto a tiled floor and were enveloped by the smell of loamy earth and fresh flowers.

The conservatory gave onto a long, high-ceilinged hall, lit by the moonlight coming through the tall windows that flanked the front door. A wedge of light showed beneath one of the doors off the hall. As they approached it, Mélanie heard a faint scrape of metal against fabric. Charles glanced at her over his shoulder and slid his pistol from his pocket. His eyes were dark blurs in the shadowy hall, but she read the question in his gaze. She nodded.

Charles rapped at the door, a clear, distinct knock. "Carevalo? It's the Frasers. We've come to negotiate, not attack. Don't shoot before you ask questions."

He stood still for a moment, his hand on the doorknob. Mélanie was just behind him.

"Fraser?" A voice came from the other side of the door panels, sharp with disbelief. Before, Mélanie could not have said with certainty that she could identify Carevalo's voice, but now she recognized it without a doubt. They had found him. Relief washed over her, followed by a frisson of anticipation. "All right, come in," Carevalo said. "But I have a pistol. No tricks."

Charles turned the knob, pushed open the door, and stepped into the room. Mélanie followed. Lamplight and fire-warmed air spilled toward them.

The room was a library, heavy with brass and dark upholstery. Carevalo sat across from the door, sprawled in the green leather of a wing chair, a decanter at his elbow. A glass of brandy tilted between the fingers of his left hand, a pistol was clutched in his right. His slight body was relaxed, but his gaze fastened on them with the intensity of a tiger bearded in its lair.

His features were the same, but the implacable determination in his eyes transformed him. It was difficult to believe this was the same man who had paid her outrageous compliments and downed bottles of claret with the British officers in her drawing room. And yet Carevalo had always thrown himself with abandon into everything he did, be it flirtation or carousing or warfare.

Mélanie stared at the sharp-boned face of the man with whom she had flirted and danced. The man who had dined at her table and patted her children on the head. The man who had mutilated Colin. Rage such as she had never known slammed through her.

Charles closed the door. "Surprised, Carevalo? I expected a warmer greeting. I thought you'd be as eager to recover your ring as we are to give it to you."

Fire leapt in Carevalo's blue eyes. "You have it?"

"We have it."

Carevalo sprang to his feet, sloshing his brandy onto the floor. "Let me see it, damn you."

"You think I'd be fool enough to bring it with me?" Charles said, quite as if the ring wasn't still hooked on his watch chain.

Carevalo set his brandy glass on the table beside him. His hooded eyes were red, but there was a gleam in their depths. "You think I'd be fool enough to hand over your son without seeing the ring?"

"No, I'm through with underestimating you." Charles walked into the room, as though he hadn't a thought for Carevalo's pistol.

Carevalo followed him with his gaze. "So I was right. You had it all along."

"No. We found it. Though to paraphrase Wellington, it was a damned close run thing. Not that I expect you to believe me." Charles moved to the fireplace and leaned his arm on the mantel, as though laying claim to it. His pistol was still in his hand, resting on the plaster. "We appoint a neutral place. You bring Colin. We'll bring the ring."

"That could be a bluff to draw me out from under cover."

"My dear Carevalo. If we didn't already have the ring, we wouldn't be wasting time with you. And if you think I'd risk a bluff with my son's life at stake, you don't know me."

"If you think I'd give up my bargaining chip without proof you have the ring, you don't know me."

"Then it seems we have each other in check."

Carevalo moved, so quickly that all Mélanie saw was a blur of movement, and then his pistol was pointed straight at her heart. "The ring, Fraser. Or I shoot your wife."

In an instant, Charles had his own gun on Carevalo. "Don't be a fool, Carevalo. Shoot Mélanie and I'll kill you."

"Oh no, Fraser, I don't think so." Carevalo's eyes had a restless glitter, but his fingers were steady on the pistol. "You'd hardly kill the only man who can restore your son to you. Let me see the ring."

"I told you I didn't bring it with me. Because I feared just this scenario."

"A good try, Fraser," Carevalo said, his gaze trained on Mélanie. "But I don't for a minute believe you'd trust the ring to anyone else. You have it on your person. Unless you don't have it at all and your coming here is a bluff." His grip on the pistol tightened.

"He's the one who's bluffing, Charles," Mélanie said, though she wasn't at all sure that this was the case. She was as conscious of the gun trained on her as if the cold metal had been pressed against her skin. "He doesn't know you well enough to realize you'd never give way to a bluff."

"On the contrary. Carevalo is displaying a disgustingly acute understanding of my character. It's difficult to call his bluff when he holds all the cards." Charles transferred his pistol to his left hand. "I'm going to show you the ring, Carevalo. Then perhaps you'll be ready to negotiate."

His movements slow and deliberate, Charles unbuttoned his coat with his right hand and unhooked his watch chain. The lamplight fell on the gold and rubies. Carevalo started as though he'd received a shock. Quicker than thought, he lunged across the room and flung himself on Charles.

Charles must have anticipated the attack. He closed his fist round the ring and struck Carevalo with his right arm. Carevalo staggered and grabbed Charles's coat, Charles's injured leg gave way beneath him, and both men crashed to the floor.

Carevalo had Charles pinned beneath him. He brought up his arm and swung the butt of his pistol at Charles's head. Charles hurled the ring toward Mélanie a split second before the pistol struck his skull. The ring skittered past her across the floor. She made a dive for it, skidded on the polished floorboards, caught her foot in the hem of her gown, and fell sprawling. Pain screamed through the wound in her side.

She scrambled to her knees and saw the ring five feet away, glinting against the corner of the Turkey rug. Booted feet thudded on the floorboards. She dove forward, her hand extended. At the same moment, Carevalo hurled himself across the floorboards with a shout of triumph. He slammed into the polished wood and lay prone, the ring clutched in one hand, his pistol in the other, pointed straight at her.

For the length of several heartbeats, Mélanie would have sworn none of them breathed.

Carevalo pushed himself to his feet, the gun still trained on her. He slid the ring onto the third finger of his right hand. The action transformed his whole demeanor, the way an actor suddenly finds a part by donning a particular piece of costume. He seemed taller, his shoulders broader, his gaze more commanding.

It was Charles who broke the silence. "My compliments, Carevalo. Though I think we might have been spared the rough-and-tumble. Now that you have your precious ring back, I assume you'll abide by your word and keep your part of the bargain?"

Mélanie pushed herself back on her heels and glanced at her husband. He was sitting on the floor where he had fallen, a red mark on his forehead, his pistol in his hand.

"Not so fast, Fraser." Carevalo's mouth curved in a smile

fraught with danger. He glanced at the ring, as though to make sure it was really there, then looked back at them. "This isn't the way this was supposed to happen. I was going to have O'Roarke here as well. But as we have reached the dénouement—"

"I'd say you handled this very well without any help from O'Roarke," Charles said, getting to his feet.

"*Help?* From *O'Roarke?*" Carevalo gave a shout of laughter that sent a chill up Mélanie's spine. "Oh, Fraser, how little you know."

Charles's fingers tightened on his pistol. Mélanie felt his unspoken warning, though he did not so much as glance at her. "At the moment I couldn't care less whether O'Roarke is your accomplice or your enemy or your long-lost brother, Carevalo. All that concerns me is my son."

Carevalo's eyes glinted with mocking triumph, a cat who has been playing with a mouse and has just moved in for the kill. Mélanie felt a prickle of sweat break out on her neck, while at the same time her insides went ice-cold.

Carevalo glanced at her, then looked back at Charles. "O'Roarke's loyal—*once* loyal—valet Tomás came to see me just before I left Madrid." He drew the words out, relishing them. "In a terrible state, poor man. He'd grown disgusted at the thought of what he'd helped his master accomplish. O'Roarke was a traitor. And so was your harlot of a wife."

Mélanie suppressed every possible reaction by holding herself stock-still. Charles didn't so much as blink. "Have a care what words you use about my wife, Carevalo," he said, his voice dangerously soft.

Carevalo stared at him. "No surprise, Fraser?"

"My dear Carevalo. A husband and wife have no secrets from each other."

"You *knew?*"

Charles raised his shoulders in a gesture of supreme unconcern. "I have known for some time."

"Then you were an agent of Bonaparte as well."

"On the contrary." Charles's fingers shifted slightly on the pistol. "It was only after the war ended that I learned my wife and I had been adversaries."

"By God, Fraser, I knew you were arrogant, but I never thought you a damned fool."

Mélanie got to her feet. "Not a fool. Just supremely chivalrous. You mustn't blame Charles, my lord. He's every bit as angry with me as you are, but he won't admit it to an outsider."

Carevalo turned to her with a gaze that singed her flesh. "You're a Spaniard." He fairly spat the words. "How could you betray your country?"

When one could not decide which lie would serve one best, one fell back on the truth. "Betrayal is in the eye of the beholder, my lord," she said. "I thought my actions best served Spain."

"To make it a vassal of a foreign power." Anger dripped from Carevalo's tongue.

Charles drew the fire away from her. "To free it from the corrupt monarchy that you yourself would now overthrow."

Carevalo swung his gaze back to Charles. "This woman betrayed you. In every sense of the word, I shouldn't wonder."

"You are speaking of my wife, Carevalo."

Carevalo gave a snort of contempt. "That's just the point." He shook his head in amazement. "It never occurred to me that you could have known the truth and continued to live with her. When O'Roarke's valet came to me, my plans for the ring fell into place. If by any chance the British didn't have it, then the French did. Either you or your bitch of a wife was bound to be able to lay your hands on it. To employ O'Roarke as an emissary in the matter seemed strangely appropriate. I was going to have all three of you there when I exchanged the boy for the ring. Once the exchange was made, I'd reveal O'Roarke and Mrs. Fraser's treachery. I did you the honor of thinking you would avenge yourself, Fraser."

"Revenge is a singularly useless response," Charles said. "Give it up, Carevalo. You're not going to produce the scene you wanted."

Carevalo's mobile face turned as austere as marble in the

lamplight. His eyes were filled with ghosts. "People died because of her."

"People would have died anyway," Charles said. "Different people may have died because of her."

Carevalo looked at Mélanie. His gaze moved over her skin, as though he was stripping away her clothing. Not for the first time she wondered why some men had the impulse to ravish women they held in contempt. "A wife who turns whore has forfeited her husband's loyalty."

"You've got the sequence of events backwards, my lord," Mélanie said, though she knew as she spoke that it would have been wiser to keep silent. "I was a whore before I was a wife."

The flare in Carevalo's eyes was like a slap. She could smell the brandy fumes coming off him, so strong surely a match would set fire to his breath. "By God, you soil the names of the innocent women of our country. I can only thank God my wife and daughters were never in your presence."

The pain in his eyes was all too familiar. For an incongruous instant, Mélanie felt her own anguish resonate with his, like two disparate voices that suddenly strike the same pitch. "I'm sorry for what happened to your family, my lord. Sorrier than I can say."

"*Sorry.*" Something shifted in Carevalo's eyes, as though a shade had been stripped away. The unadulterated anger in his gaze was that of a man with no limits left. He leveled his pistol at her. "If your husband isn't man enough to avenge your victims, I will."

Charles leveled his own pistol. "Pull that trigger and you're dead, Carevalo."

"You haven't got the guts, Fraser. I'm still the only one who knows where your son is, and you don't even have the ring to bargain with. You may be too spineless to take your revenge on this whore, but I hardly think you'll risk your son's life for her sake. I should perhaps tell you that the people holding him have orders not to let him live if more than twenty-four hours pass without word from me."

Mélanie heard a strangled sound and realized it had issued from her own throat. Charles's gaze on Carevalo was steady and implacable.

"Besides," Carevalo said, "I have the ring."

Oh, God, Mélanie thought, staring into Carevalo's wild, exultant eyes, *he more than half believes the myth. He really thinks that gold bauble makes him invincible.*

Time seemed to slow down. Reality shrank to the open maw of the gun barrel, the heavy stillness of the air, the inexorable purpose in Carevalo's eyes. Every decision she had made from the moment she stumbled down the mountainside into Charles's arms seemed to have led up to this moment. She met Charles's gaze. Difficult to put everything she felt into a single look, especially when so much was poisoned between them. *I love you. I'm sorry. Take care of the children. Take care of yourself.*

The click of the hammer seemed to echo in the still room.

"Charles, don't," Mélanie yelled.

Chapter 34

Two pistol reports ripped through the room. Pain tore through her right arm. The only man who knew where her son was hidden collapsed in a bloody mass at her feet.

The smell of gunpowder, scorched flesh, and fresh blood filled her nostrils. She flung herself down beside Carevalo. Blood spurted from a charred hole in his brocade waistcoat, but his eyes were open and stared up at her. She pressed her hands over the wound and caught his gaze with her own. "Where's Colin?"

His face was pale and twisted with pain, but his mouth curved in a grim smile.

Charles dropped down beside them. "You don't want an innocent boy's life on your conscience, Carevalo. Where is he?"

"Where you'll never find him." The words were hoarse.

Charles tugged off his cravat and pushed it into her hands.

She pressed it over the wound. Hot, sticky blood spilled between her fingers.

"I'll give the ring to your allies," Charles said. "I swear it. Tell us."

Carevalo's gaze fixed on her rather than Charles. His eyes had begun to cloud. She had to lean close to his mouth to hear his words, so close she could feel the scrape of his breath on her skin. "You won't get away with it." The faint words had a hard glint of triumph. "Bow Street. Left a letter for them."

Blood dribbled out of the corner of his mouth. His eyes froze. Mélanie seized his shoulders. "Damn you, Carevalo, tell us." She shook him, so hard that more blood spattered over her chest.

"Mel." Charles's arm came round her shoulders. "He's dead."

She released Carevalo and sat back on her heels. She felt as though all the strength had drained from her body.

Charles pulled her to her feet and gripped both her arms. "Are you all right?"

She stared down at the wreckage of what had been Carevalo. Blood and secrets spilled onto the Turkey rug. "He could have given us Colin back."

"Some prices are too high to pay." His grip on her arms tightened, forcing her attention to his face. His forehead glistened with sweat. *"Are you all right?"*

"I'm fine." Really, he was making an extraordinary fuss about it. "The bullet just grazed me."

He peered at her arm, released his breath in a harsh sigh, and pulled her tight against him. His mouth came down on her hair. His hands moved over her back and shoulders, as though to reassure himself that she was really there.

She pulled her head back. "He said they'd kill Colin if they don't hear from him every twenty-four hours. We don't know when they got the last message. Charles, you said it yourself. Carevalo's life was more precious than our own."

He took her face between his hands. "We'll find out where

he has Colin. There'll be a way." He drew back and glanced at her arm again. He tugged his handkerchief from his pocket, splashed it with brandy from a decanter, and pressed it to the wound.

Footsteps pounded in the hall. "Fraser?" Raoul called. "Mélanie?"

Charles bound the handkerchief round her arm. "In here, O'Roarke."

The door banged open. "We heard a shot. Good God." Shock, such as she had rarely heard in Raoul's voice, reverberated through the room.

"Christ, Charles." Edgar followed Raoul into the room and froze on the threshold. "I thought you wanted to avoid bloodshed. Why the hell—"

Charles dropped his arm round her shoulders. "I took exception to Carevalo killing my wife."

"He threatened to kill Mélanie?" Edgar said. "Why?"

"He was quite mad," Mélanie said. "He took it into his head that I was a French agent."

"Good Lord." Edgar stared from Carevalo's body to their faces. "He must have been mad."

"Undoubtedly," Charles said.

Raoul's gaze moved over her face. "Are you all right?"

"Only grazed." She realized Raoul was staring at her hands. She looked down. Her hands were smeared with blood and more of it had spattered over her gown, glistening against the black fabric in the lamplight. "Charles got his shot off before Carevalo did. Most of the blood must be Carevalo's." She drew a breath and went on speaking quickly. "Before he died Carevalo told us the people holding Colin have orders to kill Colin if they don't hear from him every twenty-four hours. We don't know when they received the last message."

"There has to be a clue somewhere." Charles sounded as though he would force that clue into existence by sheer power of will. He glanced from Raoul to Edgar. "You two look upstairs. Carevalo may have a manservant staying here with him. Possibly other guards, though I doubt he'd have trusted many with the knowledge of his whereabouts. It should be obvious which rooms he's used—we're looking for papers, letters, anything with writing on it, even if you can't make sense of it. Stay together. Whoever else is in the house may be armed."

Raoul nodded. "Right. Captain Fraser?"

Edgar hesitated, received a look from Charles, and strode from the room.

"Just a minute, O'Roarke." Charles crossed the room to detain him by the door. "Carevalo knew about you and Mélanie," he said, the words low and rapid. "He may have left a letter somewhere for Bow Street."

Raoul nodded without wasting time on further questions. Charles steered Mélanie toward a chair that faced away from Carevalo's body. "It's most likely any papers are in here. Sit down for a minute. I'll search the desk."

"Charles, for heaven's sake." She wiped her hands on her skirt. "I admit it was a close call, but I'm not actually hurt."

"You'd be pardoned for being in shock. I know I am." His fingers were shaking where they gripped her arm. "I thought—" He sucked in his breath. For a moment, he seemed incapable of speech. "I wasn't at all sure I could manage that shot. I thought—" His throat worked, as though he was trying to force the words out.

She laid her fingers over his own. "You should have more faith in yourself, Charles. Though I confess I had doubts about my survival myself."

He took her hand and brushed it with his lips. "I love you."

The words were clipped, almost harsh. Before she could answer, Charles turned back to the desk. "Carevalo had to have a way to communicate with the people who are holding Colin."

"A newspaper advertisement?"

"Too much like his instructions to us. He'd know we might think of it."

She lit the lamp on the mahogany desk. An innocuous, solid,

English desk. The Sheffield plate of an inkpot and penknife glinted in the spill of light. A recently mended pen lay beside the knife, and a wax jack and a small globe stood in the opposite corner. The cubbyholes and drawers were stuffed with papers, but these proved to be accounts relating to the property and correspondence by a J. Grafton, who presumably was the husband of Carevalo's mistress.

Charles tilted the lamp close to the penstrokes imbedded in the ink blotter. Mélanie tugged at a side drawer that refused to open completely. It gave way with the crack of splintered wood. She reached behind the drawer, scraped her hand on the broken wood, and felt the crinkle of paper. She drew it out. A piece of folded paper, sealed with red wax, with no imprint and no direction written on it. She broke the wax with her nail. A handful of banknotes spilled onto the desk.

"Payment to his minions," Charles said.

Mélanie smoothed out the paper wrapping. The inside was covered with writing. QAWGW UGCC EW DSMVAWM OWCYX. PWW QI GV NYLM OIWHQ OMGHB YCC QNGP. AWCC AYTW QGFW WHISRA QI OI QAYV UAWH QAGP GP OIHW.

She showed it to Charles. "Recognize it?"

"A simple substitution code, I suspect." He pinned down the curling edges of the paper with his fingers. "It's not long, but hopefully there's enough to break it. He hasn't troubled to run all the words together, which makes—"

Raoul came back into the room. "The rest of the house is empty. He only seems to have used the kitchen and one of the bedrooms. There's some food in the pantry, a change of clothes and shaving things in the bedroom. Captain Fraser's having a closer look, but I doubt we'll find anything. No sign of a letter to Bow Street, either. You've done better?"

"Perhaps." Mélanie looked up from the paper. "We've found a payment and a coded message, presumably prepared for the people holding Colin."

Raoul strode into the room and stared down at the cipher. "If Carevalo had this ready and waiting, he must have been expecting a messenger."

Charles looked up and met his gaze. "Quite."

Raoul nodded. "Mélanie's better at ciphers than I am, and you were brilliant at them even as a boy. I'll keep watch in the hall with your brother."

Mélanie looked back at the coded message. The image of Colin's severed finger swam before her eyes. This must be how Carevalo had sent the instructions. But if this was the next message he meant to send, then the twenty-four hours between messages were not yet up. She sat in the desk chair, back straight, picked up the pen, and reached for a sheet of writing paper. "*W* seems to be the most frequent letter," she said.

"It is," Charles said. "So assuming he's writing in English, *W* must be *e*."

They had both devised and decoded countless substitution ciphers in the Peninsula and later in Vienna and Brussels. It was a simple enough code, used when one wanted to conceal the message but was not expecting a serious attempt at decoding. One chose a key word (*treason* had been a favorite of Raoul's) and matched the letters of the word with the first letters of the alphabet. The rest of the alphabet was then displaced by the number of distinct letters in the key word. It was impossible to determine how the letters were displaced without knowing the key word and the number of letters it contained. But there were ways to break the code. *E* was the most commonly occurring letter in the English language, so the most commonly occurring letter in a cipher written in English was almost certainly translated as *E*.

"*W* must be the fifth letter in the key word." Mélanie copied out the cipher with *e* filled in in lowercase for all the *W*s.

She stared at the paper before her and forced her mind to focus down to those black strokes of ink. The first word was now simplified to *QAeGe*. "I'd hazard a guess the first word is 'there.' Or 'where,' but it seems more likely he'd start a letter with 'there.'"

Charles pulled up a stool and sat beside her. "The second word is a four-letter word without an *e* and with a double letter at the end. Followed by a two-letter word with *e* as the second letter. *There will be?*"

"Let's try it. If you're right, that gives us *t*, *h*, *r*, *w*, *i*, *l*, and *b*." She rewrote the cipher with those letters filled in.

there will be DSrther OelYX. Pee tI it NYLM OIWHt OriHB Yll thiP. Hell hYTe tiFe eHISRh tI FI thYt wheH thiP iP OIHe.

Mélanie studied the message. "That fourth word must be 'further.' Or 'farther.' So *D* equals *f* and *S* equals *u* or *a*. And the first word in the second sentence almost has to be 'see.' *P* equals *s*."

Charles leaned forward, elbow on the desktop. "In the second sentence there's a two-letter word starting with *t*. That can only be 'to'—so *I* equals *o*. And then we have a three-letter word ending in a double *l*. 'Ill' or 'I'll' or 'all,' but *i* is already taken, so *Y* must equal *a*."

"Which means the fourth word is 'further' and *S* equals *u*." She pulled the paper closer.

"Wait a bit, Mel, where are we on the key word?" He reached across her and turned up the lamp. "If *Y* equals *a*, we've got YEL-W-AG. Looks suspiciously as though we've got a two-word key and it's 'yellow something.' Skipping the second *l*, that makes *O* equal *d*."

Mélanie took a clean sheet of paper and copied out the message again.

There will be further delaX. See to it NaLM diWHt driHB all this. Hell hYTe tiFe eHIuRh to Fo thYt wheH this is doHe.

She chewed the tip of the pen. "What does Carevalo want them to 'see to'?" A welter of uncomfortable images crowded her mind.

Charles rested his hand on her shoulder for a moment. "Patience, my darling. Whatever it is, he can't do it anymore." He squeezed her shoulder, then looked down at the paper. "The last word in the first sentence must be 'delay.' X equals y."

Mélanie forced her attention back to the text. "And I suspect that word at the end is 'done,' making H equal n. Wait a bit, Charles, we almost have it. Look."

There will be further delay. See to it NaLM doesnt drinB all this. Hell haTe tiFe enouRh to do that when this is done.

The fingers of her left hand cramped as her grip on the pen tightened. " 'NaLM' must be a person. What were the names of the men Roth mentioned who matched the description of the man Polly saw? Stephen Watkins was the one he thought most likely. But there was also—"

"Jack Evans, a former prizefighter." Charles's eyes glinted with triumph held in check. "The one who was spotted drinking in a tavern in Wapping. Which I suspect was called—?" He pulled the sheet of paper with the key-word letters toward him. "YELOW DRAGN. The Yellow Dragon. Of course. The name of Jack Evans's favorite tavern is a key Carevalo could count on them remembering."

Fingers trembling with the relief of the finish line in sight, Mélanie filled in the rest of the code and wrote out the whole message.

There will be further delay. See to it Jack doesn't drink all this. He'll have time enough to do that when this is done.

"Not a very profound message," Charles said. "But it does tell us who."

"But not where." She threw down the pen. "Damnation."

"We know the general area—somewhere close to a tavern

called the Yellow Dragon in Wapping. And we know how to communicate with them. Perhaps—"

A crash sounded from the hall. They ran to the door and flung it open to see Edgar sitting on the chest of a prone man, while Raoul stood over them holding a pistol.

Edgar seized his quarry by the throat. "Where is he? God-damnit to hell, where is he?"

"Who?" The man's voice was thin and reedy. "I only came here because the gentleman asked me."

"Let him go, Edgar." Charles pulled his brother off the man and helped the man to his feet. He was more of a boy, actually, Mélanie saw in the moonlight spilling through the hall windows, a gangly youth with a pockmarked face and a thatch of sandy hair. Charles gripped the boy by both arms. "Deal honestly with us and you have nothing to fear. Lie and I warn you none of us has much patience left." He pushed the boy against the stair rail. The balusters shook. "Why did the gentleman want you to come here?"

"To deliver a letter, he said." The boy's eyes were enormous, his face drained of color. "Same place as before."

"Where?" Charles's grip on the boy's arms tightened.

Fear glistened on the boy's face. "I don't give them to any-one. I leave them."

Charles pulled the homespun of the boy's shirt taut. "Where do you leave them?"

"At Covent Garden Market, between the railings of St. Paul's, at the south corner."

Charles closed his eyes for a moment. Mélanie let out a gasping sigh and thought she heard Raoul do the same.

"When did you leave the last one?" Charles asked.

"This morning, round seven. Sometimes he has me go twice a day, but today it was just once. I don't know anything about it," the boy insisted in a quavering voice. "I met him when I came here to fish. My brothers and I've always fished here. There's never anyone about, 'cept in the summer. But he said I was poaching, only he wouldn't turn me in if I delivered the messages for him."

Raoul looked at Mélanie. "Did you break the code?"

"Yes."

"So we have a way to communicate with them."

"My thoughts exactly." Charles looked back at the boy. "You're coming to Bow Street with us. We may have a message for you to deliver after all."

Even on the far side of three in the morning, the candles guttering and the smell of gin stale in the air, the Brown Bear Tavern bustled with activity. Mélanie noted that her appearance in the common room drew less attention than it had in the afternoon. Perhaps the customers considered that any woman abroad at this hour couldn't possibly be a lady.

Four men of the Bow Street Patrol were clustered round a table. Yes, they said, in answer to a question from Charles, Roth was there, upstairs, writing up notes. They found him in the room where they had talked before, bent over a table in his shirtsleeves, a pencil in his hand.

He looked up at their entrance. "What's happened?"

Charles closed the door and advanced into the room, pulling Mélanie with him. He had his arm round her shoulders, as he had for the whole of the drive back from Chiswick. The ring, retrieved from Carevalo's body, was once again strung on his watch chain, though it seemed strangely irrelevant now. Their hope of finding Colin lay with the sandy-haired youth whom Raoul and Edgar were holding by either arm. "Ted here has been taking messages from Carevalo to the men holding Colin," Charles said.

Roth's gaze took in the splotches of dried blood on Mélanie's gown. "Where's Carevalo?"

"Dead."

Roth's only reaction was a brief flicker in his eyes. "Did he die in giving you the information?"

"No, we found it afterwards."

Roth pulled out a chair for Mélanie. "Then I'll assume his death was unavoidable, as I trust you would not kill the man who knew where your son was kept."

"Quite," Charles said. "You've spoken to Addison?"

"He gave an admirable account of your discovery of Mrs. Constable, especially as he doesn't seem to have been present for most of the key scenes." Roth grimaced. "Constable recovered consciousness convinced a couple answering to your description killed his wife. I think we've finally managed to persuade him otherwise. I have men searching for this Victor Velasquez, but we haven't found him yet. Don't tell me it turns out Carevalo killed her?"

"No." Charles recounted what had happened, glossing over Carevalo's attack on Mélanie as drunken madness.

Roth stared at the coded message, held down by two empty tankards on a splintery table. He raised his gaze to Ted, who was sitting quiet and wide-eyed on the cot with the blue blanket. Then he looked at Charles and Mélanie. "You could write a message in this code?"

Mélanie nodded. "We'll have Ted plant the message in Covent Garden. We have to make sure it's there well before seven. We'll cover the area and follow whoever picks up the message back to where they're holding Colin."

Roth nodded. "Seemingly straightforward. But I've known the most straightforward plans to go awry."

"Precisely. So in the letter we'll tell them to bring Colin to a rendezvous point tomorrow night. If it comes to that, we'll be there to take him from them."

Roth considered. "My compliments, Mrs. Fraser. That's not without risk, but it's about as good a plan as we could devise." He pulled his coat off a chair back. "You get to work on the message. I'll assemble men to keep watch in Covent Garden."

An involuntary noise of protest escaped her lips.

"You can't do it yourselves," he said. "You might be recognized."

"If you're going to suggest we remain behind—"

He gave her a full, genuine smile. "Mrs. Fraser, I've got to know you a bit in the last forty-eight hours. I wouldn't dream of it. You can wait in a coffeehouse on the edge of the market, as I will myself." He moved to the door. "I'll muster the troops. And then, Mr. Fraser, I'd be obliged if you'd give me any other information you have about the death of Elinor Constable."

Chapter 35

Mélanie forced another sip of lukewarm coffee down her throat. Her eyes smarted from peering through the smoke-stained glass of the coffeehouse window. She could just glimpse the south corner of the basket-hung railings of St. Paul's. The man in the anonymous brown coat and hat, leaning against the railings reading a newspaper, was a Bow Street Patrol. So was the leather-aproned coster with the applecart. Roth and Edgar were in one of the paper-screened coffee stalls under the columns of the Piazza. Raoul and Addison were in a tavern on the opposite side of the square.

Covent Garden Market was a blaze of color. Morning sun limned the scene with russet and gold, burnishing booths and carts, sieves of vegetables and bunches of flowers, kerchiefs and aprons and hampers. An ideal place for a man to lose himself, but Roth had promised that his men knew how to track a quarry in a crowd.

Charles shifted his position in the chair across from her. "It's early yet. If they only check the railings once or twice a day, they may wait until later." He picked up his coffee and stared into the dregs.

"Darling?" She scanned his drawn face. "Is something . . . ?"

"Wrong?" A bleak smile pulled at his mouth. "Just about everything, wouldn't you say?"

"Granted." She reached across the rough wood of the table, then stilled her hand, because such a gesture seemed to push beyond the boundaries that still lay between them. "But you look as though you're brooding on something besides what's in front of us."

He shook his head and set down the cup. "No. There's nothing else." He laid his hand over her own. "At least nothing else that's worth brooding on."

A man in a dark green coat and shirt points that obscured half his face slipped between a donkey barrow and a bird-catcher's stand, making for the railings. Every muscle in her body went still. The man moved on. Then she noticed the woman half-hidden behind him. A woman in a drab-colored gown with a shopping basket laden with cabbages and broccoli on her arm and a faded straw bonnet covering her apricot-colored hair. Another matron doing her marketing. And yet—

Mélanie clenched her husband's hand. "Charles."

"What?" His voice went sharp.

"I think Jack Evans's partner may be a woman."

The donkey reared up in its traces. Its owner grabbed the reins to calm it. The surge in the crowd round the barrow obscured the railings. When the press cleared, the woman was gone. It was impossible to tell about the letter at this distance. Mélanie pushed herself to her feet. Charles's hand closed on her wrist. "We can't do any good. And if we're seen, we may do harm. Roth will find us."

Mélanie subsided into her chair, hands gripped together in her lap. Each second tightened the knot in her throat and chest. The Bow Street Patrol in the brown hat and coat had gone, though the one with the applecart was still there. Perhaps it was her imagination, but his shoulders seemed to have a dejected droop. At last, Roth came into the coffeehouse, followed by Edgar, and by Raoul and Addison, whom he must have collected from across the square.

One look at Roth's face told all they needed to know. "You lost her?" Charles asked.

Roth grimaced, then frowned. "How did you know it was a woman?"

"Mélanie spotted her. It was too late to do anything."

Roth dropped into a chair. The others did likewise. "Hilton and Renford didn't realize it until they saw the letter was gone. By that time she was lost in the crowd—I suspect she caused the commotion with the donkey, though I can't be sure of it. Hilton and Renford were looking for a man. We all were. Even so, they should have been more watchful." He struck his palm against the tabletop.

"It's done." Charles drew the frayed remnants of his self-command about him. "We proceed to the next part of the plan."

On Roth's suggestion, in the coded message they had instructed the people holding Colin to bring him to St. Albans Court, off Salisbury Street, near the docks, at midnight that night.

"It's a good setting," Roth now said. He had recovered from his burst of anger. He pulled his notebook and pencil from his pocket, tore out a sheet of paper, and spread it on the table. "There was a bad fire last summer, and it's not a part of town where repairs are done quickly. The houses are unoccupied. The two at the front form a passageway. Their front doors open onto the street, their back doors onto the court." He inched his paper toward the light from the window and drew a quick sketch. "Two more houses front on either side of the court, two at the back. Once we get them to bring the boy into the court, my men can close off the passageway and we'll have them pinned."

"Won't they be suspicious when they don't see Carevalo in the court?" Edgar asked.

"They'll think they do see him." Mélanie looked at Raoul. "Let's see if your Carevalo impersonation is as good as it used to be."

Raoul turned to her, his voice slurred, his shoulders set with Carevalo's swagger. "My dear Mrs. Fraser, I'd hardly call it an impersonation."

"Good lord." Surprise momentarily overcame Edgar's distaste for Raoul. "That's him to the life."

Charles nodded. "Before dawn, with O'Roarke in a dark cloak, in the doorway of one of the burned-out houses, it should be enough to draw them into the court. He won't have to keep it up for more than a minute or so. They won't have weapons drawn. We'll get Colin safely away." He looked at Roth. "Then you can arrest them, though that's the least of my concerns."

Roth nodded. "It's as foolproof a plan as we can devise."

"Quite." Charles's gaze swept the five of them with the level intensity of a commander before a battle. "This is the night that makes us or fordoes us quite. We all know the parts we're to play. There's no room for error."

St. Albans Court was a comforting mass of shadows, lit only by the cloud-shrouded moonlight that slipped between the tall, close-set buildings and shone against the cracked, grimy cobblestones. Mélanie shifted her shoulder against the charred wall and twisted her neck so she had a better view out the window. She and Charles were in the left-hand of the two houses that fronted on the street and backed onto the court. The interior was little more than a burned-out shell, half the first floor missing, fragments of wallpaper clinging to charred beams, floorboards rotted away to reveal gaping holes beneath. It was difficult to tell what the room they were in had once been, but it had a wide window that afforded a good view of the court. Half of one of the panes was gone, letting in the chill air and the creaks and stirrings of the night.

Raoul leaned in a doorjamb on the far side of the court,

swathed in a hooded cloak, his posture aping Carevalo's casual sprawl instead of his own catlike elegance. Roth and Edgar were in a house to the right. Addison and four of Roth's men were scattered about the other buildings, while another Bow Street Patrol kept watch on the street at the mouth of the passageway.

A pigeon fluttered from the broken rafters, flapped its wings, and settled again. A gust of wind rattled through the window, ruffled the clouds over the moon, bit through the thin velvet of her cloak. It wasn't possible to talk, let alone look at a watch, but surely it must be past midnight. She felt as if she were being pulled a dozen different directions at once.

Time dragged on, grating on her nerves, fraying the already frayed threads of her sanity. She felt the vibration of Charles's breath on her neck, less regular than it had been a few minutes before.

And then a foot thudded on pavement, and a shadow and a flutter of cloak flashed into view at the far corner of the window. The breath froze in her throat.

Raoul turned his head. "Evans?"

"No, it's me." A woman's voice, low and clear. She walked a few feet farther into the court, fully visible now from their vantage point. No small person stood beside her. Mélanie suppressed a stir of agony. Charles squeezed her shoulder, part comfort, part reassurance, part warning.

"I see." Raoul's voice had just Carevalo's note of frustrated impatience. "I believe I asked for the boy. Where is he?"

"Jack's waiting with him off yonder. We want our money."

"But of course." Raoul held up a bag.

The woman took a step forward.

"Not so fast, my dear." Raoul's voice stopped her, the lazy drawl giving way to sword-cut sharpness in a way that was pure Carevalo. "I don't entirely trust those pretty hands of yours not to be armed. And if you think I have any intention of handing over this money before you deliver the boy, you're very much mistaken."

The woman stopped ten feet away from him. Her back was

to them, but Mélanie could see her fold her arms over her chest. "It's not so simple, your lordship. Seeing as how bloody much work we've been put to, the price's gone up."

"Damnation," said Raoul, though they had in fact anticipated such an eventuality.

"Seems to me the boy's worth a king's ransom, given the fuss you've made."

"Seven hundred pounds." It was a guess, rounding up from what they thought Evans and his partner might have been offered. Raoul had a thousand with him, procured that afternoon from their startled banker.

"Two thousand."

Fear and anger washed over Mélanie like a cold sweat.

"That's outrageous." She felt Raoul funneling his outrage through Carevalo's personality.

"And hacking off that kid's finger wasn't?" The woman's voice had a sting of anger.

"That's my business."

"And the money is ours."

Charles squeezed Mélanie's shoulder again. They could not risk speech, but the message was clear. *Stay here. I'll see if I can discover where Evans is with Colin.* He moved soundlessly toward the remnants of the doorway to the room that fronted on Salisbury Street.

"You bloody bitch." Raoul sounded on the edge of losing control. Mélanie suspected it was not entirely an act. "I don't have that much with me."

"Get it."

Mélanie held herself immobile. She heard the faint scrape of the door behind her. Charles had gone into the street.

"You give me the boy." Raoul's words sounded as though they came from between clenched teeth. "I'll give you a thousand tonight and get the rest tomorrow."

The woman gave a harsh laugh. "Do you think I'm a blithering idiot, your lordship?"

"I don't see your options."

"Go to your precious banker and get the rest of the blunt. Meet us here tomorrow night. We'll bring the brat."

"That does not suit my plans, madam."

"Too bloody bad, your lordship."

Raoul took a menacing step forward. An effective gesture, but the wind whipped up at the same moment, tugging back the hood of his cloak and parting the clouds over the moon. The light fell full across his face.

"Look here—" The woman peered at him, then gave a scream followed by a piercing whistle. "Run, Jack. It's a trap."

Raoul lunged at her. Mélanie turned and flung herself across the burned-out building, through the ruined doorway, and across the next room to the front door that gave onto Salisbury Street. The courtyard was irrelevant now. Jack Evans was somewhere in the streets beyond with her son.

Salisbury Street was thick with shadows, but nothing moved. The Bow Street Patrol must have run into the passageway at the eruption of noise in the court. Mélanie scanned the street and saw what Charles must have remembered from their earlier scouting of the area. Almost directly opposite the passageway was a dark, seemingly empty house. She could make out boards nailed over the lower windows, but one of the attic casements gaped open. A perfect place to wait concealed with a six-year-old boy for a summons or a signal for flight from the court beyond.

She ran to the door. It was unlatched. She pushed it open and stepped into a musty, unlit hall. A silent musty, unlit hall. No whisper of breathing, no footsteps, no telltale creaks. She moved toward the dark outline of a staircase, then saw the door at the back of the hall. That must be how Evans had brought Colin in. If they'd used the front door, the Bow Street Patrol would have seen them. Perhaps he had fled through that same door. If a struggle was in progress above, surely she would hear it.

She went the length of the hall in a handful of steps and pushed the door open onto a narrow alley that stank of mildew and rotting food and stale urine. Shafts of moonlight pierced the slabs of shadow and gave the grimy cobblestones the sheen of marble. A clatter from above pulled her out into the alley and drew her gaze upward. The house next to the one she had just left was slightly lower and its roof slanted up to a peak with a towering brick chimney at one end. A bent figure was inching up the slope of the roof. He seemed to be wearing a pack on his back. And then she realized that the pack was her son.

She forced down the scream that rose up in her throat.

"Give it up, Evans." Her husband's voice echoed down into the alley. He was half out of the attic window through which Evans must have escaped, hauling himself onto the roof where Evans crawled with Colin. "Carevalo's dead. Hand Colin over and it will go easy with you."

At the sound of Charles's voice, Colin jerked, loosed his hold on Evans, and went slithering across the roof at a diagonal, toward the alley.

This time Mélanie could not contain her scream. She ran to catch her son. Colin slid to the edge of the roof overhanging the alley and stuck there, his coat caught on some blessedly placed nail. He gripped the coping with both hands, his upper body on the roof, his legs swinging free.

The force of Colin's action had knocked Evans's legs out from under him. He flung his arms round the corner of the chimney to stop his slide and lay sprawled, legs flailing for a purchase on the roof tiles.

Charles, halfway up the slope of the roof, began to crawl sideways toward the outer edge where Colin clung. Evans kicked out and struck Charles in the face. Mélanie heard the thud of a heavy boot connecting with flesh and bone.

Charles slid down the slope of the roof, feet and hands scraping over the tiles. Evans pulled himself upright, clinging to one of the clay chimney pots, recovered his balance, and took a step down the roof toward Charles's prone figure. Mélanie saw the glint of a knife in Evans's hand. She shouted a warning to her husband.

Charles sprang to his feet and launched himself at Evans. Evans drew back his knife hand. Charles caught Evans by the wrist. The two men grappled together midway up the slope of the roof, Evans trying to turn the knife on Charles, Charles trying to wrest it away from him.

Colin was clinging to the edge of the roof in terrible silence. She couldn't see his face, but he must be gagged. "It's all right, darling," she called, over the groans and thuds from above. "Just hold on."

She was standing where she could catch him or at least break his fall. She had her pistol out of her reticule, but she couldn't shoot at Evans without risking Charles.

Evans went for Charles's throat with his free hand. Charles fell back, throwing Evans off balance, tightened his grip on Evans's right wrist, which held the knife, and twisted. Evans gave a grunt of pain. The knife flew in a glittering arc, bounced off the roof, and clattered to the cobblestones in the street below.

Evans clawed at Charles's eyes. Charles ducked. Evans kicked Charles in the shins, then screamed as his foot slipped out from under him. He slid beyond Charles's grasp and tumbled to the edge of the roof, lower down the slope than the point where Colin clung. His fingers scrabbled against the tiles for a moment. His legs swung wildly. Then the coping gave way in his hand. He fell with a cry that echoed through the alley, slammed into the cobblestones not a dozen feet from Mélanie, and lay still.

"Colin." Charles's voice was level and conversational. Mélanie nearly sobbed in relief. "It's all right. He can't hurt you anymore. All you have to do is hold still. I'm coming to get you."

It looked as though Colin nodded his head. Mélanie glanced at Evans, but he had plainly broken his neck in the fall. "Charles?" she called. "Shall I come up?"

"Stay there until I have Colin. Then meet us at the attic window." Charles lowered himself to his hands and knees again and crept down the sloping roof, his bad leg dragging awkwardly, his hands sure and steady. The short expanse of roof tiles seemed to stretch endlessly, like a chessboard with the black and white of the squares blurred to gray.

A wrench of fabric sounded through the night air. Colin's coat had given way, but Colin still lay half sprawled on the roof, clinging to the coping.

Charles stretched out his hand. "Colin? Don't move quickly, but can you reach out to me?"

Colin put up one hand. Charles closed his fingers round Colin's own.

Mélanie released her breath and clamped her jaw to hold back the press of tears. Footsteps sounded in the alley. She tore her gaze from Charles and Colin to warn the new arrival to be still, but he had already stopped. It was Edgar, his hat gone, his hair golden in the moonlight, his gaze trained on the roof where Charles was pulling Colin to safety. He didn't seem to see her in the shadows of the overhang. She turned her gaze back to the scene on the roof. As she did so, Charles dropped flat against the roof tiles, holding Colin against him. He shouted his brother's name, not a warning but an anguished plea.

Mélanie looked at Edgar and saw the gleam of a pistol in his hand. He leveled his arm and took aim at the roof, his intention written in the lines of his body.

She had no time to think or plan. She raised her own pistol and shot her brother-in-law in the chest.

Chapter 36

The report of the gun echoed through the narrow alley. Edgar collapsed onto the cobblestones with a thud. His fair hair and the pistol that had fallen from his fingers shone bright in the moonlight. The rest of him was a mass of blue-black shadows. Mélanie lowered her smoking pistol.

The sound of booted feet came from the other end of the alley. Mélanie turned her head to see Raoul pull himself up short, his cloak swirling round his shoulders.

Charles lifted his head from the roof tiles. "Mel?"

"It's all right, Charles. Just get Colin down."

She started toward Edgar, but Raoul ran forward. "Go up and help your husband with Colin," he said. "I'll see to Captain Fraser."

The need to hold Colin in her arms drove her back into the house and up three flights of sagging stairs at a run. A door was open on the attic level. She ran in, stumbling against the rotted wood, and flung open the casement to see the welcome sight of her husband's now-grimy boots. He was crouched on the edge of the next roof, holding Colin in his arms.

He handed Colin down through the window to her. She touched her son's feet and then his waist and then she had him in her arms and his own arms closed tight round her neck. Her heart seemed to burst inside her.

She kissed him and set him down. "Help me help Daddy, darling."

Charles already had his feet on the window ledge. She and Colin guided him down. Colin flung an arm round each of them and they landed in a three-way hug on the dusty, splintery floorboards.

Her chest shook as though she'd forgotten how to breathe. She was aware only of the solid warmth of Colin's body, the reassuring clutch of his hands, the softness of his hair beneath her fingers. He smelt of mildew and grime and little boy. Laughter bubbled up inside her, as though any control she had left had split open and shattered.

She wasn't sure which of them drew back first, but she found herself looking into Colin's face. The moonlight from the window slanted over him. Charles had got the gag off him. He was wide-eyed and pale, but he was smiling. "I knew you'd find me."

"I'm glad, darling." Her voice stuck in her throat. She forced it past the knot of anger and regret. "I'm sorry it took us so long."

He looked from her to Charles. "I was brave, like you would have been. I cried a little bit, though."

Charles's fingers trembled through Colin's hair. "Sometimes crying is the bravest thing to do, lad."

"Mélanie? Fraser?" Raoul's voice came from the stairs. Mélanie realized she could hear shouts and the tramp of boots from the street below.

Charles got to his feet. "In here, O'Roarke."

Mélanie stood, her arms round Colin. At least Evans and the

woman had dressed him in breeches, a shirt, and a thick wool coat and given him a pair of shoes.

Raoul's footsteps pounded on the stairs. He came through the door and checked on the threshold. His gaze went to Colin in her arms. His face went completely still save for his eyes. She couldn't have put a name to what she saw in their depths. Relief. Regret. And something else that was suspiciously close to longing.

Raoul turned to look at Charles. The two men regarded each other for a moment, gray eyes meeting gray. Even Mélanie could not completely read what passed between them. Charles cupped his hand over Colin's head. "This is Mr. O'Roarke, Colin. You haven't seen him since you were a baby. We wouldn't have got you back without him."

Colin turned in her embrace to look at Raoul. "Thank you, Mr. O'Roarke."

A host of emotions flickered over Raoul's face in an instant. "It was the least I could do, Master Fraser." He looked at Charles and Mélanie. "We've got the woman in custody. Evans is dead. Roth and the men are downstairs seeing to him and—"

"My brother," Charles said.

"Yes." Raoul flicked a glance at Colin, then looked back at Charles. "Captain Fraser's asking for you."

"Then we'd better go down," Charles said.

Colin turned his head to look up at Mélanie. "What happened to Uncle Edgar?"

Mélanie looked into her son's eyes and tried to find a way to tell the truth. "He was hurt, darling. We don't know how badly yet. Daddy's going to talk to him."

Colin insisted that he could walk, though he clung tightly to her hand and Charles's as they descended the stairs. When her fingers closed around his own, she felt the stiff cloth of a bandage. Where his little finger had been. She swallowed an upwelling of rage.

The alley that had been so empty only minutes before was

now full of people. The Bow Street Patrols had lit torches that cast a molten glow over the dark stone and rotted wood. Two patrols were bent over Evans. Addison, Roth, and another patrol hovered over Edgar. Roth straightened up. His shoulders sagged with relief at the sight of Colin. The torchlight caught the smile in his eyes as he walked toward them. "Master Colin Fraser, I presume?"

"Inspector Roth of Bow Street." Charles bent over Colin. "He helped us find you, too."

Colin returned Roth's smile. "Thank you, Mr. Roth."

Roth dropped down to Colin's level and rested a hand on his shoulder. "I only wish we could have found you more quickly, lad." He straightened up and cast a glance at where Edgar lay, then looked back at Mélanie and Charles. "Perhaps we should—"

Charles gave a quick nod. He glanced at Raoul, hesitated, then touched Colin's hair. "Listen, old chap, Mummy and I need to talk to Mr. Roth for a bit and see Uncle Edgar. Could you stay with Mr. O'Roarke? We won't be out of sight."

Colin's eyes went wide, but he nodded with a trust that squeezed Mélanie's heart. Raoul crouched down beside him. "I knew your father when he was your age, Colin. He was a brave boy, though not as brave as you, I think."

Colin smiled and tucked his hand into Raoul's own. Charles looked down at them for a moment, his face raw with fear and love. Then he, Mélanie, and Roth walked over the rough cobblestones to where Edgar lay sprawled across the alley with Addison kneeling beside him and the patrol holding a torch aloft.

"The bullet went through his chest," Roth said. "Mr. Addison stopped the bleeding as best he could, but my guess is he's bleeding on the inside as well. It's too risky to move him. I don't know how long— He hasn't said anything except to ask for you."

Addison had stripped off his cravat and was holding it over the wound in Edgar's chest. Blood had spurted onto the cobblestones. Mélanie stared at the sticky, red-black pool. Like her sister's eleven years ago in the Spanish village. She gagged on the sickly stench, though she could not have said whether the smell was real or a trick of memory.

Dear God, she had shot Edgar. Charles's laughing, light-hearted brother; Colin and Jessica's affectionate uncle; the man who had teased her and danced with her and welcomed her into the family without a qualm. The man who had been about to kill Charles, for reasons she could barely begin to guess at. If the memory of what she had seen had not been imprinted on her senses, she would have sworn it could not have happened.

Mélanie looked at her brother-in-law through the eye-sting-ing torch smoke. His face was pale, but his eyes were open and alert. Charles dropped down beside him and put his hands over the makeshift bandage Addison was holding to Edgar's chest. Addison met Charles's gaze for a moment, his cool blue eyes uncharacteristically soft. He shook his head slightly and got to his feet. The patrol with the torch drew back a few paces, leaving the brothers alone in a small circle of torchlight. Mélanie stood between Roth and Addison and watched her husband kneel beside his brother, the way she had once knelt in a filthy street and watched the lifeblood drain from her sister's face.

Edgar's gaze fastened on Charles. "Don't waste your ener-gies, brother. I've seen death enough on the battlefield. I know I'm done for." He stared at Charles for a moment. "How much do you know?"

Charles's face was as still and hard as Highland granite, but his eyes held the pain of a death blow. "Nearly all of it, I think," he said.

"Damn you, why couldn't you have come into the Mar-shalsea two minutes later? I'd have had the ring and got rid of that wretched carnelian pendant and the letter that was wrapped round it. I suppose you recognized the pendant at once?"

"I should have," Charles said. "I bought it at a jeweler's in Lisbon and gave it to Kitty a month before she died."

Mélanie stared from her husband to his brother. The pen-dant in which the ring was concealed had belonged to Charles's mistress? *Kitty* had had the Carevalo Ring? Images shifted like fragments of mosaic in her head. She remembered the look Charles and Edgar had exchanged when Edgar pulled the pendant from its hiding place in Hugo Trevennen's rooms. The pieces must have fallen into place for Charles then, but she could still not make sense of the whole picture.

Edgar's gaze was fixed on Charles with a pain that had nothing to do with his wound. "I never would have touched her. How could you? How could she? How could she cheapen herself so?"

"People will do a great many things in the name of love."

"You call *that* love?"

"Yes," Charles said.

Edgar's face twisted. "She sought me out at that damned embassy party and said she was in need of help. She looked so sweet and artless. I'd have done anything for her. I thought perhaps she'd lost too much at cards or run up bills at the dressmaker's. Or that she was desperate for news of her husband. Jesus, I was a fool. It never occurred to me—"

"That she was pregnant by your brother. Your bastard half brother."

The pain in Edgar's eyes gave way to bitter, molten hatred, hatred such as Mélanie would never have thought to see in that sunny gaze. "You don't even appreciate it, that's the hell of it," Edgar said. "I think I could have borne your stealing my heritage if you'd had the faintest respect for what it means to be—"

"A British gentleman?"

"You bastard. You can't even say it without irony."

"What was it you couldn't bear?" Charles asked. "That Kitty wasn't the chaste wife you thought her to be or that I'd taken her, too?"

"Both, damn you."

"And so you killed her."

Edgar drew a rasping breath. "I never meant to. I still can't quite remember—"

"Strangling her?" Charles said in a cold voice.

"I didn't— I know I reached for her. She was dead in my arms before I realized what was happening."

Edgar's eyes closed, his golden lashes spiky against his bloodless skin. For a moment, Mélanie thought he had gone. Roth stirred at her side, as though about to speak. Then Edgar's eyes flickered open again. "Jennings saw the whole thing from the shrubbery. I couldn't—I wasn't thinking very clearly. It was Jennings's idea to push her into the water and make it look like an accident."

"For which he made you pay," Charles said.

"Greedy blighter. I didn't know about the ring. I don't think Jennings did at the time, either. She was wearing the pendant on a long chain tucked inside the neck of her dress. The dress got torn when—"

"You grabbed her."

"It got torn," Edgar repeated, as though he had had no part in the action. "Jennings saw the pendant and decided to take it. He must have found the ring later and realized what it was."

"So Jennings set up the charade with the bandits to sell the ring to the British."

"And it was my rotten luck you got sent to retrieve the ring. I was terrified you'd tumble to the whole thing. But you didn't have the least idea, did you? Not then. For once I'd outwitted my clever brother." Pride glinted in Edgar's fading voice. "And Jennings managed to get himself killed. I'd have been safe if he hadn't written to that bitch of a whore of his."

Edgar's eyes were beginning to cloud. Charles leaned closer to him. "You never tried to find Miss Trevennen and silence her."

"She told me she'd entrusted Jennings's letter to someone who'd reveal the truth if anything ever happened to her. I thought I was done for last night when you told me she was dead. But the bloody letter was just sitting in that idiot's rooms in the Marshalsea the whole time." Edgar's fading gaze fastened on his brother. "When Castlereagh sent me to follow you and I learned you were looking for Helen Trevennen, I thought you must be onto the truth somehow. I knew I had to stop you. But when you told me about Colin— I'd never have let Colin be hurt, you have to believe that, Charles. I knew we had to get the ring back, but I couldn't risk you finding the pendant and the letter. I was trying to delay you and Mélanie so I could look for the ring myself."

"A knife in the ribs and a sniper's bullet are fairly strong delaying tactics."

"I was careful just to give Mélanie a flesh wound," Edgar said, as though aggrieved Charles could have thought otherwise. "I wanted to stop the two of you long enough to find out what you were up to. Later I was trying to put you out of commission so I could take over the search. But I made sure the sniper knew only to shoot at your leg."

"You weren't aiming for my leg in the alley just now."

"No." Edgar's voice was faint, but he stared back at Charles without flinching. "After you saw the pendant and the ring, I realized you'd put the truth together. It was one of us or the other."

Charles drew in his breath. "How little you know me, brother." His voice had a harsh, uneven rasp Mélanie had never heard before. "I don't know what I'd have done with the truth. But I wouldn't have killed you."

"But in the end you did," Edgar murmured, the words slurred. "You always were damnably good with a pistol, but how the hell did you manage that shot from the roof?"

Charles opened his mouth to speak and then fell silent. Edgar's gaze remained fixed on Charles as the life fled from his eyes.

Charles knelt staring at his brother in the guttering torchlight for a long moment, his eyes haunted by ghosts far older than the events of the past few minutes. Mélanie stayed absolutely still, as did Roth and Addison and the patrol who held the torch. At last Charles leaned forward, closed his brother's eyes, and brushed his lips across Edgar's brow. Then he got to his feet and held out his hand to Mélanie. When she put her own into it, his fingers closed round hers as though he was hanging on to his sanity.

Charles glanced down the alley. Raoul was crouched beside Colin, an arm round their son's shoulders. He appeared to be speaking to Colin. It was too far away for the voices to carry, but Colin's posture betrayed no fear or tension. He wouldn't know what had just transpired with Edgar.

Charles turned to Roth. "I don't know how much of that you understood. I'm sure you have questions. It will take a while to explain. I'd like—" He glanced at Raoul and Colin again. "I'd like to take my family home first."

Roth nodded. "Take the boy home. We'll see to Captain Fraser. I'll call in the morning. We can keep this quiet until then."

Mélanie unwrapped her son's hand from her collar. His eyes were shut, his face purple-shadowed but reassuringly at peace. She twitched the green quilt smooth. Beside her, Charles disentangled his fingers from Colin's freshly bandaged right hand and pulled the quilt over his shoulders. He kissed Colin's brow. She did the same.

They left the room and walked down the corridor without speaking. By the time they reached the door of their bedchamber, she realized she was shaking. By the time they got inside, she realized she couldn't stop.

Charles's arms closed round her. His breath washed over her skin. For a moment he simply stood holding her, anchoring her with the warmth of his body. "Three days ago," he said into her hair, "I would have sworn nothing could change the way I feel about you."

She tried to speak, choked, tried again. "And now?"

He kissed her temple. "Now I know it's true." He scooped her into his arms, carried her to the bed, and lay down fully clothed, holding her against him. The feather bed was deliciously soft beneath her aching body. The sheets smelled of starch and lavender. She and Charles smelled of soot and mildew and the grime of the streets and God knew what else. She wanted to burrow into him and never come up for air.

She didn't want to talk, but there were things that had to be said, if only she could find the words. "Charles— I'm sorry. So very, very sorry." It sounded pathetically inadequate, like a cloak too full of holes to provide warmth. "I know how you loved him."

She felt Charles's sharp intake of breath. "If you hadn't shot him, I'd quite certainly be dead, and God knows what would have happened to Colin. You didn't have any choice, Mel."

She turned her face into his throat, above his crumpled collar and stained cravat. His skin tasted of salty sweat and sweet familiarity. "How long have you known?"

"I pieced the story together over the last twenty-four hours, but it was still speculation. There was nothing to be done until we had Colin back. Then I was going to give Edgar a chance to explain himself." His voice sagged with exhaustion. "You said it yourself. Edgar was an Othello."

"Kitty wasn't his wife. But—" She thought back to the discussions about Kitty Ashford in the past days. She remembered the lines Charles had quoted earlier. " 'And when I love thee not, Chaos is come again.' He put Kitty on a pedestal."

"Pure and untouchable. A chaste wife. My brother's view of the world leaves—left no room for ambiguity."

"And Kitty had the Carevalo Ring." This was still the incredible part. Mélanie forced her exhausted brain to work. It was a sort of relief, a refuge from the tumult of feeling. "Perhaps we should have guessed. You said her grandmother was a Carevalo."

"Yes, it should have occurred to me that there might be a connection. The exact time the ring disappeared is open to debate, but Kitty's grandmother, Cristina Carevalo, could have witnessed the events. Various stories blamed Cristina's father or uncle or one of her brothers for its disappearance. Perhaps the truth is that Cristina smuggled it away with her when she left the family to marry. Or her father or one of her brothers gave it to her to keep for some reason. It's impossible to know, but she must have bequeathed it to her daughter, Kitty's mother, who bequeathed it to Kitty. A sort of secret family trust. Whatever the reasons for the secrecy, Kitty would have valued that trust. I told you she took the family honor seriously."

Mélanie tugged at the rumpled folds of her skirt, which were tangled about her legs. "So Jennings ended up with the means to blackmail Edgar and with the ring as well. And he wrote an account of Kitty's murder in the letter to Helen Trevennen that he used to conceal the ring. I suppose he thought he'd be safer if someone else knew the story."

"But he didn't tell her about the ring. Perhaps he was afraid of letting anyone, even his mistress, know he meant to swindle the British army." Charles shifted his booted legs so he wasn't lying on her skirt. "In the end it was a bloody mess of miscommunication and cross-purposes, like most of war. The French patrol blundered upon us, without the least idea that I was after the ring or that you'd been sent by their own side to retrieve it. You and I both wanted the ring and it was there tucked inside Jennings's letter to Helen Trevennen the whole time we were tending to his wounds."

"Until Baxter found the letter and sent it to Helen. At least now her reaction to the letter makes sense. She had a murderer in the palm of her hand—she knew she could blackmail him for a small fortune, but she must have feared he'd kill her, too, if he could get his hands on her."

"So she disappeared." Charles tightened his arms round her. "Helen Trevennen as good as admitted it was Edgar she was blackmailing, though I was too blind to see it. Remember Jemmy Moore said she told him she'd be well looked after thanks to 'Poor Tom.' You're not the only one good at Shakespearean references."

Mélanie groaned. "*Sacrebleu!* Of course. *King Lear.* Where Edgar disguises himself as Poor Tom."

"Lear's Edgar also happens to have an illegitimate half brother. Miss Trevennen couldn't have known how spot on her reference was."

Mélanie sorted back through the events of the last three days. "According to Edgar, Castlereagh really did ask him to find out what we were up to."

"That's the only way Edgar could have tumbled to what we were doing. I think he was telling the truth when he said he was trying to put one or both of us out of commission so he could search for the ring himself."

She forced her brain to work again, like the gears on a sluggish engine. "Edgar stabbed me at the Marshalsea and paid someone to shoot at you in the street outside the Gilded Lily. And he loosed the dog at the stables yesterday?"

"I'm sure of it. That's what really convinced me he must be behind the attacks. Startling the horse was a mad enough scheme, but the only way it made a scrap of sense is if one could be sure of having the intended victim in the right place at the right time." He turned his head on the pillow so she could look into his eyes. There was a jagged scrape on his cheek and a day's growth of stubble on his jaw. His gaze was weighted with grief and an unexpected tenderness. "You remember what happened when the horse reared up? Edgar and I both reached for you like foolish, solicitous males and managed to get tangled up with each other."

"Edgar and I fell to the side and you ended up under the horse's hooves. Edgar pushed you?"

"Looking back, I'm sure of it. I think I knew it all along, but I couldn't bring myself to admit it. At that point he must have been desperate. I don't think he cared if I lived or died. And then once I saw the pendant and the ring, he knew he had to kill me."

"He was bargaining that you hadn't told anyone, that he could make murder look like an accident again."

"Without my story, there'd have been no motive. I doubt

even you could have worked it out. I only hope he really did mean to spare Colin, though we'll never be sure."

She laid her hand on his chest. His pulse pounded beneath her fingers. "Even Edgar may not have known how far he meant to go. You can't know what you're capable of until you actually commit an act."

He was silent for so long she wasn't sure he meant to answer. "I didn't really know either of my parents," he said at last. His voice was low and rough, as though he was feeling his way over unfamiliar ground. "I don't think I'll ever understand my mother, not completely, though occasionally I get glimmerings. God knows I didn't know my father—Kenneth Fraser. To do him justice, O'Roarke made more of an effort to be a parent to me than Kenneth Fraser ever did. I missed half of my sister's childhood because I ran off to Lisbon. But I thought I knew Edgar. I can't remember a time when I didn't love him. Even when things went wrong between us, I never realized— He must have hated me."

"And loved you."

"Perhaps. I'll never know. In the end, it turns out I really didn't know him, either."

"Charles."

He looked at her, his face inches from hers on the embroidered linen of the pillowcase. She felt him brace himself against any inadequate attempt at comfort.

She touched his unshaven cheek. "I love you."

He pulled her against him and held her tighter than she could ever remember.

Forgiveness was in the force of his arms, the stir of his breathing, the brush of his lips on her brow. Tears welled up, ran down her cheeks, pooled onto his cravat. And yet . . . In the end, forgiveness was not all of it. "We'll never be able to forget," she said when she could speak.

"Then we'll have to find a way to remember."

"Carevalo's letter to Bow Street is out there somewhere. Roth may find it, or someone may send it to him."

He shifted against the pillows, settling her more comfortably against the curve of his body. "There won't be anything he can prove."

"It will be awkward, at the very least."

"We'll brazen it out. If necessary, we'll leave the country. The children will still have our love and a secure fortune. It's more than most children have."

"Don't pretend you wouldn't miss—"

"Perthshire? The House of Commons? Of course. But if I have to choose between losing them or losing you, there's no contest."

It was a moment before she could speak. "You're a much better person than I am, Charles."

"Am I?" His mouth was against her forehead. "You put your talents to use fighting for something you believed in. I employed my energies in a war over which I had increasing doubts, for a government I opposed, who later did exactly what you feared for Spain." His fingers moved against her arm. "Edgar accused me of not knowing what it means to be a British gentleman. You accused me of taking the gentleman's code too seriously. In the end I think you were both right. At the same time I was rejecting the values of my world, I was bound by them in ways I didn't even realize." He kissed her hair. "Can you forgive me?"

She jerked in his arms. "My God, Charles, forgive you for what?"

"For judging you so completely. For viewing everything you've done as though it centered round me. Look, my darling. I realized I've been looking at this the wrong way round."

"How?"

"I've been thinking of you as my wife."

"I am your wife, Charles. That's the point."

"But you aren't just my wife." His breath brushed her skin as he framed the words. "You had your own loyalties, your own code before you met me. You put your loyalty to your allies and your cause first. Which is much what I might have done in similar circumstances."

His words held an absolution she had never thought to find. She realized her fingers were clenched on the linen of his shirt. She forced a touch of lightness into her voice. "Charles, that sounds suspiciously like 'I could not love thee, dear, so much, Lov'd I not honor more.'"

"An apt sentiment."

"Since when have you taken to quoting Richard Lovelace?"

"I didn't, you did. But the man does have a point."

She stared up at the leaf pattern on the damask canopy. "You wouldn't have married someone knowing you would betray her."

"No? I think you were right earlier. We never know what we're capable of until we actually commit an act." He stroked her hair. "You accused me of marrying you to pay a debt to Kitty and avenge myself on my father. The truth is, I can't say where guilt and duty and wanting to replay my own childhood left off and love began. Yet surely— Sweetheart, after seven years surely why we got married matters far less than why we want to stay married."

She turned her face into his shoulder. "I don't deserve you, Charles."

She felt him smile against her hair. "You'll get used to it."

"Charles," she said after a long moment, her cheek pillowed on his chest, "do you think they were happy?"

He was twining his fingers in her hair. "Who?"

"Princess Aysha and Ramón de Carevalo. Do you think he abducted her or that they eloped because they'd been lovers all along?"

"Who knows?" He tugged another lock of hair free of its pins. "Perhaps they were soulmates who shared a love of poetry. Perhaps he carried her off for purely political reasons. Perhaps she was an intelligence agent and she arranged the whole thing so she could spy inside his court."

Mélanie reached up and laced her fingers through his own. "Perhaps she told him the truth eventually."

"Perhaps he believed her." Charles brought her hand to his lips and kissed her palm. "Perhaps, just possibly, they ended up being happy anyway."

Mélanie curled her fingers against his face. "It may not be the truth," she said, "but it's a lovely story."

Chapter 37

Colin took a sip of milk. His fingers were curled tight round the blue-flowered mug, as though he was afraid to let go of it. Charles felt much the same about his son. He sat back and studied his children across the nursery breakfast table. The toast crumbs on the white cloth, the steam curling above the porridge bowls, the silver gleam of the butter knife. Hallmarks of normality in a world that had not yet returned to normal. He glanced sideways at Mélanie. Her gaze was fastened on Colin as though making up for lost time.

Too much had happened in the past three days for Charles to begin to comprehend it. He knew better than to try. Every so often, the pain or fear or sorrow would break through, like glass slicing into his brain. For a moment, he would be unable to think or even breathe. And then everyday life would close the wound over and the feeling would recede to a dull ache on the edge of his consciousness.

Laura Dudley was sewing by the window. Berowne, the cat, was curled up on the hearth rug, as though this was a normal morning. But of course it wasn't anything of the kind. The children didn't know about Edgar yet. He and Mélanie would have to find a way to tell them. Roth would call soon, wanting answers. Blanca was closeted with Addison in one of the parlors, telling him she had been in the employ of a French agent. It would not be easy for them, but Charles had great faith in his valet's innate good sense winning the day.

Jessica pushed her spoon through her porridge and looked at her brother. "Will your finger grow back?"

Charles's breath caught in his throat. He sensed Mélanie's do the same.

A shadow crossed Colin's face. He shifted his mug in his hands. "No," he said. "Fingers aren't like hair and nails."

"Oh." Jessica regarded him with wide, appraising eyes. "So you'll be a hero like Uncle Fitzroy."

Jessica was very fond of Fitzroy Somerset, who had lost his arm at Waterloo. Colin took another sip of milk. To Charles's intense relief, his son's face lightened a trifle. "Not quite," Colin said. "A finger isn't nearly as bad as an arm."

Jessica added another spoonful of sugar to her porridge. "I think you're a hero."

Colin looked from Charles to Mélanie. "What's going to happen to Meg?"

It was a shock to hear Colin use her name, a shock to realize she and Evans were people to him, however monstrous their actions. "She's being held at Bow Street," Charles said. "She's going to go to prison for a long time. You don't ever have to see her again."

He expected to see relief or the remnants of fear on Colin's face, but instead Colin frowned, the way he did when he was puzzling through a problem in the schoolroom. "She was beastly," he said. "But not all the time. She brought me food and made sure I had enough blankets."

Charles heard Mélanie draw in her breath, as though to say

Meg was the lowest form of humanity possible. Then she checked herself, her gaze on Colin.

Colin bent down to pet Berowne. "Meg had a little boy who died. She missed him." His scowl deepened. "I don't understand her."

Mélanie reached across the table and touched their son's hand. "It's never easy to understand another person, Colin. But it's important to try, even when the people are beastly. Maybe especially then."

Jessica, who hated to be ignored for more than a minute or two, tugged at Colin's sleeve. "Can we play knights later? With the sword and battle-ax?"

Colin set down the mug of milk. A genuine smile broke across his face. "All right. But we have to be careful."

"I won't cry if you hit me this time. Well, not unless it *really* hurts."

Charles's shoulders relaxed, as though a weight had been lifted from them. He heard Mélanie release her breath.

The door eased open. "I'm sorry, sir, madam." Michael stepped into the room. "Mr. Roth and Mr. O'Roarke have called. Shall I—"

"No, we should see them." Charles got to his feet.

"We'll be back." Mélanie knelt between the children's chairs. "As soon as possible." She kissed both of them. Charles ruffled their hair. Laura moved to the table.

Michael had shown Roth and O'Roarke into the small salon. A wash of sunlight lent warmth to the cool sea green of the walls. Or perhaps the warmth came from the circumstances rather than the light. Roth walked forward as they entered the room. His face had the gray, worn quality that comes from a string of sleepless nights, though he had shaved and changed his linen in the few hours since they had seen him. "How's the boy?" he said without preamble.

"Remarkable, all things considered." Charles closed the door. "It will take time, but he's going to be all right."

Relief showed in Roth's eyes. "Children are remarkably

resilient. When my wife left, I thought it would take my boys years to grow accustomed to it, but they seem to have adjusted far more quickly than I have."

It was a surprising personal admission, and in its own way an offer of friendship. Charles held Roth's gaze for a moment, acknowledging the offer and responding with a like one.

"I asked Mr. O'Roarke to come with me," Roth continued. "I thought it would be simplest if I talked to all three of you at once, since you were all bound up in the events of last night."

"Of course," Charles said.

O'Roarke had waited by the fireplace throughout this exchange. They joined him and seated themselves round the warmth of the fire.

Roth settled himself in a chair and crossed his legs. He looked far more at ease in the room than he had a mere three days before. "Margaret Simmons has made a full confession. Carevalo hired her and Evans a fortnight ago. He promised them five hundred pounds to take Master Fraser and keep him until the matter was resolved. Meg Simmons thought the job was worth four times that. She figured once they had the boy in their hands they could extract the money from Carevalo."

"Did she know about the ring?" Mélanie asked.

"She doesn't seem to have done." Roth frowned. "She asked if Master Fraser was all right. She sounded as though she meant it."

Mélanie tugged at the ruffle on her sleeve. "That didn't stop them from cutting off Colin's finger."

"No." Roth pulled out his notebook, opened the cover, flipped through the pages, then closed it again. "Victor Velasquez turned himself in at Bow Street in the early hours of the morning. He made a full confession to the murder of Elinor Constable, also known as Helen Trevennen, though it sounds as if it was more accident than murder." He took his pencil from his pocket and chewed the tip. "So that would seem to tie up all the loose ends." He looked up at Charles. "Except for your brother's death."

"Yes." Charles leaned forward and drew a breath. He was prepared, but the words still stuck in his throat for a moment. Such revelations seemed to belong to the cloaking, whisky-scented shadows of night, not the clear, revealing light of morning. Mélanie reached out and took his hand. Her presence beside him on the sofa was like a touchstone. He let himself meet her steadying gaze for a moment. Then he recounted his surmises about Edgar in as straightforward a manner as possible, neither dwelling on unnecessary detail nor shirking what needed to be said.

When he finished, silence hung over the room, punctuated by the reassuring crackle of the fire. O'Roarke sat very still, his gaze intent. Roth sucked in his breath and released it in a long sigh. His shoulders slumped against the chair back.

"There's no way to prove any of it, of course," Charles said. "But it's the only way I can make sense of my brother's actions."

Roth nodded and stared down at his notebook. He smoothed his fingers over the worn brown leather of the cover. He had made no notes during the story. "I asked Velasquez about the ring this morning. I said we had reason to suspect it had been in his cousin Kitty's possession."

"And?" Charles said.

"He was surprised. But not as surprised as I would have expected. He said his great-grandfather must have decided the ring was more a curse than a blessing. The great-grandfather's two sons were fighting over it, and there was a history of duels and even murder in the Carevalo family to gain possession of it."

"Not to mention its role in the Crusades," Mélanie murmured.

"Quite," Roth said. "Velasquez said his great-grandfather must have decided the family would be better off if the ring disappeared, but he couldn't bring himself to destroy it. So he gave it to his daughter, Kitty Ashford's grandmother, and charged her to watch over it but to tell no one she had it."

"And she gave it to her daughter, Kitty's mother," Charles

said. "I suspect Kitty's mother gave it to her when Kitty married or when she turned twenty-one or perhaps on the mother's deathbed. I remember Kitty saying that it was when her mother died that she understood just how much she owed to her family."

Roth leaned back in his chair, frowning. "I can see how that could have gone on for years. Generations. But if the ring could have meant what you say to the war—"

"Politics mattered a lot less to Kit than family loyalties," Charles said. "She told me once that a vow to a blood relative came before all else. If she'd promised her mother to keep the ring for"—his voice went unexpectedly tight; Mélanie's fingers tightened round his own—"for her daughter, she wouldn't have gone back on her word."

Roth shook his head, as though he would never understand the inner workings of such a code. "If this whole story comes out, it can only tarnish your brother's memory and hurt his widow and the rest of your family. Not to mention embarrassing the army and government."

"Very true," Charles said.

Roth looked up at him. "There was a lot of confusion last night. Who's to say the exact sequence of events? The only people who were actually present at the shooting were you and Mrs. Fraser and the boy and Evans."

"Evans was dead."

"Was he? Or did that happen later?" Roth spun his pencil between his fingers. "Perhaps Evans had a gun."

"Your men know otherwise," Charles said.

Roth gave a half smile. "That won't be a problem."

Mélanie pushed a loose strand of hair behind her ear. "From the angle of the shot that killed Edgar it's plain it didn't come from the roof."

"I think we can account for that." Roth turned his head. "Mr. O'Roarke? Do you have any objections?"

"Certainly not. I saw none of it, after all."

"Good." Roth inclined his head. "What do you mean to do with the ring?"

Charles looked at O'Roarke. "I assume I can count on you to convey it to Carevalo's heir?"

"Who is his heir?" Roth asked.

O'Roarke smiled for the first time since Charles and Mélanie had come into the room. "A first cousin. Not as active as Carevalo, but with similar political ideals. And a much less volatile personality."

Roth returned the smile. "I'm glad to hear it, Mr. O'Roarke. It seems neither Spain's government nor our own need be troubled with the ring's discovery." He sat forward in his chair as though to rise, then tapped his pencil against his notebook. "Oh, there is one more thing. Meg Simmons gave me this." He drew a sealed paper out of his coat. "Apparently Carevalo left it with her to give to Bow Street if anything happened to him."

It was as though the fire had been extinguished and the lamps turned down. Charles felt Mélanie go still beside him. "How interesting," he said. The red seal on the letter appeared unbroken. He stared for a moment at the impression of the Carevalo crest. "A confession?"

"I don't know. I haven't read it." Roth leaned forward in his chair, the letter dangling from his fingertips. His gaze moved from Charles to Mélanie to O'Roarke. "I can't imagine what a twisted mind like Carevalo's could have to say that's worth my time. Perhaps you have more use for the letter than I would." He got to his feet, held out the letter, and placed it in Mélanie's hand.

The vellum trembled between her fingers. She looked down at it, then raised her gaze to Roth. "Thank you, Mr. Roth." She drew a breath. She was nearer to tears than most people could have guessed. "Thank you for everything."

Roth looked into her eyes. Charles thought perhaps he could tell how fragile her control was. "It's been a pleasure, Mrs. Fraser. Though I fear this was not one of my more brilliant cases. I did little more than follow your lead and your husband's." He coughed and glanced at the mantel clock. "I'd best be on my way. I have to meet with the chief magistrate about this Velasquez business."

Mélanie and Charles walked to the door with him. They both shook his hand. "I hope you will dine with us one day soon, Mr. Roth," Mélanie said. "And bring your sister. And perhaps your sons could visit Colin and Jessica."

Roth looked down into her eyes, a friend addressing a friend. "I'd like that, Mrs. Fraser. We all would."

The door closed behind him. Mélanie leaned against the door panels and put her hand to her mouth. Hysterical laughter burst between her fingers. "Dear God, what have I done to deserve such generosity?"

"Don't question it, *querida*," O'Roarke said. "Just be grateful." He picked up Carevalo's letter from the sofa where she had left it and held it to the light. "Steamed open. Crafty devil, Roth. Crafty and damnably generous."

Charles crossed the room and took the letter. He glanced down at it for a moment, then looked at Mélanie. At her nod, he held the letter to the fire.

He felt O'Roarke's gaze upon him. "I'm sorry about your brother, Charles. That can't have been easy."

"None of this has been easy on any of us." Charles dropped the burning missive into the flames.

"No. But some things are more easily mended than others." O'Roarke's gaze was understanding without being intrusive. "I didn't know Edgar well, even as a boy. But— He was your brother. And he was Elizabeth's son."

Charles said nothing. He didn't trust himself to speak.

O'Roarke regarded Charles in silence for a moment. "Do you think that was why Captain Fraser told you the truth of your parentage last night? To distract you?"

"I suspect so." Charles watched the flames lick at the cream-colored paper. "We'd just found Helen Trevennen's body. He was probably desperate for anything to buy himself time."

O'Roarke nodded. "I must confess, I'm not entirely sorry for it."

Charles looked into the gray eyes of the man who was his

father. Who had lied to him and used him but perhaps had had more of an impact on him than Charles had ever guessed. Certainly far more than Kenneth Fraser had had. "You gave me a copy of *The Rights of Man* once, O'Roarke. I don't know if I ever properly thanked you for it."

O'Roarke returned his gaze. "I've read your speeches, Charles. That's thanks enough." He turned, a little too quickly perhaps, and picked up his gloves from the sofa table. "I'm sure you're eager to get back to your children. I'll see myself out."

Mélanie was still standing by the door. She hesitated, then went to O'Roarke and pressed his hand. "Thank you, Raoul. We wouldn't have got him back without you."

O'Roarke looked down at her. "It was, to put it mildly, the least I could do." He lifted her hand to his lips and kissed her fingertips with a formality that could not be mistaken for flirtation. "Take care of yourself, *querida.*"

Charles crushed the ashes of Carevalo's letter with the poker, then crossed the room to stand beside his father. He took out his watch chain, unhooked the Carevalo Ring from it, and held it out to O'Roarke. "I trust you'll do what's best with it, O'Roarke."

O'Roarke looked down at the dull gold and gleaming rubies. "I'm flattered that you trust me in any way at all, Fraser." He took the ring and pocketed it. "We'll see if it means as much to the people of Spain as it has meant to us." He met Charles's gaze but did not attempt to offer his hand. "You've been a much tried man these past days. Don't think your forbearance has gone unnoticed."

Charles swallowed, aware of Mélanie's gaze on the two of them. "O'Roarke?"

"Yes?"

Charles stretched out his hand. "Thank you."

O'Roarke clasped his hand, inclined his head, and moved to the door. But he turned back at the last minute, gripping the brass doorknob. His gaze moved from Charles to Mélanie. "I only spent a few minutes with him last night, but he's a remarkable little boy. He couldn't have better parents."

He opened the door without waiting for a reply and strode from the room. Charles released his breath, though he hadn't known he'd been holding it. He stood still for a moment, listening to the retreating click of booted feet in the hall, the murmur of Michael's voice, the muffled thud of the front door.

Charles turned to his wife. She looked more or less herself, the cinnamon-striped stuff of her gown falling gracefully about her, her hair looped and curled and pinned, her pearl earrings gleaming beside her face. But her face itself was marked by indelible shadows.

She rubbed her arms. As usual, she knew what he was thinking without him putting it into words. "It's one of those clichés of life that it's hellishly easy to make promises in a darkened bedchamber. And then one wakes up and has to put them into practice."

His gaze flickered to the hole in the plaster where he had smashed his fist a scant seventy-two hours ago. "Constructing a thesis is often easier than testing it."

She stared at the rumpled sofa cushions, and then at the painting of her and the children on the overmantel. "It's never going to be the same."

"No." He watched her. The sunlight shot through the stiff lace of her high-standing collar and dappled her collarbone. A loose ringlet fell against her cheek. A scrape showed on the back of her left hand, a relic of one of their brushes with danger. In seven years, there was not a moment when he had felt he knew her so completely.

"It might be better," he said.

She looked at him, her eyes wide and bruised and tinged with something desperate—hope, relief, fear perhaps. "Oh, darling. I don't even know where to begin."

"One step at a time." He closed the distance between them and held out his hand. " 'What's past is prologue.' "

"Yes, but prologue to what?"

"What we make of it."

She hesitated a moment, then she gave a smile that drove the shadows from her eyes. She reached out and put her hand into his own.

Historical Note

$\mathcal{M}$élanie and Charles and the other principal characters in this book are entirely fictional, but I have endeavored to make the London in which their adventures take place and the Britain and Europe against which their story is set as accurate as possible. For this, I am indebted to the Stanford and University of California at Berkeley libraries for keeping a wonderful collection of early-nineteenth-century letters and diaries (some of which hadn't been checked out in years), and to U.C. Berkeley for its invaluable microfilm copies of the *Morning Chronicle*.

The Carevalo Ring and its history are also fictional, but had such a ring existed, I think it is not entirely implausible that the British, French, and Spanish would all have sought to make use of it during the Peninsular War and its aftermath.